DESIRE

"You would have me believe that a man like you has never desired a woman before me?" There was mockery in Sabine's voice as she leaned toward the duke, her hand touching his arm.

"I have desired many women," Garreth replied, "but never one that muddled my reasoning to the point of madness, as you have."

Sabine turned back to the window, where silvery moonlight played across her face. "I suppose I am the most beautiful woman you have ever seen?" she challenged him with skepticism.

"I have known some women that were as beautiful," he admitted, "but what I feel for you goes beyond beauty, and beyond mere desire."

Sabine saw the amazed expression on his face as he realized what he'd said.

"I never thought this could happen to me," he admitted, taking her hand. He shook his head as if to clear it. "The most maddening thing is that I don't know how you feel about me."

Books by Constance O'Banyon

Forever My Love
Song of the Nightingale
Highland Love Song
Desert Song
La Flamme

Available from HarperPaperbacks

Harper Monogram

La Flamme

⋈ CONSTANCE O'BANYON ⋈

HarperPaperbacks
A Division of HarperCollinsPublishers

This is a work of fiction. The characters, incidents, and dialogues are products of the author's imagination and are not to be construed as real. Any resemblance to actual events or persons, living or dead, is entirely coincidental.

HarperPaperbacks   *A Division of* HarperCollins*Publishers*
10 East 53rd Street, New York, N.Y. 10022

Cover photograph by Chase Swift/Westlight
Cover illustration by Doreen Minuto

First printing: September 1995

Printed in the United States of America

HarperPaperbacks, HarperMonogram, and colophon are trademarks of HarperCollins*Publishers*

❖ 10 9 8 7 6 5 4 3 2 1

This is lovingly dedicated to the real talent in my family, Glen Hoyle, artiste extraordinaire. Your magnificent talent has earned you a place of honor in the art world. I am so proud of you, my dearest brother.

A special thanks to Judie Hall, PhD, RN, CEN, for being my medical advisor on this book. Your help is most appreciated.

La
Flamme

To that sweet thief which sourly robs from me, which though it alter not love's sole effect, yet doth it steal sweet hours from love's delight.

I may not evermore acknowledge thee, lest my bewiled guilt should do thee shame.

—WILLIAM SHAKESPEARE

By King's Command

1

1630

The sky was the color of smoke and there was a chill in the air as a weak sun strained to penetrate the high clouds. A wide circle of colorful tents dotted the meadow while crested banners of the noblest families in England snapped and waved in the light breeze that stirred the late spring wildflowers on Heyworth Moor.

Charles Stuart had only been king for five years and already he'd made powerful enemies by disbanding Parliament whenever its members disagreed with him. His despotic actions had split the nobility; some supporting him, while others favored Parliament. Thus far the quarrelling factions had stopped short of armed conflict, but civil war would surely come if the two sides did not heal their differences.

Apprehension was reflected on the faces of the highborn lords and ladies who had once rebelled against their king but now had gathered to pledge him their fidelity because Lord Woodbridge had asked it of them. Many here would face old foes today, not on the field of battle, but by attending the wedding that everyone hoped would unite a troubled England.

The hope for the future of the realm came in the form of the young daughter of the powerful earl of Woodbridge and in the son of the equally powerful duke of Balmarough. The houses of Woodbridge and Balmarough had divided loyalties; Woodbridge was Catholic and staunchly supported Parliament, while the house of Balmarough was of the Anglican faith and unquestioningly supported the king. Since the lords were still distrustful of each other, this mutual ground had been agreed upon for the nuptials.

King Charles's advance guard had already arrived to make certain that everything was in readiness for the monarch's appearance. Holding their breath, many turned toward the woods from whence he would come—watching . . . waiting.

It was rumored that Lord Blackthorn, the son of the duke of Balmarough, had disagreed with his father and refused to submit to the marriage. Those who were acquainted with Lord Woodbridge knew he would never tolerate such an insult to his daughter, Lady Sabine. So an air of uneasiness settled over the moor, for everyone realized that there might yet be conflict if the young lord rejected a marriage that had been arranged by Charles Stuart himself.

Surely Garreth Blackthorn would not disobey the king.

Fourteen-year-old Lady Sabine limped across a meadow where a sheen of dew still clung to the grass. Several years earlier, her leg had been broken, and it had never healed properly. Awkwardly, she lifted her gown to keep the hem dry. When she entered her mother's tent, Lady Woodbridge came forward, smiling, and pressed a kiss on her daughter's cheek. But Sabine's father scowled at her.

"You are late for prayer," he said. "Your pleasure can be delayed, but God is not to be kept waiting."

"Yes, Papa," she said, dropping to her knees. In the inner circle of light, she knelt beside her parents, while her mother's ladies and her father's attendants knelt just behind them.

Sabine looked up at her mother and received an understanding smile that comforted her. Then Lady Woodbridge lowered her head and reverently clasped her rosary. Sabine was certain her mother's prayers were for her and Lord Blackthorn.

The girl's mind was not on her prayers as she looked from her lovely mother to her stern-faced father. Her father's features were angular and his brows met across the bridge of his nose. He was a harsh man, but in rare moments he could show affection with a pat on the head or restrained praise. Sabine had gotten her curly auburn hair from him, although she'd always longed for flaxen-colored hair like her mother's. She knew she was not beautiful but her mother told her that with her striking amber-colored eyes and even features she would one day be a beauty. Sabine did not believe her—her mother looked at her with love, and not as she actually was.

Lady Woodbridge was lovely of heart and face. She was devout in her religion and insisted that her family be the same. She was French by birth, and had taught her children her native language even as they learned English.

Sabine squeezed her eyes together tightly and whispered a prayer that God would take pity on her and deliver her from this marriage. She paused to wonder if God had the authority to change the mind of a king.

After prayer, which Sabine thought would never end, her father left the tent while her mother came to her. "My dearest, I have something to give you. It was given to me as a wedding gift by someone very special."

Sabine's gaze dropped to her mother's hand and she saw the locket that her mother had never removed until now. "Surely not your locket. I know how you treasure it."

"As shall you." Lady Woodbridge fastened the locket around her daughter's neck. "As you know, my sister, Margretta, gave this to me before I left France to marry your father. There is still a lock of her hair inside, and I have added a lock of mine."

"Oh, thank you, *Maman*," Sabine said, touching the locket reverently, knowing that it was a true gift of love.

Suddenly they both fell silent and there were tears in their eyes. "This will never do," her mother said lightly. "We must make haste, dearest. My ladies are waiting to dress you."

Sabine looked ruefully at her mother. "Some say that Lord Blackthorn will not come today. I hope he does not."

"Make no mistake about it, Sabine, he will come. Like you, he'll do the king's bidding, and not dally past the appointed time."

"But, *Maman*, I don't want to marry Lord Blackthorn. I have never seen him. He's in his twentieth year and that's too old for me."

Ryanne Woodbridge sat down on a velvet stool and held her arms out to Sabine. "I know what you are feeling, but I can assure you that it won't be so bad as you imagine. Your father is fourteen years older than I."

"Were you frightened on your wedding day?" Sabine asked. In truth, she was amazed that her mother had ever feared anything.

"Indeed I was. I had traveled from France to be your father's bride. When we were married, I was but three years older than you, and I had seen your father only twice before our wedding day. He seemed so stern, and I was terrified. I was far away from my home and about to marry a man I hardly knew."

"But you love Papa."

"I grew to love him, Sabine. I bore him seven children, though five died in infancy. We have shared the good and the troubled times, but not once have I regretted being his wife. It will be the same with you."

Tears filled Sabine's eyes, and she stared at the tips of her green velvet slippers, hoping her mother would not notice. Unconsciously, she rubbed her aching leg.

"Does your leg pain you, Sabine?"

Sabine shrugged, unable to tell her mother that the real pain would come if she saw disgust in the eyes of her bridegroom, because she was crippled.

Lady Woodbridge wiped her daughter's tears with a delicate finger. "Sabine, remember that nothing really changes today. You will continue to live with me and your father until your sixteenth birthday."

Sabine glanced at her mother's slightly rounded stomach. "When this baby is born, I pray it will be a son like Richard so it will not have to leave you at marriage."

"I only pray that the baby is safely delivered, Sabine, and it matters not to me if it is a son or daughter." Her mother's expression was tender. "I would not mind having another daughter as dear as you, even if she had to leave me as you will."

Sabine moved to the cot where her three-year-old brother lay sleeping. Lovingly she touched his cheek. "When the time comes, how will I leave you, Papa, and Richard?"

Her mother ushered her into the inner room of the tent,

where her ladies waited. "Let us have only happy thoughts this morning. This is your wedding day, dearest!"

With that, Sabine was disrobed, and submitted to having her long hair brushed and braided, then interwoven with fragrant red roses. She was dressed in a beaded crimson gown with yards of gold braid at the sleeves and hem. The gown was so heavy that it was even more difficult than usual for her to walk. It was grander than anything she had ever worn, yet it gave her no pleasure.

"There, my dear," her mother said, pushing an errant curl behind Sabine's golden headdress. "You look very like a bride."

Sabine limped to the mirror that Thea held out to her and stared at her reflection. "I look like an overdressed child." She turned sadly to her mother. "Lord Blackthorn will not treasure me as his wife."

"Nonsense, dearest. You are from one of the most influential houses in England. Your hand has been sought by royalty and nobles alike. You take with you a dowry of three manors that bring in over a thousand pounds a year, as well as a fortune in gold, silver, jewels, and furnishings. What man would not want you for his wife?"

No one, Sabine thought in despair, understood what she was feeling.

"We must make haste," Lady Woodbridge added. "I am told that his majesty approaches."

With a resigned sigh, Sabine raised her head and met her mother's challenging gaze. The young girl thrust her shoulders back and held her head at a proud tilt, knowing it was expected of her.

"I am ready," she said.

2

The sudden blare of a trumpet broke the afternoon stillness. Fifty horsemen, riding two abreast, with King Charles at their head, emerged from the woods, their brightly colored banners snapping in the breeze.

The king's colorful standard of the lion was not a call to arms, but displayed in honor of the union of two powerful houses.

Sabine stood stiffly beside her mother and father, nervously clasping her hands. There was a dull ache in her heart as she watched the advancing riders, their giant warhorses thundering ever closer. She held on to the hope that Lord Blackthorn was not with the king, and therefore there would be no wedding.

As the cavalcade approached, she noticed the surly expression on her father's face. It had been difficult for him to yield to a king he so adamantly disliked and distrusted. What kind of marriage would they have if Garreth Blackthorn felt the same? she wondered.

The king dismounted, and Sabine dipped into a curtsy after being prompted by her mother. Her father, however, merely lowered his head. If the king noticed the lack of deference from Lord Woodbridge, he made no mention of it.

Sabine had not expected King Charles to cut such a dashing figure. He had an elegant beard and mustache, and looked handsome indeed as he stood imperiously before her father.

The king had a speech impediment and he spoke slowly and distinctly so he would not stammer. "Lord Woodbridge, this is indeed a glorious day for us all. It is time to lay aside our swords of distrust and pick up the banner of unity."

With a stoic expression, Lord Woodbridge turned to Sabine's mother. "Your Majesty, may I present my wife, Lady Woodbridge, and of course, my daughter, Lady Sabine."

"Your son is not present?" the king asked.

"You will have to excuse Lord Richard, Your Majesty," Sabine's father said. "Being only in his third year, he is napping, and unaware of the importance of this day."

"Quite so—quite so."

King Charles exchanged polite greetings with Sabine's mother. "My Lady, you are from France, as is my wife. The queen has long expressed a wish to meet you. I hope that it will be possible in the near future."

"I would be most happy to meet Her Majesty, Sire. Doubly so since she is from the country of my birth."

His expression became serious. "Then we shall arrange it." When he reached Sabine he took her hand and covered it with his, and the smile on his lips seemed genuine.

"It's hard to imagine that the fate of so many has been placed on such small shoulders."

Sabine tried to smile, but it came out as a sigh when she let out her pent-up breath. Nervously, she took several steps backward, and the king immediately became aware of her limp. To her surprise, his eyes softened with understanding.

"Lady Sabine, know you that I could not walk until I was in my seventh year because I was stricken by a congenital weakness?"

Her eyes rounded in surprise. "No, Your Majesty, I did not know that. I am so sorry."

He raised her hand to his lips. "Have no pity, Lady Sabine, because I am completely recovered. I overcame my impairment by strenuous exercise, and perhaps you shall also."

Before Sabine could answer, a shadow fell across her face, and she moved closer to her mother as a young nobleman dismounted and approached her father.

The stranger's dark eyes held a look of insolence as they swept over her family. With an expression of total indifference, his gaze lingered for a moment on Sabine's face.

Unlike most of the gentlemen present, including the king and her father, this man was clean-shaven. He wore tan breeches and a matching velvet doublet. His thigh-length boots were of the same color, and in contrast, he wore a rakish black hat with a green plume, which he removed as he bowed before the king.

This could only be Lord Blackthorn. Sabine stepped forward, trying to get a better look at him. The sun seemed to reflect off his shoulder-length, ebony hair. He was tall and broad-shouldered. His features were handsome, his eyes deep brown. He was too handsome, too arrogant. Sabine was terrified of being his wife.

King Charles spoke authoritatively. "The wedding will go forth as planned."

Sabine felt panic, knowing the moment she had dreaded was upon her. If only Garreth Blackthorn were not so fair of face, he would not expect her to be a beauty. Why couldn't he be ordinary?

At last, he stood before her. "So, My Lady, you and I are to be a pair."

She feared that she would see distaste in his eyes when he looked at her, but there was merely acceptance in the cold, brown depths.

"Are those tears because you must have me for husband, My Lady?"

She looked up at him earnestly. "No, Your Grace. I feel pity that you have so recently lost your father, and your sadness strikes at my heart."

His eyes did not waver, nor was there any warmth in them. He merely removed his leather gauntlet and held out his hand to her. "Come, let us get this thing done."

His dispassionate manner caused her to draw back. Then, knowing what was required of her, Sabine placed her hand on his sleeve and raised her chin. "As you wish, Your Grace."

When he led her forward, he became aware of her limp and slowed his steps so she could keep pace. Sabine searched his eyes. "Did no one tell you that I am lame, Your Grace?"

"No one told me anything about you." His voice was devoid of emotion, so she could not discern his feeling about her deformity.

"I was not born this way, but suffered a riding accident which resulted in a broken leg. Although a physician attended me, the leg did not heal properly." She did not tell him that her leg ached constantly and that when she was tired the limp was more pronounced.

King Charles presented him to her mother and father. "I understand you have not as yet met the bridegroom. This is His Grace, the duke of Balmarough."

Lord Woodbridge looked baffled. "Say you that he is the duke, when I know that his father carries that title?"

"My Lord, My Ladies," Garreth Blackthorn said, bowing slightly. "I can see how you might be confused. My family has met with a grave tragedy and my father is dead."

Lord Woodbridge was clearly dismayed. "When did this occur?"

The young duke raised his head. His dislike for Sabine's father was clearly reflected in his eyes, but there was no feeling in Garreth Blackthorn's voice as he replied. "Sorrowfully, my father has been ailing for some months, and died but three weeks past."

"Most unfortunate," Lady Woodbridge said, placing her hand on the new duke's. "Please know that you have our family's deepest sympathy."

"Thank you for your compassion, My Lady. My mother sends her regrets for her absence and asks that the marriage go forward since it was my father's dying wish."

Sabine sensed that he had only agreed to the marriage for that reason. She looked into his piercing eyes which appeared unfeeling, and yet she felt he was striving to hide his grief.

She felt such pity for Garreth Blackthorn that her eyes filled with tears. Surely it must be difficult for him to proceed with the wedding when his father had so recently died.

Lord Woodbridge looked undecided. "We would readily agree to postpone the marriage for a decent interval and allow you time to mourn your father."

"'Tis of no matter," he said, his mouth set in a grim line. "The pity is that you are hardly out of the nursery. You should be amusing yourself with childish games, not dressed in that ridiculous gown that makes it appear that you're playing at being grown."

Sabine's spine stiffened. "My situation will one day be remedied—for I will surely grow older, Your Grace. But is there a remedy for your bad manners?"

His lips curved into a grim smile. "Not even married and already you give me a dressing-down. I see no wedded bliss for us, My Lady."

By now they had reached the glen that had been chosen for the ceremony. The wedding party stood beneath a grove of oak trees that arched together in a natural canopy. Lord Woodbridge had insisted that the family priest, Father Santini, perform the wedding mass, and the king had reluctantly agreed.

Sabine knelt beside Garreth Blackthorn, with her small hand in his, while she pledged her heart and her liege to the house of Balmarough. When Garreth slid a ring on her finger, she stared at the Balmarough crest, a dragon in flight, reflecting through a sparkling ruby. She felt hysterical laughter bubble up inside her when the ring almost slid off her slender finger.

Garreth Blackthorn stood and pulled her up beside him. She trembled with fright when he brushed a chaste kiss on her cheek.

"I fear that you have the worst of the bargain, little Sabine, for I am now your legal husband."

His hand tightened about hers as he turned to Lord Woodbridge. "The agreement you made with my father is met, My Lord—the deed is done."

Bishop Laud, the Lord Mayor of London, who had organized the wedding celebration, appeared beside them, his face glowing. "A banquet has been set up in the large tent. Shall we all proceed to the feast that has so generously been provided by His Majesty?"

Garreth turned to the king. "I pray Your Majesty will understand when I beg to be excused from the festivities. There is much that requires my attention at home."

King Charles looked disapproving. "I prefer that you remain, young Garreth."

Sabine spoke up. "Please give him leave, Your Majesty. It must be difficult for him to celebrate with his father so newly deceased."

The king smiled. "I yield to the wisdom and compassion of your new wife, Garreth. We shall excuse you from the banquet—though some will view it as unconventional."

Garreth turned his attention back to the child he'd just married. "Will you walk with me? There is much I would say to you."

Sabine nodded and placed her hand on his extended arm. As they moved away from the noise of the crowd, Garreth shortened his long strides to match her slow limp.

"I know that you must be feeling frightened and resentful, Sabine, so I want to assure you that you have nothing to fear from me. As you know, you will go home with your parents until such time as you reach your sixteenth birthday. Only then will you move to Wolfeton Keep to be under the tutelage of my mother."

"Wolfeton Keep?"

"'Tis my home." For the first time he smiled. "I believe you will like it."

She merely nodded, knowing that it didn't matter if she liked it or not. From this day forward, this man had the right to decide her future.

He mistook her silence for concern. "You do understand the terms of the wedding contract? You shan't be expected to be a true wife to me until you reach your eighteenth birthday."

Again she nodded. Her mother had explained this to her. When she would have turned away, Garreth took her hand and pulled her back to him.

"Little girl, you will not find me a demanding husband."

Suddenly, for reasons she did not fully understand, Sabine reached up to her hair, withdrew a crimson rose. "A token for your father," she said softly, and a tear rolled down her cheek and fell upon the petals of the rose.

As a heavy mist swirled about them, Garreth took the rose and tucked it into his doublet. "My father would have liked the gesture. Until we meet again, keep well."

At last, she found her voice. "When will I see you?"

He arched his dark brow. "Do you want to?"

"Perhaps, so I won't forget what you look like."

He smiled, and she felt her heart thump against her breasts. "Then you shall see me." He raised her hand to his lips and kissed the tips of her fingers. "Grow strong and wise for the day when you will come to me, my little duchess."

Without another word, he turned and moved away from her.

Sabine Blackthorn, the duchess of Balmarough, watched her husband mount his giant warhorse and ride across the moor until he was out of sight. She felt very unlike a bride.

The banquet was an ordeal. Sabine was seated between the king, who was in a jovial mood, and her father, who was not. Several times her mother tried to mediate between the two men, but her attempts did not meet with success.

Sabine pushed the food around in her plate, feeling that if she took a bite, she would surely choke.

She glanced about at the people at each table—some

she knew, many she did not since they were the bride-groom's friends and family. She was weary and only wanted to go to bed. At last the king rose, wished them well and departed—now Sabine could leave.

Lord and Lady Woodbridge were still conversing with the guests, when Sabine slipped away. She wanting only to get out of the heavy gown and lie down because her leg ached so wretchedly. She was approaching the clearing near her mother's tent, when the sound of voices reached her.

"The jest is on Garreth," a young courtier said with a laugh. "Imagine, married to a child, and a cripple at that. I could see nothing to admire in her. You are Garreth's cousin, Cortland, what do you think of the new duchess?"

"She brings great wealth with her," he said. "For such a dowry, I could join with a squint-eyed, pock-marked hag and call myself well-satisfied."

Spiteful laughter filled the night air, and Sabine slumped against the wide trunk of a gnarled oak tree and buried her face in her hands. The physical pain that she lived with daily was nothing compared to the agony she felt at the cruel words that had been spoken so carelessly and in jest.

Then she heard an angry voice cut through the laughter. "Don't speak of the child so. She was frightened and unhappy, and deserves our compassion. And as for Garreth, think you that he cares about her wealth? He merely fulfilled his father's pledge to the king."

"We meant no harm, Stephen," said a gruff voice. "We are all friends here. I'm Garreth's cousin. Come, everyone, fill your glasses and drink a toast to the duke of Balmarough and his duchess, that they shall know true wedded bliss."

Sabine couldn't see what happened, but the laughter started again.

"Aye," the man named Stephen called out contemptuously. "Drink to Garreth's health, and then mock him. We are all friends here indeed!"

Then Sabine heard what sounded like a silver goblet hitting the tree she was leaning against.

"What ails Stephen?" someone asked, "and where is he off to in such haste? Could it be that he goes to offer comfort to his beauteous stepmother now that Garreth is wed?"

"Nay, Stephen has no liking for his father's wife. And as for Garreth, many women will weep tonight because he's wed."

Cortland Blackthorn spoke maliciously. "Think you the new little bride knows that Stephen's stepmother is Garreth's mistress and true love?"

"Better you should ask what Lady Meredith will say about the little bride. The child had best have a care or that cat will scratch her eyes out."

"It would be a pity," Cortland Blackthorn mocked.

Although Sabine had never met Garreth's cousin, she could tell by his voice that he had no love for her husband, and she was certain she did not like him.

"Come, Cortland," someone cajoled. "Don't be so harsh about the lovely Eugenia. Lord Meredith is old and ailing—some say he won't live past the summer. I have heard Lady Meredith say that she fancies herself as Garreth's wife. She had her heart set on one day being a duchess."

"Mayhap she would do better to remain Garreth's mistress. A wife is only a necessity to beget sons, while a mistress is for love and pleasure," another said.

The laughter cut into Sabine's heart. She wanted to leave, but dared not for fear of being discovered.

"Truth to tell, Garreth's child bride looked sickly to me. She may not even outlive Lady Meredith's husband,"

Cortland said. "My cousin may yet be free to marry whom he chooses. Fortune seems to always favor him, rot his soul."

Sabine clamped her hand over her mouth, wishing she were dead. The man she had just vowed before God to love and honor, did not honor her, nor did he love her. He loved someone called Lady Meredith.

3

When Lady Meredith heard the sound of a coach arriving, she jumped up from the chair where she had been lounging and rushed to view her reflection in the mirror. At last Garreth had come, and her long wait was over! She smiled at her reflection—long golden hair, deep blue eyes, and a figure that a sixteen-year-old girl would envy. She pinched her cheeks to give them some color, then moistened her lips with her tongue.

No one would suspect from her appearance that she was thirty years old. She had told Garreth that she was twenty, his same age, and he had believed her. She would tell any lie, do anything, to make him love her, and she had succeeded!

She had used all her wiles to overcome his reluctance to become entangled with a married woman. His friendship with her stepson, Stephen, had also been an obstacle.

But now Garreth worshipped her, and for him she would control her natural urges and pretend to be the proper wife who was torn by her love for him.

Eugenia fantasized about Garreth touching her and making love to her. Thus far she had played coy and not allowed him to bed her. But he wanted her—she knew that. It had taken more scheming to entrap him than any of her former lovers, but one day Garreth would be the duke of Balmarough, and she intended to be his duchess.

Her eyes gleamed as she thought of lying in his arms with his hot kisses on her lips. This would be the night that she would pretend she could no longer hold out against her feelings for him. Tonight they would become lovers.

Eugenia patted her curls into place, and satisfied with her appearance, returned to a chair by the window and busied herself with some needlework she found in a basket on the floor. It would never do to let Garreth know that she had been watching for his arrival.

As she heard voices coming from the entryway, her heart started racing and every nerve tingled with anticipation. She managed to look startled and innocent when the door to her sitting room was flung open unceremoniously.

"Oh, 'tis only you," she said to her stepson, Stephen.

He swept his plumed hat from his head and bowed in the same movement. The smile he gave her was mocking and his gray eyes were filled with dislike. "You were expecting someone else, Stepmother?" he asked in feigned surprise. "I crave your pardon if my message failed to precede me."

Every gesture he made and every word he spoke to her was exaggeratedly polite, and she hated him because she knew that his actions thinly masked his contempt. In her anticipation of Garreth's visit tonight, she had forgotten that Stephen would be arriving today.

"Your father is confined to his chambers with some new malady, if you were looking for him," she said.

"No, 'tis you that I came to see. Had I wanted my father, I would not have come to your salon, madame, since one never finds the two of you together."

Eugenia's hands tightened, and she ached to slap the polite condescension off his face. "Everyone knows that Bertram is no husband to me. He's an old man, sick and dying."

Stephen ignored her affront to his father—he had heard this all before. "I hope that you will excuse my travel dust," he said, indicating his mud-spattered clothing, "but I hastened so that I could be the first to tell you that Garreth has wed and is safe from your wiles." With satisfaction, he watched Eugenia's face pale.

"You lie!" she cried, coming to her feet. "Garreth loves me, I tell you, ME!"

Stephen was unmoved by her histrionics. "I don't think what Garreth feels for you is love, Eugenia. He loves what he thinks you are. Pity he cannot know your true character."

"How self-righteous you are. Why should you care that Garreth loves me?" Eugenia asked pointedly. Her eyes were full of contempt. "Your father doesn't care."

Stephen shrugged. "My father knew the kind of woman you were when he married you. He wanted you as an adornment on his arm, and you've been that. If he has no complaint in the way you comport yourself, then neither do I. But I blame myself that Garreth has fallen into your little trap since he met you through me."

"Garreth is the love of my life. Nothing you can say will stop his loving me."

Stephen looked incredulous. "Did you tell him about Lord Havisham and Lord Early, Eugenia? Or how about Daniel Goodman? I believe that Goodman was a butcher by trade, but that didn't keep him out of your bed, did it?"

"You beast! Garreth would love me no matter what I did in the past."

Stephen smiled slightly. "Then why don't you tell him about the night three years ago? As I recall, I was sixteen at the time."

Grimly, she waited, knowing what Stephen was going to say. Until now, neither of them had spoken of that night.

"Father unexpectedly became ill at your twenty-seventh birthday party, so the guests left early," Stephen continued. "That was the night I became disenchanted with you, Eugenia—the night you tried to climb into my bed. You had been married to my father for less than a year." He was thoughtful for a moment. "Was it boredom that brought you to my bedchamber that night? You were no longer the loving stepmother after I refused you—were you, Eugenia?"

"You dare say this to me!" she shrieked, running at Stephen and scratching at his face. "You were just a boy with no experience—why would I have wanted you?"

Stephen grabbed her wrists, restraining her. "This is the real you, Eugenia. If only Garreth could see you now."

There were voices coming from the entryway and Eugenia could hear Garreth speaking to the butler.

"Stephen," she warned, "if you say anything to—"

"I won't have to tell him, Eugenia. Unless I am mistaken, Garreth has come to do the honorable thing and bid you adieu. But then you wouldn't understand about honor, would you, Stepmother?"

Garreth entered the room and when he saw Stephen, he paused, looking from Eugenia to his friend.

Eugenia shot her stepson a triumphant look before going forward to greet her visitor. "You need not pretend with Stephen, Garreth. He knows about us, and has for a long time."

"Leave us alone, will you, Stephen?" Garreth asked, hoping Stephen would understand. "I'll have a word with Lady Meredith."

Seeing Stephen's hesitation, Garreth added, "You need have no fear for your stepmother's reputation when she is with me."

"Think you that I care who my stepmother beds? There have been many before you; there will be many after you are gone."

Eugenia cried out in rage, and Garreth moved to her side, unbridled anger coursing through his veins. "You go too far, Stephen. I will not allow anyone, not even you, to speak of Eugenia in this manner. It matters not if you are my friend, you will not defame her. I love Eugenia."

Stephen laughed, but it was without humor. "How can it be, Garreth, that you are older than me by a year, worldly and sophisticated, yet you have so little knowledge of my stepmother's sort? Think you that my father doesn't know about all her lovers? Did you really believe that you were the first?"

Eugenia watched helplessly as Garreth's face paled. She could see the growing distaste in his expression. He must not believe Stephen. She had to do something quickly. "You are simply jealous, Stephen."

"Madame, I may be the only man who finds nothing in you to love or admire," Stephen replied as he walked toward the door. He could only hope that Garreth would see Eugenia's true character for himself.

Garreth was confused. He did not want Stephen to think that he and Eugenia were lovers. "Before you go, Stephen, I would ask your pardon for deceiving you. You must believe that we have done no more than profess our love, but for the one time I kissed her."

Eugenia could see that she was losing Garreth. She lashed out at him. "Don't be so noble, Garreth. You didn't have me because I deemed it so. Had I wished it, you would have come to my bed fast enough."

When Stephen saw the sickened expression on Garreth's face he almost found it within himself to pity his stepmother—almost, but not quite. "If you need me, Garreth, I'll be with my father," he said as he left the room.

Slowly, Eugenia raised her eyes to Garreth. "If I spoke unkindly it's just because you've wounded me so deeply. Was Stephen mistaken when he told me that you are married?"

"He was not mistaken," Garreth admitted. "Although I would have preferred to tell you myself. I could not write you about the marriage and there was no time to come to you before the wedding."

She felt unbridled fury. "You said you loved me. Why would you marry someone else?"

"I was compelled to take a wife," he said. "That's why I'm here. To tell you."

Eugenia's eyes flashed and her breath came out in a hiss. "You betrayed our love, Garreth! How long have you professed to love me, while scheming to marry another? For the first time in my life, I discovered the true meaning of love. I wanted to live with you as your wife, to grow old with you, to have your children."

He looked stricken and confused. "That could never be—you have a husband, and now, I have a wife."

Eugenia's voice rose. "Could you not have waited for me? My husband is old. Each day I watch as he grows weaker—he is dying. If you had been patient, we could be together!"

Garreth saw her clearly for the first time. "If I am not myself, you will have to forgive me. My father has but recently died."

Her eyes gleamed and her hands laced together. "You are a duke now! Oh, Garreth, I knew this day would come."

He was stunned. There was no pity in her. She saw only his new rank, not the grief his father's death had caused. What had happened to the shy, helpless woman that brought out the protectiveness in him? This woman was a stranger to him. It didn't even matter anymore whether Stephen's accusations about her infidelities were true, though they probably were. How could he have thought he loved her?

Eugenia fortified herself—she would not give up so easily. She smiled, and her tongue flicked out to moisten her lips as she moved toward him, ever the seductress. "Garreth, Stephen has always hated me. Surely you see that he would discredit me in any way he can."

Her lower lip trembled and her eyes grew teary—a ploy that had worked on Garreth in the past. But she could see coldness in his eyes, and it pierced at her heart.

"Would you take Stephen's side against mine?" she asked softly.

"I'll take no one's side. I want only the truth." His eyes bore into hers and she quickly dropped her gaze.

"I thought . . . everyone thought that I was to be your wife." She buried her face in her hands. "How will I face the humiliation?"

"Eugenia, at no time did we discuss marriage."

"You said you loved me."

Garreth pondered his feelings. "To me, Eugenia, love and honor are one and the same."

He watched as her lip curled and an expression not unlike a predatory cat's masked her face. "Spare me your boyish romanticized illusions of love," she said. "And you have no honor!"

"I admit that I have not acted honorably with you. All

the blame is mine, and I can only apologize if I conducted myself badly. It was never my intention to hurt you."

"Hurt me. You tore my heart out! I was going to give myself to you tonight."

Garreth looked at her with pity. "And I had come here to tell you that we could not see each other again."

She was frantic now, her hands like claws, clutching at his shirtfront. "No! That cannot be! We were meant to be together. You must not leave me!"

He pried her fingers loose and walked toward the door, only to pause in the archway. "I wish you happiness, Eugenia."

She was gasping for breath. She wanted to see him dead! "And I wish you and your new bride a life of misery." Her breasts were heaving and her lips curved in anger. "If possible, I'll send you both to hell, no matter how long it takes!"

4

Eugenia Meredith was becoming more agitated by the moment. She had been waiting beside her disabled coach all afternoon. She was chilled, dusty, and hungry for that matter, but she would not leave until she had accomplished her objective. She must get inside Woodbridge Castle.

No little chit was going to take Garreth away from her. And if she could not have him, no one else would.

Her scheme to gain admittance to the castle was ingenious. She had instructed her driver to stop within sight of the estate and remove a wheel from her coach in such a manner that it would appear they'd had an accident. Of course, when someone from the castle recognized her plight, she would be invited to rest there until her coach was repaired.

Once a man on horseback stopped to lend assistance, but when Eugenia discovered that he was merely a traveler on his way to London, she refused his help.

It would soon be dark and she was becoming desperate. Eugenia had decided to send her footman to ask for assistance, when she noticed a girl walking across the meadow and assumed she was a servant. She had her footman attract the girl's attention.

"You there, girl," he called out through cupped hands, "come here at once."

Sabine stopped, undecided as to what to do. After a moment, she limped toward the coach. When she reached the road, Eugenia motioned her closer.

"Are you from that castle?"

Sabine immediately saw the broken wheel. "Yes, madame, I am. It appears that you need help."

"Then hasten to your master and beg his aid. Hurry, girl, it'll soon be dark, and I am weary and in need of nourishment."

Sabine agreed with a nod. "If it is your wish, you may accompany me across the meadow to my home—it is but a short distance. Or, if you prefer, I can send someone to fetch you."

The girl's cultured speech caused Eugenia to give her a closer look. She wore a brown woolen gown with a wide lace-trimmed collar and elaborate lacework on the cuffs and hem. Her red hair was pulled away from her face and secured with pearl-studded combs. Her brown boots were of the finest leather. This was no servant girl as she'd first thought; perhaps she was a member of the family.

"Are you mayhap a relative of the earl of Woodbridge?" Eugenia asked in a more courteous manner.

Sabine had been admiring the woman's yellow gown with its gold trim. It was a most elegant creation, and the woman herself had the kind of beauty anyone would admire.

"I do have the honor of being Lord Woodbridge's daughter, madame."

Eugenia gave her a tight smile. "How fortunate for me that my coach broke down near your home. I would be delighted to accompany you across the meadow, although my shoes were not meant for walking."

"Do not be concerned, madame. I shall hasten to my father and he will send a coach for you."

"I know little of your family," Eugenia said slyly. "But I thought Lord Woodbridge had only one daughter, and she was much older. Was I misinformed?"

"You were not misinformed, madame. I am my father's only daughter."

Eugenia stared at the girl long and hard. Was this some kind of jest? She was only a child; how could she possibly be Garreth's wife? And she was certainly no beauty. Eugenia tried to see her as Garreth might. There was nothing outstanding about her. She was such a tiny little thing, and so childlike. And as for her hair, men didn't like females with red hair. No, Garreth would not have taken such a child for his wife.

"You must think me rude, but may I ask your name?"

"Forgive me, madame, I should have introduced myself right away. I am Sabine Blackthorn."

Eugenia clamped her mouth together, trying unsuccessfully to bring her sudden rage under control. "Garreth's wife!" she shouted. "That cannot be! He would never marry someone like you. You are not even passingly pretty."

Sabine blinked at the unkind words that had been spoken with such venom. "Nevertheless, madame, I am the duchess of Balmarough. Garreth Blackthorn is my husband."

For a moment Eugenia could not speak as her glacial gaze fastened on the ring the girl wore. There was no mistaking the coat of arms; it was Garreth's. There arose in Eugenia a compulsive need to punish the girl that had taken her love from her. "I can see why

Garreth has not taken you to reside at Wolfeton Keep," she said spitefully. "He could hardly show you off to his friends, could he?"

Raising her head and staring squarely into the woman's eyes, Sabine realized this had to be the woman Garreth loved. "Lady Meredith?" she asked, already guessing her identity.

"So you have heard of me?" Eugenia replied with satisfaction. "I hope it will not take long to repair my coach," she sighed, plucking at the lace on the cuff of her gown and giving Sabine a sidelong glance. "Garreth always worries so if I am detained." Then she reached out and placed a cold hand on Sabine's arm. "Perhaps I shouldn't have said that."

Sabine hardly knew how to answer such viciousness. "I will not keep you waiting," she said with quiet dignity. "You will understand if I retract the invitation to my home. I will, however, send someone to assist you."

Eugenia's voice was shrill. "Insolent brat!"

"Good day, My Lady," Sabine said, fighting back tears. She turned toward home and limped away, wishing she could close out the malicious laughter that followed her.

"Garreth could never love you!" Eugenia cried. "He loves me!"

Sabine paused and turned back to her, now more angry than hurt. "If you believe that, why did you take such drastic means to make my acquaintance? If you had wanted an invitation to my home, you need not have troubled to disable your coach. You could have come to the front door."

Sabine walked with her head high, and her eyes on her home in the distance. She resisted the impulse to clasp her hands over her ears to shut out the hurtful words that followed her.

"You are nothing but a cripple. Garreth must loath

the sight of you." Eugenia fell quiet, suddenly realizing that she had lost. Sabine Blackthorn might be young and she might not be a beauty, but she was Garreth's duchess.

Sabine was still shaking when she was in sight of the castle. Rather than going inside, she made her way to the stable, where she found the head groom.

"Go at once to the outer road where you will find a coach in need of repair and lend what assistance you can. And whatever you do, do not invite the lady to Woodbridge. She is not welcome here."

The groom nodded in obedience although he found her request rather odd. "I will see to it at once, Your Grace."

Cortland Blackthorn sat in the common room of the Duck and Fox Inn, his feet extended toward the warmth of the hearth. He raised a tankard of ale to his lips as he watched the door, waiting. An hour passed and then another. He had drunk too much and he raised his voice, demanding more ale.

The brawny innkeeper moved with purpose toward the objectionable gentleman. If the man continued to be belligerent and quarrelsome, he was prepared to toss him out.

"Do you know who I am?" Cortland demanded.

"I've no knowledge of you, sir," the landlord replied.

"What's your name, landlord?" Cortland asked.

"Harold Ludlow, sir."

"Well, Mr. Ludlow, mark this well. I'm the man who's going to destroy my cousin, the duke of Balmarough. I'm sure you've heard of him. Everyone's heard of him."

Harold Ludlow was not impressed by the boasts of a man who'd had too much to drink—he'd seen it all too often. Braggarts rarely acted on their threats once they were sober. "Of course, sir, I've heard of his grace. He married Lord Woodbridge's daughter."

Cortland took another drink. "He's a stone around my neck. He has to die!"

"Of course, sir," the landlord said, absentmindedly humoring the drunken man. "Of course."

At that moment, the door opened and a woman entered. Harold Ludlow could only stare at her. His inn seldom entertained such a fine lady. She wore an elaborate yellow gown, and her face was hidden behind a heavy veil, but he could tell that she was a lady nonetheless.

Eugenia Meredith looked about the nearly empty taproom, and when her gaze rested on Cortland, she moved in his direction and sat down on a bench across from him.

"I thought you weren't coming," he said.

Her voice sounded irritated. "You're drunk."

"Damned right, and I'll be a lot drunker before I'm finished."

"I don't talk to men in their cups." She started to rise, but he reached out and clasped her hand.

"I do my best thinking with a tankard of ale in my hand."

"Lower your voice," she warned. "The ale has loosened your tongue. You asked me to meet you to talk about Garreth."

"Ah, yes, the man of my loathing and your affections. I live to see him suffer—I dream of him crying out in agony and pain. He's always had everything—wealth, power, the king's favor. You've been at Court and noticed the women vying for his attention. Then the ripest prize in all England falls into his lap. He marries Lord Woodbridge's only daughter, who brings to the marriage great power and wealth."

"I just saw his wife," Eugenia said grimly. "That's why I'm late."

"She's just a child, but she reminds me of someone I once cared for. Garreth's little wife is delicate of face, and when she is older, she may be a beauty—her mother is."

Eugenia looked at Cortland distastefully. Another drink and he would probably tell everyone their plan. "I don't want to hear about her virtues. What I must know is how Garreth feels about her."

"How should I know?" Cortland bit out venomously. "I was not even presented to her, although I was at the wedding. I was not even considered important enough to sit with the family members at the banquet."

"Garreth could not want her with him or she would not still abide with her father and mother," Eugenia speculated.

"There was an agreement that Garreth's little duchess would remain with her family until she was older."

Lady Meredith looked at Cortland through her veil, trying to see into his black heart. "I know my reasons for wanting to punish Garreth, but why do you hate him?"

"Many are his sins against me, though there was a time when I actually admired him. When we were only lads, my father would always compare me to Garreth in an unfavorable light, stressing Garreth's accomplishments and reprimanding me because I was not more like my clever cousin." Cortland laughed evilly. "He even saved me from drowning once. I'll never forget that day—he was proclaimed a hero, by his father and mine, while I was sent to my room and admonished for being a fool."

Eugenia leaned forward so she could hear his whispered words. It was rumored that Cortland was deeply in debt and that his estates were in disarray—still he continued to live well, and she wondered how he managed that, if not with Garreth's assistance.

"You haven't the power to touch him without my help," she said.

Cortland stroked his well-trimmed beard. "Together we will be formidable, My Lady. And the best part of this plan is that no one will ever suspect us." He looked pleased with himself. "The plan is ingenious."

"Don't be so pompous. You are acting out of anger, and if we are to succeed, we must use caution."

"I'll see Garreth dead, along with everything he cherishes. But I'll need money."

"Lower your voice, fool! The ale has gone to your head, and people are beginning to stare. You will have the money, but you must promise me that Garreth will not be harmed. I still have hopes of one day becoming his duchess. And you, Cortland, will be well rewarded when that day comes."

Cortland looked at her through blurry eyes. His plan differed from Eugenia Meredith's, although she would not know it until it was too late. He would be satisfied with nothing less than the death and dishonor of his cousin. First he would see Garreth imprisoned in the Tower, and then beheaded for the crime of slaying Lord Woodbridge's family.

"When will I have the money?" he asked.

"I'll let you know. I had hoped to be invited into Woodbridge Castle today so I could gauge their defenses for myself. But Garreth's little bride spoiled my plans."

"Make it soon."

Eugenia still wondered if she could trust Cortland Blackthorn. "You have not told me the real reason you became my ally in this."

Cortland's hand balled into a fist. "Her name was Anna. She was beautiful and from a good family—Lord Timothy Dryson's youngest daughter."

"I've never heard of her."

"That's because she's been dead for three years. I loved her as I've never loved another woman. I wanted to marry her, but she wouldn't have me."

"Why?"

"Because she was so smitten with my cousin, and the bloody bastard hardly knew she existed." Rage blazed in Cortland's eyes. "Do you hear me? She killed herself—just walked right into the river that ran through her father's estate. They found a note saying she didn't want to live if Garreth didn't love her."

Eugenia did not admire weakness in anyone. "It sounds as if her mind was unhinged."

Cortland's eyes narrowed. "Do not speak of Anna that way. When I told my cousin about the tragedy, he looked blank and informed me that he knew of no one by the name of Anna Dryson."

"Oh, yes, Garreth has no end of admirers; one cannot expect him to remember all their names. But he will remember mine," Eugenia vowed.

"It was I who found Anna's body," Cortland continued with a shudder. "So pale she was, so swollen with river water, that I hardly recognized her. Garreth must be made to suffer for her death!"

Eugenia reached for his wrist and her long fingernails dug into his skin. "I told you that Garreth is not to be harmed in any way, Cortland. Is that understood?"

He twisted his hand out of her grasp, staring at the deep nail marks. "I understand."

Eugenia looked into his eyes. His mind was twisted, and he would surely end up on the executioner's block. But little she cared as long as he didn't implicate her. Perhaps she would have to take him as a lover to assure his loyalty—but not unless it became necessary. She did not find him appealing.

She rose to her feet. "My coach is waiting. I'll send a messenger to you when everything is ready."

Suddenly Cortland reached out and took her hand. "Remain with me tonight."

She flung his hand away as if his touch was defiling. Then remembering that she must pacify him, she spoke softly. "You sorely tempt me, but we must be discreet. There is time enough for our own pleasures when we have carried out our plan." Eugenia tugged on her wrist-length gloves. "I advise you to seek your bed before you draw more attention to yourself."

He watched her leave and then called loudly for another drink, gaining notice of everyone in the tap-room.

"Anyone who has ever slighted me will rue the day." He raised his tankard over his head. "Death to my enemy, Garreth Blackthorn!"

5

Sabine corresponded regularly with Garreth's mother, although she heard nothing from Garreth himself. Not that she wanted to after meeting Lady Meredith. The crested ring she wore was the only reminder that she had a husband.

It was a crisp morning as she walked down a grassy path toward the meadow. She tried to walk every day, hoping it would strengthen her leg. If only she'd thought to wear her leather boots because her thin-soled velvet slippers were wet clear through. In irritation, she removed them and climbed onto a stone wall to bask in the warmth of the sun.

Sabine had not heard the sound of riders emerging from the woods, so she was startled when she saw Garreth and another gentleman ride across the grassy meadow toward her.

Garreth greeted her as he dismounted. "Good

morning to you, Sabine. Your mother told me that I'd find you here."

She pulled her gown down, hoping to hide her bare feet. "Your Grace, I had no notion that you would be calling on us today."

"Perhaps I should not have come unannounced?"

Sabine met his eyes, determined that he was not going to make her feel insignificant. She was still angry because of his mistress's visit. "Perhaps, next time you will give us some forewarning so we can prepare a fitting welcome."

His lips twitched in amusement. "I stand rebuked, and you are right, of course. My only excuse is that I joined Sir Clander's hunting party, and since he's your neighbor, I took the opportunity to pay you a visit."

Garreth turned to the gentleman beside him. "I do not believe you have met Sir Stephen Meredith, although he did attend our wedding."

Stephen bowed gallantly to her. "Your Grace, I searched for you after the wedding so that I might be presented to you, but you had already retired. I am glad for the honor of meeting you today."

She remembered well the conversation she had overheard between Sir Stephen and the other gentlemen the day of her wedding. He had been the only one loyal to Garreth, and he had also attempted to defend her. There was genuine warmth in her voice when she greeted him. "I am glad to know you, Sir Stephen."

"I am your servant," he replied, flashing a most infectious smile. It would be hard not to be charmed by him and she liked him at once.

Reluctantly, Sabine turned her attention to her husband. He wore dark green tight-fitting breeches, a matching doublet, and black-cuffed boots that came halfway up his thighs. She noticed the way his black hair lay against his shoulder. He was even more handsome than she remembered.

When Garreth's gaze swept across her face, Sabine was mortified by the blush that tinted her cheeks. If only she could think of something clever to say to him.

He stared transfixed at his family ring circling her finger. His mother had taken it off the day his father died and placed it in his hand, knowing he would do as his father had wished and marry where the king commanded.

"My mother sends her regards and thanks you for your letters," Garreth said awkwardly.

"Her grace has been most kind. I await the day we meet."

Sabine became distressed when Garreth noticed her bare feet, and she cringed at the half smile that curved his lips. How childish she must seem to him compared to the beautiful Lady Meredith. She felt unattractive under the probing gaze of this sophisticated man.

Garreth sensed Sabine's discomfort and attempted to lighten the conversation. "How are you faring?" he asked. "How do you fill your days?"

"Mostly I take care of my brother, Richard. And I'm very well, thank you, Your Grace. I trust you are also well?"

"Indeed I am." He was silent for a long moment, not knowing what else to say to her. Finally, he suggested that they walk toward the castle.

With a resigned sigh, Sabine dropped her slippers on the grass with the intention of pushing her feet into them. But before the deed was accomplished, Garreth knelt to assist her, which only made her feel even more humiliated. She was grateful that Sir Stephen had tactfully turned away and appeared to be absorbed in examining something in the branches of an oak tree.

When Sabine's slippers were firmly in place, Garreth stood, towering over her. He had almost forgotten how young she was. He certainly didn't remember her having such spirit. At their first meeting she had been a frightened child. Now there was a spark of life and a hint of defiance in her strangely beautiful amber eyes.

When he offered her his arm, she hesitated for only a moment before she placed her hand on it. As they followed the stone wall, Stephen gallantly walked behind them, leading the horses.

The air smelled of wood smoke, crisp and clean. In the distance they could hear the cowbells tinkling as her father's herd was driven in from the meadow for milking. When they proceeded down a worn tree-lined path, a shower of multicolored leaves fell about them, a sign that autumn had arrived.

"Your mother was just telling me some of your accomplishments," Garreth said. "Lady Woodbridge is quite proud of the fact that you speak French as easily as you speak English."

"That is not such an accomplishment when you consider that my mother is French and taught me from early childhood."

There was sharpness in Sabine's tone, and Garreth wondered at the reason for it. He stopped, holding her away from him and inspecting her closely. She was a slender child, and there was a sprinkle of freckles across the bridge of her nose. The most remarkable thing about her was her extraordinary topaz eyes. He felt a twinge of guilt. In truth, she hadn't crossed his mind until Stephen reminded him that the Woodbridge estate bordered Sir Clander's land.

Garreth was staring at her so intently that she looked away. "You haven't had much dealing with children, have you, Your Grace?"

He looked stunned. "I . . . no, I haven't. Do you consider yourself a child?"

"It matters but little what I consider myself because you think of me as a child. But I shan't be young forever." She frowned thoughtfully. "Actually, I am considered by most to be a young lady now that I am your . . . your . . . wife."

"I see."

Sabine could tell that he was uncomfortable with her. She gazed out at the pasture land without seeing it. "If it had been within my power, I would not have married you, Your Grace. But no one asked me what I wanted." She turned back to him. "I was told that if I didn't marry you our families might one day be on opposing sides in a conflict."

He stared at her in amazement. "I cannot imagine being your adversary, Sabine. Like you, I had little to say in the matter of our marriage. Perhaps, in time, when we come to know each other, we will deal admirably together."

She wanted to ask him about Lady Meredith, but she knew that would not be proper. "If you were free to marry where you chose, who would now be your wife?" she asked instead.

He laughed, knowing better than to step into that old female trap. With a courtly manner he bowed before her. "Perhaps I would still have chosen you."

She didn't think he would, but it was gallant of him to say so.

"Regrettably," Garreth went on, "I must leave for London at once. But first I would ask a boon of you."

"I will grant you what I can."

"Since I am your legal husband, could you not call me Garreth?"

"Yes, if that is your wish, Garreth."

"Much better." He turned to look at the imposing castle that appeared to be rising out of the mist. "It's lovely here. I am sure you will miss it when you leave."

"Yes, I shall. I am extremely close to my family. My mother does not often feel well, and my brother is so spirited that he quickly tires her, so I spend most of my day with him."

"That's very admirable of you. Was your childhood a happy one?"

"Exceedingly happy." Mischief danced in her eyes. "It still is."

Garreth laughed heartily. Taking her small hand in his, he stared once more at the Balmarough ring. "Now, lady wife, I fear I must leave you."

To her surprise, she felt a sharp pang of disappointment. "The day grows late. I suppose you must hurry or you will lose the light. Unless," she added hopefully, "you and Sir Stephen would like to bide the night with my family."

"I fear that we cannot. By morning we'll be halfway to London."

She wondered if he was rushing to see Lady Meredith.

Garreth had been watching Sabine out of the corner of his eye. There was pain etched on her face with each step she took, though she tried to hide it. He had the strongest urge to lift her in his arms and carry her so that he might ease her suffering, but he knew she would not welcome his assistance.

"Your leg troubles you, Sabine?"

"'Tis of little consequence."

Garreth had discovered two things about his wife today: She didn't complain, and she was no one's fool.

"I wonder if you would allow me to send the king's physician to examine you? William Harvey is of some renown. It was he who first discovered that blood circulates through the whole body. I daresay that he can help you."

"It would not be wise to bring the king's physician to Woodbridge," Sabine said hurriedly. "Papa would never welcome him. Even if he did agree to our marriage, he still distrusts his majesty, and I don't believe he trusts you either."

"Do you trust me, Sabine?"

She considered his question seriously, and thought of his mistress. "I don't know you very well."

Her honesty was refreshing, and he realized it sprang from her youth. Unfortunately, as she grew older she would learn to hide her feelings and dance around the truth. "Perhaps William Harvey can examine your leg when you move to Wolfeton Keep. 'Tis a pity to wait so long, though."

By now they had reached the castle and Stephen joined them.

"I have brought you a surprise, Sabine," Garreth said. "You will find it in your room. I hope it pleases you."

Her eyes were shining. "I am fond of surprises, Your Grace—Garreth. What is it?"

"Uh . . . if I told you, it wouldn't be a surprise, would it?" He softly touched her cheek and her eyes widened at his gentleness. "My mother is often lonely. It will be most pleasant for her when you move to Wolfeton Keep so you can be a companion to her."

Sabine quickly looked up at him, wondering if he had intended to insult her by suggesting he only wanted her as a companion to his mother. There was controlled anger in her words. "It is always important to meet with the approval of one's mother-in-law."

Garreth looked bewildered, trying to think what he had said to displease her. "You have no cause for worry. I believe my mother will be enchanted with you." He raised her hand to his lips. "Farewell, until we meet again." Then he pushed his booted foot into the stirrup and mounted his horse.

Stephen bowed to her. "I hope to see you again soon, Your Grace."

"I would like that, Sir Stephen. You will always find a welcome at Woodbridge."

She watched them ride away, wondering why she suddenly felt lonely. With a deep intake of breath, she moved up the steps, pausing often to rest her aching leg.

When she reached her bedchamber, she found that a neatly folded length of red velvet lay across her bed. Eagerly, she lifted the fabric and gasped. It was a floor-length cape, completely lined with ermine. Sabine flung it around her shoulders and moved before a mirror. She buried her face in the silky fur that almost felt alive as it softly caressed her skin. She had never possessed anything half so fine. She picked up the note that had fallen to the floor and read the bold script.

For my duchess. Let this serve as a twofold gift—to keep you warm and remind you of me.

How kind of Garreth to think of her, she thought. It was a gift she would treasure always.

She had no way of knowing that the words she cherished had not been written by her husband, nor had he chosen the gift.

．

Garreth and Stephen had been riding for over an hour when they reached the Duck and Fox Inn.

"My throat's dry. I could use a tankard of ale," Stephen said.

"Very well," Garreth agreed. "I could use one myself. It was damned hard talking to Sabine today. What do you say to one so young?"

Stephen laughed. "The first time you've met a female who didn't swoon at your feet and she's your wife. Could this mean that you're losing your way with the ladies?"

Garreth scowled as he dismounted and handed his reins to an attendant. "I find nothing humorous in the situation. Sabine is too young to be a wife. Most probably she still plays with toys. Besides, she liked you better than me."

Stephen laughed. "I don't think so, Garreth."

They entered the inn and found a table near the hearth. After the landlord had served them, Garreth took a sip of his ale and leaned back thoughtfully. "She has spirit—the kind I would wish for in a little sister, if I had one. I don't know that it's a quality I want in a wife, however." He looked at his friend inquiringly. "What is your impression of her?"

Stephen hid a smile behind his tankard. Garreth was more taken with his new bride than he wanted to admit. "I believe that she is the loveliest little girl I have ever seen. I could look into those golden eyes for hours."

"She's in pain," Garreth said in a troubled voice.

"I saw that. 'Tis a pity."

Garreth slammed his tankard down so forcefully that ale splashed onto the table. "Damn the forces that control my life! Sabine is too young to even understand what goes on between a man and woman. When a beautiful lady catches my eye, I feel damn guilty for what I am imagining. Being a husband does not set well with me."

Stephen leaned against the high-back bench, unconcerned by Garreth's outburst. "Whatever troubles you,

I'm sure you'll overcome it." He took a sip of ale. "I noticed you were struggling to make conversation with Sabine today. Why don't you just treat her the way you would any other woman?"

"She's not a woman. I can't imagine ever . . . well, you know what I mean. I will never be able to be a husband to her because I'll always see her as a child."

"I saw something in her eyes today that you obviously missed. She likes you, and I'd say more as a woman than a child."

"Damn!"

Humor danced in Stephen's eyes. "So you said several times. But don't worry, by now she is probably wearing the gift you brought her and thinking of you fondly for your thoughtfulness."

"I doubt it—she still doesn't trust me." Garreth leaned forward. "I must remember to thank your sister for selecting Sabine's gift. What was it?"

"Betty said it was a cape befitting a queen. When you get the accounting, you'll think you bought the Crown Jewels."

"That would be your idea," Garreth said dryly.

"It was. I told my sister not to consider the cost, and she didn't." Stephen drained his ale. "By the way, you wrote your little wife a charming sentiment."

"I suppose that was your idea also."

"Of course." Then Stephen became serious. "I pity the little duchess, Garreth. Be kind to her."

"Perhaps you should have married her," Garreth said sourly.

"The king didn't ask it of me. Of course I don't hold the power and rank of your family. But mark this well, Garreth, Sabine Blackthorn will one day make you proud to be her husband. Even though she's young, she has pride and conducts herself with honor and dignity.

Those are rare qualities and you should cherish them in her."

"This conversation begins to weary me," Garreth said, coming to his feet. "If we are going to make London, we had best be away."

6

Sabine was bent over her father's desk while his steward explained to her about keeping household accounts. Her mother had begun to train her more diligently in the management of a large household as she prepared to become mistress of Wolfeton Keep.

Thea, her old nursemaid, appeared at the door. "No more lessons today. Her ladyship's asking for you."

Sabine closed the ledger gratefully and stood. On her way out of the room she stopped at the window to look at the gathering clouds. "It looks as if it'll storm before nightfall."

Thea nodded while peering over Sabine's shoulder. "Aye, that it will."

They had just stepped into the entry when the storm hit. A sudden gust of wind rattled the windows and one flew open, blowing out the candles and casting them into darkness. Servants rushed about, latching windows and relighting candles.

"'Tis an ill omen," Thea said. "Something bad is going to happen."

Sabine shivered, not knowing why. She, too, had been feeling restless and uneasy all day, and now that night was approaching, the feeling only intensified.

At that moment, her mother's personal maid came rushing down the stairs, her face red as she gasped to catch her breath. "Everything's astir, Your Grace. Her ladyship is giving birth! I was sent to find your father."

Sabine hurried toward the stairs. "I must go to her at once."

"No!" Thea said emphatically, planting her body in Sabine's path. "Even though you're married, you have no place in a birthing chamber."

Sabine looked stricken, and Thea spoke to her soothingly. "You must think of what's best for your mother. This is no time for her ladyship to be worrying about you. Wait in your room, and I'll come to you as soon as the baby is born."

Reluctantly, Sabine went upstairs, where she settled Richard for the night and then went to her own bedchamber. She tried to concentrate on her needlework, but it was useless, so she set it aside. She turned her head to the window, watching rain patter against the glass, and prayed that this baby would live.

It was not yet midnight when Thea entered the room, sorrowfully shaking her head. "I'm sorry, Sabine, the baby died. Her ladyship's asked to see you."

"No, Thea! How will she endure this loss?"

"'Tis a tragedy. I don't believe she'll have anymore children—this birth was hard on her. Go to her and give what comfort you can."

Sabine hurried down the corridor and into her

mother's bedchamber. Lady Woodbridge was pale and her damp hair clung to her face. When she looked at Sabine, her eyes were dull and so sad. She reached for her daughter's hand. "Do not look so distraught, dearest. It was not meant that the child should live."

Sabine dropped to her knees, pressing her lips to her mother's hand. There were no words she could utter that would bring comfort. "Please rest now, *Maman*. I shall stay beside you tonight."

Her mother managed a weak smile. "You have always been so dear to me, Sabine. Promise that you will take care of Richard."

Sabine exchanged a puzzled glance with her father, who stood at the foot of the bed, looking miserable. "But you will care for Richard yourself, *Maman*. Tell her, Papa."

"Do not speak thus, Ryanne, lest you bring it about," Lord Woodbridge said harshly.

"But if anything should happen—it will not—but if it should, Sabine, you will give Richard the love that I would have given him?"

Sabine could see that her mother needed her assurance. "I promise, *Maman*."

"Nothing will happen to you. I won't allow it, do you hear," Lord Woodbridge stated firmly.

Sabine felt a stab at her heart when she saw the uncertainty in her father's eyes. Something was dreadfully wrong. She clasped her mother's hand tightly, willing her strength to flow into her weakened body.

Ryanne Woodbridge's eyes were soft and loving as she looked at her husband. "Go to your bed, William. I will rest now, with my daughter beside me."

He nodded and moved away, his shoulders hunched as if he had been dealt a mortal blow.

Sabine remained with her mother throughout the

night. Sometimes Lady Woodbridge would fall into a restless sleep, and other times she would just quietly stare out the darkened window. Her skin was hot to the touch, and she complained of thirst.

The midwife had come in during the night and assured Sabine that her mother's condition was normal and that she would grow stronger each day.

But Lady Woodbridge did not grow stronger—five days after her infant son had been placed in the family crypt, she died. The midwife said that it was milk fever, but Sabine believed her mother had died of a broken heart from the loss of another baby.

A dark pall hung over Woodbridge Castle and in the surrounding village, for Lady Woodbridge had been well loved. The day she was entombed, a storm raged and rain poured down as if the whole sky wept for the gentle lady.

Sabine bowed her head and listened to the glowing words Father Santini spoke about her mother. She held Richard's hand, grateful that he was too young to understand what had happened. He just looked about with interest and kept asking Sabine why all these people had come to Woodbridge.

Before the funeral mass was over, the skies cleared and the sun was warm on Sabine's face. She heard magpies chattering in a nearby oak tree and wondered how everything could go on as if nothing had happened, when her world had been shattered.

Her father stood apart from everyone, his shoulders hunched, his face a mask of grief. Sabine had tried to comfort him, but he had brushed her aside. She managed for Richard's sake not to cry. Later, when she was alone, she would grieve. She felt a presence beside her, and a hand lightly touched her arm.

Sabine turned to stare into the sympathetic eyes of

Garreth Blackthorn. She had not expected him to come, and she was surprised at how grief-stricken he looked.

He stood beside her, his arm going about her shoulders, lending her his strength. If only he could know what his appearance there meant to her. In the last few days she had been forced to shed all vestiges of her carefree childhood. Her father was not thinking coherently, and it was she who had made all the decisions that kept Woodbridge Castle running smoothly.

At last the service was over. Garreth reached down and lifted Richard in his arms and the boy lay his head against his shoulder sleepily. Garreth took Sabine's hand and led her away from the mourners.

"I'm so sorry," he said gently. "I know well what you are feeling, Sabine."

It was becoming more difficult not to cry. "Thank . . . you, Garreth."

"I came as soon as I heard." He was concerned because of the constraint she was keeping on her emotions. "It's all right to cry, Sabine."

"I dare not. My father is not taking this well—I must be strong for him and my brother."

Thea came forward and took Richard from Garreth and carried him toward the castle.

"Shall we walk, Sabine?" he asked.

"The guests—"

"They can wait."

He drew her closer to him and they moved into the walled garden that had been Lady Woodbridge's pride. Garreth led her to a bench and sat down beside her.

"I have no words of comfort, Sabine. I just wanted you to know that I share your loss."

Now she lowered her head and great sobs tore at her

throat. She was supported in comforting arms and Garreth lightly stroked her hair. "There, there, cry all you want. It is fitting to cry for the mother you loved."

And she did. She cried so hard it hurt. Great, deep sobs tumbled from her lips, as her husband gently held her to him. She hadn't even known she needed him until now. All the anger Sabine had felt because of Lady Meredith's visit melted away when she looked into his dark misty eyes and knew that he did share her anguish.

After a while, he wiped her eyes with his handkerchief. "It is good to grieve. The ones who keep it inside will suffer longer."

She nodded. "That's what my father's doing. He won't allow himself to cry."

"Sabine," Garreth said, lifting her chin so she met his eyes, "when my father died, someone gave me something that meant more to me than all the heartfelt condolences I'd received."

"What could that be?"

He reached into his doublet and withdrew a rose that had been slightly crushed. "A rose, my lady wife. 'Tis a marvel that I found it growing wild beside the road, and this late in the season."

She took a deep gulp of air and looked at him questioningly.

"Yes," Garreth said, "like the rose you once gave me." He touched his lips to the delicate flower and handed it to her.

She clutched it to her like a lifeline and dropped her eyes, fearful that if she looked at him, she would surely cry again.

"Thank you, Garreth."

"Is there anything you need?"

She shook her head. "No, nothing."

"I regret that I must leave you now." He stood and

brought her up beside him. "My mother sends her condolences."

"Thank her grace for me."

He took her hand and brushed his lips against it. She raised her head to him, wishing he would take her in his arms again. Like one in a daze, she moved closer to him, raising her head and parting her lips.

Instantly Garreth lowered his head and touched his lips to her mouth as softly as gossamer wings. It was a gesture intended to give comfort, but without him even being aware of it, his hand moved to her silken hair and he held her while deepening the kiss.

Inexplicable, disturbing feelings raced through his veins like molten lava. Suddenly he tore his mouth from hers and stared into her misty golden eyes. What had he done!

Trying to gather his composure, and bring his thundering heart under control, he planted a chaste kiss on her forehead. "Good-bye, Sabine," he said gruffly.

Her heart was beating so loudly that she could not speak. Her first kiss had stolen her breath and sent the blood pounding in her body. Oh, how she wanted him to remain with her. "Good-bye, Garreth," she said softly.

Sabine sat back down on the bench and lowered her head, unwilling to watch him walk away, but she heard the sound of his boot steps fade into the distance, and then there was only silence.

In wonder, she touched her mouth that was still soft from his kiss. With tears in her eyes, she raised the rose and touched its velvety petals to her lips.

Sabine thought it was strange, that on such a sad day, she had come to love her husband.

7

Sabine's mother had been dead for five weeks, and still her father was inconsolable. He'd shut himself in his study, taking his meals and sleeping there, refusing to see anyone.

Sabine hardly recognized him as the man who had once been the strength of the family. On the rare occasions when he did venture forth from his seclusion, he was subdued, as if he'd lost direction.

Sabine kept her promise to her mother and took over the complete care of Richard. On his fourth birthday, she threw off her grief to make the day special for him. If Richard was aware that his father did not attend the celebration, he did not mention it.

Now, Sabine stood at her bedroom window gazing out at the crescent moon that strained through the ebony sky, lending only a pale light to the land and shrouding the village from her sight. On the eastern horizon, dark

storm clouds gathered, making their presence known by
the rumbling thunder and the lightening that split
through the air like sword shafts.

She wondered what Garreth was doing tonight. Did
he ever think of her? He was constantly on her mind,
and she often relived the moment of their first kiss.

Thea bustled about, going to the small room that had
once been Sabine's dressing closet but was now Richard's
bedroom. She smiled at the sleeping boy before returning
to Sabine.

"It's late, Thea, why don't you go to bed," Sabine
urged her.

"I couldn't sleep. My bones ache, so it'll soon storm.
It'll be raining in the hills now."

Sabine realized she'd been clasping her hands so
tightly that she had dug her nails into her palm. "I've
been restless all day, Thea. I don't know how to explain
it because I don't believe in premonitions. It's just that I
feel something is wrong."

"And why shouldn't you have feelings of doom? You
have the running of Woodbridge and cannot go to his
lordship for guidance. It's too much to bear for one so
young."

"Oh, Thea, what will happen to Richard when I
leave? Papa must realize that his son needs him now
more than ever."

"What Lord Richard needs is you, with no mother to
love him."

"Thea," Sabine said wearily, "I only hope—" Her
voice trailed off when Richard started to whimper in his
sleep. She hurried to him and gathered him into her
arms. The child clung to her, sobbing for his mother,
and not understanding why she no longer came to him.

"There, there, dearest. Do not fret. Sabine is here for
you."

Richard curled up in his sister's arms, sighing contentedly. Each day he seemed to remind her more and more of their mother, with the same light-colored hair and blue eyes and the same sweet temperament. Sabine sat on the edge of his bed and hummed softly until his eyes grew heavy and he drifted off to sleep, his small hand clutching the front of her gown. Her eyes were filled with pity as she gazed down at him. Richard would never remember the love of their gentle mother, but she was determined to give him a mother's love.

Laying him back onto the bed, she covered him and tiptoed to her own chamber.

Thea went about the room, collecting discarded gowns and slippers and putting them away in the trunk at the foot of the bed. After the room was straightened to her satisfaction, she turned to Sabine. "You get into bed. You've carried the load for us all. Rest now."

"I am fatigued," Sabine admitted.

The old nurse wondered sadly what was to become of her charge. She couldn't remain in her father's home forever. Soon her husband would come for her. Then what would Lord Richard do with neither mother nor loving sister to help shape his growing years when he would develop as a man?

The storm was intensifying and lightning illuminated the bedchamber. "I'll just get you something warm to drink, mayhap then you'll sleep," Thea said, lifting a candle and moving into the hallway and down the stairs on her way to the kitchen.

Thea's footsteps were noiseless as she moved through the halls that she had walked for many years. When she passed Lord Woodbridge's study, she noticed that the door was ajar. Thinking that was odd, she reached to close it, but paused when she heard his lordship speaking angrily to someone.

"He dares send an underling to escort my daughter to Wolfeton Keep? I'll not tolerate it! Return to your master and remind him our agreement was that my daughter would remain with us until she reached her sixteenth birthday. And even then, she will not leave unless Garreth Blackthorn comes for her himself."

Thea heard scuffling and flattened herself into the shadows. Her hand was trembling so badly that she dropped the candle, thus casting the corridor into darkness. She heard a muffled cry and then someone brushed past her.

She moved quickly into the study to find Lord Woodbridge on the floor, the front of his doublet stained with blood!

He attempted to rise, but fell back gasping in pain.

"M'lord," Thea cried, grabbing his arm and trying to aid him to his feet. "What has happened?"

Lord Woodbridge collapsed in a chair, a bloody hand clutching his chest. "Go to Sabine . . . at once. Get her and my son to safety . . . hasten! There is danger!"

"But, M'lord—"

"Do it now, woman! For reasons unknown to me . . . Garreth Blackthorn has sent his men to do murder. I am trusting you . . . to save my children. Impress upon my . . . daughter that it is her duty to—" A cough rattled in his chest, and it was a moment before he could catch his breath. "It is her duty to keep Richard . . . safe."

Thea reached out to him. "I must first see to your wound M'lord."

He shook his head. "There is no help for me . . . but my son must live. You are the only one I can . . . trust, Thea."

Lord Woodbridge's face was devoid of color. Blood gushed from his chest with every beat of his heart.

Thea knew that he had been mortally wounded—he

could not live past a few moments. "M'lord," she asked urgently, "why would the duke—"

"Go, Thea!" His voice came out in a gasp, and he was having trouble focusing his eyes. "Save my children! Do not let that monster . . . get his hands on my . . . daughter."

Spurred on by her love for the children, Thea obeyed, leaving the earl to his sad fate. Cautiously, she left the room and moved like a shadow toward the stairs, knowing there must be more of the duke's men about.

Suddenly sounds of fighting and struggle reached her. The castle was in turmoil—servants were scattering frantically, being chased by sword-wielding soldiers who were dressed in the duke of Balmarough's blue and white livery. Knowing where her duty lay, the old nurse hurried up the stairs, often peering behind her to make certain that no one was in pursuit.

She reached the top step and was running along the hall, when she heard the clamor of the intruders as they reached the grand staircase. They would soon be searching every room, and they must not find Sabine and Richard.

With breath trapped in her throat and eyes wild with fear, Thea burst into Sabine's room.

Sabine was just getting into bed. "What's amiss? You look like something—"

"There is no time. Make haste—make haste, there is danger!"

"What are you saying?" Sabine demanded.

"No time to talk." Thea moved quickly into the next room and lifted a sleeping Richard and thrust him into Sabine's arms, grateful that the young lord did not awaken.

"We must hurry if we are to escape!"

Sabine stared at her in disbelief. "I will not go one step until you tell me what is happening."

Without ceremony, Thea shoved Sabine toward the door. "You can flee now and ask questions later. To delay may mean the death of you and your brother."

"Father would never allow that," Sabine protested.

"It was his lordship who sent me to save you and Lord Richard. Do you talk until those men are upon us, or do you come with me?"

There was something frantic about her, and Sabine was suddenly terrified. "Tell me what to do."

"Follow me. I don't believe the duke's men will know about the secret passage in your father's room."

"What duke, what men?" Sabine asked.

"Shh! Just hurry."

Sabine wore only her nightgown, so Thea grabbed up the red velvet cape and slipped it around her charge's shoulders.

Then, Thea cautiously opened the door and glanced into the hallway, first one way, then the other. When she was satisfied that it was safe, she motioned for Sabine to follow her.

"They're already on the second floor. I hear them searching the rooms—hurry—it won't be long until they will be upon us!"

Sabine clutched Richard to her and followed the nurse down the dimly-lit corridor. Thea extinguished the wall sconces as they passed, thus casting darkness behind them.

When they reached the master bedchamber, Thea closed the door and turned to Sabine. "I know there is a secret panel in this room and you know how to open it—do so with all haste."

"Where is my father? Why isn't he coming with us?"

"I told you that he ordered me to take you to safety,"

Thea said, knowing this was not the time to tell Sabine that her father was probably dead.

With her mind in a quandary, Sabine moved to the fireplace and pulled down the lion's paw on the ornate facade. Slowly a panel slid open to reveal a dark cavity. Thea pushed Sabine inside and followed, then pulled the latch that closed the panel, throwing them into total darkness.

Leaning against the dank, cold walls, Sabine tried to catch her breath. Richard's added weight, slight though it was, made it more difficult for her to stand. "Now, Thea, you must tell me what is happening."

"He sent his men to destroy this family." There was a catch in the nurse's voice as if she could not go on. "I don't know why he has done this."

"Done what? Who are you talking about?"

"The duke—your husband."

"Surely you are mistaken," Sabine said in disbelief. "Why would Garreth—" She had a horrible thought. "Where is my father?"

Thea's hand came down on her arm. "His lordship . . . was mortally wounded. I'm grieved to tell you that he . . . will be dead by now."

A moan escaped Sabine's lips, and she fought frantically to reach the latch to open the panel. "I must go to him at once! He needs me."

Thea placed her body between Sabine and the lever, hoping she could make her understand the danger that lurked on the other side of that panel. "Your father is beyond help—you must think of your brother."

A deep sob was building up inside Sabine, and she choked it down. "How can this be? Why would Garreth do this thing?" She remembered his kindness to her after her mother's death. "There is no reason for such an action."

"There's no mistake—his lordship told me it was your husband's men. Shh," Thea cautioned in a whisper. "I hear someone. Let us be silent."

Sabine wanted to confront the men who had dared to invade her home and she wanted to go to her father, but she could only stand there in the dark, hiding like a frightened animal. Her brother had been entrusted to her, and she must keep him safe—this she owed her father and mother.

Richard moved in her arms, and she rocked him back and forth, hoping he would not awaken. Soon he became still, and she drew in a relieved breath.

Sabine heard the sound of smashing furniture and breaking glass—the men were destroying her father's bedchamber. At last it was quieter, and she could hear the muffled voices of the men beyond the wall. One of them must have moved close to the fireplace, for she could now understand his words.

"It'll go hard with us if we don't find the duchess and her brother. We aren't to return until they're dead."

Sabine now fully realized the danger. Those men must not discover the hidden panel.

"You are certain that Lord Woodbridge is dead?" a commanding voice asked.

The voice that replied was farther away, and the only thing Sabine could distinguish was when he said yes.

She turned her face to the wall, feeling a pain so sharp it was like a knife cutting into her heart.

"Find his grace's wife and we'll find the boy," the man who was apparently the leader ordered impatiently.

Aching with grief and overcome with anger, Sabine cried silent tears. She cried for her father, she cried for her brother, and she cried because the man she had begun to love wanted her and her whole family dead.

But why?

Time had no meaning there in the darkness. They dared not move or make the slightest noise lest they give away their hiding place.

All was quiet but for the breathing of the three in the darkened room. Sabine's arms were aching from supporting Richard's weight, and she moved to brace her back against the wall.

"Thea," she whispered, "dare we leave now?"

"I'm afraid we must. If they question the servants, some may know about the existence of this secret room."

"No one outside my family knows how to open the panel, Thea. Even you didn't know the secret. Let us go forward. It will be difficult without light to guide us. We should move along the wall, for it narrows into an earthen tunnel and slopes downward toward the stream."

"Do you want me to carry his lordship?" Thea asked. "You might trip with your leg."

"No, I will carry him, but you be careful, Thea. My father once told me that this was built during the bloody reign of Queen Mary so my ancestors could smuggle priests in and out of the castle. But they had torches to light their way, and we have none." She paused to catch her breath. "How can we know who is friend or foe?"

"First we escape," Thea said practically, "and then we think about that."

Their progress was slow in the inky darkness. Several times Sabine felt something scurry across her feet, but she did not fear the rats that infested the tunnel—there was a far greater danger than the rodents.

When they reached the end, Sabine handed Richard to Thea. Feeling frantically in the dark, she discovered that the passage had been blocked! She tried not to panic at the thought that they might be trapped.

"This entrance has not been used in years," she said, trying to sound reassuring. "I believe I can clear away the rubble without much difficulty." Feeling around in the dark, Sabine began moving heavy stones and boulders. Her hands were scratched and bleeding, but she continued her task until, at last, the passage was clear.

Pulling the lever that was imbedded in stone, she was relieved when the panel slid easily open. Taking Richard from Thea, she stepped out into the night.

It was raining, so Sabine enfolded Richard in her cape to keep him dry. She could only wonder how he had slept through all the turmoil.

Thea, who had been so forceful in the beginning, now turned to Sabine for guidance. "What do we do now?" she asked.

"Let me think," Sabine said. "We can't go into the village, for that is the first place they will search."

Suddenly the decision was taken out of their hands. Sabine heard the sound of galloping horses and realized that several men were riding toward them, their sabers gleaming from the lightning that flashed across the sky. With Richard's safety foremost in her mind, Sabine moved back against the wall with the intention of returning to the cave.

"You cannot go back," Thea said in a resigned voice. "There is only forward, for there are men coming at us from both sides. We are trapped between them."

"Then let us escape by the stream, Thea. I'm a good swimmer."

Thea hesitated only a moment. "Give me your cloak," she urged. "I know what's to be done."

"Tell me then."

Thea's voice was insistent. "Give me the cape at once!"

Without hesitation, Sabine complied, unwrapping her brother from the warmth of the red cape and handing it to the nurse.

"You take his lordship and hurry to the stream. It's raining and they won't be able to track you—mayhap they haven't even seen you yet. Hasten, they are nearly upon us. Run, and don't look back!"

"I will not leave you to face them alone," Sabine said stubbornly.

Thea was determined to do what she must to give the children she loved time to escape. "You *will* do as I say—go!"

Not knowing what else to do, Sabine tightened her grip on Richard and hurried toward the stream. It was raining harder, and she almost lost her footing several times. At last she stood on the embankment, realizing that the stream was now a raging river—swift and swollen from the storm.

Sabine was a strong swimmer, but could she save Richard? The water was dark and so swift, she was afraid.

The sound of thundering hooves was drawing nearer, and she stood, undecided, then turned to look back at Thea.

Thea wasn't anywhere in sight, but Sabine could hear raised voices. "There she is, after her—stop her, don't let her get away!"

A bolt of lightning danced jaggedly across the sky, momentarily illuminating the landscape. Sabine cried out when she realized what had happened. Thea was wearing the cloak and running in the opposite direction, to draw the men away from her and Richard!

Sabine moved back up the slope, only to hear a strangled cry of pain and then an angry voice. "You fool, you killed her—ran her down with your horse." Then a pause. "It isn't the duke's wife. Look, by the stream—there she is!"

In her haste to escape, Sabine lost her footing and

slipped. She and Richard went tumbling down the muddy embankment until she slammed forcefully against a large boulder. Terrified, Richard began to cry, and when she reached for him, pain shot through her leg so agonizingly that she knew it was broken. With difficulty, she gathered Richard to her and dragged herself to the stream, plunging into the icy water.

Richard clawed and clung to her neck, pulling them both under—down, down they went, swallowed by the dark, murky depths. Sabine felt as if her lungs would burst, but she did not loosen her grip on Richard as she struggled to take them both to the surface.

She finally managed to bring their heads above water. Richard was still fighting her, and she spoke to him sternly. "Don't struggle. Just trust me and I will see us safely through this."

That seemed to calm him, and he relaxed against her.

Sabine concentrated on keeping them afloat, but the icy water numbed her, and she was helpless to prevent the swift current from carrying them downstream.

Suddenly Richard was ripped from her arms and she frantically grabbed for him in the darkness, only to have him slip out of reach. At last she gripped his arm and pulled his limp body to her.

"God help me," she cried. "Help me save my brother!"

As if in an answer to her prayer, a floating object brushed up against her—it was a log! With renewed hope, she pushed Richard between her and the log so she could retain a grip on him and keep them both afloat.

She didn't know from whence came her strength, but she was able to cling to the log even though her injured leg felt like it was on fire. But at least the flood waters were sweeping them away from Garreth's soldiers.

Sabine heard one of them call loudly. "They've drowned. No one could survive in that. Let's go—we've done what we came to do."

Sabine clung to her lifeline, knowing that now was not the time to mourn her father and Thea. She had to save her brother.

Richard was strangely silent, and she spoke soothingly to him, trying to reassure him. Blackness was all about them, and the bitter taste of death lingered in Sabine's mouth.

After a while, the rain stopped and the clouds parted to allow a weak moon to shine down on them. Sabine prayed for strength, and it seemed God had granted her prayer, for she was able to keep Richard's head above water.

In her heart anger and hatred raged. She would live—she would come out of this, and so would Richard. They had a debt to pay—a debt of honor—a debt of revenge that would one day destroy Garreth Blackthorn!

8

Two brightly painted wagons blocked the roadway. The first one was helplessly stuck to its axle in mud, trapping the other behind it.

Monsieur Jacques de Baillard swore in his native French and kicked at the offending wheel. He was a tall man with an angular nose and dark hair and eyes. Not handsome, but a man with refinement and polish, that drew one's attention.

"How can we leave this cursed land if the rain continues to impede our progress?"

His wife, Marie, sat in the driver's seat, her wet, straw-colored hair plastered to her head. She called for the saints to give her patience and cast her husband a disparaging look. "If you had waited until the roads dried, as I told you, Jacques, you would not be stuck."

He looked at his wife in exasperation. "Madame, if you cannot help, don't hinder."

"I married a fool, and that is the burden I must bear all the days of my life. Why did I listen to you, Jacques?" she asked, not expecting an answer. "Come to London, you said, where we will make our fortune on the stage. The nearest we got to a stage was when we performed in that little park across the street from the theater."

Jacques had heard this all before. "Marie," he said patiently, "this is not the time to criticize. Do you not see that we are stuck?"

She snorted, then picked up a wide-brimmed hat and clamped it on her head, hoping it would offer her some protection against the rain. Then she continued to rebuke him.

"All we got for our trouble here were riots and condemnation. I can't believe you did not bother to find out before we arrived that the English do not allow women to act. You made fools of us all because you did not know that their female roles are played by men dressed as women. It was humiliating to have rotten fruit thrown in my face. And poor Odette Broglie was driven off by a deranged mob, in fear of her life."

"Do you not think I know this, Marie?" Jacques glared at her, his mind more on the wagon than her vocal complaints. "Was I not there?"

"What wonderful idea do you have now, Jacques? The Broglie brothers and sisters have deserted us. All that is left of the de Baillard Players is you, me, and Ysabel—we are hopelessly stuck, and have no funds to buy passage back to France."

Jacques was not listening to his wife. "I must hitch all four horses to the wagon to pull it free," he muttered.

"Humph," Marie said, glancing back at the second wagon. "Why don't you ask that crazed old Ysabel Agostino to conjure up something to help. Pity she didn't leave with the others."

Jacques was not deceived by his wife's shrewishness, because in spite of her complaints, she had a kind heart. Marie was a handsome woman of thirty with regular features and a stout body—just the way he liked her. He knew he would have given up long ago if she had not prodded him—she believed he was a master *artiste*, and her faith in him made him believe it also.

"Leave me in peace. I'm trying to think, Marie."

She turned her head toward her husband, her chin trembling with emotion. "I will say no more."

Two hours later they managed to free the wagon and made camp in the woods near a stream, where Jacques decided that they would remain until the road dried.

By mid-morning, the rain stopped and the sky cleared, giving them hope. But later, Marie's spirits plummeted when it started to rain harder than before. The campfires sizzled and went out, forcing them to seek the shelter of their wagon.

Marie, dressed in a dry gown, was feeling miserable and a long way from home. Tying a scarf around her head, she glared at her husband. "We have nothing to eat but dried meat and stale cheese. I suppose you gave most of our supplies to the Broglies when they deserted us."

"You would not have wanted them go hungry, wife, admit it."

"Just how do you expect we shall live after our food is gone?"

Jacques, as usual, suffered his wife's criticism with good grace, for she was the sensible one of the family. "I will ask Ysabel to go into the village tomorrow and tell fortunes. She will earn enough to buy fresh bread and cheese."

"That old woman thinks she's a better actress than all of us, dressing up like a Gypsy and making folks believe she can see into the future. Must we turn to her once more to put food in our bellies? She makes me shiver when she stares at me with those strange blue eyes."

Jacques sighed. "She earns her way, and we can be grateful that she stayed when the others left. You must admit that she creates magnificent costumes."

"She stays with us only because she has nowhere to go and we allow her to use one of our wagons as her home," Marie snapped.

Jacques knew that Marie was superstitious, no matter how she tried to hide it, and she somehow feared Ysabel Agostino, who claimed to be the seventh daughter of a seventh daughter. Marie believed that gave Ysabel "the sight."

"If you want her to leave, you tell her." Jacques smiled to himself. "I do not want her to cast her evil eye on me."

Marie shuddered. "I will not be the one to tell her she must leave."

"Are you afraid?" he asked slyly.

Marie looked furtively over her shoulder, fearing that Ysabel might have overheard their conversation. "She remains with us only until we return to France. I care not how masterful a seamstress she is, I want her gone." Marie looked out the door of their wagon. "Look, that crazed old woman doesn't even come in from the rain."

Ysabel tucked the hem of her heavy black skirt into her waistband and bent to dip her water jug in the stream. She did not like England with its rain and dampness. It was nothing like the land of her birth—warm, golden Italy. As the years passed, she dreamed less and less of her homeland. She could never return there, although the incident that had caused her to flee had long since ceased to be important. For many years she had wandered aimlessly, finding work wherever she could, but never finding a home until she met Jacques and Marie.

She stood up slowly, watching the swift current. There had been a fierce storm last night that had ripped trees up by their roots. Debris was floating by, and Ysabel stared intently at a log—someone appeared to be clinging to it. Now that it was closer, she could see two people, and one was a small child!

Ysabel reacted quickly, calling loudly to Jacques, all the while running along the bank and keeping the log in sight. "Come at once! Quickly, Jacques. Someone needs our help. Hasten!"

Jacques, hearing the urgency in Ysabel's voice, hurried from his wagon with Marie a step behind him.

"There," Ysabel pointed, "see them?"

Without stopping to consider the danger, Jacques plunged into the turbulent water, and with strong forward strokes swam toward the log.

Marie ran along the banks, wringing her hands. *"Imbecile!* You will be drowned, then what will happen to me—alone and friendless in England with no way to get home? Come out of there at once—do you hear me—come out!"

Ysabel saw that Jacques was having difficulty with the girl, so she plunged into the water and swam to help him, praying that her heavy clothing would not drag her under.

Sabine was almost unconscious and had long ago lost the feeling in her arms and legs, but she somehow managed to keep her brother on top of the log and out of the icy water.

Richard, confused about what was happening to him, had been terrified and had sobbed for hours. Just before daylight, he had quieted, and now Sabine feared he might be unconscious.

Sabine did not know how much longer she could cling to her brother—she was so exhausted. She'd thought that all her strength had been expended, but that was before a man appeared and attempted to take Richard from her. When he tried to pry her hand free of the log, her grip only tightened and she struck at him. Sabine saw him only as the enemy—one of Garreth's men, and she would not relinquish Richard to him.

Ysabel swam alongside Jacques and grabbed at the girl's hands. "We want only to help," the old woman said in French.

Suddenly Sabine became calm when the man also spoke to her in French. She reasoned that Garreth's men would speak only English.

"You must not fight me," Jacques told her, "or we shall all drown."

Sabine, too weak to struggle, was forced to relinquish Richard to the woman just before she lost consciousness, falling into a deep, silent void. Her last thought was that she must be drowning after all.

Jacques swam to shore and lifted the limp girl in his arms. She was so cold that he wasn't sure she still lived.

Ysabel reached shore with the young boy in her arms. She saw the rise and fall of his chest—he was alive. "First we need to get them warm," she said in a commanding voice. "Let us take them into my wagon and I will do what I can." She turned to Marie. "Warm some stones and wrap them in heavy cloth." To Jacques, she spoke quickly as he laid the girl on her cot. "I need something warm for them to drink. Perhaps you could make a thin broth by boiling dried meat."

Without question, Marie and Jacques hurried to do as Ysabel instructed.

Later, when the boy and girl had been stripped of their wet clothing, wrapped in warm blankets with warm stones at their feet, and had hot broth spooned into their mouths, Ysabel stood back wearily.

"I have done all I can until we know if they have other injuries. Now, they need sleep."

"This just will not do," Marie complained, staring at the pale girl. "Two more to feed."

Ysabel turned on Marie. "I do not believe they are in any condition to eat overmuch."

Marie backed toward the door, nodding in agreement, and feeling ashamed of her outburst.

The sun had set on the following day before Sabine awoke. She felt a sense of well-being and was wrapped in glorious warmth. All she wanted to do was sleep. When she tried to move, however, pain shot through her leg like a hot poker and she moaned.

"Sleep, *ma petite*," a soothing voice urged her in French, reminding her of her mother. "Sleep is what you need."

Sabine was too weak to protest. Every muscle in her body ached. She sighed and lost herself in the wonderful oblivion of warmth.

Marie shook her head. "Like as not, they attempted to cross the stream and got caught in the current. The world is inhabited by fools."

Ysabel picked up the young boy, who had just awakened. He blinked his eyes and smiled. Then he surprised them both by reaching for Marie.

Marie took him in her arms and her eyes softened when he lay his head against her shoulder. "This child is a charmer," she admitted. She looked from the boy to the young girl. "He looks nothing like his mother."

"I see some of her in him, but I do not think she is his mother," Ysabel said. "She is too young."

"Of course she is his mother. Most probably they belong to some peasant farmer."

"I do not think so." Ysabel lifted one of Sabine's limp hands that were soft and white despite the cuts and lacerations. "This is not the hand of a peasant. This is the hand of a lady. See the signet ring she wears."

Marie's words were harsh. "I suppose you think you know everything."

Ysabel merely shrugged. "I know that there is trouble here." She pointed to the girl. "I must go into the village and see what I can discover about her and the child."

Marie cuddled the young boy and smiled at him. "Go if you must, but be discreet, and tell no one that they are here. We do not want the magistrate poking around."

Ysabel tucked the blanket about the girl's shoulders. "Have no fear. I will use only my ears."

Sabine awoke, turning her head slowly. When she could focus her eyes, she was startled by her surroundings. What kind of place was this? It was small and cramped, and she lay upon a lumpy narrow bed. There were brightly-colored costumes from bygone eras hanging from several hooks. It took her a moment to realize that she was in some kind of wagon. She sat up quickly, reaching out her hand.

"Richard, where are you?" she said frantically.

A soft voice spoke in her mother's native tongue. "So, his name is Richard. We have become acquainted while you slept, but he refused to tell us his name."

Sabine reached for her brother and the old woman handed him to her. She unconsciously replied to the woman in French. "If you have harmed my brother, it will not go easy with you."

The woman merely smiled, showing even white teeth.

"I do not harm children. It was you who placed him in danger, not I."

Sabine examined Richard carefully. He giggled and pressed his cheek to hers. "He appears not to have suffered from the ordeal." Her eyes were apologetic when she looked at the woman. "It was you who rescued us."

"Jacques was the strong swimmer. I merely helped him, *ma petite*."

"Oh." Sabine felt ashamed. "I am sorry if I sounded ungrateful. Thank you for what you did."

Sabine looked into perspicacious blue eyes. The woman's face was wrinkled with age, her hands gnarled, yet Sabine was not afraid of her. "May I know your name?"

"I am Ysabel Agostino. Everyone calls me Ysabel."

"An Italian name, Madame, and yet you speak French?"

"You are English, and yet you speak French like a Frenchwoman," Ysabel reminded her. "But, yes, I am Italian, and was born in a sunny little village near the sea. That was long ago, though, and I never speak of it."

"Madame, I do not know how much longer I could have clung to that log. Where is the gentleman who helped my brother and myself, so that I might thank him?"

"Jacques, you will see later. For now, tell me of your family so that you may be reunited with them. They must be frantic with worry."

Sabine was suddenly terrified. In her anxiety, she tried to move off the bed, but cried out in agony and fell back, gasping for breath. After the pain subsided, she looked terrified. "I must leave at once."

Ysabel's eyes narrowed. "Perhaps you are running away from something . . . or someone, *non?*"

"I cannot talk about this with you. I only know I must get away from here or they will find us."

"You would not get far in your condition. I think you

cannot even stand on your own. I did not realize that you had been injured."

When Sabine tried to lower her leg to the floor, she cried out, falling back on the bed.

Ysabel's face was creased with worry. "I must speak to Jacques, and then I shall return. I believe your leg is broken and needs attention at once."

Ysabel did not know what the girl's troubles were, but the poor creature was genuinely terrified.

An exhausted Richard curled up beside Sabine and fell asleep while she waited for Ysabel. Her instinct was to take Richard and flee because they were still too close to Woodbridge Castle for her to feel safe. But the woman was right—she would not get far in her condition. How could she help Richard, if she could not even help herself?

When Ysabel entered a short time later, she was accompanied by two other people, a man with a ready smile, and a woman who looked distrustful.

The man spoke kindly. "Ysabel informs me that your leg is most probably broken."

"I pray it is not so," Sabine said. "It was broken when I was younger and has pained me every day since. I do not want to live through that again."

Ysabel had been mixing a yellow powder with water and handed a cup to Sabine. "If you drink this, it will dull your pain."

Without hesitation, Sabine gulped down the bitter liquid, hoping the old woman spoke true. Almost immediately, she felt herself becoming drowsy and soon her eyes drifted shut.

Ysabel pushed Sabine's gown up past her ankle and hissed through her teeth. "What butcher did this to her? She was right that her leg was broken before, but it was not properly set. She's crippled, and has been for some time. I only hope that I can undo the harm that was done her. I once healed a horse with a broken leg; I can surely help her."

Jacques looked doubtful for a moment, and then his rugged face eased into a smile. "A horse is always destroyed when its leg is broken. I have never heard of one that was cured. But if it could be done, surely you would be the one to do it."

Ysabel focused her eyes on the girl. "I speak only the truth."

"Do what you can to help her, Ysabel. There is not time to send to the village for a physician, and I am not sure one would attend us here, even if we asked."

"We have no need for a physician, but I shall need your help, Jacques, for I am not as strong as I once was."

The Frenchman trusted the old woman because he had often observed her skill in healing. When any of his troupe had become ill, they would always seek Ysabel for a cure. "You have only to tell me what to do."

"First, I will need four sturdy pieces of wood to make a splint. Then, when I tell you, I shall want you to yank hard on her leg. When this is done, you must hold the leg fast while I do the rest. I warn you, that even with the medicine, the girl will be in extreme pain. No matter what she does, it is most important that you do exactly what I tell you. Do not loosen your grip on her leg."

Marie de Baillard, who had been merely an observer up to now, reached for Richard and lifted him in her arms. "I'll just take him out, lest he become disturbed by what must be done."

When Jacques's wife had departed, he smiled ruefully at Ysabel. "Marie is not nearly as hard as she would have everyone believe. You can see that the child has already softened her."

"I have often seen the yearning in Marie's eyes while she watched children at play."

Jacques liked children, and his most profound regret was that he and Marie had never had any of their own. "I will go now and find wood, then you will tell me how to make the splints," he told Ysabel.

Sabine was reliving her nightmarish ordeal. She was running, trying to get Richard to safety while her pursuers drew ever closer. Then she was falling, and it felt like someone had taken a red hot poker to her leg.

Jacques took the girl's leg in a firm grip.

"Tell me when to pull," he said.

"Now—hard!"

Sabine heard someone screaming, and she did not know that it was her. Blackness surrounded her, but it did not shut out the searing, burning waves of pain.

Ysabel laid the flat boards against Sabine's leg and bound them tightly with strips of linen. Then she stood back and frowned. "I have done all that I can."

"Is it enough?"

"The blessing is that this break is at the same place as her old injury. She will either walk without a limp, or forever be a cripple and in pain, which would be a pity. I have a feeling that this child has known much pain. She is now in God's hands."

9

Word traveled swiftly concerning the raid on Woodbridge Castle, and fear ran rampant in the surrounding village. Many were sure that war had come to England because the duke of Balmarough had attacked the earl of Woodbridge.

Two days after the incursion, a messenger arrived at Whitehall, where King Charles was conversing with William Laud, the former Bishop of London, whom he had recently appointed the Archbishop of Canterbury.

Charles Stewart read the dispatch, then turned to the archbishop and thrust the message at him. "This is preposterous! I will not tolerate such acts of violence against my nobles."

The archbishop could not believe what he read. "Lord Woodbridge dead, and his children probably suffered the same fate. This is unpardonable."

The king turned to the young messenger. "It says here

that the raid on Woodbridge was executed by men wearing the livery of the duke of Balmarough. Can you confirm this?"

"I can and do, Your Majesty." The messenger produced a bloodstained blue and white doublet and held it out for the king's inspection. "This was taken off the body of one of the dead invaders. As you can see, my liege, it has the duke of Balmarough's coat of arms, a dragon in flight."

King Charles looked at the offending garment and waved the man away. "Leave me now. Later, I will have a dispatch for you to deliver to the village of Woodbridge. Impress upon the citizens that this matter will receive our immediate attention, and until it is resolved, I will send troops to protect them."

The king was silent while the young man bowed and backed to the door. Then he sent a page to fetch his ministers. "I know of no grudge that Garreth has against his father-in-law. There is no reason to this madness."

The archbishop's red robe swirled out about him as he paced the floor. "I cannot credit that his grace would commit such an atrocity. He is a man of honor, as was his father."

"I admit that this does not seem like something Garreth would do. But then, does one man ever truly know another? Who can say what madness could drive a man to such extremes?" The king's eyes narrowed in anger. "Send soldiers to Wolfeton Keep, where they will place Garreth Blackthorn under arrest. Instruct them to bring him to London, where he will be immediately confined to the Tower."

The archbishop came up beside him. "Your Majesty, have you thought how this incident will give your enemies more reason to incite the people against you?"

"Of course I have! I will do whatever I must to satisfy

Lord Woodbridge's supporters. Whether Garreth Black-thorn is guilty or not, I'll have his head on a pole for all to see! Someone must be blamed for this atrocity, and it will not be the Crown!"

Garreth was in the gatehouse conversing with the captain of his guards when his mother came rushing to him, her face ashen, her eyes wide with concern.

"I must speak with you at once on a matter of great import," she said.

Garreth dismissed Captain Barkley with a nod, then turned his attention to his mother. "You seem distressed. Tell me what has upset you."

Adrienne Blackthorn stood before him, her hands clenched so tightly that her knuckles were white. She was a small woman who only came up to her son's shoulder, and her once dark hair met across her forehead in a widow's peak.

"It's too dreadful to contemplate." She shuddered. "Even now, I cannot comprehend it. That poor little girl has already had so much sadness in her life."

Garreth gripped her hands, trying to calm her. "Of what little girl do you speak?"

"Oh, Garreth, it is so dreadful." She took in a deep breath before continuing. "Woodbridge Castle was attacked." She paused, unable to go on for a moment. "Lord Woodbridge . . . was slain, and it is supposed that Sabine and her young brother met the same fate, although no one has yet found their bodies!"

His heart contracted. "Who has dared do such a thing?" he asked hoarsely.

The dowager duchess searched his eyes, reluctant to add to his woes. "My son, it is said that the horrible deed was mastered by you."

Now Garreth's anger turned to burning rage. "Who has made this accusation? Let him come forward and confront me, so that I might show him for the blackguard he is."

Adrienne placed a hand on his arm. "I don't know all the details. I can only tell you what your cousin, Cortland, told me. He was at a nearby estate when the horror occurred. He said that the village of Woodbridge is turning into an angry mob and demanding that your life be forfeit."

Garreth could not believe what he was hearing. "Where is Cortland—I would have him relate this to me."

"I beseeched him to tell you this, but he said that he was but an hour ahead of the king's soldiers, who are on their way here to arrest you. He wanted me to impress upon you that there is damning proof the men who attacked Woodbridge Castle wore our livery. Cortland urges you to leave Wolfeton Keep with all haste and hide where no one can find you until the truth has been uncovered. He said that he was going directly to the king to plead your case."

Garreth waved his hand dismissively. "I don't know what Cortland thinks he can accomplish. The king will not listen to anything he says—he doesn't even know Cortland."

"That may be true, but I agree with him that you should leave before the king's soldiers arrive. Who knows what their orders are?"

"A Blackthorn does not run and hide like a coward," Garreth said grimly. "Sabine was my wife; therefore, it is my duty to discover who has committed this abomination and tried to blame me. *I* will go to the king—he will listen to me."

His mother's eyes were fearful. "No, Garreth! Who knows what danger you may encounter?"

"Have no fear, Mother. After I talk to the king, he will agree that I must go to Woodbridge and uncover the truth."

Adrienne had learned that once Garreth set himself upon a course, he could not be deterred. "Then I shall go with you. His majesty will surely listen to me."

"No, Mother. I must travel swiftly and avoid the main roads. The journey will be too strenuous and dangerous for you. I would prefer that you remain safely here."

She lifted her chin and moved to the door. "I can still sit a horse and ride with the best of them, Garreth. I will not remain here in the country, worrying about what is happening to you. Come, we must make haste before the soldiers arrive."

It was but a short time later that Garreth and his mother rode through the open gates of Wolfeton Keep. He had no valet, and she took no lady to attend her because they needed to move quickly. Instead of keeping to the road, they traveled cross-country, thus saving time and also avoiding the soldiers.

At first, Garreth was concerned for his mother, but she kept pace with him, and the one time he suggested that they stop and rest, it was she who urged him onward.

It began to rain as night approached, and still they continued. After midnight, the rain stopped and the clouds moved away, leaving the countryside awash in moonlight.

Garreth had much time to think, and still what had happened at Woodbridge was a mystery to him. He felt a heaviness in his heart when he thought of Sabine. Soon she would have come to live in his house and eventually she would have shared his bed. She would have borne the next generation of Blackthorns, and now she might be dead.

He glanced at his mother and noticed the tiredness etched on her face. "I see the lights of a village just ahead. We will rest awhile there," he said.

Wearily, she nodded in agreement. "We cannot face the king in our bedraggled condition. We will sleep for a few hours, refresh ourselves, and then be on our way again."

Long before the sun came up the next morning, Garreth and his mother were once more on the road to London. By midday, they were approaching the city. Mother and son glanced at each other uneasily; they were uncertain what would happen when Garreth faced the king.

They reached the palace without trouble, but on asking for an audience with his majesty, Garreth was immediately put under arrest by the palace guards. Against his mother's protest, he was taken directly to the Tower.

The dowager duchess was allowed to pass into the palace, where she was confined to the same chamber she had shared with her husband in happier times. She was told that the king would see her only at his convenience.

Garreth stood at the barred windows of the Tower, looking down on the courtyard below. Although the rooms he occupied were well-furnished, they were damp and dismal. He was informed by the unsympathetic guard that this was the same apartment that had been occupied by many notables, including the tragic Queen Mary of Scotland before her head was severed from her body. That thought gave Garreth little comfort.

Daily, he sent messages to the king, but there was never a response. He was being treated like a criminal and denied the right to defend himself. He was desperate for news of the outside world, but he was kept in ignorance. By detaining him, the king was allowing the guilty more time to hide their crime.

After Garreth had been in the Tower for three weeks, he was finally given a letter from his mother. It was dated a week before, and it stated that she was soon to be granted an audience with his majesty. She urged Garreth to keep faith. Because he was innocent, she was sure he would be exonerated.

He thought sadly of Sabine and closed his eyes as words came tumbling from his lips.

"I may not have protected you in life, Sabine. But I shall avenge you in death—this I swear!"

10

Sabine rolled her head from side to side, biting her lip to keep from crying out. Why was the woman, Ysabel, hurting her?

"Please, no more," she groaned. "Do not touch my leg. Leave me alone!"

Had Sabine looked into Ysabel's eyes, she would have seen the compassion there. "This I must do, if the leg is to heal properly, *ma petite*."

Sabine pushed Ysabel's hand away. "I was not tortured when I broke my leg the other time. Even though the bone had punctured my skin, still it was not this painful."

"Whoever attended you then was more butcher than physician," Ysabel said scornfully. "I do not like inflicting pain on you, and if it were not necessary, I would not do it."

Ysabel was tall for a woman, and it was difficult to judge her age. Her hair was mostly gray, and she wore it away from her face and hung over her shoulder in a long braid. The blue of her eyes was so pale, that at times they appeared to blend with the whites. At the moment those eyes gleamed with determination.

"Why must you hurt me?"

Ysabel pulled up a stool and took Sabine's hand in hers. "It is for you to decide if you can endure the pain. I will tell you only this—if I stretch the leg and massage the muscles twice a day, it might be that your leg will heal properly and you will no longer be crippled."

Sabine was afraid to hope; surely she had misunderstood. "Are you saying that I will no longer walk with a limp?"

"Of this I cannot be certain. But if you will trust me, I may be able to help you."

Sabine hesitated for only a moment. "I do trust you."

"Then you must decide if you can endure the pain."

"I have not known a day without pain in a very long time. I will endure what I must."

"Shall I continue?"

Sabine licked her dry lips before she answered. "Yes, please do what you can."

"If you feel like screaming, no one will mind."

She nodded as Ysabel began tightening the splints. The pain was so intense that Sabine did indeed scream until she finally lost consciousness.

Three weeks passed and the roads were still unpassable for the heavy wagons. It rained daily, adding to Marie's misery and fueling her temper. Only Richard seemed to calm her.

It was nearing sundown as Sabine sat huddled near

the waning campfire, a blanket about her shoulders, her aching leg propped on a low stool. The weather had turned colder, a reminder that winter would soon grip the land.

Sabine watched Marie de Baillard balancing Richard on her knee, while singing a French children's rhyme.

Ysabel approached Sabine, her eyes always searching, probing, as if she could extract the deepest secrets from the young girl's mind. The old woman pulled up a camp stool and sat beside her. "Today I ventured beyond the nearby village to the village of Woodbridge. There is much crying and sadness there."

Sabine gazed into the fire, afraid to look at Ysabel. "Why should I care about that?"

"I moved among the crowd, telling fortunes to those who would pay, and I am certain their sadness concerns you personally."

Sabine hurriedly attempted to change the subject. "Can you really see into the future?"

"No more than you," Ysabel replied with honesty. "But I long ago learned that people are willing to pay if you tell them what they want to hear. They resent paying for ill-tidings, therefore, I always predict good fortune and great love. It matters little what I say, for I am gone long before they discover the truth."

Sabine couldn't keep from laughing. "You are wicked."

Ysabel smiled, easing the deep wrinkles about her mouth. "Perhaps I am. Or, perhaps, I merely play the fox and use my cunning."

Sabine wiggled her foot and stretched it toward the fire. Although the leg still ached, Ysabel had her walk about once in the morning and then again in the evening, and Sabine felt that her leg was growing stronger.

"Sabine, would you not like to hear what I learned about the people in the castle?" Ysabel asked.

A lone tear rolled down Sabine's cheek. "I know what happened—I was there."

Ysabel nodded. "I was certain of that."

She raised her eyes to Ysabel. "Did you hear about . . . have you word—what happened to Lord Woodbridge?"

Ysabel shifted her weight and poked a stick at the fire, seducing the burning embers into a warming flame that licked at the pot that hung suspended above it.

"It is whispered that the great lord died by treacherous means."

Sabine wiped her tears on the sleeve of her gown. "Then he is dead?"

"*Oui.* The great lord was entombed while you were still out of your head with fever. It is said that his friends and allies are many and that they rally to the castle and village to protect the people. Even the king has sent soldiers."

Sabine glued her eyes to the stew that bubbled in the pot. She would not cry—she must not cry. "Is there nothing more you can tell me?"

"It is also said that the villagers still comb the woods and search the banks of the stream that ran through their master's estate, in hopes of finding the lord's daughter and son. It is feared that they drowned. The people want to find their bodies so they can have a proper burial. It seems that the Woodbridge family was much revered."

Sabine lifted her eyes to Ysabel and saw pity there. "You know who I am, do you not?"

"You are the great lord's daughter, and Richard is his son. From what I gleaned, I should call him Lord Richard, and you are a duchess, are you not?"

Fear tore at Sabine's mind. "No, please do not do use

a title when addressing my brother or myself. Did you tell anyone about us?"

"I told only the fortunes of those who paid me the price. No one asked if I knew of you or the child, and I did not volunteer any information."

"I don't understand any of what happened," Sabine said, her eyes swimming with tears.

Ysabel watched the girl carefully as she began to speak. "They said also that the duchess's own husband instigated the raid."

Sabine buried her face in trembling hands. "I believe it is the truth. If Garreth Blackthorn has done this, then he may yet be searching for us. Richard and I must leave before we are discovered."

"You cannot leave until your leg knits," Ysabel said firmly. "I will not allow you to undo the healing."

Sabine closed her eyes. "There is no refuge for us. I don't know the faces of all my enemies, or even who I can trust."

"You can trust Jacques and Marie, and you can trust me. You will, I believe, journey with us to France, where you will be safe." Ysabel's eyes grew reflective. "When one has enemies, one must become shrewd."

"My enemy is more influential than you can imagine. He sits on the right hand of the king. With that kind of power, he can reach across the Channel to me."

"Everyone has a weakness, and so does your Garreth Blackthorn. You will allow him to believe that you drowned, while you come to France with us. One day you shall grow strong and confront your enemy—but that day is far away."

Sabine merely lowered her head. "Do Monsieur and Madame de Baillard know our true identities?"

"They have not said so to me—but I believe they have

guessed the truth. I shall ask them if you can go with us. I believe they will agree."

"I have been nothing but a burden to the de Baillards and have contributed nothing to our keep." Sabine tugged at the golden chain about her neck. "I have this locket that belonged to my mother—I believe it is very valuable. You could sell it when we are far away from my father's village. Many may have seen my mother wear the locket and recognize it." Sabine held her hand out to Ysabel. "There is also this ring that was given to me by my . . . husband on our wedding day. I fear there is nowhere to sell it because it is engraved with a dragon, the Blackthorn coat-of-arms. There are few in England who would not recognize it."

"Why have you not removed the ring?"

"I . . . do not know. Perhaps I wear it to remind myself to despise the man who put it on my finger."

Ysabel closed her hand over Sabine's. "Keep them both for now. You may have need of them later."

Sabine glanced across the camp where Madame de Baillard still held Richard on her lap. "If anyone objects to our accompanying you to France, I believe it will be madame."

"I do not think so. Marie will be loath to part with your brother, for she has become quite attached to him."

"France," Sabine said wistfully. "I have always wanted to visit the land of my mother's birth, but not as a fugitive."

Ysabel lifted Sabine's hand, turned it over, and studied the palm for a long moment. "France will be good to you. You shall walk in the footsteps of fame."

Sabine smiled. "So, you would practice your witchery on me? Did I not hear you say that you tell people what they wish to hear?"

Ysabel tossed a stick in the fire and watched the sparks fly. "Sometimes the truth comes disguised in the remnants of suspicion to a nonbeliever—but it is the truth nonetheless."

Sabine touched Ysabel's arm. "I know not where my path will lead, but I do know that there are those who wish to harm me and my brother. I would be less than honest if I accompanied the de Baillards to France without informing them of the danger to anyone who aids us."

The more Ysabel came to know Sabine, the more she liked her. The young girl was frightened and she did not know where to turn for help, but still she possessed honor and would not put others in danger. "Come, I will assist you into the wagon."

Sabine leaned heavily on Ysabel. Once inside, she eased her weight onto the bed, then Ysabel lifted her foot, placing it on a cushion.

"You are yet young, Sabine. Soon you will take the first step toward tomorrow—there will be pain, but this too shall pass."

"You are not speaking of my leg."

"I speak of your inner self. You have much courage, and it will take you through many difficult times."

"I do not feel that I have courage." Sabine stared down at the ring for a moment before yanking if off her finger. "I no longer need this to remind me that evil often appears in the form of goodness. How could the same man who held me comfortingly in his arms while I wept for my mother, take the life of my father?"

"Have courage, *ma petite*. Tomorrow the roads will be dry enough to travel, and we will leave this place."

"Ysabel, you have taken Richard and me into your wagon, giving us your bed, while you sleep on the floor. How can we repay your kindness?"

"Kindness is its own reward. Once someone helped me when my need was great."

"Who, Ysabel?"

"The de Baillards."

Sabine studied her bare hand, wishing she dared throw Garreth's ring out the window, for the sight of it offended her. Instead, she clutched it so tightly it cut into her palm. "I am angry that I was forced to leave my own home. I want to go to my husband and . . . and plunge a knife into his black heart for his treachery."

"Face your grief now, and later, when you are stronger, you can face the anger. I would caution you that revenge is destructive, oft times harming the innocent." The old woman moved toward the door. "I will go now to speak to Marie and Jacques, then I shall bring Richard to you."

When Ysabel left, Sabine allowed hot tears to flood her eyes. "Oh, *Maman*, the pain in my leg is nothing compared to the pain I feel in my heart. What shall I do—what shall I do?"

Marie de Baillard still sat on the steps, holding Richard, while Jacques was gathering their supplies and loading the wagon.

"I'll take Richard to his sister," Ysabel said, reaching for the young boy. "I will surely miss them when we leave tomorrow."

Marie tightened her arms protectively about him. "What do you mean, old woman? Those two children will be coming with us."

"I merely supposed that you would not want to be bothered with them, and that they would be left behind."

"The girl is not well enough to be on her own, much less take care of this precious child," Marie stated, glancing at her husband. "Tell Ysabel that they must come with us, Jacques."

He smiled at Ysabel, realizing the game she was playing, then turned to his wife and sighed regretfully. "We cannot keep them with us, Marie—you know this. We have no coins for food. We may even be forced to sell the wagons to pay our fare home."

"You will not sell my wagon. We will find another way to get home. Have we not always managed? This wagon is the only home that ever belonged to me, and I will not return to France without it."

"We have never been this desperate," Ysabel said.

Marie stood up, her eyes sparkling angrily. "Do you think me a fool, old woman?"

Ysabel met her gaze squarely. "I have never considered you a fool, Marie."

Marie nodded. "I know the identity of the girl and boy, and I know that they are in danger. So, I refuse to leave them behind to be murdered. They go with us when we leave in the morning." Marie looked first at Ysabel and then at her husband, daring either of them to contradict her. "That is the way it's to be, and I've said my last word on the matter."

Ysabel feigned hesitation. "The girl is concerned that she is a burden."

"She is no trouble to me since you have had the care of her. And she eats very little." Marie's eyes were soft when she looked down at Richard. "Besides, he has become attached to me."

It was all Ysabel could do to keep from smiling. "I'll just see if I can convince the girl to come with us. She may not want to leave England."

"Then you must make her realize that it is best for them to remain with us," Marie said, finally relinquishing Richard to Ysabel.

As the old woman passed Jacques, he chuckled and said in a low voice: "Have you no shame, Ysabel, that you trick my poor unsuspecting wife so?"

"I did not trick her," Ysabel replied. "As she said, she is no fool—she knew what I was doing."

11

Sabine had been tense on the long journey, cringing with fear whenever riders would come upon them. She felt safer when they came within sight of Dover.

Jacques got permission from a farmer to camp on his land, where they would remain until they earned enough money for passage to France.

Each morning Ysabel would go into Dover and move among the populace, telling fortunes, earning what money she could. Jacques had been a tinker before he became an actor, so he traveled to the outlying farms, offering to mend pots and pans and reweave cane-bottom chairs. Marie took in washing and mending for several young sailors.

Sabine felt guilty because she was the only one who contributed nothing to their care. One morning, she awoke early and dressed herself and Richard in the warm clothing Ysabel had made them from old costumes.

Taking Richard's hand, they walked the short distance to Dover. Because of the splint she still wore, Sabine's steps were stiff and slow. The town was just coming to life when she and Richard moved down the cobbled streets. The bustling activity caught their interest. One man was washing his storefront windows, while another was sweeping the steps to his shop. In colorful stalls, tradesmen were displaying their wares. Richard held his nose when they moved past the fishmonger's stand.

Sabine was distressed by what she must do; it was with a heavy heart that she stopped to look in the window of a goldsmith's shop. Her hand trembled when she entered and handed her mother's locket to the gentleman who was bent over a worktable.

"How much will you give me for this? It is very valuable."

The goldsmith examined it closely. "I sell gold, little miss. It is not my habit to purchase from others."

"Please, sir, would you look at this carefully? It is truly beautiful."

He saw the desperation in her eyes. "Yes, I can see that the stone is a rare pink diamond. It is indeed of great value."

"Then will you consider buying it from me?"

The goldsmith was an elderly man with thinning hair and soft brown eyes. He had grandchildren of his own, who were much the same age as this young girl, and he hoped someone would help them if they were ever in need. "Are you certain that you want to part with this?"

Sabine swallowed the aching lump in her throat. "I must."

He was silent for a moment. "I am an honest man, so I will strike a bargain with you, little miss. I will buy this from you for five pounds—"

She was so distressed that she held her hand out for

the locket. "You profess to be an honest man, and yet you attempt to cheat me! Because I am young, do not think I don't know the locket is worth ten times that amount."

A wide smile softened his face. "You did not allow me to finish. I shall buy the locket for five pounds and keep it for the period of one year. If within that year, you have the price to buy it back, I will sell it to you for six pounds. After all, I do have to make a profit."

Sudden tears glistened in Sabine's eyes, and she was ashamed of her earlier outburst. "You are indeed kind and generous, sir. And if it is within my power, I shall most certainly return within the appointed time and buy back my mother's locket."

He grinned at the young girl with shimmering red hair. Although she was dressed simply, she was delicate and had the bearing of a born lady. "I will keep it safe, and it will be here waiting for you. I have little doubt that you shall redeem it."

With the money clutched in her hand, Sabine moved out of the shop and down the street. She wanted to cry because she had been forced to part with her only memento of her mother. If only she could have sold Garreth's ring instead—but she dared not lest the goldsmith recognize the Balmarough coat of arms. She turned back to look at the goldsmith's shop and made a mental note of the name and location. One day she would reclaim her mother's locket.

Richard looked up at her inquiringly. "Sabine, where is Father? When can we go home? I want to see Thea, and sleep in my own bed. When we fell in the water, did we get lost?"

"No, Richard, we're not lost." It was the first time he had asked to go home. He was too young to understand about the tragedy that surrounded them. Eventually she

would have to tell him everything that had happened—
but not for years.

She knelt down so she was eye level with him.
"Richard, you are very young, and I don't know if you
can understand, but we cannot go home just yet. Instead,
we are going to have a great adventure. How would you
like to go on a big ship?"

His eyes brightened, and he jumped up and down,
clapping his hands excitedly. Then he looked at her
questioningly. "Will Father allow it?"

"He would wish it, Richard. There is just you and me
now, and we shall survive as long as we have each
other." She hugged him to her, and his little arms went
around her neck. "I will not let anything harm you,
Richard."

He drew back and smiled at her. "And I shall take
care of you, Sabine."

She stood and gripped his hand. "You will be my
champion." She gave him a mock curtsy. "Now, sir
knight, would you like a twopenny cake with raisins? I
see a confectioner just across the street, and his goods
smell wonderful."

He nodded eagerly. "Oh, yes, may I, Sabine?"

She would give the rest of the money to Monsieur de
Baillard, but Richard would have his confection.

When they came out of the shop, Richard's tongue
darted out to lick the crumbs from his lips. "I could have
eaten everything, Sabine."

"Thea would say it is wrong to overindulge. I believe
one was enough."

"You did not have one."

"I . . . wasn't hungry."

"Where is Thea? Why is she not with us?"

He adored the old nurse and missed her dreadfully, as
did Sabine. She would one day tell him how Thea had

sacrificed her life that they might escape. "She could not come on our great adventure, Richard."

His eyes suddenly darkened. "I want to go home. I don't like it here."

"We cannot go home, Richard," she said patiently. "Don't you like Ysabel and the de Baillards? They certainly like you."

"Yes, they're very nice. Could we take them with us on our adventure?"

She fastened his cap against the sudden cold wind. "Yes, they will come with us."

Jacques took the money Sabine gave him and placed it in Marie's outstretched hand. "With this, we shall soon have enough to sail for home," he said.

Marie counted all their money and shook her head. "It is still not enough. Besides passage and the transport of the wagons, we shall need thirty francs to repay the moneylenders when we reach home."

Jacques sighed. "We also have to eat until we find more actors to join our troupe."

"What troupe?" Marie asked. "There is no de Baillard Players."

Jacques looked miserable. "If only we could stage a play in Dover to raise the fare."

"That is impossible, my fool of a husband. You are the only one they would allow to act since you are the only male except Richard and he's too young. We will just have to work harder, and it will take longer to leave this cursed country, but leave it we shall."

Richard was asleep, so Sabine and Ysabel huddled near the campfire to keep warm. It was a calm, clear night, and the sky sparkled with thousands of stars.

"If we were in the village where I was born," Ysabel said reflectively, "there would be a warm breeze blowing off the sea. You would only have to reach up and pluck an orange from a tree."

"Why do you not return, Ysabel?"

"For many reasons. You would not know it to look at me now, but I was quite pretty when I was young, and had many suitors."

Sabine settled comfortably. "Do go on," she said.

"When I was in my seventeenth year, the lady of the great house, where my father was master of horses, engaged me to work as a maid. Within a year, I became her personal maid." Ysabel closed her eyes, as if it was painful to remember.

"Do not speak of your past if it distresses you."

"Only my father, and later the man I loved and married, knew what I now tell you. Perhaps it will help me put the past to rest if I speak of it. Since you also have troubles, I believe you will understand."

Sabine placed her hand on Ysabel's arm. "Then I will listen."

Ysabel laced her gnarled fingers together and stared at them, remembering a time when they had been soft and unlined. "I was my lady's maid only a few weeks when her husband began to show me marked attention. He would touch me in a way that was offensive, and say things to me that no girl should have to hear. I was frightened of him and tried to avoid him whenever I could."

"How dreadful for you."

"One night he came to my bedchamber and pressed his attentions on me. I struggled and fought, but he was too strong. I shall not speak of the things he did to me. But after that, he came to my room almost nightly. Each time he came, I fought and begged him to leave me alone. I was young and frightened, not knowing who to trust. I could not tell my father, for he would have demanded justice, and he would have lost his position as master of horses and my family would have gone hungry."

"Oh, Ysabel, how horrible for you. What did you do?"

"The worst thing I could have done—I informed my mistress. She was livid, and accused me of lying. She confronted her husband in front of me, and he called me names that I had never heard before. It would have been better if they had been satisfied by just dismissing me, but they also ordered my father to leave. And even that was not the end of it."

Sabine felt Ysabel's pain. "I am so sorry. You have suffered greatly."

Ysabel nodded. "The punishment for telling the truth was severe. In an act of revenge, the lady accused me of stealing her jewels, and had it not been for my father's quick action, I would have spent my life in prison. He hid me, and then when it was safe, smuggled me over the border into France. He gave me what little money he had, and I don't know what became of him or my family after I left."

"Have you never returned to Italy?"

"Never—nor shall I, *ma petite.*"

Sabine was saddened by what her friend had suffered. "Dear sweet Ysabel, have you known any happiness in your life?"

"Oh, yes," she said, smiling at her memories. "I was married for five wonderful years to an Italian shopkeeper in Paris. Maurizio and our two sons died of a fever one winter, and the creditors took the shop. He was the love of my life, and I never wanted to marry again, although several gentlemen asked for my hand. For many years, I struggled just to live. Then I met Jacques and Marie, and they gave me a home. The rest you know."

Sabine realized that there was much Ysabel left

unsaid. "It is a very sad story. You deserve happiness, Ysabel, for I have known no one kinder than you."

Ysabel decided to distract Sabine and speak of other matters. "You walked into town today, did you not?"

"Yes. It was quite glorious."

"Did your leg pain you?"

Sabine looked surprised. "I thought little of my leg. No . . . it did not pain me!" She turned to Ysabel in surprise. "It does not hurt in the least. I can hardly recall a time when my leg did not hurt. Now it's merely uncomfortable because of the splint."

"I find encouragement in this, Sabine."

Sabine looked hopeful. "If only it has healed."

"We shall soon know. I do not wish to plant false hope in your mind. It may be that the leg is the same as before and the splints keep it from hurting."

Sabine startled Ysabel when she reached over and hugged her. "You are better than any physician."

Ysabel looked pleased, but she did not indulge in false modesty. "I was well taught. It was said that my father was of Moorish descent—if he was, he never said so to me. He did have skills that made others marvel. Since he had no sons and eight daughters, and I was the only one who showed an interest in his trade, he taught me many of those skills. I am not yet certain what my father showed me will heal a human."

"So you would practice your animal husbandry on me?" Sabine laughed, and the sound of her laughter warmed the old woman's heart. "When will you remove the splints so I will know if I limp?"

"Not for a time yet. We must first make certain that the leg is fully healed."

"Would it not be a marvel if I were no longer a cripple, Ysabel?"

Ysabel looked at the young girl in amazement. She

was sweet-natured and seldom complained, though her life was filled with sorrow. "To walk without pain is what you deserve."

Then Ysabel stood. "I am to bed. Put out the fire before you leave," she said, ambling toward the wagon.

Sabine nodded. She wasn't sleepy, so she sat by the fire for a long time, wondering what was happening at home. She suddenly noticed that Monsieur de Baillard had left his book behind. She picked it up, knowing that if it rained during the night, the book would be ruined. Her eyes moved over the first page and it caught her interest. It was William Shakespeare's *Henry IV* Part One, which Monsieur de Baillard was translating into French. She leaned more into the light and began to read aloud, changing her tone when she switched from Prince Henry to Falstaff.

She started Prince Henry in a deep voice. "What none?"

She spoke in a high tone. "No, by my troth; not so much as will serve to be prologue to an egg and butter."

"Well, how then? Come, roundly, roundly."

Jacques startled Sabine when he moved into the ring of light, applauding. "You are a natural. You have a voice that carries, and you speak clearly and distinctly. If only you were a lad, we could easily earn enough to sail for France."

Sabine drew in an aggravated breath. "'Tis a silly rule that a female cannot act in public. Ysabel said it is not so in France."

"True, true. But France is an enlightened country. In Paris the great actresses obtain respect and fame. They are *feted*, admired, and lavished with jewels and fortunes that lesser mortals only dream about. The female luminary is often more loved than the royal family."

They both stared into the fire. At last Sabine spoke. "I

have oft times been told that I have the appearance of a lad." She smiled mischievously and stood for his inspection. "Do you not agree?"

"What? Oh, yes—yes, you do. But—"

"Monsieur de Baillard," she bowed before him, "may I present myself to you? A son of France, my name is Antoine de Chavaniac. My profession is actor for the de Baillard Players, and I am at your service."

Jacques smiled first and then roared with laughter. "It would fool no one. You would be stoned as an imposter."

"Not when I finish with her," Marie said, joining them at the campfire. "The idea is sound, and we are desperately in need of funds. Jacques, I believe that I can make Sabine look like a lad."

He still was not convinced that Sabine could fool an audience. "I do not know. Dare we try it?"

"We dare," Marie said, moving around Sabine and eyeing her speculatively. "The worst that can happen is that they run us out of town. We have been run out of towns before." Marie turned Sabine to face her. "How did you come to choose the name de Chavaniac? Near the village where I was born, there lived the marquis de Chavaniac and his family."

Sabine hesitated only a moment before she answered. "If you were born near the mountains of Auvergne, then the marquis of whom you speak would have been my mother's father. My grandfather has but recently died, and my Uncle Joseph is now the marquis de Chavaniac."

"Then you will go to your uncle when we reach France, *non*?" Marie inquired.

"Although I have never met Uncle Joseph, or any of my mother's family, I shall certainly inform them that Richard and I are still alive. They must have heard what happened by now, and most probably believe that we are dead."

"Your uncle is a powerful man, and he will see that everything is put right for you," Marie said with assurance.

"I hope that is so, Madame."

Jacques had heard little of the conversation between Sabine and Marie because he was busy rifling through papers, searching for a certain play. At last he found what he wanted and nodded, shoving several pages at Sabine. "Read this. Take the part of the knight."

Sabine put all the feelings she had in the lines she spoke. When she had finished, Jacques nodded eagerly.

"If we do this, it will not be easy because the two of us will have to play all the parts. And you must know my parts as well as you know your own." He had given this speech many times, but never to a more eager listener.

"Do you think I can?" Sabine asked.

His voice was stern. "That will be for you to prove. Acting requires much study and preparation. When you perform you are not there to be entertained—you are there to entertain others. You must speak loudly and distinctly at all times—never allow your voice to falter. Even those who have not paid admission should be allowed to hear you."

Marie rolled her eyes at her husband. "The child cannot be expected to remember all that you are telling her."

"I would not want to disappoint either of you so I shall strive hard to do as you ask, Monsieur."

"You can do it," Jacques said confidently. "An actor gives his all to his audience. You shall use not only your voice, but also your body to express what you are implying."

"I understand."

"If you are performing a comedy," he continued, "you must not laugh—if you deliver your lines correctly, the audience's laughter will be your reward."

"How will I know I have done well?"

"If you're a good actor, the audience will let you know."

"If you are not," Marie sniffed, "they will also let you know by jeering and throwing unpleasant and smelly things at you."

"Do not scare the child—she will do well."

"Jacques, do not be a fool. Can't you see that you are filling her head with too much?"

Ignoring his wife, he handed Sabine several more pages. "Charge these to your memory. Tomorrow we shall see if we are applauded or run out of town."

12

Madame de Baillard was as good as her word. When she brought Sabine before Jacques the next morning, there was a look of triumph on her face. "Did I not say I would make her look like a boy? The only thing that concerns me is the stiffness in her walk. You will notice how cleverly I have disguised the splint with the long surcoat?"

Jacques inspected Sabine carefully. She wore a green tunic and low boots. Her hair had been cropped to shoulder length, and she wore a rakish black hat with a wide brim. "The disguise does not fool me; I can clearly see that she is a female."

Sabine's face fell, and Marie started to protest.

"But," Jacques continued, holding his hand up for silence, "while this disguise would never fool a Frenchman, the English will be easily duped."

Sabine happily turned to Marie. "I will make everyone believe that I *am* Monsieur Antoine de Chavaniac."

Later, Sabine recited her lines with Marie prompting her, until she could say them in her sleep. She practiced walking, but with the splint she could not disguise the limp. She lowered her voice so she would sound less feminine, and strutted about as she thought an arrogant young knight might.

At last, the moment came to step onto the makeshift stage. Monsieur de Baillard had chosen a small park near the more prosperous part of town, hoping to draw a generous crowd. At first Sabine was nervous even though there were only three people watching. Amazingly, as the play progressed the crowd began to swell and she became more confident.

With Jacques beside her, Sabine moved easily through the scenes. Soon they could hear uproarious laughter, and Sabine felt her spirits soar.

Marie passed among the audience, asking for donations. Her eyes gleamed as money continued to tinkle into the cup.

Sabine found that in acting a part she could forget about her own sadness. She was sorry when the play was concluded.

During the enthusiastic applause, Monsieur de Baillard held his hand over Sabine's head while she bowed to the audience. His eyes were sparkling when he whispered to her. "You made a convincing boy, and you made them laugh. Would that I'd had you with me in London."

For three weeks, Sabine and Monsieur de Baillard put on daily performances and the crowds grew larger as word of their entertainment spread to nearby villages. Jacques was delighted when the Lord Mayor of Dover invited them to entertain at the local theater.

They performed in the Dover Playhouse for two weeks. Even Marie was smiling as she counted the money each night. At last she announced that they had more than enough to sail for France.

Ysabel removed the splint from Sabine's leg. She then joined the de Baillards by the campfire while they silently waited for Sabine to emerge from the wagon. There was a tenseness on each face, and they held their breath, hoping the girl they had come to love had healed.

Unaware of the importance of the moment, Richard sat upon Ysabel's lap, blowing on the wooden whistle that Jacques had carved out of a reed.

At last, Sabine appeared on the steps, her face soft in the moonlight, her expression unreadable. She moved down the first step and then the second. Once on the ground, she closed her eyes, putting her right foot forward. She let out her pent up breath and took a faltering step and then another. At last she laughed happily and threw her arms up in the air.

"Oh, Ysabel, you did it—you did it! I can walk without pain for the first time in so long!"

Marie dabbed at her eyes with her apron. "You did good, Ysabel. I have often been unkind to you, and I am sorry for that. From this day forward, I will say no word of harm against you, nor will I allow anyone else to. And should the time ever come when I am ill, I want only you to tend me."

"I have always liked you, Marie. If I had not, I would have left with the others." Ysabel looked into Sabine's happy face. "The girl has taken her first step toward tomorrow. I know not where that step will take her, but it will take her there without a limp." Ysabel motioned to Sabine. "Walk toward me, *ma petite*. I want to know if the pain returns."

Sabine was testing her leg further, and happiness soared within her heart. "Look at me," she cried, jumping on the leg that had been injured. "I can walk!"

Richard glanced at his sister and then went back to blowing his whistle. He could not see why everyone was making such a fuss—to him Sabine had always been perfect.

Garreth heard a commotion at the door. He leaned against the mantel and watched, feigning disinterest as the Archbishop of Canterbury entered. This was the same man who, as Bishop of London, had helped arrange his marriage to Sabine.

The archbishop looked about the room with interest. It wasn't often he visited the Tower, and never on a mission of such importance. "Your Grace, pardon this intrusion, but I must talk to you."

Garreth nodded toward a chair. "Then pray be seated, Your Excellency. I would offer you refreshments, but as you can see, I have nothing to offer."

The archbishop ignored the chair, preferring to stand since Garreth was standing. His eyes were watchful. "It is his majesty's wish that we clear up this misunderstanding with all haste, since to prolong it would only serve his enemies. I have much to relate to you today."

Garreth tried to keep his anger under control. "What do you have to say that would be of interest to me, Your Excellency? Will you have me confess to crimes I didn't commit to save his majesty embarrassment? My loyalty does not go that far, and his majesty's loyalty to me is in question."

The archbishop dropped down on the chair, and was forced to crane his neck upward at the young duke. "Have a care what you say. And as for your anger, I can understand it. In this most unhappy event, I have endeavored to seek the truth, and I believe I have succeeded."

Garreth stared at him for a long and poignant moment. "Have you indeed?"

"I know quite well how difficult this had been for you and your mother."

"I care not for your sympathy unless it will translate into gaining my release."

"Your mother is a very persuasive woman, Your Grace. She would not relent until she had an audience with the king. They talked for hours. On her insistence, others were questioned, and some interrogations lasted for days."

Garreth picked up a log and tossed it onto the fire, causing sparks to fly. "Why was I not allowed to speak, since I am the accused?"

"I know only that the king has sent me to put questions to you now."

Garreth appeared uninterested. "I have questions myself, but I have doubts that you can give me the answers, Your Excellency."

"Hold your bitterness, Your Grace. In due time, you will understand what I am about. I beg you to be seated so I won't have to look up to you."

Reluctantly, Garreth sat on a frayed, velvet-covered stool, his eyes riveted on the archbishop's face. "How is my mother?"

The archbishop allowed himself to smile slightly. "Her grace is most formidable, charming, and loyal to you. In truth, I believe the king was quite intimidated by her."

Garreth could imagine his mother daring to take King Charles to task. Still, he doubted that the archbishop was here for his benefit. "Say what you will and leave me in peace. I'm certain that my fate has already been sealed."

"Not at all, Your Grace." The archbishop met his eyes. "Have you any knowledge of the identity of your accuser?"

Garreth's lashes swept over his eyes and he stared at the man. "I've heard that the servants at Woodbridge Castle unanimously agree that it was my soldiers who attacked them. I had supposed that they were my accusers."

"Many of them were questioned, and most of them were confused. They say it happened so quickly. But there is one who spoke loudest and crows longer about your guilt."

Now Garreth's eyes flamed with smoldering anger. "Tell me who it is, and bring him before me. It is only just that he face me as he weaves his lies."

The archbishop watched Garreth carefully to gauge his reaction. "Your accuser is your cousin, Cortland Blackthorn."

There was a note of disbelief in Garreth's voice. "Cortland. But why?" He fell silent as he tried to remember what his mother had told him. "It was Cortland who first informed my mother that Woodbridge Castle had been attacked. He was most adamant that I go into hiding while he tried to clear my name."

The archbishop nodded. "That's much the same as what your mother told us."

"Did the king believe her?"

"It would appear so," he said. "On his majesty's instructions, Cortland Blackthorn was brought to London for interrogation. We also questioned many from Woodbridge Village and the surrounding countryside. As you can see, we were most diligent in our quest for the truth."

"No doubt," Garreth said dryly.

The archbishop continued. "Some of the most damn-

ing testimony against your cousin came from the landlord of an inn near Woodbridge. It seems that Cortland
Blackthorn was there one night boasting about what he
intended to do to you."

"Cortland always was a fool."

"Mr. Ludlow, the landlord, told of the hatred your
cousin has for you, and how he bragged about bringing
you down. Apparently he hoped to see you imprisoned
and eventually beheaded."

Garreth waved his hand dismissively. "Cortland isn't
capable of such a plan. He has never been accused of
being overly intelligent, and he's certainly not skillful
enough for such an immense undertaking."

"We do not believe that he acted alone in this treachery. The innkeeper, and other witnesses, spoke of a
mysterious woman who met Blackthorn at the inn. But
we were unable to discover her identity, and your cousin
insisted that he met no woman at the inn, but his denial
was unconvincing."

Garreth was still skeptical. "While imprisoned here, I
have had much time to reflect. I have lived every day
under the threat of death, so it no longer holds any fear
for me."

"We were fortunate in finding the guilty one."

"So you say, but I am still not convinced. What does
Cortland have to say about the accusations?"

"I questioned your cousin myself, and after three
hours, he began ranting about how you were responsible
for the death of the woman he loved. He had for years
plotted your downfall. And he almost succeeded, at least
in his majesty's eyes."

Garreth was astounded. "I hardly know my cousin. And
as to my knowledge, I have caused no woman's death."

The archbishop related the details of Cortland Blackthorn's plan, while Garreth listened in disbelief.

"I cannot credit that he caused the murder of innocent people out of revenge for me." Garreth was stunned by the truth. Then he asked the question that was uppermost in his mind. "Is there news of my wife and her brother?"

"There was a wide search along the stream and surrounding area," the archbishop said sadly, folding his hands in a pose of prayer. "I'm sorry, Your Grace, but it is assumed that they both drowned, and the search has ended."

"I can't accept that."

The archbishop was again watchful. "His majesty has a dilemma. We need to have the boy declared dead so his great-uncle can inherit. But the king does not want your wife to be declared dead because those that support the Woodbridge family might object."

Garreth's lip curled cynically. "You keep her alive to safeguard the alliance. The boy can be proclaimed dead because another member of the Woodbridge family will take his place and reside at the castle."

"You have great insight."

"Archbishop, you know me so little. Even if you had asked me to declare my wife dead, I would not have done so. I still need positive proof before *I* believe that Sabine no longer lives."

"Perhaps it is too soon to speak of such matters, Your Grace. In the future, when she has been forgotten, we shall most certainly sign her death certificate. After all, you will eventually need an heir."

There was hostility in Garreth's dark eyes. "Such a practical decision."

The archbishop stood, knowing the duke's anger was justified. He felt shame for having participated in such an injustice. "You are free to leave. His majesty asks only that you go directly to your country estate and remain there until tempers cool. There will be many who will still insist that your cousin was innocent and sacrificed on your behalf. They will find a way to blame the king."

"What will happen to Cortland?"

"There will not be a public trial because he has already admitted the crime. His death will be forthcoming. The sooner this incident comes to a conclusion, the sooner people will forget."

Garreth stood, wishing it could be his hand that would strike Cortland dead for the black deed he had done and the dishonor he had brought to the Blackthorn name. "I want to see my cousin—there are questions I would put to him. Perhaps he has knowledge of my wife and her brother."

"He has been questioned repeatedly and will say only that the death of your wife is his revenge on you."

Garreth had not known that Cortland hated him—it was so unbelievable. "I must be allowed to speak to him," he insisted.

"That will not be permitted. His majesty wants you to leave London tonight, drawing as little attention to yourself as possible."

Garreth had always revered his king, but now he was disillusioned. He looked about the room that had been his prison for so many weeks. "I leave with no regret. I have been imprisoned here without being allowed a voice to defend myself."

"You are feeling embittered, and I cannot blame you."

"May I see the king?"

"Not at this time, I'm afraid."

"So, I have become an embarrassment to him."

"You must not think—"

"Where is my mother? I am eager to leave London; there is a stench coming all the way from St. James Palace."

The archbishop offered his hand to Garreth, but the duke ignored the gesture so he let it drop to his side. "Her grace is waiting for you in a boat outside the Tower gate."

Garreth picked up his cape and flung it about his shoulders. "It will be a long time before I return to London."

"I would feel much the same as you, Your Grace. These are troubled times, and one does not always know where to look for one's enemies."

"Or one's friends. Those who have come to me under the guise of friendship have turned away when my need was the greatest. Will you give his majesty my . . . regards."

The archbishop looked away. "Go with God and with my blessing."

13

Sabine stood on the rolling deck of the ship that would take them the short distance across the Strait of Dover to Calais. She glanced down at her simple blue woolen gown and reached up to adjust the peasant scarf that covered her red hair, hoping no one would recognize her in this disguise.

Her eyes lingered on the mammoth chalk hills until they began to fade in the distance. A sudden ache of homesickness struck her, and she reached out, taking Richard from Marie. She watched England disappear in an eerie fog, wondering how long it would be before they returned.

Marie saw Sabine's forlorn expression and wanted to cheer her. She touched Richard's curly head. "I find joy in watching this child grow. The two of you will always be welcome with us."

"Thank you, Madame. We will try not to be a burden, and I will help in any way I can."

Marie watched Sabine closely as she spoke. "Jacques' genius is in knowing how to make the people laugh, and what will make them cry. His burden has been that he has never had an actress who could do equity to his direction."

"'Tis a pity, Madame."

Marie's eyes glittered. "I have seen him keep an audience enthralled for five acts, and have them pleading for more. Those little plays he staged in England did not show his true ability."

"I found it amusing to act in his plays, although I do not know how long I could have been convincing as a lad."

Marie leaned on the railing, watching as fog engulfed the ship. "Would you consider acting for my husband when we reach France?" she asked. "You took direction well enough and delivered in a clear voice. You speak French like one born to my country. What a great actress you will become, with Jacques and I to guide you! You will do this for us, *non*?"

"I would do that gladly, Madame, as long as I am able. But once we reach France, and I inform my uncle what happened to Richard and myself, he is certain to send for us."

Marie clasped her hands gratefully. "This is as it should be. But it will take time to exchange letters, *non*? Jacques has agreed to give a performance at the *La Monde* in Calais tomorrow night. The landlord saw a performance in Dover and was most excited when he learned that we were returning to France. He begs us to perform for him—is that not wonderful?"

"It is indeed," Sabine replied, happy for the de Baillards' good fortune.

"I go now to tell Jacques that you remain with us in Calais. Until," she said, smiling, "you go to your uncle."

"Madame, you understand that if I do this, I must perform as a boy, lest someone recognize me."

"Yes, that is understood."

Sabine watched Marie hurry across the deck. She was glad to have the chance to repay the kindness to the de Baillards for all they had done for her and Richard. She looked down at her brother, who had been listening to her conversation with Marie.

"Sabine, why do you want to act like a boy—you are only a girl."

She smiled at him. "Only a girl, am I—well you are only a small boy."

He nodded. "But everyone knows I am a boy. They do not always know that you are a girl."

She had to smile at his shrewdness. "Richard, when we reach France, I am going to ask you to help me become a deceiver. I want you to speak only French. You know the language very well, so don't pretend otherwise."

With a small boy's reasoning, Richard looked at her stubbornly. "Why do we have to speak French—we're English?"

She could understand his confusion. "Never forget who you are, Richard. But we are going to play a game. Would you like that?"

His eyes brightened. "I like games. What shall we play?"

"We are going to see how long we can fool others into believing that we are French. The first one to fail forfeits the game."

His eyes gleamed with the challenge. "I will not lose, you will, Sabine."

"There is more to the game than just speaking French,

Richard. We must change our names because we cannot play a French game with English names. What would you like to be called?"

He set his chin stubbornly, reminding her of their father. "I shall not play if I must change my name."

She relented, placing him on his feet and smiling. "Very well, but I shall change mine. You must help me keep my name a secret. When others are about, I will be known as Antoine de Chavaniac, and you will be my brother."

Richard shook his head and tears gathered in his eyes. "I want to go home."

"Richard," she said, hugging him tightly, "I have told you before that we cannot go home yet a while. It is very important that you understand this and do as I ask."

He wiped his tears with a chubby little hand. "I will, Sabine, but I won't like it."

She led him to a protected part of the deck, away from the chilling wind. For now it was her and Richard against unknown and faceless enemies. Garreth Blackthorn was a dangerous adversary, and if he suspected they were in France, he would surely send someone after them, or come for them himself.

Cortland Blackthorn smiled bitterly as he walked between the two guards who escorted him down a dark, narrow passage to his execution. He had no fear of death. He wished he could think clearly, but his mind was a dark, swirling wasteland. He wanted to feel emotions so he could take his hatred for Garreth with him to his death—he wanted it to be his last conscious thought. He'd prayed that Garreth would come today so he could taunt him as a last triumph. But Garreth had not even acknowledged him, and that was the final insult.

In all this, Cortland did have one thread of satisfaction, because, no matter how his tormenters had questioned and tortured him to make him tell who had been his accomplice, he had not told them about Eugenia Meredith. She must have known terror when he had been arrested, fearing he would name her as a companion in his conspiracy. He wondered what she thought when she learned that he had gone against their agreement and implicated Garreth in the crimes.

He gnashed his teeth. Of course, Garreth had walked free, but his name was tarnished nonetheless. Cortland's eyes gleamed. There would be many who would believe that Garreth had plotted the attack on Woodbridge and that he, Cortland, was the innocent sacrifice to save the family honor.

As the guards led him into a secluded courtyard, he looked up at the sky, thinking it would rain later in the day, but he would not see it. His execution was to be private, with only the four guards and an executioner in attendance. In this, the last moments of his life, he was still of no consequence—it was a fitting end, he thought.

When they reached Calais, Sabine immediately sent word to her uncle informing him that she and Richard were in France and wished to visit him. Weeks passed and still she waited for a reply. It was the day of their last performance in Calais when Sabine finally received a letter, but it was not from her uncle; instead it was from someone representing him. With sadness, she read the letter to Marie and Ysabel.

"Madame, on behalf of the marquis de Chavaniac, I send you a warning not to press your claims further. The marquis is very aware that his niece and nephew met a tragic end. If you persist in identifying yourself as

Sabine Woodbridge Blackthorn, you will be punished severely."

There was a long moment of silence. Then Sabine looked at Marie and Ysabel for guidance. "What shall I do?"

"The man is a fool," Marie stated flatly. "You will stay with us, of course. We soon leave Calais and play in the Provinces until we have perfected our act. Only when we are ready, will we go to Paris. There, others besides me will acknowledge my husband's genius and your great talent."

Sabine gripped the letter in her hand. "Since my uncle will not believe me, Richard has no one to champion his cause."

Ysabel, always wise, commented forcefully. "One does not need a champion when one has friends. You will remain with us until you are ready to return to England. Justice will be yours in the end."

So it was that Sabine took the name of Antoine de Chavaniac as her own. Even when not performing, she wore the attire of a young boy, to hide her identity.

Jacques brought two more actors and an actress into the troupe as they gained in reputation. However, the new members knew Sabine only as Antoine de Chavaniac, and they thought it strange that the young Antoine was so reclusive. Sabine and Richard now had their own wagon, and when she wasn't onstage, she spent her time with her brother.

As Marie had predicted, the de Baillard Players traveled the Provinces, acting in small towns and villages. Sometimes they stayed only one night, and other times they performed for a week or more.

Out of concern that Richard was growing up without direction, each day Sabine would instruct him in manners and courtly etiquette. Like most small boys, he rebelled against the refinements, preferring to run wild and free. At night, by lantern light, she began to teach him to read. She found that he had a quick mind and hungered for knowledge.

The de Baillard Players slowly began to obtain the recognition Marie felt they deserved. They received so many requests to perform that Jacques had to refuse many of them. At first, they played only the small villages, and then larger towns welcomed them as well. The crowds grew larger and a particular favorite with them was a young man of personable manner, known as Antoine de Chavaniac.

1633

It was a lovely spring morning as Sabine left her wagon to join Jacques and Marie beneath a gnarled oak tree. Jacques had written a new play that he wanted her to read. Sabine could see by the expressions on their faces that something was amiss. Marie motioned her forward while Jacques hung back allowing them privacy.

"I have something that I must say to you, Sabine," Marie told her. "I do not know how you will feel about it—but it must be said."

Sabine searched Marie's eyes. "I have done something to displease you?"

"*Non, non,*" Marie hastened to assure her. "It is nothing like that."

"Then what? Tell me."

Marie lowered her voice. "Are you not aware that your body has changed?"

Sabine had noticed that her hips had rounded and her breasts were fuller, forcing her to bind herself each morning before she dressed. She nodded in embarrassment. "*Oui,* Madame."

"Jacques has written a magnificent new play that will need the talents of a beautiful woman," Marie said firmly. "This morning he dismissed the other players. It was difficult for him to do so, but he did it for you."

Sabine was confused. "You sent them away because of me? I do not understand."

Marie was silent for a moment, as if contemplating how to proceed. "Jacques and I have decided that you can no longer play a convincing boy."

Sabine felt heavy disappointment. "Oh. I suppose if you are bringing in a new female lead, you will need an actor to replace me."

Marie shook her head, her bright yellow curls bobbing about her face. "This is a happy day for us and you must be happy with us. Jacques want you for his luminary!"

Sabine thought she must have misunderstood. "Are you certain that you want me for such an important role?"

Jacques joined them, a wide grin on his face. "We will have no one but *you*, Sabine. We have been offered the Escredil Theater in Paris. It is not a large theater, but very respectable. It is what we have been waiting for."

Sabine could hardly contain her joy. "Oh, Jacques, Marie, how wonderful for you." Then her face fell. "But I cannot be your star—one must be very beautiful to be the female luminary in Paris."

Jacques and Marie looked at each other and laughed. "Sabine, why do you think you can no longer pretend to be a boy? Have you not looked at yourself lately?" Marie asked.

"I . . . no." Her eyes widened. "What are you saying? Do you think I am pretty?"

"Are you pretty?" Marie asked, turning to her husband. "You have kept her dressed as a lad too long. She does not know how she looks." Then she turned back to Sabine. "Wait until Paris sees you. The gentlemen will lay wreaths at your feet."

Suddenly Sabine's face froze. "I cannot go to Paris. Someone might recognize me."

Jacques took her hand in a fatherly manner. "Do you still believe you are in danger?"

"Yes, I do. Garreth Blackthorn would not give up so easily."

He rubbed his forehead in thoughtfulness. "You have changed much since we first found you. I do not believe anyone will recognize you. The reason I dismissed the other players was so they would not witness your transformation to a woman."

Marie nodded. "Sabine, in the time you have been with us, your appearance has altered from that of a young girl to a woman. Your hair is a deeper red than it was then. At first you were slender and pale—now there is color in your cheeks and you are very beautiful." Marie spoke admiringly. "I have never seen hair like yours. The lights of the Paris stage will make it appear to be on fire."

"I have changed," Sabine admitted, "but what about my brother, Marie? Suppose someone recognizes him?"

"Richard has almost doubled in height, and for all anyone will know, he is a French lad."

"Yes, I suppose so," Sabine agreed reluctantly.

"Sabine," Jacques said in a soft voice, "we would do nothing that would put you or Richard in danger."

Marie nodded in agreement. "We are a family," she said. "If it is your wish, then you can remain with us even if you take no part in the plays, but you cannot remain a boy, for you would fool no one."

Jacques had been staring at Sabine's hair. "You need a name worthy of your beauty." He stroked his beard in thoughtfulness as he circled her. "I know what we shall call you—you shall be known only as, La Flamme!"

"'Tis fitting," Marie said, turning to Ysabel, who had just joined them. "Do you not think so?"

"It will suffice," Ysabel agreed.

No one bothered to ask Sabine what she thought of the new name, and Jacques seemed so pleased with himself that she didn't want to object.

"This is the day Monsieur de Chavaniac dies and La Flamme is born," Jacques said, marveling at his own brilliance.

Sabine watch her brother as he raced across the meadow in pursuit of a brightly-colored butterfly. "I will think on what you have said and let you know my decision tonight. I want first to speak to Richard about going to Paris."

Sabine went directly to her wagon and opened a trunk. Rummaging through the clothing, she found a gown that she had not worn in over a year. It was made of soft pink linen with white lace at the high neck. She quickly undressed and pulled it over her head. The gown was too tight across the bust, and so short that it showed her ankles. Even so, she whirled around the small wagon, feeling very female.

She went outside in search of Richard. When she found him, he was curled up beneath a wild blackberry bush, his lips stained purple from the berries he'd consumed.

When Richard saw his sister, he sat up, his eyes filled with amazement. "Sabine, you're a girl!"

She took his hand and pulled him to his feet. "And you, Richard, have juice on your mouth. Walk with me to the brook so you can wash."

They walked hand-in-hand while she tried to think how best to tell him about Jacques's plan for her. "Richard, how would you like to go to Paris?"

"I would rather go home," he said, "although I don't really remember much about it."

Sabine sighed. "We cannot go home just yet. Would you mind so much if we went to Paris with Madame and Monsieur de Baillard?"

"Will Ysabel come too?"

"*Oui.*"

His face was creased in a serious frown. "Then I shall go to Paris for a time."

Sabine stopped before the brook and reached into Richard's pocket to remove his handkerchief. Bending to dip it in the mirror-bright water, she paused and stared at her reflection. She ran her hand down her face and touched her red hair. She was stunned by what she saw. Marie and Jacques had been right—she had changed.

"I look so different," she said in wonder.

"Are you going to stay a girl this time?" Richard asked, taking in her transformation matter-of-factly. "I like you better as my sister."

Sabine laughed and wet the handkerchief, then began dabbing at his face. "Yes, you imp, I will remain a girl." She stepped back and dropped into a curtsy. "I am off to Paris, where men will lay wreaths at my feet, or so Marie assures me."

Richard looked puzzled. "Why would you want them to do such a silly thing?"

She tousled his hair. "So I can engage a tutor for you before you take on more Bohemian ways. And so we can live in a proper house. I grow weary of living in the cramped wagon. Wouldn't you like to sleep in a real bed?"

"Will we ever go home, Sabine?"

She hesitated only a moment. "Yes, one day."

"Make it soon."

She took his hand and they walked back to the encampment. She often thought of England, and she wondered how the people of her father's village were faring, but there was no way for her to obtain the news she craved.

Hatred still smoldered within her when she thought of Garreth Blackthorn, but she kept it under tight control. The day would come when she would return England and expose him, but that time was not now—she would know when it was right to go home.

Richard glanced up at her. "Your hair looks different. What did you do to it?"

"Do you like it?" Sabine asked.

"Yes, I do. You are beautiful."

She smiled down at him. "So says my champion."

Sabine did not know that her movements were graceful. She could not see that the red of her hair brought a rosy glow to her face. And no matter what Marie and Jacques told her, she was still not convinced that she was beautiful.

There was a dull ache in her heart. The future was bleak and uncertain, the past too sad to dwell upon. She would hold on to Richard, and together they would survive!

II

La Flamme

14

1634

     Lord Stephen Meredith was getting drowsy from the rhythmic swaying of his coach as it traveled over the rough road toward Paris. It had rained earlier in the day, but at mid-afternoon it had cleared, and a bright sun now shone down on the French countryside.

Stephen had inherited his father's title upon Lord Meredith's death six months earlier. His stepmother, Eugenia, had finally gotten what he thought she deserved. She had married an ailing old man, thinking he would soon die and leave her a wealthy widow. But Stephen's father had lived long enough to despise his unfaithful wife.

After her husband's death, Eugenia declared to anyone who would listen that she had wasted her best years on a husband who left her only a country house outside a small village. Worse than that, it was a three-day journey from the London she loved. She also became enraged upon discovering that she would only receive a yearly income of twenty pounds, which was less than she was accustomed to spending on hats. Her constant demands for money had sent Stephen fleeing to France for a respite.

Three years ago, he had inherited a small estate outside Paris from the grandmother on his distaff side. At one time he had considered selling it, for he'd had no interest in the château until now. He found it charming and had been staying there for the last two months.

At first he had enjoyed the peace and solitude of the French countryside, but this morning he had awakened feeling restless and needing a diversion. So, he was off to Paris.

As the coach slowed in the city traffic, Stephen glanced out the window with interest, wondering how he would pass his time. At the moment, the rage in Paris was a play at the Escredil Theater. It appeared that all of Paris was at the feet of some actress called La Flamme. Perhaps after dining, he would just see this La Flamme for himself.

The audience was roaring with laughter by the end of the first act, and Stephen applauded louder than anyone, although he couldn't always understand what the characters were saying since he was not proficient in French. Nonetheless, he was in love. La Flamme was the most enchanting creature he'd ever seen. He wanted to talk to her and tell her how he admired her, but how would he communicate with her? After the final act, he waited in front of the theater, hoping for his chance to speak to her. Judging from the large gathering of people, who were all pushing and shoving to get near her, he doubted he would be able to attract her attention at all.

At last, La Flamme emerged with a servant walking at her side. She moved through the crowd, speaking to admirers as they made a path for her. When she neared Stephen, he stepped forward and spoke in faltering French.

"*Mademoiselle La Flamme, vous . . .*" He struggled with his words. "er, *laide . . . a . . . faire . . . peur.*"

Sabine came to a shocked halt, and stared at the man in astonishment.

Stephen thought she would pass him by without a word. But suddenly she smiled, and then musical laughter escaped her lips. To his relief, she spoke to him in heavily-accented English.

"Monsieur, you must take care, or you will turn a woman's head with such talk."

"I had to tell you how wonderful you were," he said sincerely.

Again she laughed. "Your French is not very good, is it, Monsieur?"

"Not very, I'm afraid."

"I am relieved to hear that because what you said to me was not a tribute."

He searched her eyes, feeling a sinking sensation in the pit of his stomach. "What did I say?"

"You said, Monsieur, that I am frightfully ugly."

His face reddened. "Mademoiselle, please forgive me! I promise you it was not my intention to . . . I only meant to . . . I think you are beautiful!"

Sabine was looking at the Englishman closely, all the while trying to pretend indifference. She felt her heart thundering inside her breast. What was Stephen Meredith doing in Paris? He seemed not to know her— was that possible?

Gathering her courage, she met his eyes. "I will ignore the first compliment, Monsieur, and accept the second."

She turned to leave, when he spoke. "Please, Mademoiselle, there is no reason that you should speak to me again, but I wonder if I might introduce myself to you."

By now the crowd had moved away, and she turned back to him. "That would be acceptable." She had to know if Garreth had sent him, or if this was but a chance meeting.

"I am Lord Stephen Meredith, from England."

Her hand tightened inside her muff. "Have we met before, Monsieur?"

"I can assure you that we have not. I would remember if I'd ever met you."

Sabine let out a relieved breath. She remembered the day he'd come to Woodbridge with Garreth, and how gallant he had been. She had never forgotten how he had defended her on her wedding day when others had ridiculed her.

"It is always agreeable to meet someone from England, Lord Meredith. Are you in my country alone?" she asked, hoping Garreth had not accompanied him.

"Yes, quite alone," Stephen answered, hardly daring to hope that La Flamme was interested enough in him to find out if he was married.

Sabine turned to Ysabel, who had been patiently waiting, not knowing that this was a man from Sabine's past.

"We will leave now, Ysabel."

"Mademoiselle, before you go," Stephen said hurriedly, " . . . may I . . . call on you sometime?"

Sabine hesitated only a moment. "If you would like, My Lord, you may come to my home Friday next. I am having a small gathering, and you would be most welcome."

His face brightened. "I'll be there." Then he looked puzzled. "But where do you live?"

"Come backstage tomorrow night and ask for Jacques. He will see that you have directions."

Stephen could hardly believe that La Flamme had spoken to him, let alone invited him to her house. He was most fortunate indeed.

When Sabine was seated in her coach, Ysabel questioned her. "Why did you invite a stranger to your home, and an Englishman at that?"

"He is not a stranger. He is a friend of Garreth's, and stepson to my husband's mistress."

"Is there not danger in this, *ma petite*?" Ysabel asked with a frown.

"How better to learn about Garreth than to become a friend to his best friend? I will use Stephen Meredith to gain knowledge of my enemy—is this not cunning?"

Ysabel stared at her for a long moment. "As long as you remember it is also dangerous."

"I never forget that Richard and I live beneath a cloud of danger."

Sabine became extremely fond of Stephen. He was what Thea would have called a worthy gentleman. He was honest and caring, and he made Sabine laugh with his wonderful sense of humor. She was cautious with him, never asking about Garreth or his stepmother, although they were uppermost in her mind. She waited, hoping Stephen would speak of them himself.

A month had passed since their first meeting, and now Sabine was becoming concerned. Stephen was beginning to have special feelings for her, and she did not want to hurt him.

The night sky was alive with stars as Sabine stood

with Stephen in the garden of her home. The sound of merrymaking came through the open doorway.

"I love it here, Stephen. Paris sparkles like a beautiful jewel, *non*?"

He looked at her, his eyes openly admiring. "Not nearly as beautiful as you, La Flamme."

"Stephen," she said gently, "I treasure your friendship, for I have so few real friends. I would not like our friendship to be spoiled."

"You are saying that we can only be friends?" he asked, striving to hide his disappointment.

Sabine felt remorse because she had shamefully used him. "I am saying that you are my dear companion—and that's all we can ever be to each other."

He was quiet for a long time, just gazing up at the stars. "Then I shall consider myself fortunate to be your friend."

Sabine felt his pain and was sorry. "Friendship is often deeper and more enduring than love, Stephen."

He smiled down at her ruefully. "Perhaps in a few years, or even a few months, I'll see the wisdom of that statement, but not at this moment."

She touched his face as her eyes misted. "Perhaps you should return to England, Stephen."

"Yes, perhaps I should."

Sabine avoided his eyes, knowing that she must now use him again to find out about Garreth. "Have you many friends in England?"

"Yes, I suppose. I have many friends, but only one who is like a brother to me."

"Tell me about him."

He was reluctant to speak of Garreth, even with La Flamme. "You would probably like Garreth—all women do. But he is unaffected by adoration." He looked down at her again. "He is not unlike you in that."

"So your friend Garreth likes the women, *oui*?" she asked.

"It's more that the women love him. At one time he lived a cavalier life, but something happened to change him, and now he is much too serious. He rarely goes to London, and he never appears at Court. Garreth chooses to remain at Wolfeton Keep, in virtual seclusion."

Sabine tensed. "What happened to change him?"

Stephen grimaced. "He was imprisoned in the Tower after being falsely accused of the death of his young wife and her family."

"How dreadful," she said, hoping that Garreth was still suffering for the crimes he had committed.

"Garreth hasn't said so to me because he refuses to talk of it, but I believe that he blames himself for the deaths—especially his wife's."

Sabine tried to keep the bitterness out of her voice. "What a pity."

"If you knew Garreth, you would understand how he could take another's guilt and make it his own."

"Has he not remarried?"

"There have been women, but—" Stephen threw up his hands. "I should not be boring you with this."

"I was not bored."

He took Sabine's hands and gazed for a long time into her eyes. "I shall miss you."

"And I you. Will you return to Paris soon?"

He smiled, thinking of all the things that could never be between the two of them. "Of course. I try never to stay away from my friends for long."

"Perhaps," she said, daringly, "you should bring your friend, Garreth, to France. No one takes life seriously in Paris."

"What a splendid notion. Perhaps I shall." He raised

her hand to his lips. "Will you think of me while I am away?"

"As with any good friend, I shall think of you often."

As Stephen walked away, Sabine realized that she would miss him dreadfully, for he had brought with him a touch of England and home.

15

1636

    The de Baillard Players had obtained international fame, not only in their native France, but throughout Europe. The ultimate honor came when the company was bestowed a royal order to perform at the Theatre du Palais-Royal, where they were hailed as The Royal Acting Troupe.

King Louis XIII awarded Jacques a yearly income of fifteen hundred francs, but it was said that the lead female actress, La Flamme, received two thousand francs a year.

The theater was filled each night, and much of the crowd was turned away because it was difficult to gain admission unless you knew someone of importance, or were important yourself. The King's box was rarely empty. He applauded Jacques' genius, and stared with admiration at the female luminary of the de Baillard Players.

The enchantingly beautiful La Flamme had all Paris talking about her, with her shimmering red hair and mesmerizing topaz eyes. It only added to her mystique that no one knew anything about her personal life, although there was much speculation.

The Palais-Royal was crowded with those who had come to see the de Baillard Players perform Jacques' new romantic comedy, *La Haute Noblesse*. Sabine stood offstage, waiting for her cue to enter. She was dressed in shimmering gold, and her red hair was bound and intertwined with precious pearls.

Ysabel looked her over to make certain everything was perfect. "You will have them at your feet tonight, *ma petite*."

Sabine was going over her lines in her mind and answered Ysabel absently. "I have never wanted a man at my feet."

"That is because you lose interest in the men who are so easily conquered, and well you should. But one day, you will meet a man who will conquer you."

Sabine gave Ysabel a doubtful look. "I am not interested in any of them."

To put the finishing touch on Sabine's costume, Ysabel attached a golden rose to her red hair. "You are weary of those who would roll over and play tricks if La Flamme asked it of them."

"I ask only that they laugh when I play comedy and weep when I play tragedy."

"You cannot keep yourself apart from life forever. You are young. It is not good that you close your heart to happiness."

Sabine kissed Ysabel's cheek. "You have said this all before, and you fuss too much. I have you, Richard, Marie, and Jacques, and surely that is enough happiness for anyone."

In the darkened theater the audience waited breathlessly for La Flamme to make her appearance. In a box hung with red velvet drapes, two gentlemen also waited.

"You will lose your heart when you see her, Garreth. La Flamme is like no other woman!" Stephen exclaimed. "I saw her perform for the first time two years ago. Now, I'm glad to be numbered among her friends—it's an honor she bestows on very few."

"An enviable position, I'm sure," Garreth said. "I have listened to your tributes to her for so long that I grow weary of her without ever making her acquaintance. Tonight I shall judge for myself if the woman fits the legend."

"She does," Stephen said with confidence, a smile curving his lips. "After the performance, you will implore me to present her to you, and I may not."

Garreth leaned back in the red velvet chair, wishing he had not agreed to accompany Stephen tonight. He had always found playacting tedious. To spend an entire evening watching French actors and actresses would be more punishment than pleasure for him.

"I will be glad to quit France," Garreth said in a bored voice, "and I care not for Paris."

"Then why did you come?"

"You know well that I came only because of my mother's prodding. She insisted that I needed a holiday. I'm grateful that you agreed to accompany me, thus saving me weeks of monotony. Surely now that we have visited Florence, Rome, Venice, and Paris my mother will be satisfied."

"Her grace was right, Garreth. You've forgotten how to enjoy life. I am glad that you have finally agreed to visit my château. I've been trying to get you here for years."

"It's a charming house with an admirable setting," Garreth said politely.

"Let us watch the stage. It is almost time for La Flamme to make her entrance. At last you will see her for yourself, and like everyone else, you will be captivated."

"Come now, Stephen, I'm not as easily swayed by a woman's beauty as you are. An actress could hardly be my ideal woman."

Stephen merely smiled. "There was a time when you were susceptible to every beautiful woman. La Flamme is as perfect as a woman can be."

With little interest, Garreth directed his attention toward the stage, where two actors were dramatizing a duel. They were well-practiced, he had to admit, and each was an excellent swordsman, but they were still play-acting.

Suddenly a woman swept on stage, and there were gasps heard from the audience. She was in a halo of light, shimmering in gold—her red hair like a crown of fire.

It was La Flamme!

Garreth leaned forward nonchalantly. "So that is your paragon of beauty. I have known many English women who are more beautiful."

Stephen was not listening. He was staring at the object of his adoration. "She is magnificent!"

La Flamme's voice was musical, and she spoke with the clarity of a high-born lady. Her movements were so graceful that it appeared she was floating across the stage, coming alive like a golden goddess.

Garreth noticed her dove-white throat and her creamy skin that appeared to be shimmering like moon glow. This phenomenon he cynically attributed to the excessive number of candles that flickered on the stage.

Without realizing it, he became so engrossed with the actress that he heard little of what the other actors were saying. La Flamme knew well how to keep her audience spellbound. She raised her chin, her eyes flashing, and her soft lips curved in a smile, provocative, enticing, entrapping those who watched her.

"Who can she be?" Garreth asked, unaware that he had spoken aloud.

Stephen gave him a triumphant glance. "No one knows her true name, not even me. Have you changed your mind—shall I present you to her?"

"Yes," Garreth said, gracious in defeat. "Can you arrange it?"

"Confess that she is more beautiful than our English roses," Stephen said smugly.

"I confess that she looks perfect from a distance, but in talking to her, she will probably prove disappointing— I have oft found this to be true of beautiful women."

"You are too cynical, Garreth. Be warned that she will not be swayed by your charm. Her life pivots around a child, her brother, Richard."

Garreth glanced over at the royal box and watched the French king throw kisses toward the stage. "Does she not . . . bask in the king's adoration?"

"I don't think she even likes him, but she tolerates him for the sake of the de Baillards. She is a woman of high virtue and strict morals."

Garreth raised a skeptical brow. "An actress with high morals?"

"Scoff if you wish, but it's true. She is as pure as an angel."

Garreth had not taken his eyes off the lovely creature. "Then one would ask why she is called La Flamme—a name that would surely suggest a seductress, rather than an angel."

"A name chosen merely for the stage, I would imagine," Stephen replied. "She is accomplished and adored, dazzling her admirers and then turning them away if they attempt to get too near."

"La Flamme," Garreth said under his breath.

Stephen waved an invitation at Garreth. "Would you like to go to her house tonight? It's Marie de Baillard's birthday, and La Flamme is hosting a celebration for her."

"Yes, I would like that. I shall see for myself if your angel is as virtuous as you say."

"One does not question La Flamme's virtue. I know of two duels that were fought over her for just that reason."

"Tell me more about her."

"She lives with her young brother on the fashionable Avenue Gabriel. Only close friends are ever invited into her domain."

"So there is no man in her life?"

"No. There are those who suspect that the child La Flamme calls brother is really her son, but I do not believe it. Some people say that she's from a great noble family, while others believe that she fled from an affair of the heart with a noble prince, perhaps the father of the boy. It's obvious the king admires her, and has showered her with honors."

Garreth glanced at the royal box. "I could well understand if she does not return his affection—the popinjay. It's my guess that she is under his protection."

"No, she's not, Garreth. Why should she need the king when she is more adored than he is? After each performance, she is showered with flowers, precious jewels, and she has even been offered a palace by an enamored Danish prince. She keeps the flowers, and returns the rest with her regrets."

"You begin to weary me with your constant devotion, Stephen. I cannot imagine you being satisfied with merely being her friend."

"Tonight, you shall be one of the few ever allowed into her home. So you can be glad I am her friend."

Ysabel pulled aside the drapery and looked out the window at the line of coaches making their way down the drive. She lived with Sabine and Richard, which gave her at last a family to care for, and a home.

"Sabine, it looks like all Paris will be in attendance tonight. Will not Marie be pleased?"

"*Oui.* I believe even King Louis will be attending."

Ysabel moved to Sabine and began lacing her gown. It was a frothy creation with white lace and white pearls decorating the hem and sleeves. The lace collar was modestly high. Her only jewelry was her mother's locket that had been reclaimed from the goldsmith in Dover by Jacques on one of his voyages to England.

"Please go downstairs and greet the guests, Ysabel, while I tell Richard good night."

The old woman nodded. "Do not leave me alone for long with all those handsome young men. They come to see you, not me."

Sabine took a last look at her hair. "Tonight is for Marie. She was as excited as a child about the party."

Sabine left her dressing room and went across the corridor to Richard's bedroom. She found him curled up on his bed, reading by candlelight.

She took his book and glanced at the title. "History of England?"

"It's fascinating," he said, coming to his knees. "Do you know what I remember most about England?"

She smiled and sat on the edge of his bed. "You were very young when we left—what can you possibly remember?"

"The smells; like rain on a spring morning—a hillside

covered with wildflowers. Even the musty smell of the stables and kennels."

At nine, Richard was a striking youth and reminded her of their father, at least physically. But he was not hard or forceful, as their father had been. He was patient and possessed great kindness, and it was a pity that he lived such a solitary life.

Her heart contracted as he went on sadly. "I have been trying to remember what my father looked like, but his image is unclear. I have heard you speak of my nurse, Thea, but I do not remember her—is that wrong?"

Sabine bent to kiss him on the forehead. "No, dearest. You were so young when we left. Some day I will tell you all about our life in England." She moved across the room to close his draperies. "Do not read more than another hour in this light. It isn't good for your eyes." She smiled to herself, thinking how like Thea she sounded.

Already Richard's interest had returned to his book. Sabine quietly left, closing the door behind her.

Richard had made her think of England tonight, and she was overcome with homesickness.

Oh, what she would give to smell the wildflowers at Woodbridge and to walk through the marble halls of her home. She pushed the thoughts of England to the back of her mind.

Home was a fanciful dream, and she wondered if they would ever return.

16

Music wove its way through the house and up the stairs. With her foot on the top step, Sabine was almost knocked over by Richard's two golden Afghan hounds when they joyfully came bounding up to her. With a dog on either side of her, she patted them both and then grasped a collar in each hand, continuing her descent.

Garreth paced the room with a scowl on his face. France was not like England. Here, the nobility moved freely among actors and actresses. The hostess, who had not appeared yet, was apparently playing the old game of grand entrance. Somehow that disappointed him—a flaw in her character. But then she was an actress, and she would no doubt play her part on- or offstage.

He saw Stephen conversing with several people, apparently enjoying himself. Garreth turned away from the tables that were heaped with food, deciding to go outside for a breath of fresh air. He regretted the impulse that had brought him here tonight.

He walked into the deserted hallway and drew in a deep cleansing breath, glad to be away from the noise. He had lived too long in the country to enjoy such frivolity.

A movement at the top of the curved stairway caught his attention, and he watched as a vision in white seemed to float downward. It was La Flamme, and she was flanked on either side by two enormous hounds. While he could not tear his eyes away from her, she seemed totally unaware of him.

Sabine pulled one reluctant dog forward. "Come on, Maurice," she said playfully. "You must go outside before you can return to Richard. "Come on, I have to join my guests."

Garreth stepped back in the shadow of the stairs, watching as she guided the playful hounds outside. She was shimmering, beautiful, intriguing. He followed her almost against his will.

Stars seeded the night sky like sparkling diamonds as Sabine walked through the garden, watching Richard's hounds romp and play. She scolded Ginger when she rolled in the flower bed, then both dogs bounded around the corner toward the front of the house.

Knowing they would soon return, Sabine waited for them, turning her gaze, as she always did, toward her homeland. "Oh, England, how far away you seem tonight," she said.

She was startled when an English voice spoke up from behind her. "Your English is quite good, for a French-woman, Mademoiselle."

Sabine froze—oh, how well she knew that voice! It was deeper than she remembered, but still held the same hint of sarcasm and arrogance.

Garreth Blackthorn had found her!

Frantically, she wondered if she dared scream for help—no, she would never be heard above the music and laughter.

Sabine had known that she would one day face Garreth, but she'd thought it would be at a time and place of her own choosing.

She attempted to hide her fear as she turned slowly to face him, ready to continue her disguise. She could hear the trembling in her voice when she spoke in French. "Pardon, Monsieur?"

Garreth emerged from the darkness to stand beside her. "You spoke of England with the yearning of one who is homesick, Mademoiselle."

Could it be that he did not recognize her? Or, was he only taunting her? She must know. The lie came easily to her lips. "I merely recited a part in a play that I am to perform."

He stepped closer, and she felt as if her legs would not support her. Slowly she looked up at him. He was dressed in formal black, and still clean-shaven, though the stylish gentlemen wore beards and mustaches. As his dark gaze settled on her, she realized how devastatingly handsome he was.

"You will be performing the play in English?"

"Perhaps, Monsieur. We have been invited to England by your Queen Henrietta. She is French, you know, and has asked us to perform for the king, but we have not yet decided if we will accept the invitation."

"An invitation from her majesty—that is an honor." His tone of voice suggested that he was not impressed.

Garreth stepped further into the moonlight, and Sabine could only stare at him. He seemed older than she remembered, and there was the hint of sadness about him. Though he was no longer the dashing young man she had married, maturity had only made him more appealing.

Her throat tightened in fear—or was it excitement? Looking into his eyes, she saw no recognition there. Was it admiration she saw? Sabine was confused. What was he doing in her home? How had he found her?

"I do not know you, Monsieur," she said hurriedly. "If you will excuse me, I must see to my invited guests."

When she would have stepped around him, he blocked her path. "Allow me to introduce myself. I am Garreth Blackthorn." He swept into a bow. "I add my invitation to the queen's for you to visit England."

"This is not a suitable introduction, Monsieur Blackthorn," she said, pretending a haughtiness she was far from feeling. "I do not know what you have heard about me, but you would not have heard that I speak to those who have not been properly presented to me."

Garreth was not accustomed to women acting indifferently to him. He was intrigued. When she had been on the stage, he had thought her beautiful, but now standing close to her, she was flawless and enchanting. She was all in white except for her glorious flaming hair.

"Would you acknowledge me if I were introduced to you by a friend we share, Lord Stephen Meredith?"

"You know Stephen?" she asked innocently.

"I am staying at Stephen's château, and I'm here tonight at his invitation."

"So you are the friend he spoke to me about. I believe you are a duke, *non*?"

Garreth smiled slightly. Perhaps La Flamme wasn't so different from other women after all. "Yes, does that matter?"

"Not to me, Monsieur. I know many dukes."

"What if I told you that my great-grandmother was

French, would you then agree that we have something in common?"

"Then you have very little French blood in you, Monsieur le duc, therefore that gives us very little in common."

This man was her enemy, and he had invaded her sanctuary. Even though he had not realized who she was, she didn't want him here. She had suggested that Stephen bring Garreth to Paris—but not to her home!

"Please excuse me, Monsieur," she said. "I must see to my guests."

Sabine hurried inside, feeling safer once she entered the brightly-lit salon that was filled with familiar faces. After her encounter with Garreth, she was trembling, and thought surely everyone would notice.

In the corner of the room, the harpist and flautist played their music, but she did not hear. Her pose was rigid, her eyes wide with terror when she realized that Garreth was standing beside her.

She deliberately turned her back on him to greet one of her guests. "Monsieur Rabaut, how kind of you to attend my little soiree for Madame Marie." She moved away from Garreth, talking to guests as she went. Her smile was forced, and she pretended a cheerfulness she did not feel. She moved from one gentleman to another, dulling their amorous advances with laughter. She was aware that Garreth watched her from across the room, but she refused to look in his direction.

Sabine raised a glass and offered a toast to Marie. She went through the motions of the perfect hostess, but she felt as if the evening would never end.

At last, the moment she had dreaded had come. Stephen approached, with Garreth at his side.

"La Flamme, I haven't been able to get near you all evening," Stephen said, smiling. "Would you permit me to introduce my friend from England, His Grace, the duke of Balmarough? If you will remember, I have spoken often of him."

Garreth bowed before her mockingly. "Will this satisfy you as a proper introduction?"

Sabine pressed her lips together tightly against the angry retort that begged to be spoken. When at last she did speak, there was an edge to her tone. "Such an illustrious person. Will my heart ever be stilled from beating?"

Garreth arched a brow at her, and Sabine stared coldly into his eyes. In that moment, they each issued the other a silent challenge.

"What would you have me do, Mademoiselle La Flamme? It seems that I have offended you without intending to, and I would like to make amends."

She linked her arm through Stephen's. "You are of course my welcome guest, Your Grace, since you are a friend of my friend." She smiled brightly at Stephen. "And a dear friend he has been to me."

Stephen looked pleased, and Garreth was puzzled. No matter that her words were courteous, she was angry for reasons that eluded him.

"If I have offended you, I can assure you it was unintentional," he said. "With regret, I take my leave of you."

"*Adieu*," Sabine said.

Garreth stared into her golden eyes, trying to read her thoughts, but she was too complex. "We shall meet again, I think, Mademoiselle La Flamme."

She turned deliberately to Stephen. "I will see you soon, Stephen," she said, trying to catch her breath and appear unaffected by Garreth's presence. "You have been away from Paris much too long."

By now, Stephen was aware that something was wrong between La Flamme and Garreth. "I will be here for several more weeks," he replied. "Although I am not certain that I can convince Garreth to remain—he insists on returning to England."

"Then you must use your persuasion to make him stay." Her statement sounded as false as she intended. She kissed Stephen's cheek, gave Garreth a weak smile, and moved away, her back straight and her chin high. She would never again run from Garreth Blackthorn—no matter how frightened she was.

With relief, she caught Jacques' arm as he came by. "Let us find Marie and drink another toast to her," she said, feigning a cheerfulness she was far from feeling. "Have you told her that you purchased the house she has been wanting?"

Jacques smiled down at Sabine. "Remember when she would not give up her wagon?"

"She was most insistent, was she not?"

"Now, she will have the home she deserves," Jacques said with feeling.

"*Oui*. The house you both deserve," Sabine said, kissing his cheek.

On the coach ride home, Stephen was bemused. "What did you say to La Flamme to make her so angry? I have never seen her react to anyone the way she did to you. She is usually so agreeable."

"Lofty, I'd say. Perhaps too aware of her own worth." Garreth's eyes sparkled with anger. "I like her not."

"But surely you did something to offend her. Why else would she have reacted so coldly to you?"

"I neither know what I did, nor do I care."

Stephen was clearly disappointed. "I had hoped the two of you would like each other. She is lonely, and I thought with your knowledge of women that—"

Garreth interrupted him. "Surely you don't intend to play matchmaker."

"I suppose that was in my mind at first. But as we saw, she did dislike you."

"Let's forget about her," Garreth said.

They were silent until the coach made the last turn before coming to the château. Then Garreth spoke. "What are La Flamme's habits?"

"I don't understand what you mean by that."

"Where does she spend her days?"

"I don't know. She seldom goes anywhere without her brother. Of course, she always takes him to the church on Wednesday afternoons. But at those times, she will not allow anyone to approach her. She's very protective of him."

"If he's her brother," Garreth said, doubt lacing his words.

Stephen looked uncomfortable. "I believe that the boy is her brother. She would not have told me so if it were not true."

"You have this saintly vision of her, and if the boy is her son, that would refute your insistence that she is pure."

"You were there tonight and saw that she singled out no man."

"Except you, who received a kiss on the cheek."

Stephen smiled in triumph. "So I did."

"At what hour does she attend church on Wednesdays?" Garreth wanted to know.

"I'm not certain. I recall that she once told me she goes there after luncheon to avoid the crowds that might recognize her and intrude on her privacy." Stephen eyed his friend suspiciously. "Surely you would not disturb her at prayer. No one would be so bold."

"I would," Garreth said with determination. "She is a

mystery which I intend to solve. She also issued me a challenge that I cannot refuse."

"What challenge? I saw only that she cut you dead, Garreth."

"Then you do not know women, Stephen. There was something between us that I cannot explain. It's strange, but I could almost believe that she fears me. I wonder why?"

Stephen felt the need to defend her. "La Flamme fears no man."

"And yet, for some reason I do not understand, she fears me."

Sabine was relieved when the last guest had departed. Her encounter with Garreth had so shaken her that it had been difficult to speak of trivial matters and make polite conversation for the remainder of the evening. She grew weary of constantly having to sidestep some gentleman who insisted that she was the love of his life. She had no love to give to any man. Her heart was barren, but for her brother and her close friends. There was room only for one other emotion—hatred for Garreth Blackthorn!

She stood in the doorway of the salon, watching the servants busily tidying the room. She had been content in this house, thinking it was a haven for her and Richard. Now it had been invaded by her adversary, and it was no longer her sanctuary.

Ysabel came up beside her. "I found Richard's dogs running loose in the garden and took them to his room. I cannot imagine who let them out and then forgot about them."

"It is of little consequence. Was Richard asleep?"

"*Oui.* He was sleeping like an angel." Ysabel could feel that something was wrong with Sabine. "You have been acting distracted all evening. What has happened, *ma petite*?"

Sabine's voice sounded strained. "My husband was here tonight." Fear trembled in her voice. "It was like living in one of my nightmares—I could not escape him!"

Ysabel looked concerned. "Was he the dark gentleman—the handsome one?"

"*Oui.*"

"I saw that he could not take his eyes off you." Ysabel tensed. "Did he threaten you?"

"Our encounter was very curious." Sabine moved toward the stairs and Ysabel followed her. "I believe that Garreth does not know my identity. But, how can that be?"

"If he is the one who caused the death of your father, he is a dangerous man, and you should never be alone with him or underestimate him."

"I have feared him for so long, that when I saw him tonight, all I wanted to do was take Richard and flee. I now know that would be a mistake. I am weary of living with fear, Ysabel. This time, I will not run, and I will not let Garreth Blackthorn defeat me."

"Have a care, Sabine. You have often told me that he is a powerful man."

"Perhaps in England," Sabine said defiantly, "but not in France. Here, I know the people with power, and I will not hesitate to use my influence."

"You are not alone; I am here for you and Richard," Ysabel assured her.

Sabine smiled and patted the old woman's hand. "I need your friendship and support. I cannot fight Garreth as an equal, for he would destroy me. But it is said that everyone has a weakness, and so must he. I will find his weakness, and use it against him."

They were almost at the top of the stairs, and Ysabel

paused. "I do not like this bitterness in you, Sabine. Do not let this man spoil your sweetness."

"How would you have me feel about him? He had my father and many of our people killed. And he tried to kill Richard and me."

Ysabel saw the determination in Sabine's eyes and knew that she was prepared to strike at her husband. "So the time has come to begin reclaiming your past?"

"I don't know . . . yes, I must."

Ysabel reached out and laid a hand on Sabine's shoulder, forcing the young woman to look into her eyes. "It is said that no man is immune to the charms of La Flamme, and after all, your husband is but a man."

Sabine looked horrified. "Are you suggesting that I try to make Garreth love me?"

"A man will seldom harm that which he loves. You are a beautiful woman, and your beauty may be your only weapon against him. Throughout history, beautiful women have had wars waged for them and kingdoms have tumbled because of their power over men. But to use your allure against a man can be the most dangerous weapon of them all, for it could destroy you along with him."

"I don't know what to do," Sabine said, plainly distressed. "I do not play games. I would not even know how."

She opened the door to Richard's bedroom, where moonlight streamed across his bed. He was sleeping soundly, and both dogs lay on the foot of his bed. They raised their heads and wagged their tails when they saw Sabine.

Richard was safe for now. No one could gain entrance to his room without rousing his dogs.

Closing the door softly, she turned back to Ysabel, who had waited in the hall to pick up the threads of their conversation.

"When I married Garreth, he loved another—he may still love her. She was very beautiful," Sabine said with uncertainty.

"And how old would this woman be now?" Ysabel asked with a chuckle. "Besides, I do not believe that a woman could hold a man if you decide to be her rival. Any man in Paris would leave his wife if La Flamme would have him."

"I do not know how to entrap a man, Ysabel."

"Then I shall help you."

"Tell me how to act when I meet him again."

"Aloof, cold, and disinterested. Nothing captures a man's desire more than a woman who is unobtainable. Of course, you must never see him alone."

Sabine's mind was troubled as she crossed the hallway to her bedroom. "I will think on what you say, Ysabel."

When Sabine was alone, she sank down on her soft bed and stared at the overhead canopy. She could admit to herself that the most frightening aspect of her meeting with Garreth was that he had excited her. How could it be that she still harbored some semblance of love in her heart for Garreth Blackthorn? That realization made her sick, and she despised herself for it.

Her mind was filled with bitterness as she tried to think of ways to maneuver Garreth into her trap without falling into that trap herself. Dawn tinted the sky before she fell asleep.

17

The moment Sabine walked onstage she knew that Garreth was out there in the darkness. She could feel his eyes on her, and it made her nervous and tense. Once she even stumbled over her lines, which caused Marie to give her a puzzled glance.

Gathering her courage, and determined that Garreth would not make her cower, Sabine raised her head and swept around the stage, playing her part for him alone. She had never performed better, and she knew it. She was coquettish, provocative, and flirtatious. She seemed to glow with a hidden fire, and Garreth, along with the audience, was caught by her magic.

Jacques, who was playing the part of her father, watched her in amazement. Although she was a good actress, men came to see her more for her beauty than for her acting. Tonight, she had reached for and obtained greatness, and everyone on the stage and in the audience could feel it.

After the final scene, Sabine went to her dressing room and waited, pacing the floor.

Ysabel looked at her, frowning. "Why do we not leave? The usual crowd departed long ago."

"He'll be out there waiting, I know he will."

"If you are talking about Blackthorn, he sent a note asking to see you. As you instructed, I had Henri give him your regrets. He will have already gone."

Sabine reached for her cape and flung it about her shoulders. "I suppose you are right. Let us go home."

They walked through the darkened theater, then out the door, where Sabine hurried toward her waiting coach.

She stopped in her tracks, quivering with fear when Garreth appeared beside her. She gathered her courage and prepared to face him calmly.

"You were magnificent tonight! I couldn't take my eyes off you," Garreth admitted, surprising even himself with his ardor.

"You are too kind, Monsieur le duc," she said mockingly, acting as if his praise meant nothing. In truth the blood was pumping madly through her veins, and she felt lightheaded, as if she were going to swoon at his feet.

She must fight this attraction—this feeling that drew her to him, for it was dangerous and it was wrong!

Garreth stood between Sabine and her coach, determined to make her listen to him. "I suppose you are accustomed to receiving compliments, so they are of little value to you."

She stiffened her spine. "*Oui*, I am. I usually find them wearisome. But I suppose a compliment is better than insults, *non*?"

"I spoke sincerely," Garreth said, frustrated because he could not make her believe him. "You had me so enchanted that I believed you *were* the person you played onstage."

Sabine lifted her chin. "That is what I do. I make people believe the illusion."

"So they will not know the real you?"

Her eyes locked with his. "Perhaps. Are any of us what we appear to be?"

She could feel the tenseness in him. "My carriage is waiting," Garreth said. "I wonder if you would agree to a ride through the park?"

"*Non*. I am weary, and it is late."

His expression hardened. Sabine could imagine that he was not accustomed to a woman's refusal. Ysabel had been right with her advice. To act indifferent to a man only deepened his interest.

"Then perhaps you would allow me to take you home?" he persisted.

"I regret, Your Grace, that I must refuse."

He bowed to her, his eyes probing hers all the while. "Perhaps another time."

She climbed into her coach before she answered him. "I think not, Your Grace. I hardly know you. And I do not believe that we shall ever know each other."

She watched the slow smile of assurance curve his lips when he reached out, placing his hand on hers. "I think we shall know each other very well indeed, Mademoiselle."

Sabine pulled her hand away from his as if the contact had burned her. "*Adieu*, Your Grace."

She signaled her coachman to drive away. When they were some distance, she turned back to look at Garreth, who still stood there, watching her departure. She was so badly shaken that she was forced to take several steadying breaths to calm herself. It had begun to rain, and she glanced out the window at the wet cobbles that glistened under the passing coach torches.

"Garreth will not give up so easily, Ysabel."

"He seemed surprised that you did not accept his invitation. I think he will be persistent."

"What shall I do next time, Ysabel?"

"Refuse him again, *ma petite*."

"How long will he keep coming back if I keep sending him away?"

"Until he decides it is futile. I watched him tonight, Sabine. He does not know who you are. But I'll tell you a little secret: your husband is beginning to love you."

Sabine closed her eyes. "There was a time when I ached for his love. Now there must only be enmity between us."

"Have a care, Sabine. I not only observed the duke tonight. I also watched you."

"Ysabel," Sabine admitted, "against my will, I began to think of him as a man—even while a small voice reminds me that he murdered my father."

"Your king exonerated him from the crime. Is it possible that he was innocent? I detect in him a man who does not surrender to defeat. I also sensed in him deep sadness, and asked myself, what could be the reason?"

Sabine had learned long ago to trust Ysabel's judgment, for she had an uncanny insight. "I do not know about his feelings, but what would he do if he discovered that the woman he is pursuing is his own wife?"

"You can stop this now, Sabine, and take this thing between you and Garreth Blackthorn no further. If you refuse enough, he will soon grow discouraged and pursue you no more."

Sabine pressed her hands over her eyes as her head began to throb. "I have always known the day would come when I would face him. I am fortunate that he does not know me, or recognize me as his enemy. I must bring him down, Ysabel—this I swear!"

"Again, I would caution you to be careful. He is not a man to misjudge."

Sabine shook her head. "As La Flamme, I shall draw secrets from him that will later destroy him. I must gain his confidence, and perhaps, if necessary, I shall even allow him to make love to me."

"Beware, Sabine, that you do not fall in love with him," Ysabel said, shaking her head. "Already he pulls at your heart."

Sabine wasn't listening. Thoughts of Garreth touching her intimately sent hot waves through her. She was a woman, but she had never allowed those feelings to surface. Garreth had caused wild stirring to awaken in her body, and she could not drive those feelings from her thoughts.

"Ysabel, through the years my goal has been to one day return Richard to his rightful place. I also swore that I would find justice for the people who died at Woodbridge that night. I have always thought that I would place my claim before our peers. Now, I shall be Garreth's judge, and I shall punish him severely. I must destroy him before he destroys me!"

"Do nothing in haste that you will later regret as folly."

Sabine's eyes gleamed. She had obtained fame and adoration, but it meant nothing to her. She now realized that Garreth had always been in her mind, dominating her thoughts, shaping her future. If he had not come to Paris, she would have one day returned to England to face him.

"Ysabel, like the master of a marionette, I shall manipulate his strings and make him do as I wish."

"I do not think that will happen, Sabine. But if you are determined to do this thing, I shall help you all I can."

Sabine took in a shaky breath. "I will need your wisdom. Suddenly I feel afraid, and I do not know why."

"Remember, *ma petite*, that love and hate are woven from the same tapestry."

"I have come to realize that, and I will not forget."

It was a bright day without a cloud in the sky when Sabine and Richard entered the small chapel. The first time she had seen St-Merri, Sabine had become enchanted because it reminded her of the family chapel at Woodbridge Castle. She and Richard seldom attended Mass, but instead came every Wednesday to say their prayers in seclusion. Today, however, there was a celebration Mass, and the church was filled with worshippers.

Richard couldn't understand all the Latin words that were being spoken, but he found something soothing in the ritual performed by the officiating priest. He imitated his sister as she genuflected, rose to her feet, then knelt to bow her head in prayer.

Sabine squeezed her eyes together tightly, wishing she could cleanse her heart of this bitterness she felt for Garreth. God had said to forgive one's enemies, but he also said an eye for an eye. Perhaps God would understand her need for revenge.

After Mass was over and the others had departed, Sabine remained kneeling, so Richard stayed beside her, sensing that she should not be disturbed. She was still in anguish and needed the comfort of this holy place to find answers to her tortured questions and peace for her troubled soul.

She raised her head to stare at the stained-glass windows. Oh, how she wished that God would give her direction in what she must do. Was it wrong to plot a man's destruction, even if the man deserved to be destroyed?

She lowered her head and whispered her prayer. "Heavenly Father, give me a sign, show me what I must do. I am lost, and need your guidance."

Sabine remained on her knees long after Richard began stirring restlessly. She could not say what made her raise her head and glance over her shoulder. There had been no sound and no movement, but she knew that when she turned, Garreth would be there.

He was sitting just behind her, and their eyes met. She had to tear her gaze from his. She had asked for a sign from God, and he had shown her Garreth. What did it mean?

Shaken, Sabine took Richard's hand and stood, walking silently out into the sunshine. When she reached the steps of the church, Garreth appeared beside her.

She looked fragile and ethereal, like an angel with the white filmy covering on her head. Somehow her devoutness did not fit with the picture Garreth had of her, and yet, had he not observed her piety when she had not known anyone was watching? What manner of woman was La Flamme? Why was he so intrigued with her?

"I did not know, Your Grace," Sabine said, "that an Englishman of high rank would be Catholic."

"Some are, but I am not. I came here only to see you—you know that."

She raised her eyes to his. "You would have done better had you come to pray, Your Grace."

He smiled down at her. "Do you fear that my immortal soul is in danger?"

"Only you can answer that."

"I have oft heard that a woman can save a man from his wicked ways."

She looked away. "Only if the woman is interested in saving the man."

Sabine gripped Richard's hand so tightly that he

pried her fingers loose and moved a few steps beyond her.

"Will you not introduce your companion to me?" Garreth asked.

Sabine reached out for her brother and clasped his wrist. "This is Richard. Richard, the duke of Balmarough."

Garreth dropped down to the boy's level. "I am pleased to meet you, Richard."

The boy's eyes brightened. It wasn't often that he met someone from England. But he had been trained well, so he spoke in French. "And I you, Monsieur le duc."

"Tell me, Richard," Garreth asked in French, his eyes still on Sabine. "What is your last name?"

Sabine smiled mockingly at Garreth. She knew that he was shamelessly trying to pry secrets from Richard, but her brother would not betray their secret.

"Monsieur le duc," Richard answered, his face creased in a serious frown, "you may think of me only as the brother of La Flamme."

Garreth raised his eyebrow. "So you are her brother?"

In that moment, Sabine realized that Garreth had heard the rumors that Richard was her son. Perhaps it would be safer if she allowed him to believe that false-hood.

"If you will excuse us, Your Grace," she said, "I have promised Richard an outing in the park. This is our day to spend together, and I never allow anything, or anyone, to interfere with our excursion."

Richard was so delighted to be in the company of someone from England that he spoke up. "Why do you not come with us?"

"I do not believe his grace would care for a day of frivolous amusement," Sabine said quickly. She turned, hoping to dismiss Garreth, but his words stopped her.

"You are wrong, Mademoiselle La Flamme. It would

be my deepest pleasure to stroll through the park with you and your . . . brother."

Sabine looked into Richard's eyes and saw his happiness. To keep him safe, she had isolated him, and she was aware that he was lonely. He had never been allowed to run and play with other children. He was forced to deny his own name and country and exist in a false world where nothing was real. All this she had done because of the man who now stood before them. Dare she expose her brother to Garreth Blackthorn?

"Very well," she said at last. "But I'm sure it is not the kind of recreation to which you are accustomed, Your Grace."

Garreth smiled down at Richard. "Your sister hasn't learned that all men have some of the boy still in them—has she?"

Richard nodded eagerly. "When I am old like you, I will still want to run and play games."

Garreth arched his brow and smiled at Sabine, while she burst out in amused laughter. "I'm sure the duke is not yet in his dotage, Richard."

"I suddenly feel old." He smiled at Richard. "I am not certain that I was ever as young as you."

It was apparent to Sabine that Richard liked Garreth, and she thought that might be dangerous. Without telling him why, she must warn him to be careful.

After Garreth had dismissed his driver, they climbed aboard Sabine's coach and were soon on their way. Garreth was seated beside Richard, who pointed out locations of interest.

Sabine sat silently, her eyes trained on the window as if she was hardly aware that Garreth was there—but she was very aware of him. Then she turned to him and found him watching her. Their eyes locked in silent battle.

Garreth saw no warmth in La Flamme's amber eyes. He could only wonder what had happened to make her so distrustful of men. Perhaps Richard's father had hurt her so deeply that she punished every man for his treatment of her.

He wanted to win her trust. What would it be like to see her smile, to hear her laughter—to crush those full lips beneath his?

Suddenly her eyes were no longer cold—it was as if someone had lit a candle behind them—or as if she knew exactly what he was thinking. Damn! She was the most maddening woman he had ever known.

Sabine dragged her gaze away from Garreth's and glanced out the window again. While she knew little about men, Garreth knew exactly how to make a woman ache inside. He made her very aware that he desired her.

Garreth deliberately turned back to the boy, who enthusiastically pointed out Notre Dame Cathedral.

"Your Grace," Richard asked, "did you know the conception of that church dates back to 1163? But it was not completed until 1345. I love to hear the bells ring. You can hear them from our house."

Garreth couldn't keep from smiling at the young boy. "Richard, while my French is passable, I would better understand you if you spoke in English."

"I can speak English very well, Monsieur le duc."

"You are very advanced for one so young, Richard. You cannot be over—"

"I am in my ninth year, Your Grace."

"I know of no young man your age who would be so well versed. What is the source of your education?"

"My sister taught me when I was younger and now I have three teachers. I have seventeen books, which is quite a lot, is it not?"

"Indeed it is, Richard."

"My sister makes me read. But it is no hardship because I like books." Richard smiled at Sabine. "But I do not like it when she insists that I learn politeness, chivalrous ways, and how to behave in courtly society. Why do you think I must learn those things?"

"I suppose because your sister deems it so. It would be wise to please her in this, Richard." Garreth was thoughtful for a moment. "I cannot recall when last I had leisure to read. I am kept very busy in the country."

Richard's eyes sparkled with curiosity. He was always interested in hearing about England. "What is the name of your estate, Your Grace? Perhaps I have heard of it."

"Wolfeton Keep."

"No, I have not heard of it. Are there any children there?"

Sabine pretended to be observing something out the window, but she waited for Garreth's answer.

"I have no children, Richard."

"A wife, perhaps?"

Sabine turned her head, her eyes colliding with Garreth's. She knew from Stephen that he had not taken another wife, but she wanted to know if he still considered himself married to her, or if he now believed she was dead.

"Only myself and my mother live at Wolfeton Keep, Richard," he answered, artfully sidestepping the question.

"'Tis a pity," Richard said. "When I am older and have to marry, I want many children so they won't be lonely."

"As you have been?"

"I have always had my sister, Your Grace," Richard hastened to assure him.

Shamelessly, Garreth plodded onward, questioning the child, hoping to learn about his mother—for he was now certain that La Flamme was indeed Richard's mother. "What of your mother and father?"

"I never knew my mother, and my father died when I was but a small child."

Sabine's voice was cool. "You can see, Your Grace, Richard and I have only each other."

"Tell me more about England," Richard said, settling back against the seat.

"Have you never been there?"

Richard paused but for a moment. "*Oui*. But I was too young to remember much about it."

"What shall I tell you?" Garreth asked. "Let me see—do you want to know about King Charles?"

Garreth watched the boy's eyes darken with distaste. "I do not like your king—he's a tyrant! I support the cause of your Parliament. King Charles has only one redemption—he married a French Catholic."

"I am astonished by your knowledge of my country, Richard." Smiling, Garreth looked at Sabine, who gave him an innocent look. "Who has kept you so informed about English politics?"

Richard giggled at Sabine. "My sister has taught me that those who blindly follow your king are fools."

"Oh?"

Much to Sabine's relief, they had reached their destination. Her coachman helped her to the ground, and she took her brother's hand. "What shall we see first, Richard?"

His voice was filled with excitement, his eyes gleaming. "I want most to see the boat races. May we?"

"Richard, you know the races are only on Saturday mornings, and even if we came then, we could not get close enough to see them. Many people spend Friday nights camping near the river so they will have a have a good view of the races the next morning."

Richard looked disappointed. "I love boats." He spoke to Garreth. "I have heard that you English have boat races on the River Thames—is that so?"

"Indeed it is. And it is not difficult to see the races from any vantage point."

"Some Friday night," Richard said, "I shall sleep along the river so I shall have a good view of these races."

"Come along, Richard," Sabine said. "Choose what you would like to see."

He quickly forgot his disappointment. "I want to see the fire-eater and the trained dogs and the acrobats. Then can we see the marionettes?"

Garreth saw La Flamme's first genuine smile. "Let's away to see the fire-eater. I hope, Monsieur le duc, that you will not find this all too tedious."

There were many stalls, and Richard visited them all. First he had a cream confection, an orange drink, and a bag of hard candies.

To Sabine's surprise, Garreth seemed to be enjoying himself. He laughed with Richard when a small dog leaped in and out of a rolling hoop. Later, Sabine stood to the side, watching as Richard and Garreth seemed captivated by the marionettes.

She could not help but think it was a pity that Garreth did not have a son of his own, for he seemed to have a genuine fondness for her brother. She remembered how uncomfortable he had been when visiting her as a child. When she watched him with Richard now, she wondered how he could have once planned her brother's death. Suddenly she decided to walk between the two of them and take Richard's hand, which she held for the rest of the day.

When the sun was going down, Sabine announced that it was time to leave. On the ride home, Richard lay with his head against her shoulder, his eyes closed drowsily. Lovingly, she touched his cheek as he drifted off to sleep.

"He is a very exceptional child," Garreth said, finding that he meant it. "You must be proud of him."

"I am often in awe of my brother's brilliance," she said, ready to further bait the trap. "But then it is not surprising that he is so intelligent—his father was a most exceptional man."

"You said *his* father."

"I meant to say *our* father," she corrected, pretending contrition.

Garreth stared at her through half-closed lashes. "I can see that he resembles you. But his light-colored hair he must get from his father."

Sabine tensed at the mention of her father. How could she have forgotten, for even a moment, that Garreth was the enemy? "No," she said abruptly. "It was our mother who had light hair. Father's hair was like mine."

Garreth's eyes rested on her flaming head, and he wondered what it would feel like to touch the shimmering curls.

"Where would you like my driver to take you?" Sabine asked, her voice suddenly cold.

"You could invite me to sup with you and Richard."

"I'm afraid, Monsieur le duc, that will not be possible. I must hurry as it is, to make the evening's performance."

"Then dine with me afterward."

She was silent for so long that Garreth thought she might accept.

"I am sorry, I never dine with gentlemen."

"You have dined with Stephen," he said.

"Ah, Stephen is different. He is my friend."

"And what am I?"

"That is for you to say, Your Grace. I do not know you."

She gasped when he reached out and took her hand in a firm grip. His eyes never left her face as he brushed his mouth against her fingertips.

"You will know me well, this I promise. And do not

expect me to be one of the milksops that are content to worship you, nor merely your friend." His eyes were bold, his manner insolent. "I want more than that from you."

He wrenched open the door and stepped out, disappearing in a swirling mist.

Oh, yes, she thought, taking an unsteady breath, they would know each other intimately before she brought him down from his lofty perch.

18

When Stephen entered the breakfast room, Garreth had already eaten and was having a second cup of tea. "You look like hell, Stephen," he observed cheerfully.

"Damn," Stephen groaned, as he waved the serving girl away with her platter of food. "I drank too much wine last night." He glanced at Garreth, who was immaculately dressed as always. "Where were you yesterday?"

"I went to the park and watched trained dogs jump through hoops."

"What?"

Garreth leaned back in his chair. "I accompanied Mademoiselle La Flamme and her brother on an outing."

"You jest. I don't care how irresistible you are to other women, she certainly was not charmed by you."

"She still isn't, but she invited me along nonetheless."

Stephen looked at him suspiciously. "I happen to

know that she protects her brother from all outsiders. I
have seen him only once, and then by accident when I
was at her house and the boy came back from taking the
dogs for a walk. I was not introduced to him, because
Ysabel hurried him upstairs."

Garreth eyed his friend over the rim of his cup, then set
it down and folded his hands together. "I am compelled
to ask you something, Stephen, and I want complete
honesty."

"It's about her, isn't it?"

"Yes. I need to know what your feelings are for her. If
they're deeper than friendship, I'll return to England
without seeing her again."

Stephen pondered how best to answer Garreth. "I
have always been a practical man. At one time, I fancied
myself desperately in love with La Flamme. She saw
what my feelings were, and to spare me hurt, made me
realize that all we could ever be was friends. But I have
told you this before."

Garreth lowered his head, studying the floral pattern
on the teacup. "I am not as practical as you, Stephen,
and it's already too late for me."

"I am sorry now that I brought the two of you
together. Mayhap, we should both return to England,
then you can put her from your mind, Garreth. You are
both my friends, and I see no happy ending in this for
either of you. She has already suffered because of what
some man did to her."

"So you believe that the boy is her son, and that his
father deserted them?"

"I didn't at first—lately, I'm not so certain. The
mere fact that she keeps her past so secretive makes me
question."

Garreth stood. "I won't hurt her, Stephen, and I may
even be able to help her."

"You can't offer her marriage."

Garreth walked to the door and turned back to his friend. "What makes you think she'd have me?"

Garreth presented his card to the butler. "Is mademoiselle receiving callers?"

The man glanced at the card. "She is not in, Your Grace."

"When is she expected?"

A woman came up behind the butler and Garreth recognized her as the one who always accompanied La Flamme.

"See to your duties, Cholet, I will speak to his grace," Ysabel said.

Garreth looked into the faded blue eyes of the woman. How better to learn about a person than through a personal servant?

"Madame, we have never met. I am—"

"I know who you are," Ysabel said, looking him over carefully. Her eyes stabbed deeply into his. "Cholet told you the truth, Your Grace. Mademoiselle La Flamme is not here."

He had the feeling as he stared at the old woman that she was no mere servant. She gave him the impression that she had a canny insight that could probe his mind.

"Could I come in and talk to you, Madame . . . ?"

"Just Ysabel. And to talk to me would be fruitless. After you inquired about my health and I assured you that I am hearty, we would have come to the end of our conversation."

He grinned. "It appears that you are well able to handle any gentlemen who come to mademoiselle's door. She has a protector in you."

"It is well that you remember that."

"I do not suppose it would benefit me to ask you where I might find mademoiselle?"

Ysabel was silent as if she were deciding something. At last she nodded. "This is Thursday, so she will be with her fencing master, Monsieur Daymond."

Garreth was not surprised to hear that La Flamme was doing something as unconventional as fencing. "Where might I find this Monsieur Daymond?"

Again there was a long silence as Ysabel studied the duke intently. "You will see his school once you cross the *Pont-Neuf* bridge."

"Thank you, Madame."

Ysabel saw the relief in his eyes that was quickly replaced by uncertainty. This handsome devil had never met anyone like Sabine—he was completely bewitched by her. Ysabel was beginning to believe that Garreth Blackthorn might be innocent. She was a good judge of character, and she could find nothing in him that suggested deceit.

"If you go to Monsieur Daymond's school, you may not find a welcome."

He smiled, and she could see how a woman would lose her heart to him. "I shall take my chances, Madame." He swept her a bow and turned away to mount his horse.

Ysabel was wise enough to know that nothing could stop Sabine from colliding with her past. Today, Ysabel had made certain that the duke met Sabine on her own grounds, thus giving her the advantage in the battle that would surely come.

Garreth was admitted to the fencing school by a servant who led him to a small sitting room.

"I would like to see the fencing master—is he in?"

"*Oui*, Monsieur, but he is with a special student and cannot be disturbed. If you have come to inquire about lessons, you must wait."

Garreth could hear the sound of clashing swords coming from the thin walls. When the servant departed, he moved into the hallway and entered a long gallery with high windows that caught the afternoon sunlight. Standing in the shadows, he watched two gentlemen fencing. One was tall and moved to sidestep the shorter slender swordsman, but the lighting quick blade caught him and he laughed heartily.

"Again you have mastered the master, Mademoiselle La Flamme. Shall we try again?"

Garreth stared in astonishment at the slender figure who wore the garments of a cavalier. Her breeches and doublet were rust colored, her cuffed boots were of the same color. Never had he seen a woman in men's apparel, but it suited her. On closer inspection, he saw the soft curves of her body—how could he have mistaken her for a man? He could not see her face because she wore a protective helm.

Fascinated, he watched her graceful parry turn into lethal lunges. She was damned good, he thought.

The two crossed swords, and then La Flamme went on the attack. Wielding her rapier, she struck, once, twice, thrice, driving back her opponent. When the instructor advanced toward her, she agilely sidestepped his thrust, turning it to her advantage. She was poised as she wielded the deadly blade, driving him against the wall.

"Enough, enough, Mademoiselle." He chuckled and threw up his arms in surrender. "You need no more lessons from me. But if you ever decide to give up acting, I could use your talents."

She flourished her rapier in a salute, then laughingly

removed her protective mask, allowing her crimson hair to spill down her back. "You are the master, and I believe you only let me win out of pity."

"No so. I told you when you began the lessons that I would not show mercy just because of your sex. Nor have I. You defeated me last week, and today you became the master swordsman."

Garreth clapped his hands together slowly as he walked toward her. "Quite an exhibition, Mademoiselle La Flamme."

She turned around quickly, her eyes meeting his. "I did not expect to have an audience, Monsieur le duc," she said with composure.

"I know of no other woman who would have dared such a venture." He stopped in front of her, his eyes sweeping down her slender form.

The fencing master excused himself, but neither Sabine nor Garreth noticed.

He did not flinch when her sword snaked through the air to pop loose the gold button on his jerkin without even damaging the fabric. In a smooth motion, she speared the button from the floor and offered it to him on the tip of her rapier. "Perhaps you would like a contest, Monsieur?" she asked daringly.

"Keep the button as a memento," he said in a deep voice. "When you and I meet in a contest, it will be of a different sort, Mademoiselle."

She took the black cape that was draped across a chair and threw it about her shoulders. The long folds fell to her feet, concealing her slender figure. She pulled on leather gloves, glaring at him all the while. "How did you find me here, Monsieur?"

"I have my informants," he said with a slight smile.

She swept him a stiff bow. "I'll give your regards to Ysabel. *Au revoir*, Monsieur."

When she turned to leave, his hand came down on her shoulder and he turned her to face him. "Since I have gone to all the trouble to find you, could we not dine together tonight?"

"I have a performance."

"Afterward?"

She stared into those fathomless eyes, feeling as if she were being dragged into their depths. "I think not."

"When can I see you?"

"Tomorrow," she said, taking him by surprise. "I have a chance to purchase a pair of matching grays that have long interested me. Stephen has an eye for good horseflesh, so I want his opinion. As his houseguest, you may join us if you choose."

"Does Stephen know?"

"I sent him a message."

"Do you like dangling Stephen along and the other poor devils who will beg for any crumb you toss their way?" Garreth asked with growing frustration.

Her golden eyes bore into his, and for a moment she could not answer. "He understands our relationship, and no matter what you think, I don't dangle him. Good day, Monsieur."

She rushed across the gallery, her cape flying out behind her.

He didn't know what demon had possessed him to insult her. Why must he always try to provoke her? Anger guided Garreth's steps out of the gallery. Once outside, he mounted his horse. He had made a fool of himself today and every day since he'd met La Flamme. As soon as it could be arranged, he would leave for England and put her forever from his mind.

Sabine stood in Monsieur Daymond's office, watching Garreth ride away. It was becoming increasingly difficult to act indifferently to him. She remembered the day he had come to her and held her in his arms while she cried out her grief at the death of her mother. She must not be seduced into trusting him, for that would surely cause her downfall, and do harm to Richard.

Sabine heard a man speaking to Cholet, and descended the stairs, thinking it would be Stephen. She paused on the bottom step when she saw Garreth.

"So," she said, going forward to greet him, "you decided to come with us. Is Stephen waiting in the carriage?"

"Stephen didn't come."

She eyed him suspiciously. "Did he not get my message?"

"When I arrived home, your message was on the entry table."

"Then why did he not come with you?"

He took her arm and guided her toward the door, giving her no time to protest. She stopped when he would have handed her into the open carriage.

"I demand to know why Stephen isn't here."

Garreth's hands spanned her tiny waist and he lifted her into the carriage. "It's cloudy. I hope it doesn't rain to spoil the day."

"I was asking about Stephen."

"It's quite simple." He climbed in beside her. "I did not give him your message."

She could hardly believe his impudence—how dare he do such a thing! "You are devious, sir. You deliberately kept my message from him."

"I did," he admitted. He smiled, leaning back and looking into her golden eyes. "How could I miss this chance to have you to myself?"

"This is . . . is . . . abduction."

"That's not the way I see it. Did you or did you not ask me to come with you today?"

"I . . . *oui*, but not—"

"I merely accepted your invitation."

"You, Monsieur, are bold beyond belief."

"I'm merely an opportunist." His eyes seemed to soften when they rested on her face. "Be warned, La Flamme, when I see something I want, I usually get it."

"If you think you can win me by tricks, Monsieur, you are mistaken. I do not like men who take what they want, no matter who they hurt."

He blinked his eyes in astonishment. "If that is the way you see me, I shall just have to change your opinion. The driver waits. Will you not give him direction—the team grows impatient."

Reluctantly, Sabine instructed the driver. When they started off, she refused to look at Garreth, but instead stared straight ahead.

Soon the coachman was aptly maneuvering the carriage through the crowded streets. After an uncomfortable silence, she turned to Garreth. "Tell me about yourself, Your Grace, so that I might know you better."

"I find it tiresome talking about myself. Let us instead speak of you."

She shrugged. "My life is uneventful. I would like to hear about the women in your life."

"What if I said that you are the only woman in my life?"

"Then I would pity you, for I am not in your life."

He nodded toward the coachman. "We will speak of this later, when we are alone. Unlike you, I do not perform before an audience."

"I am not certain I want to be alone with you." She batted her eyelashes. "Can a woman trust you, Monsieur?"

He laughed at her coy little trick that was most enchanting. "I believe I'm the one in peril."

To Sabine's surprise, Garreth turned his attention to the Paris countryside, asking her questions and showing marked interest.

A short time later they reached the Tournes' estate. Monsieur Tourne was a gentleman short in stature and wide in girth. He was obviously impressed by La Flamme and was almost too ingratiating in his attentions.

"May I offer you, refreshments?" he asked.

"Thank you, no, Monsieur," Sabine said. "My time is limited and I would like to see the grays."

He nodded eagerly, leading them to his stables.

Garreth surveyed the animals. "They are magnificent," he said, running his hand over the muscled flank of one of the grays.

"Then I would not be making a mistake if I added them to my stable?" Sabine asked.

Garreth examined both horses' mouths and teeth, then he walked around them, lifting each hoof. "They are in excellent health. They are of Arabian blood, spirited, and no doubt swift."

"You have a practiced eye," Monsieur Tourne said. "I would not let them go to anyone except Mademoiselle La Flamme."

"How much, Monsieur?" Sabine asked.

"For you, they are a gift," the Frenchman said, bowing before her.

"*Non*, Monsieur. I will not take them without payment. What is the price?"

He shrugged. "Whatever you think is fair."

Sabine turned to Garreth and spoke in English. "Help me, so I do not cheat this man. What price would you give for the two grays?"

"Why do you not take them as a gift and make the man happy?"

"I will accept no gift from a man, so I owe favors to no one."

"A hundred francs for each would be generous." Garreth smiled. "You wouldn't want to sell them to me, would you?"

She looked at him for a moment, and then turned to the Frenchman. "Monsieur, I will leave with you my marker for two hundred francs. Kindly have the grays delivered to my stables within the week."

"If that is your wish." There was disappointment in the man's eyes because La Flamme had refused his gift. Then he brightened. "When word reaches Paris that La Flamme has favored my horses, everyone will flock to my stables."

Sabine turned away from him. "*Au revoir*, Monsieur."

She walked to the carriage, and Garreth helped her inside. "Poor man. You dealt him a blow by refusing his tribute."

The clouds had moved away and she angled her hat to protect her face from the sun's rays. "It is always the same. I have heard that he has a wife. He would have done better to bestow his favors on her."

Garreth settled beside her. "You have an objection to being admired by married gentlemen?"

Her golden eyes bore into his. "I have an aversion to being used, for whatever the reason."

He stared at her with a strange expression on his face and then shook his head as if to clear it. "For a fleeting moment, you reminded me of someone, but I can't think who. It's like a vague memory, but the illusion is gone."

She lowered her eyes, fearful that he was beginning to remember her. "We are almost home," she said, trying to sound lighthearted.

"May I see you tonight?"

"If you like," she said, turning to look at him, jarred by the heat of his eyes. "You may dine with me at my home, this evening after my performance."

A rakish smile curved his lips. "Does it make you feel safer to invite me to your home?"

"Does it make you feel unsafe, Your Grace?"

19

Garreth was waiting for La Flamme beside his coach. When she came out of the theater, she was dressed in a white velvet gown with slashed sleeves inlaid with gold. Around the hem of the skirt were dozens of tiny golden rosebuds.

He became irritated when she was immediately surrounded by admirers. She smiled to each of them and exchanged greetings. At last she was beside him, and he opened the door and whisked her inside.

When the coach pulled away, they could still hear the loud chant of those who revered her: "La Flamme! La Flamme!"

Sabine was very aware of Garreth's irritation. He was so near her that she could feel his breath stir her hair. A strange yearning came over her, and she had an urge to lay her head against his shoulder and have him hold her as he once had. She looked down at the hand that rested on his knee. It was the hand of a gentleman, long tapered fingers, with strength she could only imagine.

She was glad that the coach lights were dim so Garreth could not see how badly her hands were trembling. She stuffed them into her white velvet muff and turned to face him.

"Your countrymen have made you famous," Garreth said, still annoyed for reasons he could not say. "I had even heard of you in England. Mostly from Stephen, I admit. Before I met you, I was skeptical that anyone could be as exceptional as he claimed you were."

"And now?"

"I agree with him." The way Garreth said the words, they did not sound like a compliment. "How does it feel to be adored by so many?"

"I have little interest in such absurdities, Your Grace. I only care to give a good performance. I owe no one more than that."

"Your Jacques de Baillard is also famous in my country—there are many who speak well of him. You mentioned the night we met that his acting troupe has been invited to perform for Queen Henrietta—will you come to London?"

Sabine put on the face of a coquette and drew her white muff across his face flirtatiously. "I do not know. It has not yet been decided."

He clasped her hand and took the muff from her, tossing it on the seat. "I would like to show you England."

"Jacques makes those decisions, not I. If he says we go, then I shall go."

"Why did you agree to dine with me tonight?"

"I'm not sure I know." She gave him her most beguiling smile. "Perhaps it is because of your extraordinary charm."

His hand moved to her chin, and he turned her to face him. "Do you mock me?"

"I," she said with exaggerated surprise, "who am merely a helpless woman, mock a great titled gentleman like yourself? I would not dare."

His hand moved to the side of her face, and he brought her further into the light so he could see her eyes. No woman had ever held him so captivated. "It is my belief that you are merely toying with me, and I don't know why."

Sabine replied using words from one of Jacques' plays. "Monsieur le duc, it is said that you have taken the hearts of dozens of ladies and dropped them with little remorse. I only pray that you will be kinder to me."

Garreth was not fooled, or amused, by her act. "Do not play a role with me. I am not one of your simpletons who sit in the audience every night just for a glimpse of you."

She looked at him innocently, knowing he had attended every performance since they had met. "Tell me, Monsieur le duc, how many times have you been in the audience?"

Suddenly he started laughing. She had cleverly trapped him with his own words. What did it matter, when soon victory would be his? "Tonight I worship you close at hand. And I'll have you to myself."

She turned away from him, studying the silk print on the seat across from her. "I do not want to be worshipped."

"What *do* you want, La Flamme?" he asked in a low, caressing voice.

Garreth had the power to seduce her with words. She decided it would be safer to make him talk about himself. "Is it not true that you have broken many poor maidens' hearts?"

"Who has told you this?"

"The distance from London to Paris is not as considerable as you might believe. There are those who have mentioned you to me. It is said that your heart belongs to a certain Lady Meredith. Will she not care that you are dining with me tonight?"

Garreth was stunned for a moment. "That information is outdated. Tonight, I only want to talk about you and how enchanting you are."

Sabine knew she had struck a nerve and smiled as she toyed with the diamond bracelet at her wrist. "I seldom believe flattery. Especially when it comes from a highborn gentleman. Most of your class would say anything in a moment of passion, *non*?"

He nodded at her bracelet. "Did one of your highborn gentlemen give you that little trinket? I doubt it came from peasant stock."

"As I told you, I would never accept something so valuable from a man. If I did, he would believe that he had some claim on me, when I belong only to myself."

"Did Richard's father give you expensive trinkets?" Garreth asked, suddenly jealous of the unknown man.

"But of course. That was different—he had the right."

Garreth was more determined than ever to break down the barriers La Flamme had built around her heart. "What would a gentleman be required to do that he might win the right to give you gifts?"

She looked directly at him. "He would have to win my heart, and I do not believe that is possible."

"Can it be that you have just issued me a challenge?"

"No, Monsieur le duc, I merely spoke the truth." Again she turned the conversation back to him. "I am sure many women have loved you."

He took an impatient breath. "Not so many."

She took her courage in hand. "It is said that you

were married to a young girl of family who died under suspicious circumstances."

She could feel him stiffen. It was so silent inside the coach that the only sound that could be heard was the clopping of the horses' hooves on the cobbled streets.

"Your informant is not precisely correct, Mademoiselle. I do not yet accept the fact that my wife is dead."

His revelation came as a surprise to her. He still believed she was alive. She must not panic or show weakness. "If you have a wife, you should not have asked me to dine with you, Monsieur. I do not consider it proper."

In a sudden move that took her by surprise, Garreth gripped her by the shoulders and brought her body against his. "Does that matter?" His lips grazed her cheek. "Does anything matter except that we are together? I have no other woman in my mind or in my heart save you—does that satisfy your curiosity?"

Sabine blinked her eyes. It was becoming harder to play the coquette. "Now it is you who is toying with me, Monsieur le duc. Surely, you do not expect me to believe that a man can feel so deeply about a woman he has known but a short while?"

He wanted to shake her, to make her admit that there was something rare and wonderful between them. "You know very well what you are doing to me, and I believe you enjoy keeping me on a hook." His eyes were burning into hers. "Do not play coy with me, for you are no innocent. You are aware of my feelings for you because you have felt them, too."

Her laughter was forced. "You think much of your prowess with women, Your Grace. Why should you believe that I feel anything for you but amusement?"

His arms tightened about her so that she could scarcely breathe. "Am I amusing you now?" His hand slid up her neck and he held her chin firm, while his lips were only inches from hers. "Why are you not laughing?"

Sabine's heart was beating wildly, and she was sure that she would be unable to catch her breath. "Release me," she said, hoping he didn't hear the fear in her voice.

To her surprise, Garreth did. "If you do not want me to make love to you, then tell me now. I cannot be with you and not touch you," he said gruffly.

"You go too far," she said in panic. "You asked for a companion at dinner, and that is all I agreed to, Your Grace."

He let out his breath and moved back against the coach seat. "You are right, of course. Forgive me."

She wondered why she suddenly felt like crying. "Is this the way you treat all your women?"

"What do you mean by all my women?" he asked in exasperation. "I told you that I have no women in my life."

"Not your wife . . . not your mistress? Deny it if you will, but I do not believe that a man such as yourself would deprive himself of women's companionship."

The hurt Sabine had felt so long ago came rushing back as if it had happened only yesterday. How well she remembered the pain of finding out on her wedding day that her husband loved Lady Meredith.

Garreth watched her golden eyes become piercing and cold, and that made him want her more than ever. The only woman who had touched his heart in years seemed to hold him in contempt, and he didn't know why. But there was something he did know about her— she was not as unresponsive to his touch as she would have him believe.

Sabine pushed her distress to the back of her mind. No matter what she had to do, she would find a way to reach Garreth's heart. Then she would rip it to shreds. Whatever she did to him would be no more than he deserved.

She laid her hand on his arm. "It's true that you are the only man I have ever agreed to dine with alone. I don't know what made me accept your invitation."

Garreth was not smiling. "Tell me about Richard's father."

Sabine tried not to feel triumphant as she realized that Garreth was tormented by the belief that she was Richard's mother. She would allow him to ask the questions, fuel his curiosity by her truthful answers—and lead him to a wrong conclusion. "I . . . loved Richard's father," she said. "I shall always love him. I was very young when he died, and I have had to take care of Richard alone. Of course, Ysabel, Marie, and Jacques have become our family. We could not have survived without them."

"Did not Richard's father provide for you?"

."He died too suddenly. He could not help us." She paused, fearing that she might cry. "I am told that his last thoughts were of us."

Garreth did not understand the burning jealousy he had for a dead man, but there were questions he must ask. "Have you loved no man since Richard's father?"

"Not in the same way I loved him. But Richard's father is dead, and I am alive."

"How do I contend with a ghost?" Garreth asked, voicing his frustration.

"Indeed," Sabine said, hatred battling for dominance within her. "Richard's father's ghost does stand between us!"

"It's difficult for me to believe that a woman as beautiful as you has lived a chaste life. Yet, that is what is said about you."

Sabine bit her trembling lip. "I am gratified that you

think me beautiful. But I do not believe you should concern yourself about my life."

"Whether you welcome it or not, I'm in your life." His eyes were suddenly piercing. "You want something from me, and I do not know what it is."

By now the coach had reached its destination, and Sabine glanced at the brightly-lit château. She had been so engrossed with their conversation that she had not noticed they had driven into the country.

"What is this place, Monsieur le duc? This is not my home."

"We have arrived at Stephen's château."

"Why did you bring me here, and where is Stephen?"

"I brought you here so we could be alone. Stephen will be staying in Paris tonight."

Before Sabine could protest, the coach door was whisked open and a footman lowered the steps, offering his arm to her. She reluctantly stepped down and allowed Garreth to lead her inside. Her plan had been to be alone with him, but at her home, not here.

"Do not be concerned," he said next to her ear so the butler could not hear. "We shall be quite alone except for the servants, and they will serve us and leave."

She stiffly allowed him to lead her down a hallway.

"Why did you not ask me if I would come here with you?" she demanded. "I do not like to be tricked."

He merely smiled. "I did not trick you. Had you asked where we were going, I would have told you."

"I find your manners questionable. Do you not think I should have been given the choice of accepting or refusing?"

"If I am in error, I will take you back to Paris at once. You have only to say the word."

"I have given you no reason to believe that I am promiscuous and would welcome such an arrangement."

His eyes settled on her lips. "Forgive me. You are right, of course—I did take liberties."

She reconsidered. "I will have dinner with you, but then you must take me home."

She expected him to look triumphant, but he merely nodded. If she didn't know better, she would have thought he was unsure of himself.

"I believe everything is in readiness." He offered her his arm. "Shall we dine?"

Sabine laid the tips of her fingers on his sleeve. "One can only hope that I shall still have a reputation by morning."

Garreth was mystified. An actress, after all, was not considered a lady. Why did he have the feeling she was an innocent? Because, he reminded himself, she was an actress, and that was what she wanted him to believe.

Instead of escorting her to the formal dining room, he led her to a salon on the second floor, where a table had been placed in front of a window with a sweeping view of the Seine.

She watched tiny lights bobbing up and down and realized that they were fishing boats.

"I've never been here. It's quite lovely." She turned to him, smiling. "Have you brought many women here?"

She had thought he would laugh or make some humorous remark. But he steered her to the table and seated her before he answered. One hand came down on her shoulder, and he raised her chin with the other. "You are the only woman I have ever brought here, but as you are aware, this is not my home."

Shame and anger washed over her at the reminder of Stephen. Did he know of Garreth's plans with her this evening? "Surely Stephen was not a party to your bringing me here."

"No, of course not." Garreth wondered who La Flamme thought she was fooling by pretending to be so maidenly, when they both knew she was not. "You will find that I have been discreet."

His hand seemed to burn into her skin, and Sabine was frightened by her reaction to him. She started to rise. "I should leave."

"Please stay. You have my word that you are safe with me."

She dropped back into the chair while he moved around the small table to sit opposite her. For a long moment, his eyes lingered on her face.

"Tonight, let us play a game," he said at last.

"Before I agree to that," she replied, intrigued, "you must first tell me what kind of game."

He had a scheme that he hoped would draw her secrets from her. "It's simple. We shall be totally honest with each other." He arched his brow. "Dare you play my game?"

"I will agree to be honest, but I shall also add rules of my own. If the question becomes too personal, and if either of us do not wish to answer, we shall keep our silence. Agreed?"

A servant entered, placed covered dishes on the table, then quietly withdrew. Garreth poured La Flamme a glass of wine before he answered. "I agree to your terms."

She raised the glass to her lips and took a sip. "You go first, Monsieur le duc."

"Could you not call me Garreth?"

"Of course, Garreth," she said with a smile. "Is that your first question?"

He watched her carefully. "And what shall I call you?"

She raised her glass to his. "You may, as you already know, call me La Flamme."

"What do your friends call you?"

"I have few friends."

"You dance around the truth very cleverly. By what name does Monsieur de Baillard call you?"

"I choose not to answer."

"Which is an answer in itself," Garreth observed. "Your reluctance proves that the de Baillards know your real name—true?"

"True," she agreed. "Now it's my turn, Garreth Blackthorn."

He sat back in the chair, his eyes on her. "I am ready."

"You said you had been married?"

"Yes."

"And you consider yourself still married?"

He hesitated, wondering if he could make her understand. "It is accepted by most people that my wife is dead, but I am not so sure."

Sabine tensed, swallowing her fear. "Did you love your wife?"

The food on the table went uneaten as they both became engrossed in their game, and in each other. "In truth, I hardly knew her. She was little more than a child. I never knew her as a husband."

She gathered her courage to question him further. "How can that be? Was she so repulsive that you could not tolerate the sight of her?"

"I have tried to recall her face, and all I can remember is a pair of golden eyes, not unlike your own. She was merely a lovely child."

Sabine dropped her eyes. "Tell me more about her."

This game was not going as Garreth had intended, but he would answer her questions. "I have spoken to no one about her for so long because everyone else believes she is dead and encourages me to do the same. Her name is Sabine, and she was a frightened little girl who had been forced to marry a man she didn't know. I can recall feeling mostly pity for her."

The candles flickered and burned low in their silver holders, but neither Garreth nor Sabine noticed, as their game continued.

Sabine brushed a stray curl from her face, a movement that caught and held Garreth's attention.

"What happened to your pitiful little wife?"

"'Tis over, 'tis done," he said bitterly.

"That is no answer."

"I have no answer." He fortified his patience. "I searched for her for many months, but found no trace of her. There are those who would have me petition the king to put the marriage aside so I might remarry and beget an heir, but I am not willing until I know what happened to her."

"Poor unfortunate girl, to be married to a man who loses his wife and cannot find her."

Garreth reached across the table, took her hand, and laced his fingers through hers. "It's my turn now. Tell me, La Flamme, have you ever loved a man?"

"Yes, of course."

"Richard's father?"

"Deeply."

"Have you never loved a man save him?"

She smiled. "I once thought I was madly in love with a young man, but as you cannot recall your wife's face, I cannot remember his."

"His name?"

She withdrew her hand, remembering the day she had fallen in love with him. "I have been well brought up," she said at last, "and know one does not discuss old lovers with another man. And besides it was long ago."

He smiled ruefully. "Have you ever been married?"

She hesitated only a moment. "Everyone knows that La Flamme has no husband."

Garreth was no longer smiling. "Richard's father did not marry you?"

There was a scowl on his face, and she wanted to laugh at the irony of the situation. He was now the hunted, and she was becoming the hunter in their game. Her heart felt lighter and she managed to laugh. Garreth had no notion that he was sitting at the same table with his poor, pitiful little wife. She would twist him and manipulate him without him knowing.

"Richard's father already had a wife when I met him."

There was an edge to Garreth's voice. "You must have been very young."

She found humor in baiting him by telling the truth. "Love knows no age."

Garreth was tight-lipped, and it was clear that he was no longer enjoying their game. "If I am wrong, I shall ask your pardon, but I must know. Have you any feelings for me?"

Sabine stood. "I know so little about you, Garreth."

"Dare I hope that your feelings could deepen if you came to know me?"

Sabine did not like where his questions were leading. He was forcing her to examine her inner feelings, something she was not prepared to do. "How can I answer that, when I do not know myself?"

She moved to the door, and would have opened it, but Garreth stopped her. He took her by the shoulders and turned her to face him. She was trapped between his hard body and the wall. Her throat suddenly closed, and she could scarcely breathe.

She turned her head to follow the mouth that was so near, wanting to feel his lips on hers.

20

Garreth's lips were soft when they settled on Sabine's. Tenderly, he nestled her against his body and heat simmered inside her. His hands moved up to clasp her head, and he deepened the kiss. He held her so tightly that she could feel the muscles of his body.

Wild and wonderful feelings ripped through Sabine like a churning sea, and her lips parted as she sought more of what his kiss promised.

When he raised his head, his eyes held her captive, and she could only bury her face against his chest, feeling suddenly shy. She heard the beating of his heart—he was as moved by the kiss as she had been.

Garreth dipped his head, and once more his lips were on hers, drawing emotions from her that she didn't want to feel. It was becoming harder for her to remember that he was dangerous. She could only think that this was her husband, and how wonderful it was to be in his arms at last.

Finally he raised his head and held her at arm's length, smiling at the rosy tinge to her cheeks. "If I didn't know better," he said, "I would think you were as innocent as you pretend to be."

She said nothing, allowing him to lead her across the room, where the candles had burned low. She turned from him and moved to the window, where bright moonlight spilled into the room, lighting the darkened corners.

He came up behind her, and his hand moved up her arm.

"I should go," she said in a voice that denied her words.

His hand gently moved to her hair, and the silken strands sifted through his fingers. "Do you really want to leave?"

"*Non . . . oui*—I am confused. I do not know."

He groaned and pulled her against him, and she could feel his body tremble. "What are you doing to me?" he asked in an agonized voice.

He wanted her, and her woman's heart told her that it would take very little to make Garreth Blackthorn love her.

"You want to possess my soul, you flaming-haired enchantress," he muttered, his lips gliding sensuously against her arched neck. "Indeed, it may be too late for me because I believe you already hold my heart captive."

It wasn't supposed to be like this, Sabine thought, trying to pull away from him, but he turned her toward him and his kisses drained her resistance. He was seducing her with words and with the touch of his hands and the feel of his male body.

Sabine had acted in plays where she was supposed to love a man, but she had not known that love was such an all-consuming emotion that would leave her aching and uncertain. She wanted Garreth to touch her and go on touching her. She closed her eyes when his hands slid down her throat to the hook on the front of her gown.

"I must leave," she said, her voice trembling. "This is not right." But a small voice inside her head reminded her that this man was her husband.

"Would you leave me in torment?" he asked, his mouth touching her skin each place he unfastened a hook.

Suddenly her mind cleared, and she spun away from him, attempting to regain her composure. She had been so sure that she could control him, and instead she was in danger of losing control herself. She knew nothing about the act of love between a man and a woman. But tonight was not the time to learn that lesson.

"You go too fast," she said laughing. "That which is worthwhile should be savored, *non*?"

Garreth towered over her. "The ways of the French mystify me. What would you have me do, beg for your kisses?" His hand drifted once more through her silken hair. "I'm begging," he said, his eyes boring into hers. "I know you will not believe me, but I have never wanted a woman as much as I want you. I knew the first night I saw you onstage that I would have you. If not tonight, then another time—but make no mistake, you will be mine."

Sabine leaned toward him, her hand touching his arm. "If you know anything about the French, you know that we are not easily fooled. You would have me believe that a man like you has never desired a woman before me?"

"I have desired many women, but I have never had one that muddled my reasoning to the point of madness, as you have."

She blinked her long lashes and turned back to the window, while silvery moonlight played across her face.

"I suppose I am the most beautiful woman you have ever seen?" she challenged skeptically.

"I have known some women that were as beautiful, perhaps one or two even more so," Garreth admitted, "but what I feel for you goes beyond the beauty of your face and beyond mere desire."

Sabine saw the amazed expression on his face as he realized what he'd said.

"I never thought this could happen to me," he admitted, taking her hand and placing it against his heart. "I have no words to describe what I feel for you." He shook his head as if to clear it. "The most maddening thing in all this is that I don't know how you feel about me."

"Does it matter?"

"Yes, damn it, it does! For some reason, it matters a great deal."

Sabine moved her body in such a way that drew his eyes, and she purposely allowed her unfastened gown to slip off her shoulders. His breath caressed her cheek as his lips moved to her neck. She tried to remember Ysabel's warning, but it was swept from her mind as Garreth's lips nestled at the curve of her breasts. So this was what it felt like to have a man make love to you, she thought as delightful feelings engulfed her.

In the moonlight, it seemed to Garreth that La Flamme's skin was silver, while her hair gleamed as if it were spun from glistening fire.

"Garreth, this should not be happening," she whispered in a tight voice.

A tear slid down her face, and he touched his lips to it. "Of all the moments in my life that I would like to cling to and remember, I believe this is the one I would choose above all others."

How could any woman resist him? she wondered. He

was ripping her heart out, and she had to free herself before it was too late.

"You are frightening me, Garreth," she whispered.

He heard the fear in her voice, and immediately released her and stepped back, dropping his arms to his sides. His breath came out raggedly. "To frighten you is the last thing I would want to do."

She buried her face in her hands, and he wanted to hold her, to comfort her, but he dared not touch her for fear he wouldn't be able to let her go again.

Garreth fought to bring his own emotions under control. When she raised her face to him and he saw confusion in her eyes, he knew she was not acting.

He was beside her in an instant, turning her into his arms. "Do not be distressed. I will make no more demands on you. It is obvious that you still love Richard's father."

She was stunned by the mention of her father, which brought her back to reality. The words she uttered next were like a knife in Garreth's heart. "Oh, yes, yes, I'll always love him."

Garreth steeled himself against the pain. "Do we still play the game of questions?" he asked.

"What? I . . . yes."

"Did you think of me when I was kissing you, or were you thinking of Richard's father?"

Sabine saw how unsure he was of himself, and there was no mistaking the anguish reflected in his eyes.

"No," she said at last, "I did not think of Richard's father when you kissed me."

"I don't know what's happening to me," Garreth whispered. "I tell myself that I should forget you and return to England, yet I cannot go a day without seeing you." He closed his eyes for a moment. "Tell me that you feel something for me."

Sabine threw her head back, wishing she did not feel such pain in her heart. She was betraying her father by welcoming the touch of the man who had slain him. She tried to pull away, but his lips were on hers once more, rendering her helpless.

As her father's face swam before her, she tore her lips from Garreth's. "Don't touch me!" she cried, backing away. "I don't ever want you to touch me." Sabine was unaware that she had spoken in English, with no trace of a French accent.

There was a bewildered expression on Garreth's face. "Who are you? It's almost as if you're two women. One is soft and loving, and the other . . . hard and angry—perhaps even cruel."

Sabine's hands trembled as she attempted to fasten the hooks on her gown. "You should not have brought me here."

"Do not reject me until you have given me a chance to win your love."

She buried her face in her hands and great sobs escaped her lips. "I don't want to love you."

Tenderly, he pulled her head to nestle against his broad shoulder. She had not expected such compassion from him. Somehow a feeling of peace descended on her, and she wanted to stay in his arms forever, for his hands were consoling as they glided up and down her back, not evoking passion, but soothingly as if to comfort.

"Have you suffered so much?" he asked.

"Oh, yes," she replied, thinking how her life had been destroyed that terrible night her father was killed. "There are events in my life that have guided my footsteps on a path I must tread. Be warned, Garreth, that if you stay near me, my past will surely reach out and destroy you."

He raised her face up to the light. "Don't you know it's too late to warn me? Have you not guessed that I love you? If you are in danger, I will protect you and ask nothing of you in return."

She shook her head so vigorously that her auburn hair swirled out about her. "You do not have the right."

He brushed his lips gently against her tear-wet face. "Oh, but I do. I would fight the world to keep you safe. Come back to England and give me the right to protect you."

Suddenly, Sabine raised her head, staring at him. "Are you asking me to become your duchess?"

His eyes reflected sorrow. "No, I cannot do that."

There were threads of anger in her voice. "Of course not. It would never do to have an actress as the duchess of Balmarough, would it?"

He captured her chin and held her gaze. There was pain in his voice. "I don't expect you to understand how I feel, but I shall try to explain. If I were free to do so, I would not hesitate to make you my wife and hold you up with pride for all the world to see."

"You can say this while you are already married—that is your protection, is it not, Your Grace? And most convenient. How many times have you used your poor wife to keep some ambitious lover from expecting marriage from you?"

He looked stricken. "Do you think that of me?"

"Are you asking me to become your mistress?"

"Do we play the question game again?"

"*Oui*, if that is your wish."

"Then I will admit that I would take you as my mistress if that is the only way I could have you. But this is not in my control."

"Why not?"

"Because of the sad little girl that I once stood with and pledged my protection."

"Your wife?"

"Yes." His shoulders slumped. "If she is dead, the blame is mine. If she is alive, I must find her."

Sabine could not speak for a moment. She was confused. Raising her hand to her mouth, she suddenly felt sick inside. "I am not well, Your Grace. I want to go home now."

"Don't withdraw from me," Garreth pleaded.

All she wanted to do was escape. "I need time to think."

"Will you think about us?"

"*Oui*—that and other things."

Garreth took her face in both his hands and tenderly pressed his cheek to hers.

"For so many years I have been empty inside, but the moment I saw you, I came alive again. I don't know why—I cannot explain it, even to myself. I never again want to feel the loneliness."

"I do not believe you and I are suited to one another. And I shall never be any man's mistress."

"Even if that is so, I still want to be near you. For all your renown you are not happy. I want to take care of you and Richard."

He drew her tightly against him, and they stood there for a long time. Oh, how she gloried in the feel of him, and it terrified her. She tried to remember that he was devious and manipulative, and she must not trust him.

"I am capable of taking care of Richard." Her voice was suddenly without warmth. "I have done so most of his life."

"But he has no father."

She pulled away. "No, his father is dead, and no one will ever take his place. Never again imply that you want me for your mistress."

He stepped away from her. "At this time, I can offer you nothing more."

She turned her back on him. "I want nothing from you, Garreth, but one thing. And one day you will know what that one thing is."

He let out an exasperated breath. "Tell me now—why do you keep me waiting?"

Tears gathered in her eyes. "Know this, Monsieur le duc, I will be no man's whore." Before she lost her nerve she moved quickly toward the door. "I must leave. I shall ask your coachman to take me home."

He moved toward her—she was pale and did not look well. "I will accompany you."

"I would rather go alone."

He watched her move away from him, wanting to call her back. God help him, he loved her. There had been moments when he had felt she loved him too—he couldn't be wrong about that. Whatever was troubling her was also robbing them of happiness. He intended to discover what devils haunted her.

Seated in the coach, Sabine stared into the darkness. It had taken all of her willpower to leave Garreth. It was not supposed to happen like this—she had lost control tonight. The next time they met, she would be prepared. And the time and place would be of her choosing.

21

When the coach stopped in front of Sabine's house, all the lights were blazing. As the footman was helping her from the coach, Ysabel came hurrying through the door.

"It's your brother!" she cried in distress. "We have searched everywhere and cannot find him. I did not know where you were, so I sent for Jacques and Marie."

Garreth's coachman bowed to Sabine. "Is there something I can do to assist you, Mademoiselle?"

Sabine was so fearful for Richard that she could not think clearly. "No. You may leave." Frantically, she hurried into the house and flew up the stairs to her brother's room.

"Richard," she called, opening the door to his bedroom. "Richard, answer me!" His two hounds came to her, licking her hand and wagging their tails, but Richard was not there.

Ysabel entered the room, puffing to catch her breath. "As you see, he has not slept in his bed."

Sabine stooped to pick up a toy soldier, held it in her hand for a moment, and then placed it on his trunk. "Have you questioned the servants?"

"That was the first thing I did. No one has seen him since early evening."

"He has no friends. Where could he have gone?"

Ysabel was so frantic that tears filled her eyes. "I have tried to think where he would go, but I cannot imagine."

Panic was building up inside Sabine. "He would not do this to me. Richard understands that I would worry. Someone has taken him—I'm sure of it."

"No one could get into the house without our knowing. And the dogs would not have allowed an intruder into this room."

Sabine frantically looked around for some clue, anything that would tell her what had happened. "Is it possible that Garreth found out who we are, Ysabel? Could he have deliberately distracted me tonight while someone took Richard?"

"It would make no sense. He had you and let you go."

"I must find Richard. I'll report his disappearance to the authorities, and they will help us."

"Jacques and Marie have already done that and a search has begun."

Sabine was not aware that she had begun to pace. "I cannot just do nothing." She went to the window and stared out into the inky darkness. Her brother was out there somewhere, alone and frightened. "Oh, Richard, I pray that God will keep you safe."

*   *   *

On returning to the château, the coachman asked to see the duke, and was shown immediately into the salon, where Garreth was answering his correspondence.

"Ackerman," Garreth said in surprise, "did you deliver your passenger safely home?"

"I did, Your Grace; but I thought you might like to know about her brother."

Garreth frowned. "What about Richard?"

"Mademoiselle was told that her brother was missing, and she was most distraught."

Garreth stood, his face creased with worry. "La Flamme is famous, so some deranged person might have taken the boy, although I think that is unlikely. It's more likely, with his adventuresome nature, that the boy struck out on his own." He looked at the coachman. "Where would you go, if you were a young boy looking for adventure, Ackerman?"

"I can't say that I ever had an adventure, Your Grace."

Suddenly Garreth smiled. "I believe I just may know where to find him. Have you unhitched the horses?"

"No, I came directly to you, Your Grace."

"Then let us hurry."

It was raining when the coach reached the park where Garreth had spent the afternoon with La Flamme and Richard. Now the park was dark, and the empty stalls cast grotesque shadows in the misty rain.

Garreth hurried toward the river, where several people were camping beneath makeshift tents, so they would have a good view of the boat races at sunrise.

He called Richard's name and questioned several people, but no one had seen the boy. Garreth was just about to give up hope when he saw a lone figure huddled against the side of a statue, trying to keep dry.

"Richard," he said, bending down to the boy.

"Monsieur le duc," Richard said with relief, "I was

praying that someone would find me, and you came. I was so frightened, and I am so cold." He threw his arms about Garreth's neck, and Garreth lifted him up and hurried toward the waiting coach.

"Your sister is worried about you, Richard," Garreth said, as he placed the boy inside the coach and covered him with a lap robe.

"How did you know where to find me?"

Garreth looked at him sternly. "I merely thought as a young boy would think, and I remembered how badly you wanted to see the boat races."

Richard looked up at Garreth searchingly. "My sister is going to be angry with me, is she not?"

"I believe you worried her a great deal. You know you did wrong?"

Richard nodded, his face full of misery. "I would do anything to see the boat race, but I am sorry if I caused my sister distress."

"You must promise her that you will not do this again. Will you promise, Richard?"

He nodded. "I only want to go home."

Marie had returned, but Jacques was still searching. Sabine paced the floor, often going to the door to listen. "I hear a coach," she said hopefully.

"Perhaps Jacques has returned with news of Richard," Ysabel said.

Sabine rushed into the entry with Ysabel and Marie, just as the door opened to admit Garreth, who was carrying Richard in his arms.

Sabine snatched her sleeping brother from him, looking him over carefully. When she was sure he was unharmed, she hugged the boy tightly.

"Richard, what happened to you?"

"He will tell you later," Garreth said. "He's wet and tired—you should get him into some warm clothing as soon as possible."

Sabine glared at Garreth over Richard's head. "What did you do to him?"

Garreth shook his head, and turned to the door. This wasn't quite the reaction he had hoped for. "I shall leave you to tend to your brother. Your gratitude is not necessary for what I did. Good night, La Flamme."

Sabine opened her mouth to protest, but he had already gone.

Marie and Ysabel were fussing over Richard, and he opened his eyes sleepily. "I didn't mean to worry anyone. I only wanted to see the boat races. Remember, Sabine, when you told me that people camp there so they can have a good view?"

Marie lifted Richard in her arms and walked toward the stairs. "First we get you tucked into bed. You have worried us all. A boy should not do this to those who love him," she scolded.

Sabine followed them up the stairs. "I want to know exactly what happened, Richard."

After he was in dry clothing and under the blankets with a warming pan at his feet, Sabine sat beside him.

"Now, tell me everything."

"Are you angry with me, Sabine?"

"I believe I am. But it's just that I was so concerned about you because I love you."

"Monsieur le duc has told me I must promise never to worry you so again."

"How did he know where to find you?"

"I don't know, but I'm glad he did."

"How did you get out of the house without being seen?" Sabine asked.

"I slipped down the stairs when no one was looking

and walked all the way. I hoped you and Ysabel would think I was asleep. I was going to return in the morning, after the races."

Marie was hovering over him like a mother hen. "You are a naughty boy to worry us so."

He hung his head. "I'm sorry." His eyes sought Sabine's. "I was frightened," he admitted. "It was like the night we fell into the water—do you remember?"

It had been a long time since her brother had mentioned that horrible night, and she had hoped he had forgotten about it. "What else do you remember about that night, Richard?"

"I remember being cold and frightened, like someone was chasing us."

She held her breath after she asked the next question. "Did you tell this to the duke?"

"Of course not. He was nice, Sabine. When he came for me, I wasn't frightened anymore."

Sabine kissed his cheek and moved to the door. "Go to sleep, Richard. We will talk more about this tomorrow."

"I'll sit with him for a while," Marie said, pulling a chair to the side of the bed. "I hope my fool of a husband comes in from the rain soon."

"I'll go below and make Richard something hot to put in his stomach," Ysabel said, moving out of the room.

Sabine went to her bedchamber across the hall. Tonight, for just a moment, she had thought that Garreth had abducted Richard. Instead, he had found him and brought him safely home. She was becoming confused about her feelings for him. It was strange, but she no longer feared him. Was there danger in being lulled into complacency?

She had to do something soon to bring these years of

uncertainty to a conclusion. It was time for her move against Garreth, and she knew just how she would do it.

Garreth stared at the note he had just received from the housekeeper.

"A love note?" Stephen asked, smiling.

"It seems to be from La Flamme. I told you that I found her brother last night."

"Yes, but you told me little else."

Garreth broke the seal. "I believe this will merely be a note expressing her gratitude."

He read the note to himself:

Your Grace,
I am ashamed of my actions last night. I was most ungracious to you after you had rescued Richard. I am having a supper party tonight, at eight, and wonder if you might attend. I look forward to seeing you and expressing my appreciation.

He raised his eyes to Stephen, who was waiting expectantly. "Did you receive an invitation from La Flamme?"

"No I didn't," Stephen said, glancing over Garreth's shoulder. He smiled. "Perhaps she has invited only you."

"Not likely." After last night Garreth had decided that he would no longer pursue La Flamme. She loved a dead man, and he could not compete with her memories.

"I shan't be attending her little party," Garreth said, wadding the note and tossing it on the table. "Tomorrow I'm going home."

Stephen was more perceptive than Garreth had realized. "Distance will not cure what ails you, my friend. I have never before seen you this besotted over a woman."

"Leave it alone, Stephen. It is over. She has made her feelings quite clear. She has ice in her heart and is content to live with the memory of Richard's father."

Sabine watched for Ysabel's return and met her at the door. "You delivered the invitation?"

"*Oui*, but still I do not like this thing that you do."

"Did he say he would come?"

"I did not stay to see him, but no doubt he will come."

"Tonight," Sabine told Ysabel, "you will take Richard to Marie's and remain with him until I come for you both tomorrow. I have already told the servants that I will be closing the house after our possessions are packed today. When I leave this house tomorrow, La Flamme will cease to exist."

"So it's time for you and Richard to return to the past," Ysabel said sadly. "Are you certain?"

"It is the only way, Ysabel. I sent another message to my uncle, the marquis de Chavaniac. This time I included my mother's locket, in hopes that he would recognize it. Apparently he did because he has invited Richard and me for a visit as soon as I can arrange it."

Ysabel's heart was heavy as she moved to her basket of mending by the door. Sitting in a chair, she took one of Richard's shirts and begin making small stitches on the torn sleeve to keep her hands busy. "I will miss you both; you have become my life."

Sabine took the wrinkled hand gently in hers. "Dear Ysabel, put aside your sewing. This is something you will never have to do again."

Ysabel dared not meet Sabine's eyes. "It is what I am accustomed to. My hands go to it."

"Did you think I would leave without you? You will be coming with us, of course."

The faded blue eyes widened with joy, and for a moment she couldn't speak. "I do not know what I would have done had you left me behind. I ask only to be your personal maid and look after your needs."

"You will have to do nothing but pass your days in leisure, Ysabel, as my dear and trusted companion."

"No, this I will never do," Ysabel said quickly. "I am happiest when I look after you."

Sabine understood Ysabel very well. She was not suited to a life of idleness. "If it is your wish to continue as you are, it will be so."

There was a smile on Ysabel's face. "I will go now and make certain that everything is properly packed." She started to leave the room, and then paused. "Do you intend to be alone in this house with Blackthorn?"

"Yes. It's the only way. I believe Garreth loves me, and tonight I will use that love against him."

"Ask yourself why you do this. Is it to punish him or because you love him?"

"My feelings do not matter. What I do tonight is for my father—at last he will be avenged! Tonight is only the beginning. The rest will be played out in England, and I do not know what will happen."

Ysabel watched Sabine's face carefully. "There is peril in this."

"He doesn't know who I am."

"I would remind you of the day Jacques and I pulled a half-drowned girl out of the stream. If Garreth Blackthorn was the man responsible, who is to say he will not try again—and next time, he might succeed."

"By the time he realizes who I am, it will be too late, for we shall be under my uncle's protection."

Sabine glanced out the window and watched as crates

were being loaded onto several wagons. "You will see that everything is stored with Marie?"

"Of course. What have Jacques and Marie said about your leaving?"

"They were sad, of course, but they understand."

"I still do not like you being alone in this house with that man."

"Understand what I must do, Ysabel. It was you who told me that a woman only has one weapon, and I shall use it tonight."

It was later in the day when Ysabel came to Sabine and handed her a small vial containing blue liquid. "This is a powerful sleeping draught that is my own concoction. Just two drops will put anyone to sleep. But I would caution you to use only two drops."

Sabine looked at the vial curiously. "You want me to use this on Garreth?"

"It will do him no harm and will allow you time to escape. Otherwise, he may not let you leave when the time comes."

"It seems such an . . . odious thing to do to anyone."

"Use it only if you feel the need." Ysabel's wise old eyes looked deeply into Sabine's. "If a woman loves that which could harm her, she should cut it from her life. Turn away from the plans you have made for this night. Just walk away."

"If I do not face him now, I shall only have to face him later." Sabine moved toward the stairs, dreading what she must now do. "For now I want to talk to Richard. He is confused by the closing of the house. It's time I told him his identity, and that we are returning to England."

"Yes, it is time," Ysabel agreed.

Sabine found Richard sitting on the window seat in her bedchamber, watching a servant packing her trunks.

Sabine sat down beside him. "Richard, you will be happy to meet our Uncle Joseph, the marquis de Chavaniac."

Richard was immediately excited. "Why did you not tell me before that we had relatives living in France, Sabine? We have a family, and I did not even know about them."

"There is much you do not know, Richard." She watched the smile leave his lips and his eyes become sad.

Concerned, Sabine dismissed the servant and gave Richard her attention. "I have kept many things from you, Richard, because you were too young to understand. Until now, the time was not right."

He ducked his head, avoiding her eyes. "I know more than you think I do, Sabine. I've heard people talking about me." His lips trembled, and she could see that he was trying to control his emotions. "You are not my sister—you are my mother! And do not pretend otherwise."

Sabine was so startled that she could hardly find her voice. "Is that what you think, Richard?"

"Why else would we leave England, keep our names secret from everyone, and you keep me hidden? It's because you were ashamed of me." He raised clear eyes to her and placed his hand in hers. "I want you to know that I love you, no matter what. And I'm glad that you are my mother."

Sabine realized that he'd heard the cruel rumors and had been hurt by them. He thought that he was illegitimate, and yet, he had never spoken of it to her.

She gathered him to her and he leaned his head on her shoulder. "Oh, Richard, dearest, why didn't you ask me about this before?"

His arms tightened about her neck. "You don't have

to feel guilty, Sabine. I know everything, and I do not blame you—I love you."

"Oh, Richard, you are wrong."

"I know that you loved my father and that he was a great nobleman. He could not marry you because your family was not of the nobility, and he already had a wife."

Sabine held him away from her, looking into his eyes. "Who has been filling your head with such absurdities?"

"I've heard the whispers among the kitchen scullions and the other servants. I realized why you never allowed me to use a surname—it's because I don't have one—do I?"

She took both his hands in hers, feeling like crying. He had been so dreadfully hurt, when all she had meant to do was protect him. "Richard, listen to me. You have a fine old name, one that has known great honor and is respected throughout the whole of England."

"Yes, I know, but it is not my real name. It was my father's and he could not give it to me. I remember so little about him—but it seemed that we lived in a big house with many rooms and many servants. My father must have loved you."

"What else do you remember?"

"I remember the water and the cold."

"That was because we were running, Richard. We escaped death that night, only because I took you into the stream."

"I have somehow known that we were in danger that night, and I have thought about it many times. Was it my father who wanted us dead? Had we become a humiliation to him?" There was pain and bewilderment in Richard's voice.

"No, Richard. What I am going to tell you now is the truth—I want you to believe that. I have not told you this before because I thought I was doing what was best for you. Little did I know what you were suffering because of my silence."

His eyes were filled with hope. "My father did not want us dead?"

"*Our* father, Richard. No matter what you have heard, or what you believe, I *am* your sister. The truth is going to be as painful as anything you may have imagined, for it is a tragic story that I now reveal to you."

He listened intently as she explained the events that led to their escape from Woodbridge Castle. Tears swam in his eyes as she told them how their father had died, and how his last thought had been for their safety.

"So you see, Richard, I am your sister. I wish you could have known our mother. She was gentle, kind, and lovely, and she was so proud of you. Our father was a man of honor, though sometimes intimidating. He was not afraid to tell even the king himself when he thought his majesty was wrong. He was a great man, and you are his legal heir."

Richard was quiet as he contemplated everything Sabine had told him. "I have a family name," he finally said in wonder.

"Indeed you do. You are also lord of vast lands and holdings and have great wealth." She brushed her lips against his cheek. "In truth, you have so many titles, I cannot remember them all. I do know that you are the viscount of Ironsworth, baron of Rummedale, baron of Wimsley, and most important of all, you are the earl of Woodbridge!"

Richard's eyes were round with amazement as he stared at her. "We are of the nobility?"

"Indeed, M'lord," she said smiling.

Suddenly his eyes flamed with anger, and she was reminded of their father.

"I must avenge my father!" Richard said. "Who is the person that caused his death?"

Sabine realized that she must still keep secrets from him, at least a while longer. "Richard, trust in me, for I cannot reveal anything more to you until we reach England. The day will come when father will be avenged—this I swear. And it will not be long in coming."

He leaned his head against her shoulder, and her arms went around him. She smiled. "So you thought I was your mother?"

His shoulders slumped. "It was not so bad to think that, even when I believed you were ashamed of me. I love you better than anyone. I realize now that for all the years we have been in France, you have guarded and protected me." He looked up at her. "You still believe that our father's enemies want to harm me, don't you?"

"I have never been willing to take that risk. I may have been too cautious, but you're still alive."

They sat there for a long time, drawing comfort from each other. At last Sabine stood. "Enough of this. We are off to the province of Auvergne to visit our mother's brother. While there, we can both be ourselves."

"Will our uncle know us?"

She walked to her dressing table and opened a wooden chest where she kept her jewelry. "This is the letter I received from him." She smoothed out the pages and began to read:

"My dear niece, it is with great happiness and much astonishment that I received your letter with the locket. It was my unhappy understanding that you and my nephew, Richard, were missing and were ultimately considered deceased. I await your arrival so I may judge for myself the validity of our relationship. I have many questions that beg to be answered."

Sabine smiled. "There you have it, Richard. An uncle that is looking forward to your visit."

He was looking over her shoulder, and he reached into her jewel chest, lightly touching a diamond necklace. "I wish we could leave today."

"Tomorrow will be soon enough."

He picked up a ruby ring with a dragon carved in the stone. "This is not our family crest."

Sabine took the ring and closed her hand around it. "No, 'tis not your crest."

He could tell that she was being mysterious again. "Do not keep secrets from me, Sabine."

She laid the ring in his hand so he would not think she was deceiving him. "It belongs to a man I know. I have no wish to speak of him tonight. One day I will tell you about him."

"He gave the ring to you?"

"Yes." She kissed his cheek and led him across the room. "Now off to the kitchen. You may ask cook for a sweet."

Reluctantly, Richard moved out the door, but stood in the hall, looking back at Sabine. "I will have many responsibilities when we reach England."

"Yes, you shall."

Suddenly his face brightened. "Do Jacques and Marie know that I am of noble birth?"

"Of course. They have known for a very long time. You have my permission to ask Jacques tonight how they pulled us from the stream and saved our lives."

He nodded solemnly and walked to the stairs.

Ysabel entered the room, a wide smile on her face. "I passed Richard on the stairs, and he informed me that in the future, I should address him as my lord, but that you could still call him Richard."

Sabine couldn't help laughing. "There will be no living

with him now that he knows his true identity. Perhaps I need to tell him that I outrank him."

Ysabel went about the room, gathering up items and placing them in a trunk, then slammed the lid shut. "That's the last of the clothing." She raised her eyes to Sabine. "There is still time to reconsider."

"Oh, Ysabel, I want desperately to get through this night. If only it did not have to be—but Garreth Blackthorn must be punished!"

22

The fire had long since died down and was now only glowing embers. Sabine sat alone in the salon, unmindful of the chill in the room or the candles that had burned low, casting the room in shadows. Eight o'clock had come and gone, and still she waited for Garreth. She glanced at the mantle clock as it struck the eleventh hour.

She had been so confident that he would come. She had taken particular care with her toilette, pulling her hair away from her face and fastening it with diamond clips. She wore a sweeping, red velvet dressing gown that was trimmed with silver lace. Her heart was heavy with disappointment as she bent to blow out the candles, when she heard the front door open. She held her breath as she heard Garreth calling her name.

She straightened and watched him enter the room. Their eyes met, and she was unaware that she moved across the room to meet him halfway. They did not touch, but stared into each other's eyes.

"Your other guests have gone," Garreth said at last.

"There were no others. I invited only you."

His eyebrow arched in mockery. "Had I known that, I would have arrived earlier."

She licked her dry lips. "You're here now."

"I tried to stay away. But as you see, I could not."

There was nothing of the coquette in her now. "I am glad you came."

He glanced about the room. "No servants?"

"I sent them away. There is no one in the house save you and me."

His voice was deep and resounded through her like a caress. "Not even Richard?"

"Not even Richard." She laid her hand on his arm. "I want so much to thank you for finding him last night. I was very unkind to you after you brought him home. Can you forgive me?"

"There is nothing to forgive. It's understandable that you were frightened for his safety."

She smelled of some strange exotic flower, and he ached to crush her in his arms. Instead, he moved away from her. "Did you change your mind about me, or is this merely your way of showing your gratitude because I found Richard?"

A slight smile flickered across her face. "Does it matter?" She walked to him, and in a gesture that took him by surprise, lay her head on his shoulder. "I asked you to come because I wanted to be with you."

His arms went around her, and gently, he pulled her close. His lips brushed against her hair, gliding down her neck to nuzzle the lobe of her ear. "I have been in torment since last night," he admitted. "I had decided to return home, but I could not leave you."

Sabine had also been tormented, but she would not

admit this to him. She understood about love now. Why did they have to be enemies? She pressed her lips against his, lightly touching, and then pulling away. "I am glad you did not return to England."

"I could not go until I made a confession and extracted one from you." His eyes softened with an inner glow. "It's very simple, really. I love you." He gripped her arms, jerking her forward, his mouth grinding against hers in a kiss that made her feel as if she were falling into a bottomless chasm.

He raised his head and stared into her eyes. "Tell me that you love me," he whispered in her ear. "Say it."

The admission was torn from her lips. "I . . . do love . . . you." She loved him in every way a woman could love a man. She pressed her head against his shoulder as he triumphantly lifted her into his arms.

"I knew you had to love me, or else there would be no meaning in this life."

"I . . . don't want to love you."

He carried her into the hallway and up the stairs. "Love does not seem a free choice." He smiled down at her. "Yet, I would have chosen you above all other women."

She pressed her face against the rough fabric of his jerkin, too overcome with tenderness to speak.

"Which is your room?" he asked, and she could feel the urgency in him, for it matched her own.

Sabine nodded at her door and he opened it, carrying her inside.

A single candle flickered low. He placed Sabine on her feet and untied her belt, sliding the dressing gown off her shoulders and allowing it to fall to the floor. He could only stare at her in wonder, for she wore nothing beneath the dressing gown.

Sabine could hear his sharp intake of breath. When he unfastened her hair and allowed it to fall freely across her shoulders, she shivered as delightful feelings moved through her.

With masterful hands, Garreth stroked up and down her arms, then lightly touched her breasts.

Once she tried to protest, but he turned her toward him and smothered her lips with his, stopping her objections and cutting off her speech.

She was existing in a dream state where touching, feeling, and the spoken word were all that mattered. Emotions exploded within her, and fire burned in her veins. His touch, his voice, his mouth were all that existed for her.

She threw back her head as his mouth moved over her body in the most sensuous way, causing her to tremble in anticipation of what else he would do. He lay her on the bed and came down beside her, trailing his finger down her shoulder. "Are you sure you want this?"

"Yes, Garreth, I am sure."

Her eyes glistened like liquid gold in the soft candle-light. He was drawn further into her spell. He lifted a flaming curl and caressed it between his fingers. "I have thought of little else save this moment. Now that it is here, I hesitate only because if I have you, I will never be able to let you go."

His words were like wine to her. "Perhaps I shall be a disappointment to you," she murmured.

His hand moved lower to lay gently against her flat stomach. "No, you could never be that."

Sabine closed her eyes and groaned when his lips softly touched one breast and then moved to the other with the same gentleness.

"I will make you forget everything but me," he said, allowing his hand to move lower, and still lower.

Her skin was like velvet to his caress, and when she moved closer to him, inviting his kiss, he was mindless with desire.

Cupping her head, his mouth moved against hers. Garreth knew he wanted her for the rest of his life.

When he drew her against his naked body, Sabine pressed tighter against him, reveling in the feel of his muscled thighs, and wanting to be closer to him—to be a part of his warmth—to be a part of his body.

His breath was warm against her skin. She touched his hair, his face, running her finger over his lips.

He groaned as her hand moved boldly across his hips.

A sudden realization brought a stabbing pain to her heart—she loved him—oh, how deeply she loved him.

She submitted willingly when he gently moved her legs apart and hovered above her. He attempted to keep his passion under control, but he had ached for her, and now he could not stop the fire in his body or the desire that raged out of control. His body trembled as he stabbed into her.

Sabine had not expected the pain that ripped through her virgin body, and she cried out in surprise.

She could feel Garreth tense, and he withdrew from her. Rolling over, he took several deep breaths to calm the thundering of his heart. "Why didn't you tell me?" He grabbed her by the shoulders and shook her. "Why did you allow me to believe you had already been with a man?"

Sabine was glad for his anger, because it helped cool the intensity of her own feelings. She moved away from him, pushing her tumbled hair out of her face. "Is it a requirement that every lady you make love to tell you that she is a maiden still?"

She was on her knees; the silky red hair that fell over her shoulder did little to cover her nakedness. It was difficult for Garreth to keep from reaching out and bringing her against his body.

"You deceived me into thinking that Richard was your son," he accused.

"No, I did not." Her eyes glinted and her breasts were heaving. "I told you that he is my brother."

He did touch her now. His hand drifted through her hair. "You are every man's fantasy, but you have become my nightmare. Nothing about you is real. Are you an illusion that will disappear with dawn?"

He had come too close to the truth. Boldly, she took his hand and laid it against her breast. "This is real. Is it not enough to know that you are the first man I have ever wanted to give myself to?"

He jerked his hand away and drew in his breath, closing his eyes. "It is not enough. You have pulled me into a web of mystery that I don't understand. I sense destruction in you, and yet, I cannot leave."

She tossed her hair and pressed her body against his, and he quaked from the magnitude of his need.

"You do not want me?" she asked in a soft voice.

"Want you? I know that if you left me now, I would never know a contented day for the rest of my life." He pressed her to him. "God help me, for I cannot help myself."

That was the confession she had been waiting to hear. Her lips parted as she moved toward him, and he was lost. The sweetness of her filled his mind, his heart, his whole being.

Sabine did not remember drifting back against the pillow. She only knew that he was kissing her and calling her name over and over. When he entered her body this time, it was with gentleness, and she gasped with each thrust he made. The love between them seemed so pure, so right. If only . . . if only. . . .

She tried not to think of the wonderful feelings that he aroused in her. In a moment of desperation, she sought his lips, biting until she brought blood.

Pushing her away, he laughed and tested his lip. "Temptress, your teeth are sharp."

Gathering her in his arms once more, his lips slid over hers, and she groaned as he moved sensuously within her. She gasped and her body trembled as his warmth spilled into her body and her body answered.

His kiss was long and drugging. It felt as though every breath he took circulated through her body and they breathed as one.

They lay there holding each other, both affected by what had happened between them. While Sabine curled against him she turned her head to look out the window, wondering if it were possible to love where one hated.

Garreth allowed his hands to say what he was feeling as they gently slid over her body and then into her hair.

The light fell across the bed, and Sabine turned to look into his eyes that were soft with an expression that took her breath away.

"Garreth, I have often wondered about lovemaking, but I never imagined it would be so . . . wonderful."

He pressed her tighter to him, as if by doing so, he could absorb her into his body. "I have never felt this way before." He touched his lips to hers and smiled. "You leave me breathless."

"Then I pleased you?" She dropped her head against his chest, suddenly shy because of the intensity she saw reflected in his eyes.

"I will never let you go now. We belong together, and you cannot deny it."

She raised her head, daring to look into his eyes once more. This was the moment she had waited for, the moment she would seal her revenge—then why did it hurt so much? "Do you truly love me, Garreth?"

He placed his finger over her lips. "I have an ache

within me that only you can soothe. I want to be with you every day, to spend the rest of my life with you. What else can it be, if not love?"

She hated the tears that spilled down her face at his admission. Sabine was caught in a trap of her own making. Was not this her moment of triumph? Why then did she want to feel his arms about her, holding her so tightly that when he took a breath she would feel it?

She leaned back on her elbow, watching his handsome face in the soft moon glow. She could not think of him as the man who had destroyed her life. He was loving and kind. And, oh, how she wanted to be with him again.

Garreth pushed her hair aside and touched her ear with his lips. "Let me hear you say how you feel about me."

She let out her breath, knowing that the words she must speak were indeed the truth. "I love you from the depths of my soul, and I will love you until the end of my life."

She heard his sharp intake of breath as he held her tightly. "And yet," he said in a painful voice, "I do not know who you are. I do not even know what to call you. I despise the name, La Flamme, because I know it is not really you."

"I cannot tell you my name at this time. But I promise you, Garreth, that when you awake in the morning, the mystery about me shall be unraveled."

He smiled softly and touched his lips to her cheek. "Why must I wait?" He kissed her lips and then raised his head. "I warn you, I am a jealous lover. I no longer want you to be onstage where other men can watch you and want you. You belong to me alone."

How simple it would be, she thought, to admit to him

that she was his wife, and that this was the last time she would ever be known as La Flamme. The words ached to be spoken, but she dared not. "I belong to you tonight, but beyond that, I can promise nothing."

He laughed, feeling too sure of their love to be concerned. "You will never be free of me, nor, I think, will you want to be."

"What future can we have together? You are an important man, a friend to the king, and I am merely an actress. Would you dare to introduce me to your king? Would you dare make me your duchess?"

"Yes!" he said, coming to his knees and bringing her up with him. "Yes, I shall certainly present you to King Charles, and I will make you my duchess. I want you for my wife so no one will doubt that you belong to me."

She knew what it meant for a nobleman as important as Garreth to offer marriage to a mere actress. She turned her face up to his and offered him her lips. There was beauty in their love, but there were also dark and sinister shadows that would soon rip them apart. It had to be, because the blood of her father stood between them like an avenging sword.

Once more Garreth made love to her, and again she reveled in his touch. The night was spent in loving discoveries, and Sabine was saddened to see it end.

It was almost morning when she slipped out of bed and moved to the bottle of wine on the low table. Garreth watched her in all her naked glory, thinking she was more beautiful than he had imagined. He, who had often scoffed at love, would never do so again.

She returned with two glasses of wine, offering one to him. "A toast, I think."

He smiled, taking the glass. "What shall we drink to?"

"To the new day, when there shall be no more secrets between us, Garreth."

"You make it sound so mysterious." He raised the glass to his lips, thinking it tasted bitter, but he drank it nonetheless.

"When will you return to England?" she asked.

He felt suddenly dizzy and waited for the sensation to pass. "As soon . . . as you can . . . come with me."

He closed his eyes as her soft body pressed against his. Her lips covered his, and he could not stop the room from spinning.

"Sorry, I . . ." He could not keep his eyes open and fell back against the pillow, lying very still.

23

Sabine kissed Garreth's lips tenderly before moving off the bed. There was an urgency about her as she quickly dressed. As she stood over his sleeping form, she thought how vulnerable he looked. Gently, she pushed a lock of dark hair from his forehead and bent once more to kiss his lips. To leave him was like tearing her heart from her body.

She felt a pang of guilt for drugging his wine, but it had been necessary. She wanted desperately to lay down beside him and have his warmth fill her once more, but that could never be again. Last night was all they would ever have.

"I love you," she whispered. "But you will never believe that after today."

She placed a letter and Garreth's family ring on the pillow beside him. When next they met, the love she had seen in his eyes last night would have turned to hatred.

She couldn't seem to leave. Her hand drifted across his chest as she memorized the feel of him.

"You will understand many things when you waken, my dearest love," she whispered. "It was predestined that we would be enemies from the day we stood beneath the bowed branches and became man and wife."

The blackness of night had given way to golden dawn when Sabine entered the de Baillard's home. Marie met her at the door with tears in her eyes. Sabine was enfolded in her arms and they wept together.

"I always knew this day would come," Marie said, trying to regain her composure. "I told myself I would not cry when you left."

"Dear Marie, Richard and I shall never forget you and Jacques. You have been our family for so long."

"I'm glad you are going to have Ysabel with you. I would worry about you otherwise."

Richard appeared beside them with Ysabel. "Marie," Richard said with a serious expression on his face, "when I am earl of Woodbridge, I shall expect you and Monsieur Jacques to visit me often."

Marie tried to hide her tears, but still they spilled down her cheeks. "You'll be too grand for us, Richard."

"Not you, Marie," he said earnestly. "As my sister told you, we are family."

Sabine nodded in agreement. "You will be welcome wherever we are, Marie. Richard and I shall always want you and Jacques to be a part of our lives. Do not disappoint us."

Marie looked doubtful. "There will not be a day goes by that we won't think of you. But we shall be happy in knowing that you will both be in your rightful place."

"You will make certain to tell no one where we have gone," Sabine said.

"No one will hear it from us. As you know, we

arranged to leave for Florence this very day. When we return to Paris, we will simply say that La Flamme has retired from the stage."

Jacques hung back in the shadows, and Sabine saw that he was having difficulty expressing his feelings. She moved into his outstretched arms. "I'm going to miss you, Jacques." She kissed him on the cheek. "You have been like a gentle father to me. I hope you will find another La Flamme."

His eyes were swimming with tears as he raised her hand to his lips. "There was only one La Flamme, and Paris will never see the likes of her again."

Garreth woke slowly, blinking his eyes and staring in bewilderment at the unfamiliar room. His head ached and his mouth was dry. When he sat up, he felt the room spin, so he buried his head in his hands.

"Where the hell am—" Suddenly he remembered the night he had shared with La Flamme, and he jerked his head up, looking for her. She was not there. Her red dressing gown lay on the floor where he had dropped it when he undressed her last night.

He staggered to a standing position, holding on to the bedpost to keep his balance. What had happened to him? He shook his head to clear it, then dropped back on the bed, trying to keep the room from spinning.

Standing, he slowly dressed, then walked to the window, discovering to his surprise that it was long past noon. Sleeping late was not one of his habits. He smiled, but then last night had been like no night he'd ever known.

His eyes softened when he thought about La Flamme. Even in the light of day, after his passion had been spent, he still wanted to take her back to England. He wanted to marry her with all haste. His mother might object until she came to know La Flamme.

He frowned. It would mean that he would have to declare Sabine dead. Something inside of him made him reluctant to let her go. Of course, she was dead, or she would have been found, after all these years.

With a sudden burst of happiness, he remembered that La Flamme had promised to reveal her true identity today. After last night, there would be no more La Flamme.

Still feeling somewhat dazed, he sat on the edge of the bed and was pulling on his boot when he noticed a note laying against the pillow where La Flamme's head had lain last night.

Looking puzzled, Garreth picked up the ring that lay atop the note. How could La Flamme possibly be in possession of the ring he'd given Sabine the day of their wedding?

He ripped open the letter. There were only a few words written on the page.

Garreth,
I promised to reveal my name to you today. I am Sabine Blackthorn, duchess of Balmarough. Some will never believe that you did not know your own wife. We shall meet again, never fear.

He was too stricken to react for a long moment. Stunned and sick of heart, he reread the note, thinking there must be a mistake. What kind of cruel jest was this?

He ran from the room, calling her name. "La Flamme, where are you—answer me!"

Once he was downstairs, he went from room to room,

his voice echoing in the emptiness. "Where are you?" he called out with trepidation. "Why did you tell this lie? Did you think I would be so easily fooled?"

At the front door, Garreth closed his eyes against the bright sunlight. He realized that she had drugged him. He walked into the salon, the one downstairs room that still had furniture, and dropped down on a chair. If only he could think clearly.

La Flamme claimed to be Sabine, but that could not be. Sabine had been a sickly child, a cripple, and La Flamme was a beautiful, graceful woman.

The breath was trapped in his throat as he compared the two of them. Sabine had red hair, but not so bright as La Flamme's. Sabine had a brother and his name had been Richard. Richard Woodbridge would be about the same age as La Flamme's brother, but anyone could know that. Perhaps she had only used the boy—but to what purpose?

Then he remembered her strange reaction to him the first night they met in this house. She had been frightened of him, but why?

All these years he had thought of Sabine as a child. Of course, by now, she would have grown into a woman. No! he thought in disbelief. Sabine and La Flamme could not be the same person!

He stood and walked to the double doors, throwing them wide and walking outside, hoping the fresh air would clear his tortured mind.

What else did he remember about Sabine? Her eyes—yes, her eyes had been the deepest amber, almost jewel-like. He had never seen their like before . . . except . . . except, oh, dear God no—La Flamme's!

"No," he moaned. "It can't be."

Garreth looked down at the ring he clutched in his hand. La Flamme had been in possession of the ring he had given Sabine. How could she have come by that if they were not the same person? And where was she now? Why had she not stayed to face him? Because she was afraid he would discover her deception. How dare she try to pass herself off as his wife. No matter where she went, not matter how she tried to hide, he would find her.

A short time later, Garreth entered the Palais-Royal, demanding to see La Flamme.

The portly attendant shook his head. "Monsieur le duc, Mademoiselle La Flamme has gone."

Garreth's eyes were burning with anger. "Where?"

"I do not know. Monsieur de Baillard informed me only yesterday that they would all be leaving Paris for an extended time."

"I demand to know where they went."

"I was not told. It's very mysterious—no one seems to know. I can tell you that it's awkward trying to satisfy the questions of everyone who inquires of La Flamme and the de Baillards. Do you not think they should have told me where they were going, Monsieur le duc?"

After leaving the theater, Garreth went to the fencing master, who could tell him nothing. And for two weeks, he frantically searched the city, trying to locate someone who might know what had happened to La Flamme. If anyone knew, they did not tell him.

He began to realize that if La Flamme did not want to be found, he could not find her. As each day passed, and he could not find her, his heart turned to stone.

At last, Garreth decided to return to England and Wolfeton Keep. When next they met, it would be on English soil. She would come to him there . . . this he knew.

24

Seated beside Richard in the travelling coach, Sabine merely glanced at the farms and villages they passed. It was approaching sunset when the coach began its ascent into the Auvergne Mountains.

Much of the scenery seemed familiar to Sabine because her mother had described it to her so often. Before they reached the summit, the landscape was broken by a large meadow that seemed to go on forever.

At last, nestled in a meadow, there rose a great house, which dominated even the mountains. This was the birthplace of her mother, the Château de Chavaniac.

"Ysabel, it is beautiful here, is it not?" Richard said in French and then happily spoke in English. "I have been so long in Paris, that I have seldom seen the country."

Ysabel nodded. "It is beautiful, Richard."

Sabine tried to imagine her mother here as a girl. She could almost see her in the meadow with her favorite sister, Margretta, picking wildflowers.

As the coach slowed in the circular drive, Sabine became nervous and wondered if she had been wise to come to her uncle. Suppose she failed to convince him that she and Richard were the children of his late sister? Where then would they go for protection?

She stared at the towering castle as the coach door was opened by a footman. They ascended the steps of the ancient gray stone castle while Ysabel walked just behind them.

The massive front door swung open, and a servant greeted them. "Your Grace, My Lord, the family waits for you in the morning room. If you will follow me, I will instruct the housekeeper to take your maid to your chamber so she might unpack for you."

Richard looked at Sabine quizzically, wondering why she had been addressed as a duchess. It was also the first time that anyone had used his title, and he was uncertain how to react.

Sabine gave him a reassuring smile and took his hand. When they were led into a large room, she was surprised that there were so many people present.

"My Lord," the butler announced, "Her Grace, the duchess of Balmarough and Lord Woodbridge."

Richard gave Sabine a sharp look, and she saw the questions in his eyes. There was no time to explain, for a tall stately gentleman came forward to greet them while the others waited.

Sabine knew that this was her uncle, the marquis, even though he looked nothing like her mother. His features were angular, his nose slightly hooked. He had dark eyes, and they were going from her to Richard, as though assessing them. His expression was stoic, and she saw no sign of welcome.

Sabine dipped into a curtsy. "Uncle, I am happy to meet you at last. This is my brother, Richard. Our mother told me so much about you, I feel I know you already."

The marquis looked into her golden eyes searchingly. "Welcome, Sabine and Richard. Now the family can know contentment. At last, to know that my sister's children are not dead as we were told."

Sabine could see that there was something guarded in his expression and a stiffness in his manner. She realized that he was being cautious because he wasn't certain of their identity.

"Is Aunt Diane here, Uncle Joseph?" Sabine asked.

He shook his head. "My wife has been deceased these last two years." He motioned for a woman to come forward who so closely resembled Sabine's mother that it was almost painful for Sabine to look at her.

"I am Margretta. Did your mother mention me to you?"

Sabine smiled, wanting to reach out to the aunt she had heard so much about. But she did not because she realized she was being tested. "*Oui. Maman* often mentioned you, Aunt Margretta. You are my mother's sister, older than her by one year."

Margretta held the locket out to Sabine. "Did your mother ever tell you how she came by this?"

"*Oui*. The locket belonged to you, Aunt Margretta. My mother so admired it, that when she left France to marry my father, you gave it to her as a wedding gift."

Margretta's eyes were searching Sabine's face. "Did she tell you what I placed inside the locket?"

Sabine nodded solemnly. "Inside, you placed a lock of your own hair." Sabine pushed the catch, and the locket opened. "As you see, it is still there, along with a lock of my mother's hair, which she added when she gave it to me on my wedding day."

"My dearest," Margretta said, hugging Sabine affectionately, "you look very like Ryanne did at your age, but we had to be certain."

Suddenly the other relatives surged forward, and

Sabine and Richard were engulfed in affectionate greetings that made them know they were welcome. Two more of her mother's sisters were present, as were numerous cousins, great-aunts and great-uncles. There was such a genuine outpouring of love that Sabine and Richard were overwhelmed by it all.

Richard was smiling, and when a boy his age approached, it wasn't long until the two of them had bounded off, in search of adventure.

Sabine was asked so many questions that her head was reeling. At last, her uncle Joseph stood, calling for everyone's attention. "My niece must be weary after her long journey. All of you go to your homes. You can return for the weekend and we shall give Sabine and Richard a grand welcome." He turned to his sister, Margretta. "You alone shall remain."

Margretta slipped her arm about Sabine's waist. "You do look weary. I'll have the housekeeper show you to your chamber." She smiled. "You will be staying in the room that was your mother's."

When Sabine was alone, she walked around the chamber, exploring every cranny. It was just as her mother had described—the yellow bed covering and canopy, the white marble fireplace with faces of cherubs carved across the top. There was a miniature of her mother on the dressing table, which Sabine lovingly picked up and examined.

She heard the sound of children's laughter, and hurried to the window, where she observed Richard running and playing with his cousins. There was love and warmth in this home, and she was sorry she had not brought Richard here before now.

That night, after they had dined and Richard had gone to bed, Uncle Joseph and Aunt Margretta took Sabine into the library, where she was made comfortable in a large, overstuffed chair.

"As you can imagine, Sabine, we are mystified by much that has happened," Uncle Joseph said. "Are you rested enough to answer our questions?"

"*Oui*, that is why I have come."

Her aunt and uncle listened quietly as she revealed the events of her life, starting with the death of her mother. She told about the night she had fled Woodbridge with Richard. They made little comment, but often her aunt would wipe tears from her cheeks.

Sabine did not tell them that Garreth had come to Paris and that she had become acquainted with him as La Flamme.

Her uncle frowned. "When you first came to France, you wrote to me for help, and I turned you away. Can you ever forgive me?" His voice was gruff with emotion.

"There is nothing to forgive. I would have reacted no differently, had I been in your place. Even now, I hesitate to make our troubles yours."

"Nonsense! You are my dear sister's children. Your welfare is my concern. I will not be content until you have both resumed your proper places."

Margretta took Sabine's hand, her expression compassionate. "Tell us about your life with the de Baillards. I have heard of their fame, of course. It was kind of them to take you and Richard to their hearts."

She looked into eyes so like her mother's, begging for understanding. "*Oui*, but there is more to it than that. I had to take care of Richard. I did not plan what happened, and I hesitate to mention it, fearing you will disapprove."

"Tell us what it is," Uncle Joseph insisted.

"Have you heard of La Flamme?"

"Everyone has heard of her," Margretta said. "I have intended to see her in a play when I go to Paris, but have not yet done so. Did she help you and Richard?"

"No, Aunt Margretta—I am . . . I was La Flamme."

The marquis' breath came out in a hiss. "This is not possible. What must you have been thinking?"

Her aunt was clearly shocked. "*Non*, Sabine—to be on the stage is acceptable for the common people, but you are of the nobility."

"Please understand—I had no money and nowhere to go. No one, save Ysabel and the de Baillards, knew my true identity. I trust them completely with the secret of my past."

Her uncle became serious. "You must not again appear as the actress. And Richard must return at once to England so he can claim his titles and holdings. You, Sabine, must be installed in your husband's household without delay."

"I want Richard to regain his title, but I do not want to be a wife to Garreth Blackthorn."

"We are aware that he was accused of your father's death. But you must remember that the guilty one was punished. I corresponded with the Lord Mayor of London and the Archbishop of Canterbury, and they both assured me that the duke was innocent of any wrongdoing. I am certain that he will allow you to take your rightful place beside him."

"I . . . have no wish to reside at Wolfeton Keep."

"Nonetheless you must," her uncle stated flatly. Seeing Sabine's distress, he softened his manner. "But we will not rush you in this. Leave it to me to deal with your husband."

Sabine wondered how everyone so readily accepted that Garreth was innocent. Had they been at Woodbridge the night of the raid, they would not be so quick to believe in him.

"Do not worry, Sabine," her aunt assured her. "Everything shall be put to right."

Sabine's eyes glistened with tears and she could not speak past the lump in her throat. "I have waited long for Richard and I to go home."

Margretta took Sabine's hand and talked soothingly. "You have been carrying a heavy burden, but you can now rest, Sabine, for you have a family to help you."

Sabine's eyes were bright with gratitude. "When will we leave for England, Uncle?"

"Within three weeks time, I shall send you and Richard to London. There are letters I must write and people that I must contact on your behalf. And I shall go ahead of you to make certain that all arrangements have been made."

"Shall I accompany Sabine and Richard?" Margretta asked.

"That will not be necessary. By the time they arrive, I shall already have spoken with King Charles on their behalf."

"I long for England," Sabine said. "And I know Richard will be happy to return to Woodbridge."

Her uncle nodded. "When you arrive in England, you will draw no attention to yourself. I have a friend in London who will find a house for you and Richard. I will send him a message by courier so everything will be in readiness when you arrive. You will remain secluded until I contact you."

"I will do as you say," Sabine agreed. She was relieved to put Richard's future in capable hands. "Thank you both. I was not certain how I would get Richard's titles and lands back for him. But the king will surely listen to you, Uncle."

"*Oui*, he will listen to me," her uncle said. "Just to make certain, I shall have you, Margretta, write to the queen." Sabine's uncle turned to explain to Sabine. "Your aunt was once Queen Henrietta's friend when she was a princess of France."

"That is so," Margretta said. "I was lady-in-waiting to her mother, and I was quite fond of Princess Henrietta. I shall now use that friendship to help you and my nephew."

Sabine could hardly speak for fear she would cry. "I have lived for so long in terror and confusion, I can hardly believe it is over."

Margretta pressed her cheek to her niece's. "You have been brave, but you need have no more worries. My brother will take your burdens and make them his own. You will soon be home."

Sabine spent happy, glorious days with her mother's family, but as a week passed, and then another, she began to long for England.

When the time of their departure arrived, it was with a heavy heart that Richard and Sabine climbed into the coach that would take them to Calais.

The members of the de Chavaniac family stood on the steps of the château, waving until they were out of sight.

Sabine clasped Richard's hand. "You liked it there, didn't you?"

"Yes, I did," he admitted. "I would like to one day return. But now, I want only to go home."

"Yes, as do I. Perhaps, when you are settled at Woodbridge, the family will visit you there."

"Sabine," he asked, with troubled eyes. "I know that I will have many responsibilities when we reach England—would you object if I attend school? There is so much I do not know about my own country. I have discussed this with Uncle Joseph and he has said that he will arrange it, if you are in agreement."

"I believe that once your claim to Woodbridge has been established, it would be prudent for you to acquire an education." She smiled. "Yes, I'm certain that would be best for you."

His face brightened. "I have always wanted to attend Eton."

"Then you shall certainly do so."

"In England," he said emphatically, "I shall speak only English."

She laughed and hugged him to her. "You may start now. Even though you still speak English with a French accent."

He was thoughtful. "I shall make a good earl, I believe, once I am educated."

"Yes, Richard, you shall," Sabine assured him, smiling.

III

The Duchess of Balmarough

25

Garreth looked puzzledly at the Frenchman who handed him a letter from the marquis de Chavaniac. "I am sorry," he told the man. "I am not acquainted with your lord. What can you tell me about him?"

"Your Grace," the man said bowing, "I was told to say that my lord is uncle to Your Grace's wife, Sabine Blackthorn. If it pleases you, I am instructed to wait for an answer to his letter."

Garreth disguised the tumult within him behind a face of indifference. At last, he would know what Sabine intended. "Very well," he said. His hand trembled as he broke the seal and hurriedly read the letter:

Your Grace:
This is to inform you that my niece, Sabine, and her brother, Richard, are returning to England, under my protection. I shall be speaking with King Charles on

*their behalf and I have my eye on their future. I am certain
that you will want only what is in their best interests.*

Garreth glanced up at the messenger. "You may tell
the Marquis de Chavaniac that I will do what I can to
help Lord Richard establish his claim to Woodbridge."

The Frenchman swept him a bow. "I shall deliver
your message, Your Grace. If you wish to send a letter, I
will wait."

"That will not be necessary. Just tell his lordship what
I have told you. You are dismissed."

"Very well, Your Grace."

Garreth stared at the letter long after the man had
departed. Here was final proof that La Flamme was
Sabine. He found no joy in knowing that she was at last
in England.

Sabine and Richard walked through the small but comfortable house with Thomas Yielding, the man who was
acting on their uncle's orders to settle them in London.
They were situated some distance from the city, and
through the woods at the back of the house she could
just see the roof of Hampton Court, one of the many
country homes of the royal family.

"May I inquire, Mr. Yielding, why you chose a house
so far from London?" Sabine asked.

He adjusted the spectacles on his large nose, and
squinted through the lenses. "It was your uncle's wish
that you not be subjected to the atrocities of London. If
you will excuse me for speaking of indelicate matters,
London is overcrowded and noisy. Open drains run
down the middle of the streets, and you would find the
stench offensive. My wife swears that the poor sanitary
conditions are why many in London suffer from the

fever. I wouldn't live there myself, and I would not put anyone I know in that pesthole either."

"Thank you, Mr. Yielding, I'm sure my uncle will be pleased with your concern on behalf of my brother and myself."

"I have engaged a housekeeper, Becky Struthers, and a cook, Mrs. Laurly, who came to me highly regarded by their former employers."

Having explained the arrangements, Mr. Yielding excused himself, and Ysabel escorted him to the door.

Sabine walked through the rooms that looked so wonderfully English. It felt good to be home. She had rarely allowed herself to think about how much she'd missed England.

Richard, who had been exploring, came bounding down the stairs. "When do we go to Woodbridge?"

Sabine laughed and gave him a hug. "When Uncle Joseph arranges it, you will go home. Try to be forbearing"—she smiled and dipped into a curtsy—"M'lord."

"I have been reading about the peerage of England, Sabine," Richard said seriously, "and you should not curtsy to me. You are a duchess and far outrank me."

She brushed her lips against his cheek. "I also outrank you by being the eldest. So, My Lord Earl, I will say to you to wash those hands so that we may dine."

He grinned and nodded. Sabine realized that for the first time, he was truly happy. When he went bounding up the stairs, Ysabel shook her head. "He is young to be faced with the responsibility of running a large estate."

"Speak English, Ysabel," Sabine reminded her gently. "This is now your home."

The dear old woman looked into Sabine's eyes, and there was tenderness and caring there. "My home is wherever you are."

"And it always will be so, Ysabel. But to answer your

concerns about Richard, Uncle Joseph will find a capable
man to manage the estate until Richard is of age. For
now, my brother is going to school."

Events moved swifter than Sabine had expected. Her
uncle had already gained an audience with King Charles.
On the day he came to see Sabine and Richard, Uncle
Joseph was smiling. He brushed a kiss on Sabine's cheek
and took Richard's hand.

"I explained everything to his majesty, Richard, and
your claim has received favorable response for several
reasons. Sabine, you and Richard are to appear before
the Archbishop of Canterbury, who would put questions
to you both. It is to be a closed session that even I shall
not be allowed to attend unless summoned."

"So it has begun," Sabine said.

"Your father's uncle, an elderly gentleman, inherited
the lands and titles after you were declared dead,
Richard. He will be one of those who will be questioned
on your behalf and is ready to yield to you if your claim
is proven."

Sabine looked uncertain. "Have you had word from
my . . . husband?"

"Only that he will support Richard's claim."

"Nothing about me?"

"Not as of yet. I expect he will be at the hearing."

Sabine turned away, not wanting to think about
Garreth. She must consider only Richard's claim. Later,
she would face Garreth, and that thought terrified her.

Sabine clutched Richard's hand as they moved slowly
across the black and white marble floor. Her gaze was
fixed on the man dressed in red regalia, who seemed

detached from the proceedings. But on drawing nearer, she could see that his eyes were alive with interest as he looked from brother to sister, his hands poised in a prayerful position.

The archbishop's voice was sharp, as if he were delivering a sermon. "Since it has not yet been established that you are the earl of Woodbridge, and that you are her grace, the duchess of Balmarough, I shall address you by no title, but rather by name. "You, young Richard, and you, Sabine, please be seated so that we may begin."

The archbishop's chair was higher than the others, and Sabine thought this might be done to intimidate those he questioned.

She could see by the archbishop's eyes that he was both cagy and wise. He would try to expose them as impostors by his questions.

The archbishop first turned to Richard. "I assume, young lad, that you have not neglected your faith while you have been in France."

"No, Your Excellency, we attended church every Wednesday, although we did not often go to mass."

"So, then, you are Catholic?"

"Yes, Your Excellency, as were my father and mother before me."

"Tell me, Richard, what do you remember about your mother and father?"

"Your Excellency, my mother died when I was very young. I was also young when my father was slain. I have only a vague memory of him, and I remember nothing of my mother."

Sabine was proud of her brother. His answers were clear, and it was obvious that he was not intimidated by the archbishop.

The archbishop turned to Sabine. "I was present the

day of your wedding. Will you not tell me something of that day?"

She went over in her mind what she could say that would impress him the most. "I remember that the king told me that he had once been crippled, as I was."

The archbishop's eyes bore into hers. "Indeed, I remember that as well. What else impressed you that day?"

"Many events. My father was unhappy because he was not certain that Garreth Blackthorn would attend the nuptials."

"Many people had that knowledge. Your father's voice carried when he was angry. Can you tell me anything further that might convince me, for you do not look like the child I saw that day."

"Garreth . . . my husband's father had died, and I was sad for him."

She saw his eyes narrow, and Sabine feared he did not believe her. "Again, anyone would know about the death of his grace's father."

He signaled to the guard, who immediately opened the door. Sabine did not know the man who entered. He walked slowly, for he was a man of advanced age. When he was near Sabine, she thought he looked familiar, though she could not think why.

"This," the archbishop said, "is the earl of Woodbridge. Do either of you know him?"

Richard shook his head, but Sabine looked him over carefully. "I do not remember him well, but he is our great-uncle, Simon."

"My Lord, do you recognize these young people as your grand-niece and grand-nephew?"

The earl looked at each of them closely. "I never saw my grand-nephew, but I saw Sabine when she was quite small." He smiled slightly. "I have to say you do hold a remarkable resemblance to my nephew's wife. She was a handsome woman. Of course, your red hair you would have gotten from your father."

Sabine had thought their uncle would deny their claim so he could retain the title—yet he seemed kind, and not at all what she had expected.

"If you are my grand-niece and grand-nephew as you say, I will welcome you. I am an old man—I did not ask for the title, and I shall give it up without hesitation."

"Thank you, My Lord," the archbishop said. "I know the journey from Woodbridge has wearied you, so you may withdraw. I will speak to you after I have rendered my judgment."

The earl nodded and ambled out, but Sabine kept her eyes on the archbishop. "You have neither proved nor disproved my brother's claim, Your Excellency. Have you no one who can say who we are for certain?"

"I have one more witness. She was the old nurse. Can you say what her name is?"

Richard shook his head. He did not remember.

Sabine came to her feet, quickly suspicious of his words. Surely he was trying to trick her. "You are cruel, Your Excellency. I heard the men who raided my home say that Thea was dead. Do you think I would have left her if I thought she was alive?"

The archbishop nodded toward the door where a fragile woman moved forward as if each step was an effort. Her hair was completely white, and it was apparent that she was in ill health. But it was Thea all the same! Sabine held her breath as the nurse came near. She wanted to run to her and tell her how happy she was that she still lived, but there was no recognition in Thea's eyes.

Thea greeted the archbishop and then looked from Sabine to Richard, her eyes probing.

The archbishop motioned Thea to be seated. She gratefully eased her body onto the chair, her eyes now fastened on Sabine's red hair.

"Thea Mertson," the archbishop said, "I was told that you knew the Woodbridge children better than anyone. I will depend on you to tell me if these two are impostors."

Thea nodded at Sabine. "Let me see you walk."

Sabine felt her heart sink. Thea would expect her to limp. "Thea, don't you know me? How could you not?"

The old woman's face was ashen, and she paused to catch her breath. "I'll see you walk before I decide who you be."

Sabine stood and moved around the room and back, stopping before the nurse. "It's me, Thea, even though I no longer limp."

"My Sabine was crippled—you're not," Thea said accusingly.

"Oh, Thea, you must know me. If I were an imposter, could I not have contrived a limp?"

"You do resemble her grace's mother. And Sabine did have red hair, though not so dark as yours."

Sabine knelt before Thea. "Don't you remember how you were always scolding me, trying to get me to eat? And remember how you could predict when it was going to rain because you said that your bones ached? Remember the terrible night when you came to me and saved me and Richard from those men who had killed Father? We hid in the secret room in my father's chamber, and later went down the dark passage that led to the river. You took my cape and—"

Thea was nodding her head vigorously, her trembling hand going to Sabine's face. "Bless you, child," Thea said. "No one but Sabine would know about that secret passage." She withdrew her hand. Then her expression became doubtful again. "You could have guessed about the passage. Most old castles have secret rooms."

The archbishop had been listening intently. "You have doubts that these two are Sabine and Richard?"

"I have one sure way to prove it, Your Excellency, that will leave no doubt in my mind."

"Then I suggest you tell us what it is, so we might put this incident to rest, one way or another."

"Only myself and Sabine would know this—young Richard had a birthmark. What is the birthmark, and where is it located?"

Sabine closed her eyes, trying to remember. Where was it . . . where was it? Her eyes brightened. "It is a perfect circle, and it is located on my brother's upper leg—his right leg."

Thea's face crinkled into a smile, and tears swam in her eyes. "You'd be my Sabine right enough. No imposter could have known about the birthmark."

The archbishop held up his hand. "I will require further proof. We shall see the birthmark."

Richard came to his feet. "I will not disrobe before women—not even my sister."

The archbishop's eyes were piercing as he motioned his guard forward. "Take this young man and examine his upper right leg. Then return here and tell me what you have observed."

The moments seemed like hours while they waited for the guard to bring Richard back. Sabine reached out her hand to Thea, and the old nurse took it.

Thea was already convinced. Softly she touched Sabine's red hair.

"Dear Thea, I thought that you were dead, or I never would have left you that night. You offered your life so that Richard and I might live—I have never forgotten that."

"I would do it again if the need was such. Knowing the strong swimmer you were, I never gave up hope that you would one day come home."

The door opened, and all eyes turned to the guard who ushered Richard into the room.

"Tell us if you found anything on the lad's leg," the archbishop demanded.

"I found, Your Excellency, a round birthmark, just as the woman said."

The archbishop turned to Richard and nodded. "Your claim had been proven, My Lord Earl. Henceforth, you shall be known as the earl of Woodbridge, and shall be entitled to all monies and estates accorded to that title."

Sabine grabbed Richard and hugged him to her. "It is done! Oh, Richard, father would be so pleased; his heir has come safely home."

The archbishop interrupted them. "I will ask all of you to leave with the exception of you, Your Grace."

Sabine nodded reassuringly to her brother. "Go with Thea, Richard. I shall soon join you."

When they left the room, Sabine turned her attention to the archbishop, her chin set in a stubborn line. "I have nothing more to prove, Your Excellency."

"What shall we do about your situation, Your Grace?"

"I have put no petition before you, so my future is not your concern."

He smiled wryly. "Your tongue is sharp, like your father's. I should have seen the resemblance sooner."

"I am going home with my brother, where I intend to petition the pope for an annulment from my marriage with Garreth Blackthorn."

"I wonder what his grace will say about that?"

"That is no concern of mine."

"A marriage is not so easily put aside, Your Grace—the king does not wish this marriage to end. You will remember the particular interest he took in this union."

"While it is true that I married to please the king, I shall seek an annulment to please myself."

The archbishop was laughing so hard that he was shaking. "If I were your husband, Your Grace, no pope would take you away from me."

She raised her head. "You seem to believe that Garreth Blackthorn was innocent of any wrongdoing to my family— I am not so convinced."

He looked shocked. "You cannot believe that. The king has pardoned him of that crime. I, myself, drew a confession of guilt from his cousin, Cortland Blackthorn."

Sabine remembered that name from her wedding. She also recalled the hatred in Cortland Blackthorn's voice when he had spoken of Garreth. "It may have been the cousin who drew the bow, but perhaps Garreth aimed the arrow."

"That is a dangerous assumption, Your Grace. I have here a letter from your husband. Would you like to know what it says?"

"I'm not interested."

The archbishop unfolded the letter slowly and deliberately. "I feel obligated to tell you that it was because of this letter more than anything else that persuaded his majesty that young Richard's claim should be investigated. His grace interceded on Lord Richard's behalf and asked that we return all titles to him. He has also asked to be notified immediately about the results of this hearing today."

For a moment, she looked fearful. "He is here?"

"No. He remained at Wolfeton Keep."

So Garreth acknowledged her as his wife. She had not been certain that he would, and she had not expected him to help her brother.

"Richard and I did not ask for his assistance."

"It's a pity. He never gave up believing that you were alive."

"If there is nothing else, Your Excellency, I would like to join my brother."

"Before you go, may I inquire what you have been doing all these years—his majesty will want to know why you did not return sooner."

"I'm sure my uncle has told you I was in France—tell his majesty that." She turned to look at the door. "If there is nothing else, I'm anxious to see Thea. She seemed very ill. And it is a long journey to Woodbridge—I want to go home."

"The king will not allow you to remain at Woodbridge. You will soon find yourself installed at Wolfeton Keep."

She raised her eyebrow, reminding him again of her father. "Tell his majesty not to concern himself with me."

He chuckled. "I don't believe that would be wise. Rather, I shall give him your regards."

She started to object, and then reconsidered. "Do as you will."

He smiled at her. "Go with God, and may God help your husband—I believe his grace is going to need divine guidance."

Sabine did not smile at his humor. She turned and walked toward the door, wondering if she should be happy about Richard, or frightened for herself.

26

There was no joyful reunion between Sabine and Thea because the nurse was feverish and talking incoherently by the time Sabine left the archbishop. It was apparent that she was too ill to make the long journey to Woodbridge, so Sabine gently helped her into the carriage that would take them to the house outside London.

"It will be all right, Thea. I will take care of you now."

The old nurse mumbled over and over, "I wait only for Sabine and Richard—then I die in peace."

When they arrived at the house, Sabine helped Thea to bed and then immediately sent for a physician. After examining Thea, the man was not encouraging; he told Sabine that the old nurse would not recover from her bout with fever.

Sabine was torn. She did not want to leave Thea, and yet she had to accompany Richard to Woodbridge. She bent to kiss the old woman's cheek. "We'll soon have you well, Thea, then you will come home to Woodbridge."

Thea rolled her head. "I won't die here in this strange house. I want to go home."

"Don't talk, just rest." Sabine moved to the door, where she lowered her voice to Ysabel. "I'm concerned about her."

"I will remain with her throughout the night," Ysabel said. "You go to bed now."

Sabine nodded. She was exceedingly weary, but once in bed, she could not sleep. She rose several times during the night and went into Thea's room. Thea's condition had worsened, and she was babbling about the night Woodbridge Castle had been attacked, reliving the whole tragic incident.

It was difficult for Sabine to leave Thea the next day. She issued orders that the servants were to see to Thea's every need, and that the physician was to visit her twice a day. She left instructions that if Thea grew strong enough to travel, she was to be brought home to Woodbridge.

The closer the coach got to Woodbridge Castle, the more subdued Richard became. Sabine tried to engage him in conversation, but he remained silent and pensive.

It was a strange cavalcade, with their Uncle Joseph and Uncle Simon following in a carriage, no doubt discussing Richard's future.

At last Sabine took Richard's hand, thus forcing him to look at her. "If there is something troubling you, we should speak of it."

His shoulders slumped, and he seemed even more dejected. "I have been thinking of the obligations that face me, for which I have had no preparation. You tell me that many people will depend on me, and yet, I have not the knowledge to guide them. No one would be willing to follow the direction of a boy."

"Richard, the fact that you are our father's son makes you the rightful lord in the villagers' eyes—and they are ready to follow your guidance. You will have a host of people trained to aid you. Each of them will have a particular function and they will know well how to perform their duties. Uncle Simon will help you in matters concerning Woodbridge. And he has agreed to stay on while you attend school."

Richard looked from his sister to Ysabel. "You will soon leave me, Sabine. And you will also leave, Ysabel?"

Sabine realized what was bothering him, and it was time to tell him about Garreth. "Richard, I must tell you about the signet ring you found in my jewel chest."

"Did you think I wouldn't know that Garreth Blackthorn is the duke of Balmarough? I did not speak of him to you because you were reluctant to talk about him. But I find it confusing that he did not appear to know you in Paris. Would not a husband know his own wife?"

She gathered her strength. It would be difficult to tell him about Garreth. "I can see where it would be confusing. When Garreth and I were married, I was but four years older than you are now. I never lived at Wolfeton Keep. I saw him only on two occasions other than our wedding day. I was a child then—he did not recognize me as a woman." She dreaded what she must tell him now. "Garreth was locked in the tower because it was believed that he ordered our father murdered."

"Uncle Simon told me about that. But he's innocent, Sabine—I know he didn't do it."

She had no response to that. Everyone save herself

seemed to believe in Garreth's innocence. "Whether he is worthy of blame or not, I want never to see him again. I shall not move to Wolfeton Keep. My home is at Woodbridge—father would have wished it so."

Ysabel shook her head. "I do not believe that you can live your life by the wishes of your dead father. This is not France, Sabine, and your future will rest on the dictates of the duke. I would not so easily dismiss him from my life if I were you."

"I will expect Garreth to cause trouble and make demands. But I do not intend to obey him. I may as well tell you both now that I have decided to petition the pope for an end to my marriage."

"Sabine," Richard said, a frown creasing his brow, "I liked Garreth Blackthorn. Too much of your life has been devoted to me, and everything you have done was for me. Is it not time to live for yourself?"

"You have been doing much pondering of late, old wise one," Sabine replied, touched by his concern for her. "Let us speak of this later. Within three hours, we shall reach Woodbridge Village—consider how elated the people will be to see you."

Richard again became silent, and after a time, he fell asleep, leaning his head back against the cushioned seat.

Sabine met Ysabel's eyes. "I know what you are thinking, Ysabel."

"I was not aware that you could read minds."

"I have decided on this annulment, and I will hear nothing to the contrary."

"I believe the duke will have much to say on the matter."

"After the humiliation I've been to him, he will undoubtedly welcome the annulment. Do you think that he wants all England to know that his wife was an actress? I pray that he will be as eager to be rid of me as

I of him. For seven years, I have been married to him, and yet, for only one night was I his wife."

Sabine glanced at Richard and saw from his deep breathing that he slept soundly. "Everyone believes that Garreth was wrongly accused of my father's murder. But I will always have doubts. I want to believe in Garreth, yet dare I?"

"Only you can answer what is in your heart. I told you in Paris that I sensed no evil in him," Ysabel said.

Sabine thought back to the night she had lain in Garreth's arms while he pledged his love to her, the night she had also admitted that she loved him.

"My heart is as cold as the winter that will soon cover this land. If only I could go back and relive that last night in Paris," she said softly. "I deliberately humiliated him, and he will not so easily forgive that."

"You cannot go back—there is only forward."

"He must despise me." Sabine pulled the soft fur lap robe about her, suddenly feeling cold. "But little I care."

"So I see," said Ysabel, noting the sadness in Sabine's eyes.

The day was cloudy, and there was a chill in the air as Lord Stephen rode through the woods that surrounded Wolfeton Keep. Many of the leaves had fallen from the trees, but those that persistently clung to the branches were now ripped away by the gusting winds that sent them swirling to the ground.

Stephen urged his mount over the wooden bridge and into the inner courtyard of the Keep. He dismounted and handed the reins to the stable boy, then straightened his jerkin. Gazing up at the castle, he couldn't help but think it was very like a fortress with the thick heavy gates, turrets, and battlement towers. But there was warmth in the gray stone structure, and he knew he would find a welcome here.

Today, however, he was not pleased with the mission that had been entrusted to him. The Archbishop of Canterbury had chosen him to deliver the document because he was Garreth's friend. Stephen had spent an hour with the archbishop, during which he was informed about the importance of his mission.

Stephen still could not believe that La Flamme was the same little girl that had been so sickly and fragile at the wedding. What twist of fate had placed him between Garreth and her in Paris? He thought back to the chance meeting with La Flamme the first night he had seen her perform. Now he knew why she had befriended him—although he never doubted that their friendship was genuine. At the moment, he was concerned about what Garreth's reaction would be when he learned of Sabine's intentions. Stephen wished that the archbishop had chosen another messenger.

He was admitted to the Keep and told that her grace was in her private salon. On entering the room, Garreth's mother greeted him warmly and then offered him refreshments while they waited for Garreth.

"We don't see enough of you, Stephen, with you in London and Garreth here at the Keep." There was worry in her voice. "I don't know what to do about Garreth, Stephen. I am glad you're here."

"Is he ill?"

"His health is good, but I sense much anger and confusion in him. I believe something happened to him in France and I'm certain it involves a woman—yet he will not speak of it. Do you know what is troubling him?"

Stephen was glad that he was saved from answering

when Garreth entered the room. He immediately saw why her grace was concerned. Garreth had no sparkle in his eyes; he looked haggard, and seemed withdrawn and distant.

Garreth gave Stephen a forced smile. "I thought that was your horse I saw in the stable. What brings you to Wolfeton Keep?"

Stephen had been holding the archbishop's message in his hand, and he now offered it to Garreth. "I was asked to deliver this into your hands."

"I have been expecting this. A summons from the king, no doubt."

"It's not from his majesty, but the archbishop."

Garreth's mother stood. "I will leave the two of you alone. Stephen, I shall expect you to remain with us for a while. I will see you both at luncheon."

"Stay, Mother," Garreth said. "I believe I know what this is about, and it's time I told you." He turned to Stephen. "It is about my wife, is it not?"

The duchess looked distressed. "Oh, Stephen, they have not discovered that Sabine is dead, have they?"

Stephen looked into Garreth's eyes. "No, Your Grace."

"Tell her, Stephen," Garreth said dully. "Tell my mother about my . . . wife."

Stephen cleared his throat. "Garreth's wife has been located."

Adrienne Blackthorn looked confused, and then she smiled. "Surely this is good news! Is she well? Have they also found her brother?"

"Yes, Your Grace," Stephen replied.

"This is wonderful. I shall have everything made ready for her. When will she be arriving?"

Garreth seated his mother and turned to Stephen. "How much does the archbishop know about Sabine?"

"He told me that when he pressed her for information

about where she had been all those years, she only said that she had been in France."

Garreth's lips thinned. "I have little doubt that she does not want it known about her past."

"Garreth," his mother asked in puzzlement, "what are you saying? Have you known where Sabine was hiding all these years? Why did you not tell me?"

"I only discovered her whereabouts lately, Mother— while I was in Paris."

"So that's where she fled! It's no wonder we could not find her. You must bring her home without delay."

Stephen had been watching his friend's face and he could see the veiled anger that Garreth kept under tight control.

"In that, I believe, lies the dilemma, Mother."

The dowager was bewildered. Something was not right. "Surely you intend to bring Sabine home, Garreth. Her place is here at your side."

Garreth broke the seal on the document. There was an official-looking paper and a letter from the archbishop, which he read to himself while the others waited silently for him to finish.

Your Grace,
I am sure that Lord Stephen will have explained the circumstances concerning your wife. Against my advice, she is seeking an annulment. It is his majesty's hope that you will not allow this. It is his wish that you will take yourself to Woodbridge with all haste and bring her grace to Wolfeton Keep. His majesty will be waiting for a happy solution to this situation.

Garreth handed the letter to his mother, and when she had finished reading it, she looked at him inquiringly. "What's wrong with Sabine, Garreth? Is it possible that she still believes that you were involved in her father's death? Why else would she remain in hiding, and then demand to be free of the marriage?"

Garreth moved angrily to the window. "I care not what she does. I married her at the king's insistence, but I will not raise a hand to keep Sabine against her will— no matter what the king says. I've been in the Tower before, let him put me there again."

Adrienne shook her head. "Talk to him, Stephen. Tell my son that Sabine should be brought here at once."

Stephen shrugged and shook his head.

Garreth did not turn to his mother as he spoke. "I wonder if you would be so anxious to have her installed at Wolfeton Keep if you knew of her past?" He moved to the door and glanced at Stephen. "I give you leave to tell my mother about La Flamme."

Stephen sprang to his feet. "Not I. I have done what I came to do. Any more that needs doing will have to come from you, Garreth."

The dowager duchess looked from her son to his friend. "Will one of you tell me what has happened?"

With a resigned intake of breath, Garreth approached his mother and sat beside her. "I met an actress who called herself La Flamme while I was in Paris."

She looked disapproving. "Did Sabine find out about the actress? Is that why she wants to end this marriage?"

Garreth called on all his tolerance. "Remember, Mother, how father was fond of saying that the Blackthorn name had never known disgrace? Because of me, we have known several disgraceful moments."

"What are you saying, Garreth?" his mother asked in a voice filled with dread. "Tell me what you mean."

"Very well. What would father say if he knew that his only son had been accused of murder and locked in the Tower, and that the present duchess of Balmarough had earned money by acting on a stage under the ridiculous name, La Flamme?"

Adrienne covered her mouth in shocked surprise. "Oh, the poor dear. She was forced to feed herself and her brother. I can understand why she might do such a thing."

Garreth scowled at Stephen, who could only smile. The dowager had such an understanding heart.

"She has suffered enough, Garreth," she continued. "You must go to Woodbridge at once and bring her home."

Garreth shook his head. "That I shall never do."

27

There was celebration in the village of Woodbridge, since the rightful lord now resided at the castle. Even though Lord Richard was only a boy, he had been joyously welcomed home, and it warmed Sabine's heart that he was at long last where he belonged. They spent many hours riding over the estate so Richard would become acquainted with his holding.

An uneasy two months had passed for Sabine. Each day she waited for word from Garreth—but none came. As she stood at the window of her father's study, she watched the first winter snowflakes drift into the courtyard below. She spent a lot of time in this room, trying to recapture the peace she had known in her childhood, but it eluded her.

Every day she went to the crypts where her parents had been entombed. She would kneel for a long time, immersed in prayer. Her prayers were mostly for Richard because he was still confused and a little frightened about the future.

Uncle Joseph had returned to France, and Sabine had been sorry to see him leave. Each day Richard was closeted with their Uncle Simon while he learned about the operation of the Woodbridge estate. Richard was also preparing to leave for Eton in three weeks. The Archbishop of Canterbury had been instrumental in enrolling him in school.

Ysabel came up to the window and glanced over Sabine's shoulder. "It doesn't look like it'll stop snowing today."

"No, it doesn't," Sabine answered. She moved away from the window and sat at her father's desk. "I once loved the winters here."

Ysabel had placed a tray on the desk, and now she handed Sabine a cup of tea. "Sabine, Thea has been brought home. When I admonished the coachman for transporting a person in such ill health in this weather, he said that she insisted on returning to Woodbridge, so he brought her."

Sabine set her cup on the desk. "How did she tolerate the journey?"

"Not well, I fear. I settled her in and took her some clear broth and hot apple juice, but she would have none of it. She keeps asking for you and insisting that she must warn you about someone. I believe she will not rest until she has spoken with you."

Sabine rose. "I'll go to her at once."

Ysabel was watchful. "I heard that a dispatch came today from Rome."

Sabine nodded to the table near the door. "Yes, it was from Father Santini, who put my case before the pope. The annulment is to be granted after I put my name to the papers. I must swear that Garreth and I have never been husband and wife."

"Are you prepared to distort the truth to gain your freedom?"

"I would have done that without the slightest guilt. But now I cannot sign the papers." Sabine gave Ysabel a troubled look.

"You have changed your mind and want to remain Garreth Blackthorn's wife?"

"No, it's something else."

Ysabel was mystified. "You were so sure you wanted the annulment. What made you decide otherwise?"

There was pain in Sabine's eyes, and she clutched her hands tightly, trying not to cry. "Something unforeseen has occurred, Ysabel. If the annulment is granted, that would leave my baby without a name."

Ysabel was clearly shocked. "Are you certain?"

"Yes."

"How long have you known you were with child?"

"I suspected since our return to Woodbridge—it took me longer to accept it. Then today I received the document from Father Santini. What shall I do?"

Ysabel leaned forward, her eyes probing. "You already know what you must do. This child is issue from your husband, and there must never be any doubt that it is his child. You will have to inform his grace."

"Yes, I know that. I wish it were not so."

"The sooner it is done, the better for all."

"What if Garreth insists that I move to Wolfeton Keep?"

"He will want the baby born in his home, and it is only right that it be thus."

Sabine looked dejected. "I have no desire to go to Wolfeton Keep." She walked to the door. "I must see to Thea, and then I will write Garreth, informing him about the child."

Ysabel shook her head as she watched Sabine leave the room. It was sad that Sabine was never to be master of her own destiny. First she sacrificed herself to a marriage she did not want—then she became an actress for her brother's sake. Now, she would be under the dictates of her husband because she was to have his baby.

Sabine entered the darkened room where Thea lay pale and listless upon her bed. The old nurse was so weak that she could hardly raise her hand to motion Sabine forward.

Sabine sat beside Thea, taking her hand. "Is there anything I can do to make you more comfortable, Thea?"

"There is no comfort for me. I am dying, and we both know it."

"I will not hear such talk, Thea." Sabine tried to sound cheerful. "I didn't find you again only to lose you. Do you want me to read to you? You once liked that."

"No, I must talk. I must . . . tell you about the night your father died."

Sabine tensed. She was afraid to hear what Thea had to say—what if she further implicated Garreth? "There is no need to speak of that night. It will only cause you distress."

Thea's hand tightened on Sabine's. "You must listen to me. You still have an enemy, and you must be aware."

Sabine froze, her heart pounding fiercely. This was not the ravings of a dying woman, but the terror of one who had loved her and Richard and feared they were yet in danger. "What is it you want to tell me, Thea?"

Thea's voice grew stronger with urgency. "That night the soldiers thought I was . . . dead. I heard them talking." Her eyes widened, and she tried to rise, but Sabine gently pushed her back against the pillow.

"Please do not speak of this now. When you are better we will talk."

Thea licked her dry lips, praying for strength. "Hear me! I must tell you what I overheard."

"Very well," Sabine nodded. She must know what Thea had learned that night, even if it proved Garreth's guilt.

Thea began to cough, and Sabine handed her a drink of water after the spasms passed.

She looked tenderly at Sabine. "I always knew in my heart that you were alive."

"We survived because of the chance you gave us, Thea."

"Listen to me, Your Grace. This is what I heard one of the men say that night. He did not guard his tongue because he thought I was dead—I very nearly was." Thea stopped as if she were gathering her fragmented thoughts. "I heard a man boast that they had made it look as if the duke of Balmarough was the guilty one."

Sabine's heart contracted. "Are you certain!"

"Yes. There is more. They said that the cousin had finally avenged himself against the duke."

Sabine felt tears of shame swimming in her eyes. Though she had fought against it, she had known in her heart that he was honorable. If only she had believed in his innocence, they might have been happy together. He had loved her, but she had killed that love, and now she must face the consequences—whatever they might be.

"You are not yet safe," Thea continued. "There is another who wished you harm. It chilled me to hear the man speak of some woman wanting your death."

"What did he say?"

"He said, her ladyship won't rest until the duke's wife is dead. He said . . . her ladyship'll want proof that the deed's done."

Sabine stared at Thea. "Garreth is truly innocent."

Thea nodded. "Aye, that he is. I told as much to the king's man long ago. Your husband did not have anything to do with your father's death, as we thought that night. He was betrayed, the same as you."

Sabine glanced upward so Thea would not see her tears. "For so long I have hated and feared my husband, believing that he was a villain. I have wronged him, Thea."

Thea's eyes took on a look of fear. "Beware of this woman who wanted your death. If she is yet alive, she may still wish you ill."

"I can think of no woman who would despise me that much."

"Be alert," Thea warned. "I can no longer watch over you. But you have a good watchdog in Ysabel. She has given me her pledge that she will protect you, and I believe her."

Sabine could see that Thea was in pain. "Rest now, dear Thea. Think only pleasant thoughts."

"Yes . . . I am . . . so weary." The old nurse's eyes became misty. "I can go now that I have warned you."

Sabine sat beside Thea long after she had fallen asleep, trying to make sense out of all that she had been told. What woman had plotted with Cortland Blackthorn to have her killed? Who would have hated her so much?

During the night, Thea died in her sleep, and the next day she was buried in the churchyard in the village. A large number of friends tramped through the snow to pay their respects, the duchess of Balmarough and the earl of Woodbridge at their head.

Sabine was haunted by the thought that she had wronged Garreth. Would he ever forgive her for tricking him? She thought not—and she did not deserve his forgiveness. Once she had held his love in her hand, only to kill it by humiliating him. A man like Garreth would not easily forget such a blow against his pride.

Three weeks had passed since Sabine sent a message to Garreth about the baby. Every day she expected to hear from him, but thus far there had been only silence.

Sabine was watching Ysabel fold Richard's woolen doublet and place it in the trunk. "You must prepare yourself to face his grace," Ysabel said, pausing. "You know he will want this baby—especially if it is a son."

"I would expect that. I wonder what I'll do if he decides to take the child and reject the mother. Already I love the baby that stirs within my body. I will never give it up, not even to Garreth."

Ysabel closed the trunk. "This is a muddle of confusion."

"The waiting is the worst," Sabine said. "If he had ridden here demanding that I go home with him, I would have understood that. Now I'm afraid that he might refuse to acknowledge the child as his."

"Garreth Blackthorn did not seem a man who would put his feelings in a letter. He will come in person, I think, and he knows that the child is his."

Adrienne Blackthorn closed the door to the study and approached her son. "Garreth, I want to speak to you."

He was seated at his desk and rose as she entered the room. "I wondered when you would approach me about Sabine, Mother."

"It's not only that. I am most concerned about this bitterness in your heart. You never told me all that happened in Paris, and I don't want to know. What concerns me is this change in you." She placed her hand on his arm. "You did not want to marry Sabine, but she is your wife, and she's going to have your child, so she deserves some consideration."

He glanced up. "She was my wife for exactly one night. The results of that night is this baby. If it were not for the child, we both know that she would have gone through with the annulment."

"I wish I did not have to ask this, but I must. Are you certain that the child is yours?"

"There is no doubt."

"Of course, forgive me for questioning, but I knew of no other reason that you would be so reluctant to bring Sabine here."

"Fear not, your grandchild will be born at Wolfeton Keep."

Adrienne could see the pain he tried to hide. "I have only seen you this disheartened one other time, and that was the night you promised your dying father that you would marry Sabine Woodbridge. I now realize that the marriage has forged your life, Garreth. Had I known the unhappiness it would cause, I would have objected to the match."

"It's hardly worthwhile to lament about that now, Mother."

"I suppose not," she said. "What do you plan?"

"I go to bring my wife to Wolfeton Keep."

She smiled. "Oh, Garreth, I'm so excited about the baby, and I have wanted to meet Sabine for a very long time."

When Garreth remained silent, she looked perplexed. "Tell me about her."

He shifted some papers on the desk, avoiding her eyes. "She is the most independent woman it has been my misfortune to meet—she is strikingly beautiful, witty, and charming. You will find her honorable and ready to fight for that which she believes to be right, no matter how misguided. After seeing her with her brother, Richard, I am convinced that she will make an admirable mother." His eyes bore into hers. "What else would you like to know about her?"

The dowager heard more in her son's voice then he realized. He sounded like a man in love. "You described qualities I would want for you in a wife."

Garreth moved around the desk and turned to the door. "I have this day received a summons from the king, asking me to come to London with all haste."

"He sends for you to speak of Sabine."

"I daresay," Garreth agreed. "I shall first go to Wood-bridge Castle, and then to the king."

Adrienne rushed to her son. "Be kind to her, Garreth. And remember what she has suffered. Would it not be better to wait until after the child is born to bring her here—the journey is a long one, and the weather is unpredictable this time of year."

"I'm determined that my child will be born at Wolfeton Keep," he said, the coldness back in his voice. "After that, Sabine can either stay or leave—I care not which."

Adrienne was stunned by the callousness of his words. "Why do you want to hurt Sabine? She was a child when she married you. Her mother died, her father was killed, and she had to flee for her life. Have some compassion for her."

"For her as a child, I have compassion. For the woman she has become, I have none."

"You will regret it if you do not rid yourself of this hardness in your heart, Garreth."

He smiled sardonically. "I regret many things, Mother, and I'm sure if I live long enough, I'll regret many more."

*   *   *

Sabine was instructing the butler on shining the silver when Richard burst into the pantry. "He's coming,

Sabine. A rider came from the village to warn us. He'll be here within minutes."

She didn't have to ask who Richard meant. "Is he alone?"

"I was told that there are two coaches and ten outriders accompanying him."

She moved out of the pantry, with Richard at her side. "I have ordered the gates to be closed and locked, Sabine. I will only admit the duke if you say so."

"Let us climb to the battlement. I will see this for myself," she said, not knowing if her heart was racing from happiness or fear. He had come for her, as she had known he would.

Remembering the raid on Woodbridge, the villagers were in a panic as a column of soldiers wearing the duke of Balmarough's livery rode swiftly through, heading for the castle.

When they reached their destination, they were met with barred gates. Richard and Sabine stood on the battlement, and Richard called down to them.

"What seek you here?"

Garreth removed his hat and looked at Richard, ignoring Sabine. "Good day to you, Lord Richard. I come to pay my respects to you, and to take my wife home."

"You have no jurisdiction here, Your Grace," Richard answered with an assurance that was unusual in one so young. Sabine had taught him well.

At last, almost reluctantly, Garreth looked to Sabine, and she saw a coldness there that made her shiver. Snowflakes were softly drifting earthward, and the whiteness was the perfect backdrop for the pale blue cape that Sabine wore.

"Madame," Garreth said stiffly. "I pray you accept my escort to Wolfeton Keep. It is there that I would have my child born."

Richard stared at Sabine, seeming much older than his years. "I will turn Garreth Blackthorn away if you don't wish to see him."

Sabine was silent for a moment. "Allow him to enter, Richard. Garreth has his rights. But you might want to ride into the village and assure the people that they have nothing to fear from these men."

Richard nodded. "If you are certain this is what you want."

Sabine looked into her brother's troubled eyes. "I am carrying my husband's child, Richard. I must do what is right for my baby."

He called down to his guard. "Open the gates to allow the duke and his men to pass through."

Richard took Sabine's arm and carefully guided her back into the castle.

The meeting she had been dreading had come at last.

28

As Garreth entered the castle, he was led down marble halls so bright that the chandeliers were reflected on the walls. He moved past tapestries that had been woven long ago. Vaguely, he noticed the display of weapons that adorned the ceiling, and the suits of armor that lined the curved walls.

Silently he followed the servant up the ornate Renaissance stairs to the second floor, where he was shown into a green and gold salon. "Her grace will be with you shortly, Your Grace. Is there anything you require?"

Garreth could tell by the man's stiff manner and the way he avoided his eyes, that he was mistrustful of him. "No, I require nothing."

After the servant had withdrawn, Garreth looked about the tastefully decorated room. Everything about it revealed the wealth of its young lord.

His attention was drawn to a portrait that hung

within a large alcove. Standing beneath it, he stared at the little girl pictured there, a dull ache in his heart. The artist had deftly captured Sabine's unusual amber eyes, that even at such a young age were melancholy and sad, and seemed to be looking at him accusingly. This was the Sabine he remembered from the wedding. How could he not have recognized her in Paris? The features were exact—it was so apparent to him now that Sabine and La Flamme were the same person.

Sabine's footsteps faltered outside the door while she gathered her courage to face Garreth. Stiffening her spine, she grasped the handle in her hand and the door creaked open.

He was standing beneath her portrait and turned to watch her enter, his face an unreadable mask.

She wore a modest brown velvet gown with a wide white collar and a matronly head covering. Her only jewelry was a gold locket he had so often seen her wear. Their gazes collided, and he swept her a bow.

"So, Madame, we meet again."

She moved to the hearth and held her hands out to the fire, hoping that if Garreth noticed them trembling he would think it was because she was cold. "You come because the king commands it?"

"He has commanded me."

There was wistfulness in her voice. "Garreth, it seems destiny has once again stepped in to dictate the course of our lives."

Sabine noticed no softness in his dark eyes, no sign of the love they had shared that last night in Paris. Instead they were as cold as the wintry snow that fell past the window.

As Garreth removed his leather gloves and tossed them on a nearby chair, he glanced at her stomach. He could see a slight rounding there and it gave him a rush of pride. Then his lips twisted sardonically. "It would seem, Madame, that in your haste to avenge yourself on me, you got caught in a trap of your own making."

She met his gaze, knowing that she deserved his contempt. "So it would seem." Was he happy about the baby? It didn't appear so. His manner was distant and detached.

"I have come to escort you to Wolfeton Keep."

He had been prepared for Sabine to fight him on this, but she merely nodded.

"I will come with you. I ask only that you delay our departure for two days so that I might see Richard depart for London."

"I could never deny you anything, Sabine. I feel sure it will take you that long to pack your belongings." He dropped down in a chair and watched her for a moment, softening his manner slightly at her acceptance of his demands. "My only concern is if you are able to travel in your . . . condition."

"I will not impede your progress."

"You are welcome to bring whatever servants and possessions you wish."

"You are most kind, Garreth." She attempted to hide the rush of heat that stained her cheeks because he was staring so intently at her. "As for servants, I will bring only Ysabel with me, although she is more a friend than a servant. I would wish her to be accorded the respect of my personal maid."

"As you wish."

"I brought the grays with me from France. I would like to take them with me."

"Ah, yes, the matched grays. Of course, you may bring them." He glanced toward the door. "Where is Richard—I had hoped to see him."

"He has ridden into the village to assure the people that your soldiers have not come to raid."

A muscle twitched in Garreth's jaw. "The villagers did seem to scatter into their cottages as we passed. I should have foreseen their fear and instructed my men not to wear livery. I ask your pardon for the oversight."

"It is of little consequence. They will believe Richard when he assures them that they have nothing to fear." She searched his eyes. "There is nothing to fear, is there?"

She watched fury ignite in the depths of his dark eyes and wished she could retract the words that had been spoken in anger.

"I may ever stand accused in your eyes. If you still judge me guilty, I'll put forth no defense. My good intentions and my family honor need no vindication."

Why hadn't she told him that she believed in his innocence?

Without a word, she moved to the bellpull, and a servant immediately appeared. "Please show his grace to his room, and send his valet to him." She turned to Garreth. "Be assured that your men have been properly housed. Richard and I dine at eight. You may dine with us if you like. Or . . . if you would prefer, I can have a tray sent to your room."

He stared at her intensely. "You are the perfect hostess. It will be my pleasure to dine with you and your brother." He loomed over her for a moment. "I have a dilemma, Madame. By what name do I call you: La Flamme, or Sabine? I seem to have difficulty separating the two in my mind."

She stared at the carpet. "La Flamme was an illusion. I am, and always have been, myself."

He bowed stiffly. "As you will, Sabine," he said. Then he left the room.

She had held herself rigid during their conversation—

now she collapsed onto a chair, her heart pounding and her mouth dry. She had made it past the first ordeal, and hopefully that had been the worst. Perhaps their meeting at supper would be less strained.

That evening, Garreth was shown into a room where the amber glow of the candles fell on the stark white marble floor. An elderly gentleman, dressed in finery that had been in vogue twenty years earlier, was conversing with Richard. They both turned their attention to Garreth.

"Your Grace," Richard said, smiling. "It is a pleasure to see you again."

Garreth walked toward the young lord, returning his smile. "That was not the impression I got when I arrived this afternoon."

"You will have to understand that I was only thinking of my sister. You would not now be here, if she had not allowed it. I pray you understand my feelings on this."

"I do, Richard. And I admire the loyalty you have for your sister."

The boy let out a relieved breath. "I am glad that you were not offended by my actions. I like you, Your Grace." He turned to the gentleman beside him. "Your Grace, may I present my uncle, Sir Simon Woodbridge?"

The elderly man looked Garreth over carefully. "I am pleased to meet you at last, Your Grace, and happy that this beastly affair is ending in a happy conclusion."

"Uncle Simon became earl in my absence, Your Grace. He was only too happy to rid himself of the title, though he will be remaining at Woodbridge to manage the estate while I am away at school."

Garreth glanced around the room, noticing Sabine had not yet come downstairs. "Very admirable of you, Sir Simon."

With a rustle of silk, Sabine swept into the room with

her head high. She avoided looking at Garreth, but she could feel his presence and knew that his eyes followed her.

Richard, knowing what she was feeling, went to her, and taking her hand, led her forward. She brushed her lips against her uncle's cheek and turned to Garreth.

"I trust you have found your quarters comfortable, Garreth."

"Indeed they are."

"I believe," she said, smiling tightly, "that we can dine now."

Garreth held his arm out to her and her golden eyes flashed, reminding him momentarily of La Flamme, before she veiled her gaze and placed her hand on his arm. She walked stiffly beside him, remembering a time when she had limped and he'd been forced to slow his steps to match hers. She glanced up to find him watching her, and it was most unsettling.

Sabine wondered how she would get through this night, and how she would sit at the same table with Garreth and make polite conversation.

Silver and gold dishes adorned the dining room table, while four sober-faced servants stood at either end of the room anticipating the family's every need.

Garreth was seated, as befitting his title, on Sabine's right. Richard was at the head of the table, and his uncle on Sabine's left.

Sabine forced herself to turn to Garreth, to engage him in polite conversation. "Was your journey a pleasant one?"

"Reasonably so, considering that a snowstorm struck but a day from our destination." He raised a glass of wine to his lips and then looked at her. "You should not concern yourself about the journey to my home. I have arranged for your every comfort."

"I look forward to meeting your mother. I remember well her many kindnesses."

"Unfortunately, that will not be for a time. My mother has decided to winter in Brighton."

Sabine could not hide the disappointment in her voice. "Oh. Is it because you told her about . . . Paris?"

He lowered his voice. "I did tell her about Paris . . . with exceptions. But that is not why she decided to leave. She believes that we should be alone to become better acquainted with each other—her words, not mine."

Sabine could feel her face burn. "You must try the leg of mutton *a la braise*, Garreth. It was my mother's recipe, and quite delicious. My father always boasted that Woodbridge has the best-tasting mutton anywhere because of the sweetness of our grass."

"Why, Sabine, you're a wellspring of domesticity. Only you and I know that you also have other talents."

She could only lower her eyes, wishing the meal would end. Soon the last course had been served, and she rose, leading the way to the salon. Richard and Uncle Simon were soon bending over a chessboard, leaving Sabine to entertain her husband.

She was seated near the fire and watched as Garreth moved about the room. He was restless, pacing like a sleek cat ready to spring on its prey. At last he came to her, and she motioned for him to sit beside her.

"You are not enjoying our hospitality," she observed.

"This is not your hospitality, Sabine. Woodbridge Castle is your brother's domain—Wolfeton Keep shall be yours."

"You are right, of course," she said stiffly.

He glared at her. "I don't trust this subservient act of yours. It makes me want to watch my back."

She deliberately folded her hands demurely in her lap. "Is it not a wife's duty to obey her husband in all things?"

"God help me, but I believe I liked you better the other way."

Some of the spark was back in her eyes. "What way is that, Garreth? Did you come here expecting me to defy you? Are you disappointed that I gave in so easily?"

"I merely don't trust you."

"I take that as a compliment. I would not want you to think I was commonplace and predictable."

He stared into the fire, the licking flames reminding him of her glorious hair. "I'd like to see the man who believes he can predict what you will do."

Wanting to put an end to the evening, Sabine turned to her brother. "Richard, it's your bedtime."

"Oh, Sabine," the boy groaned, but obediently came to her. "Why must I be treated like a child?"

She smiled, clasping his hand. "At school, Richard, they will be much more strict than I. They will not allow you to sneak a book and read after you are in bed."

"Very well. It matters but little that I am lord of this domain." He bowed to Garreth. "I will wish you good night, Your Grace."

"Good night, Richard. Now that we are family, why don't you call me Garreth?"

The boy beamed. "Good night, Garreth."

Uncle Simon moved toward the door. "I'm to bed, as well. I want nothing less than a warm fire in my hearth and a warming pan at my feet."

Sabine started to rise, but Garreth reached out, placing his hand on hers. "You are feeling well?"

"Yes, of course."

"Are you"—he seemed to be struggling with his words. "Are you very unhappy?"

"If you mean about the baby, I love the life I carry within my body."

"Even if it's mine?"

She stood. "I am tired, Garreth."

He come to his feet. "Forgive me, I should have realized that. You will have to understand that I have never been exposed to a woman in your condition."

"Stay and enjoy the fire if you like," she said hurriedly. "I will instruct a servant to light your way when you are ready to retire."

He turned his back on her and walked to the window. It had stopped snowing, and a bright moonlight gave the appearance of day. "Good night, Sabine."

Everyone had wisely allowed Sabine and Richard to be alone as he prepared to board the coach that would take him to London.

"I don't like leaving you, Sabine."

She tried to make light of their parting as she took him in her arms. "We shall soon be together again."

He relaxed against her and then pulled himself up stiff, trying to act grown. "You will take care of yourself, and let me know as soon as the baby is born?"

She smiled at him. "Of course."

"It is time that I learn to take care of myself."

"It is," she said sincerely, thinking how young and frightened he seemed at the moment. She touched his cheek. "Be diligent in your work habits; father would have expected it of you."

Richard studied the tip of his boot, and she knew he was trying not to cry. "I shall."

"Good-bye, Richard. Write as often as you are able."

He nodded and climbed into the coach, waving until he was out of sight. This was the first time she and Richard had been parted, and Sabine felt an ache in her heart. She reminded herself that he needed to be with boys of his own age and rank, but the ache would not go away.

Sabine pulled her woolen cape about her to protect herself from the cold. Not wanting to face anyone at the moment, she walked toward the meadow. She took the familiar path that she had trod so often as a child. This was her last day at Woodbridge, and she wanted to imprint each memory on her mind.

She passed stone barns that brimmed from a bountiful fall harvest, then continued toward high ground, where she could see all of Woodbridge. Glancing toward the castle, she watched threads of gray smoke curl skyward from numerous chimneys, then looked around at the meadow and hills. In the spring, they would be dotted with wildflowers but she would not see it.

Sabine didn't know how long she stood there taking in the beauty around her. It stopped snowing, so she pushed the hood off her head and allowed her hair to blow free.

At last, she turned to the frozen stream, remembering the night it had been a raging torrent that had carried her and Richard to safety. There were memories here that she would always cherish, and some she wanted to forget.

She shaded her eyes and glanced upward, where a brilliant blue seemed to compete with the purple storm clouds that hovered low in the eastern sky.

With a sigh, she walked toward the castle. She had one more place to visit.

Sabine entered the family crypt and went directly to her parents' tombs. Dropping to her knees, she paid her last tribute to her mother and father. She felt so alone with no one to counsel her about the future.

Lovingly she touched each cold stone crypt and then

walked out into the sunlight. Tomorrow she would leave for Wolfeton Keep.

She heard footsteps and turned to see Garreth approach. He took her arm, wanting to reassure himself that she was there. When she hadn't returned after Richard's departure, he had feared she had run away again. "You should go in now. It's bitterly cold."

She allowed him to lead her forward. "I hadn't noticed."

"You have to think of the baby, if you won't think of yourself."

She looked into his eyes. "Do you ever think of it?"

"That's why I'm here, remember?"

"Yes, of course. You came for your baby."

He looked away from her. "That is the tie that binds us, Sabine."

She was suddenly cold . . . all the way to her heart.

29

A bright sun was shining, and the snow had melted except for the places that were protected from the sun. Sitting beside Ysabel in the carriage, Sabine refused to look out the window for a last glimpse of the castle. The procession wound its way through Woodbridge. Many of the villagers came out of their cottages to bid her farewell. There were tears in her eyes as she waved back.

Ysabel tried to distract her. "I have never known such comfort. This is a well-sprung coach; we have fur lap robes, satin pillows, and foot warmers. I am content."

Sabine's eyes were still shining with tears as she looked at Ysabel. "It seems that my husband has provided every luxury. But how will I bear his coldness to me?"

"You brought out fire in him before, Sabine, you will do it again. Time and patience will be your weapons," the old woman said cryptically.

Sabine look at Garreth, who was riding beside the coach. He wore a black cape, and his long dark hair rippled in the wind. He looked not at her, but straight ahead. Oh, how she loved him. But he must not know.

"We were never meant to be husband and wife, Ysabel," she said sadly. "There are too many differences between us, and too many wounds left unhealed."

"You will meet him more than halfway and heal the hurts—the differences do not matter. I was nothing like my husband, and yet we were happy every day of our marriage."

"Garreth and I have been unhappy every day of ours."

Even Ysabel had nothing to say to that, for it was true.

It was nearing the noon hour when Garreth stopped at a small country inn. He helped Sabine inside, where he asked for a private room. She was soon seated before a warm fire as a maid served a luncheon of mutton stew, cheese, and fresh baked bread.

Garreth sat beside her, his gaze straying often to her face. "You are not overly weary?" he asked.

She met his eyes. "Not in the least. I'm strong."

He broke off a piece of crusty bread and placed it on her plate. "So I've observed. Nonetheless, I have instructed my captain to travel slowly and stop often to allow you to rest. Arrangements have been made at inns along the way to offer you shelter."

She looked puzzled. "Will you not be coming with us?"

"No, this is where I leave you. I must be in London by tomorrow. If there is anything you need, you have but to tell Captain Barkley."

She looked away so he would not see her disappointment. "You should leave at once. It is yet a long ride to London."

He stood. "Yes, I must." He worked his fingers into his black leather gloves and pulled his cape about his shoulders. "My servants will see you settled when you reach the Keep. Should you need to contact me, I'll be staying at Blackthorn House. Captain Barkley knows how to reach me."

She made no reply, nor did she look at him. In a move that surprised her, he took her arm and brought her up beside him. "Must you do this?"

She blinked her eyes. "Do what?"

"Damn it, do you sentence me to a life of contrition?"

She shook her head as his grip on her tightened. "I don't mean to."

"You submit too easily. What has happened to your unconquerable spirit?"

Now her eyes flamed, and her lips tightened. "Do not let my obliging manner lull you into believing that I am disposed to do your bidding, Garreth. I will go to Wolfeton Keep, and I will have your baby there—beyond that, I promise nothing."

He brought her closer to him, and she caught her breath at the smile that curved his lips. "This is the woman I know." He laid his face against hers. "What new method of torture have you devised for me?"

She wanted to rest her head on his shoulder and feel his arms about her. Instead, she turned away, moving back to the fire. "If you are tortured, it is not of my doing, Garreth."

"Is it not?" He abruptly swept her a bow. "When next I see you, it will be at Wolfeton Keep."

She did not watch him leave, but she listened until the sound of his footsteps died away. She wondered why she no longer fought him. She could have told him that she was weary from years of fighting just to keep herself and Richard alive. She now had the heart of a woman, and oh, it hurt so badly.

Picking up her cape, she left the room. It was yet five days to Wolfeton Keep.

Captain Barkley was most attentive and saw to Sabine's needs before they arose. The coach moved swiftly across the wooden bridge that spanned a meandering brook with large chunks of ice floating on the surface.

"Ysabel, I never expected to feel so strongly about Wolfeton Keep—It's somehow like coming home. Why do you suppose that is?"

"Perhaps you feel that way because you have known since you were young that this would one day be your home."

As the carriage topped a hill, she could see Wolfeton Hamlet. It appeared so natural in its setting that it seemed to be woven into the fabric of the land, as if it had always been there. In the distance, Sabine caught only brief glimpses of the huge castle nestled in a wooded area high above the village they were approaching.

"I can see by the architectural style that the village was built by the Normans. Look, Ysabel, instead of thatched cottages like at Woodbridge, these are built of limestone. There must be a limestone quarry nearby."

Ysabel looked with interest at the quaint shops with pointed roofs and gables. "I do not know about such things. But I see that the village prospers."

"Yes," Sabine agreed. "It is evident that my husband looks after his people."

The horses slowed their pace as they entered the village. She had not expected to find the villagers lining the cobble streets. The men removed their caps and bowed, while the women curtsied. Children waved and ran alongside the coach.

"What a wonderful welcome," Sabine said, waving through the window and smiling at the children.

"They will have been curious about you, since you are their lord's wife."

Captain Barkley smiled at her as she opened the window. "I believe they love you already, Your Grace."

She waved at the children until the village was left behind. Now the coach travelled faster, so Sabine leaned back and thought of her new home.

They sped through a maze of narrow lanes and then began to ascend a hill. The horses' hooves clattered over a narrow wooden bridge, then down a cobble roadway. Just ahead, the turrets, battlement towers, and clusters of Tudor chimneys of the great castle rose ghostlike through a winter mist.

The massive oak gates of Wolfeton Keep swung open to allow them passage through the arched gatehouse. The horses clattered over another wooden bridge that took them into the inner courtyard of the castle.

When the carriage came to a stop, Sabine was aided from the coach by a footman, and then alone she walked toward the castle.

Two servants stood on the steps—a man and woman. As Sabine approached, the man bowed and the woman dipped into a curtsy. The woman smiled, softening her angular face, and her gray eyes sparkled with warmth.

"Your Grace, I am Ida North, the housekeeper. This is George Brook, the butler. May I say what a joyous day this is for all of us? Welcome to Wolfeton Keep."

The butler bowed to her. "I shall see to your trunks, Your Grace."

"Thank you, Mrs. North, Brook." She indicated Ysabel with a nod. "This is Ysabel Agostino, my personal maid."

Garreth's butler and housekeeper looked at Ysabel with respect, and Mrs. North spoke. "Mrs. Agostino, we all stand ready to be of assistance to you in any way."

Sabine looked up at the wide double doors and climbed slowly up the steps. At last, after all these years, she had arrived at Wolfeton Keep.

The Lord Chamberlain pushed the door open and allowed Garreth to precede him. "Your Majesty, his grace, the duke of Balmarough," he announced.

Garreth approached the king and bowed. "You sent for me, Sire?"

"I did," Charles Stuart said heatedly. "I am pleased that you arrived promptly, even though I am not pleased with *you*, sir."

There was a cynical twist to Garreth's lips. "I would not want to be the object of my king's displeasure. Pray tell me what I have done, so that I might rectify it."

King Charles glared at him. "What you've done is most distressing to myself and the queen. You live at one place and your wife at another. I won't have it! I want both of you to reside at Wolfeton Keep, or else there will be those who will suppose that you cannot control your own wife."

"Then they would suppose correctly, Your Majesty."

Garreth's manner was deferential, but King Charles was not duped, for he recognized all too well that look of defiance in Garreth's dark eyes. "This marriage has been a millstone about my neck from its conception. Would that I had never insisted on this alliance."

Garreth's eyes darkened. "It distresses me that you are displeased."

The king looked sharply at Garreth. Again the words implied respect, the tone did not. "You will obey my order at once and take your wife to your home."

"Your Majesty, I would have brought the duchess with me if she were not with child."

"What say you?" King Charles' eyes lit up and he turned to his minister. "You did not tell me this. How can there be trouble with a marriage where there is a child on the way?"

"Sire," the minister answered, "we did not know that there is to be a child."

The king turned back to Garreth, in a jovial mood. "Your wife has consented to live with you and drop this silly nuisance about an annulment."

"That is so, Your Majesty."

Now that the king was satisfied that Garreth had taken his wife in hand, he became happier still. "How is the hunting at the Keep this year?"

"Stag hunting is good, Sire, but the boar hunting is better."

"I may be coming your way, perhaps late in the spring." He smiled. "Since yours is a marriage of my choosing, I would be most pleased to see it flourish. I'll have no difficulty with Lord Richard since he's under my direction and not the troublemaker his father was."

"My brother-in-law is but a boy, Your Majesty, and boys grow into men."

"True, true." The king stroked his beard for a moment. "Then we can assume this breech in your marriage is ended?"

"You can assume that, Your Majesty."

King Charles leaned forward so only Garreth could hear. "You were quite resourceful in bringing your wife about." Then he moved back. "You may take leave of us now, but expect us at Wolfeton Keep before the year has ended."

"We look forward to the honor, Your Majesty."

Garreth backed to the door, turned, and walked into the anteroom and down the wide steps. He did not see Eugenia Meredith until she stood in front of him, blocking his path, her eyes riveted on his.

"Garreth," she said breathlessly, "I could play coy and pretend that this is a chance meeting, but in truth, I knew you had been summoned by the king and I have watched for you."

"Lady Meredith," he said absently, sweeping his hat off and bowing to her. His mind was still on his conversation with the king, and the hardness in his eyes showed his displeasure.

"Does it take a king's command to bring you to London?" she asked, linking her arm through his.

Garreth searched Eugenia's face, trying to see what had attracted him to her so long ago. She had changed but little, and was still beautiful. She was dressed in a fashionable green silk cape. From the look of the jewels that sparkled on her hands, it was apparent she was doing well.

He removed her hand from his arm and stepped back. "It's always a pleasure to see you, Lady Meredith," he said, his distant tone disavowing his words. All he wanted to do was leave, but he smiled politely. "Time has been good to you."

"Always the gallant, Garreth. You do know how to flatter a woman. But it is hardly flattering that you act as though we are only passing acquaintances. Have you forgotten so easily how close we once were, and that you once called me by name?"

He had not seen her since the day he told her about

his marriage and she had made such a scene. "I remember, Eugenia."

His obvious eagerness to leave fueled her anger. He seemed totally unaware that two young ladies had moved closer, hoping to be noticed by him. Eugenia turned to glare at them, and they hurried away.

She looked over Garreth with a ravenous hunger. He was so dashing in deep blue breeches and doublet with hip-high boots. Loving him had cost her dearly, in money and hiding after Cortland was arrested. She had lived in fear that he would betray her, but he hadn't. Now she reached out for Garreth without fear. He still excited her as no other man could. She had to make him see that they would be perfect lovers.

"I know that you have not forgotten me, and I think about you every day," she purred. "I have heard that your little wife has been located. Is she still a drab little thing, Garreth?"

"If you will excuse me, Eugenia, I must leave."

Her lip trembled and her eyes grew teary. "What about us?"

He now looked into her eyes, and saw smoldering passion reflected there. "What happened between us burned out long ago, Eugenia."

"Liar! You know you love me—why not admit it?"

Garreth was feeling uncomfortable because her voice was beginning to carry to others. "I do not believe this is the place that we should be having this conversation, Lady Meredith."

Her hand tightened on his arm like a claw and she didn't seem to hear his words. "Many times I have ridden past Wolfeton Keep, hoping for a glimpse of you. Now you are here and I shan't let you go. Come with me so we might be alone."

Garreth shook her hand off and moved down a step,

hoping to discourage further conversation. "Eugenia, there is nothing for us—there never was. What I once felt for you was nothing more than a young man's foolish infatuation with a beautiful woman."

"Deceiver of women!" Her voice rose even higher. "You allowed me to love you and then left me as if I was nothing! I shall never forgive you for the humiliation I've suffered. Everyone laughs at me because you prefer a witless cripple to me. Not once did my plight cross your mind."

Eugenia became aware of the hardness in Garreth's eyes. He was no youthful lover who could be easily manipulated. He was a man now, cold and distant, and his aloofness only made her want him all the more. "You have not thought of me at all, and I have never stopped thinking about you," she went on. "I would have done anything for you, Garreth, and I have." There was such vehemence in her voice, such passion and hatred twisted together that it was difficult to see where one ended and the other began.

Garreth looked at the pitiful creature. How could he ever have thought he loved her? His eyes were smoldering with anger. "You are mad, Eugenia."

"If I am, 'tis your fault." There was desperation in her voice. "We belong together—you just don't remember how much we loved each other, before she came along. She is nothing—NOTHING!"

Garreth suddenly felt repulsed by her. "Good-bye, Lady Meredith. I do not expect we shall meet again." He turned and hurried down the steps, knowing that she was watching him. There had been something unsettling about her actions today. She was surely demented to make such a public display of her emotions. He had little doubt that their meeting would be the talk of London over morning tea.

He thought of Sabine, and it was like a cleansing breath sweeping through him. He wanted to see her, to touch her, to know that she belonged to him.

30

Mrs. North escorted Sabine into the huge anteroom that was decorated in Roman style. The ceilings
were coffered in gold and white, while marble pillars
trimmed with gold arched along the walls, and the armo-
rial glass windows running the length of the entire eastern wall were etched with the Blackthorn coat of arms.
Sunlight reflected through the amber and blue glass, giving that portion of the hallway the appearance of a vast
honeycomb.

"You must be weary, Your Grace," Mrs. North said. If
you will follow me, I shall show you to your chambers."

As they moved past ornate salons and formal rooms,
Sabine glanced inside, noticing that they were elegantly
furnished.

Climbing the stairs, Sabine could see out the high
windows to an enormous park beyond the courtyard.

This would be a lovely place to live and raise children. She had to keep reminding herself that she was mistress of this domain.

Mrs. North threw open a pair of wide double doors. Sabine went inside, looking puzzled. Highly polished wooden floors were partially covered by a green carpet, where deer and pheasants had been skillfully worked into the nap. The huge mahogany bed was carved with the Balmarough dragon. This was definitely a man's room— the master suite.

Mrs. North saw the question in Sabine's eyes. "His grace left instructions that you were to be placed in his chambers."

Sabine was too stunned to speak at first, and when she understood the significance of this action, she realized she could not object to the housekeeper. How dare Garreth assume that she would share his bed!

"Perhaps later you would like a tour of house?"

Ysabel came forward to pull down the bedcovers. "Not today, I think. Her grace must rest from the journey. She will dine in bed. Tomorrow will be soon enough for her to see the rooms."

"Of course." Mrs. North moved to the door and turned back. "If there is anything you need, you have only to ask."

Ysabel unfastened Sabine's gown as she asked the question that Sabine could not. "Have you heard when his grace will be returning?"

"We have heard nothing, Mrs. Agostino."

Sabine was glad her back was to the housekeeper so the woman would not see the disappointment in her eyes.

After the housekeeper departed, Sabine looked at Ysabel with defiance in her eyes. "I did not expect that I would be sharing Garreth's bed."

"You have it within your hands to win your husband. You now know that he is innocent of any wrongdoing. Do not turn away from him."

After Sabine slipped out of her gown and into her nightgown she got into bed and plucked at the gilded fringe on the coverlet. "Garreth has said little about the baby, Ysabel."

The wise old woman walked to the door, knowing well what Sabine was feeling. "I would think his first concern is with the mother of his child. And, he has put you where you belong."

Alone at last, Sabine moved out of bed and walked to the dressing room that was connected to the bedchamber by double doors. She lifted Garreth's green velvet doublet from a wooden peg to hold it to her cheek. She wished with all her heart that they could recapture the love they'd shared in Paris.

A servant led Garreth into the dining room, where Stephen was having breakfast.

"Have you eaten?" Stephen asked, motioning Garreth to a chair. "Try the salmon—it's quite delicious."

Garreth shook his head. "I dined hours ago. I was on my way home when your message reached me."

Stephen leaned back in his chair, watching Garreth. "I'm glad you came promptly."

"Your note said it was urgent."

"I never liked her, but I still can't believe she is that evil. It never occurred to me that she was so desperate."

"Stephen, are you going to tell me what you are talking about, or keep rambling on?"

"Eugenia of course. I supposed her infatuation for you would pass, as it had with all the others, but she only became more obsessed with you." Stephen lifted his cup to his lips but did not drink. "I heard about the scene yesterday. Everyone's talking about your meeting with her at the palace."

Garreth shrugged. "It was of no importance. Surely you haven't asked me here to talk about that."

Stephen took a sip of tea and wiped his mouth on a napkin. "What I'm trying to tell you, if you'll stop interrupting, is that Eugenia admitted to me that she was Cortland's cohort. She gave your cousin the means to hire assassins to execute the raid on Woodbridge Castle. To hear her tell it, Cortland betrayed her by trying to make it look as if you were guilty. The plan, as she saw it, was to have your wife killed so you would be free to marry her."

"Dear God, this cannot be," Garreth said. He felt an urgency to rush to Sabine. "I felt uneasy about my meeting with her yesterday—she was distraught, but to actually . . . no, she could not be guilty of that."

"I can assure you, Garreth, Eugenia was a party to what happened to the Woodbridge family. She brazenly admitted everything to me not an hour ago. I won't even repeat the threats she made before she went storming out. I tried to stop her, but her coach left before I could reach her."

Garreth's eyes narrowed in thoughtfulness. "Now everything becomes clear. When I was in the Tower the archbishop told me that there was a woman involved with my cousin. I never thought it would be Eugenia—I still can't believe that she would go to such extremes."

"Eugenia's dangerous, Garreth. She means to harm you, I believe through La Fla . . . er, Sabine."

"I'll see that she rots in hell!"

"No doubt she'll eventually come to that. My concern for the moment is that I can't locate her. I've had men looking for her, but she has disappeared."

Garreth came to his feet. "I care nothing for her. She had not entered my mind until yesterday when she created that distasteful scene."

"Therein, I believe, lies the trouble. As much as I could make out of her ranting, she fancies herself your true and only love. She believes that you will realize that you love her. She isn't rational, Garreth. I would watch your wife since Eugenia's threats were against her."

Garreth's jaw tightened. "She dared to threaten Sabine?"

Stephen nodded. "She vowed that if she couldn't have you, no other woman would."

Garreth moved quickly to the door. "I'm going home at once."

"Yes, that would be wise. I'll continue to search for Eugenia. I'll send a messenger if I locate her."

"Have you alerted the authorities?" Garreth asked.

"I wanted to talk to you first, as I was unsure how you would want to proceed. This will no doubt cause a scandal."

Garreth's lips thinned. "Scandal and I are old friends. Go to the authorities and tell them what you have told me. Inform them that I want Eugenia detained, and impress upon them that she is dangerous. Also tell the archbishop what you told me."

"Rest assured, I shall do that."

Stephen walked Garreth to the door and watched him mount his horse. "How fares La Fl . . . your wife?"

Garreth glanced up at the sky then back at his friend. "About the way anyone would fare who is where they don't want to be."

"Give her my respects."

"I shall."

*　　*　　*

Garreth entered the small salon, where he'd been told he would find Sabine. She lay asleep on the lounge near the window, with an open book clutched in her hand.

For a long moment, he stared at her. She wore a blue gown without adornment and he thought she had never looked more beautiful. Reposed as she was, he could see the swell of her stomach and once again felt a surge of pride.

Sabine awoke and stared into the eyes of her husband. "Garreth," she said, swinging her feet off the lounge and standing, "I didn't expect you today."

Amusement twisted his lips. "I couldn't stay away from you, Sabine. I hope you have come to feel that this is your home."

Her long silken hair fell across her shoulder as she bent to retrieve the book she had dropped. "I believe there has been a mistake. Mrs. North has put me in your bedchamber."

"It was not a mistake. She was merely following my orders."

"I desire my own quarters. I remained there merely until you came home because I did not want to involve the servants in our personal lives."

Tense moments passed before he spoke. "And if I refuse, what then?"

She gave him a mock curtsey. "I have been well brought up, Your Grace. My only aim in life is to please My Lord."

He took a step closer, so near to her that they were almost touching. He held his arm out to her. "Shall we go below and sup, Madame?"

She ignored his arm and walked stiffly to the door. As they descended the stairs, Garreth suddenly felt the weight of their plight.

*   *   *

"If circumstances had been different, Sabine"—Garreth began after a long silence—"if you had come to me as my bride when you were supposed to, I wonder, would we be happy now?"

"We shall never know. But I do not believe we are suited to each other."

A mocking smile touched his lips. "I remember differently."

She blushed and lowered her head, thinking the meal would never end. At last they retired to the green salon where Sabine was seated near the window, watching Garreth conversing with a servant.

"Inform Captain Barkley that I will see him in my study within the hour."

"Very good, Your Grace," the man said, departing.

"Captain Barkley was most courteous and helpful on our journey, Garreth," Sabine said. "He is to be commended for his attentiveness."

"He was only doing what he was told, Sabine. He is, however, a good man—which is why he is commander of my guards."

Sabine stood up and began moving nervously about the room, straightening a portrait, centering an ornate clock on a table, running her finger across the mantle as if looking for dust.

Garreth watched and guessed at the meaning of her actions. "You find life in the country tedious after Paris?"

"I hope never to see Paris again."

He looked skeptical. "Think well before you speak. Did you not like being adored as La Flamme?"

"I was wondering how long it would take you to speak of my past." She walked back to him and sat beside him. "It is well that we get this finished and done."

He glanced down at her. "I believe the lady is about to make a confession. Dare I hope she will explain to me why she left me in Paris with just a letter to untangle the web she had woven?"

"It would be futile to try and make you understand."

"Understand this, Sabine—no husband likes to think that his wife had been desired by hundreds of men."

"It wasn't like that."

"Was it not?"

"You are free to think what you will. I will not speak of it at this time. I'm going to bed, Garreth."

"To my bed," he reminded her.

She shrugged. "I am but your vassal, by order of the king—where else would you find me?"

He stood, taking her hand. "Where else indeed? Your charms are many, your faults few. After all, I can boast that I am the only man who ever bedded La Flamme. Pity we cannot post it, so I could be the envy of half the world."

"Mock me if you must, but know this, Garreth—I did what I had to do to survive, and I ask no one's pardon—not even yours. I kept Richard and myself alive for all those years, and that's all that mattered to me."

"It's true, Sabine, you did keep Richard safe."

A frown creased her brow. "I'm not even sure yet that Richard and I are safe, and I worry about him."

Garreth's muscles became taut. "Why should you think that?"

"Before my nurse, Thea, died, she told me what she had overheard the night my father was killed. One of the men boasted about how they had made it look as if you were guilty."

He searched her eyes. "Thank God you at last believe that I am innocent."

"I know that now, but I didn't know it in Paris."

His jaw tightened, and his dark eyes were piercing. "Did your Thea overhear anything else?"

"Yes, and this is the odd thing. The man were talking about a lady who wanted proof of my death."

This confirmed everything Stephen had told Garreth about Eugenia. "Did the men name the woman?"

"Thea said not. Perhaps it was one of your rejected lovers," she said in jest.

He moved away from her, his manner suddenly distant and cold. She had come too close to the truth. "I do not find humor in this."

Years of hurt begged to be put into words. "I once met one of the women who loved you. I still carry the scars of that encounter within my heart."

"I can't imagine who it would be, Sabine. When did this happen?"

"Not long after we were married. Your Lady Meredith staged an accident on the road by Woodbridge. I was unfortunate enough to come upon her."

He grabbed her arm, his fingers tightening on her tender skin. Garreth could almost imagine what had transpired at that meeting. If only he had known about it before, he might have prevented the tragedy that had taken place at Woodbridge. "What did she say?"

Sabine wondered why he had such an impassioned reaction to her confession. "It was of no importance—it happened long ago." Was Lady Meredith the reason he'd lingered so long in London? She jerked her arm free of his grip. "I received a letter from a lady who refused to identify herself. She considered that she was doing me a kindness by informing me that you had met with Lady Meredith while in London in a most public place—St. James's Palace."

"It took the gossips less time than I thought to get to

you." He wished he could tell her the truth. He was almost certain the letter she had received had been written by Eugenia herself. "May I see the letter?"

"It was offensive to me so I tore it into pieces and threw it into the fireplace."

"Your informant was less than honest if she believes that the meeting between myself and Lady Meredith was of any importance. Now I must ask you to excuse me, Sabine. There is something that requires my attention."

She watched him leave the room, his back rigid, his steps purposeful. Why had she mentioned Lady Meredith to him? It was evident that he had not wanted to discuss the woman with her. Slowly, and with a heavy heart, she ascended the stairs.

Garreth had been in love with her in Paris. Had her actions driven him into Lady Meredith's arms?

31

Ysabel was waiting to helped Sabine undress. She slipped a soft nightgown over Sabine's head and tied the laces at the neck. "You look very pale—do you want me to stay with you for a while?"

"No, I'll be fine. It's late and you need your rest."

Ysabel pulled the blanket down and watched Sabine climb into the high bed. Her eyes twinkled when she spoke. "When I was with my husband, we had very few arguments that could not be solved in the bed."

"Ysabel!" Sabine said in a shocked voice. "I am not in this bed to end an argument, but rather because my husband is a proud man and does not want the servants to know that we are not happily wedded."

Ysabel moved to the door. "Just think on what I've said."

*　　*　　*

Garreth took Captain Barkley into his confidence. "You understand that there may be real danger for her grace. Have several men patrol the woods daily, and post a man in the village to watch for Lady Meredith, should she pass this way. I do not expect trouble, but I am unwilling to take any risks. Allow no strangers through the gates."

"I will see to it at once, Your Grace. No one will get past us."

After Captain Barkley had departed, Garreth sat for a long moment, pondering his situation. Since learning of Eugenia's visit with Sabine before the raid on Woodbridge, he understood the extent of her madness. She would somehow try to get into the Keep, and he intended to stop her.

He considered warning Sabine about Eugenia, but decided against it. She'd already had enough upheaval in her life, and he had to think of the child she carried.

Garreth left his study and slowly climbed the stairs. His footsteps slowed as he reached his bedchamber. Instead he entered his dressing room, where he found his valet waiting for him. After he had dismissed his man, Garreth entered his bedchamber through the connecting doors.

There was but a single candle burning, and it appeared that Sabine was asleep. She had moved close to the edge of the bed.

He blew out the candle, and moonlight spilled into the room. Quietly, he eased himself into bed, smiling because he knew she was only pretending to be asleep.

"Good night, Sabine," he whispered.

"I won't allow you to touch me," she said, coming quickly to a sitting position.

"You are assuming that I would want to touch you, Sabine."

"I . . . you . . . then it is as I suspected, you are making me share your bed because you fear the servants will talk."

"Is that what you think?"

"Y-yes."

He smiled to himself. "Servants are great gossips. We must do all we can to keep them from learning all our secrets."

There was a long, poignant silence, and Garreth could feel Sabine's anxiety. "You have nothing to fear from me, Sabine. I'm not going to attack you."

She lay back against her pillow and squeezed her eyes shut. She had expected him to make love to her—why was she disappointed because he seemed uninterested in her? She stared out the window at the branches of the tall oak tree that swayed like dancing shadows in the wind. She tried not to think about Garreth, but he was so near, she could reach out and touch him.

The tension was so heavy that she could scarcely catch her breath. At last she spoke. "Did you see Stephen while you were in London?"

"Yes, he asked that I give you his regards."

"I often think of him. He was a good friend to me."

Garreth was surprised by the sudden feeling of jealousy. "He's enjoying the attentions of many young ladies. I believe before the year is over, he will have chosen a bride."

"Surely Stephen has not been ordered by the king to marry as you were?"

"No. Fortunately for him, the king has no particular interest in his marital situation."

She winced. "Unlike yours, Garreth."

"No, not like mine." She heard his deep intake of breath. "I was going to tell you in the morning that I spent an afternoon with Richard. I also spoke to his headmaster, who praised Richard and told me that he was his most promising student."

"Is he . . . did he seem lonely to you?"

"Yes, somewhat, but give him time, Sabine. I could see that he cultivated many friends."

"Thank you for seeing him."

"I asked him to come here in the summer, and he's agreed, although he feels obligated to go to Woodbridge first."

"I worry about him. After all, he's just a boy and this is his first time on his own."

"I never saw a more mature and responsible lad. You taught him well, Sabine. Now, let him stand on his own. He will soon face a great responsibility, and he needs to be prepared for that."

She held her breath when she felt him move, then her heart sank when she realized he had merely shifted his weight.

"Good night, Sabine."

She did not answer. Long after she heard the steady breathing that made her think he was asleep, she lay awake, wanting to reach out and touch him. She had wronged him so—and he must have suffered because everyone had believed him guilty.

She had never known a more honorable man than Garreth, and she was proud to be his wife. Turning slowly, so as not to wake him, she watched him sleeping in the faint moonlight. Her heart drummed inside her, and she thought it would burst from the love she had for him. At last, she could no longer resist the urge to touch him—he was asleep, he would never know.

Lightly she touched his face. She gasped when he gripped her hand and opened his eyes.

"You should not have done that, Sabine."

Roughly he slammed her body against his. "I vowed I would not touch you unless you wanted me to." His lips brushed through her hair, and his voice deepened. "The most difficult thing I have ever done was to lay beside you and pretend indifference."

She closed her eyes tightly as her skin tingled everywhere his lips touched.

His hand moved to the tie at her throat, and he yanked it, causing the nightgown to spread open and one of her breasts to fall into his hand. Gently he caressed it, sending shivers of delight through her every nerve end.

"Do you want me to stop touching you, Sabine?"

"Garreth, I was just . . ."

His fingers circled her nipple, and she could no longer speak. "You were just what, Sabine?"

She moaned, moving her head so her lips were near his. "Oh, Garreth, I don't know."

His hand slid up her arm. "Why did you come to Wolfeton Keep?"

"You ordered me to." Her voice was tremulous.

A slow smile curved his lips. "And you always do what you are told, my flaming-haired wife."

His mouth slid down her face and settled near her lips in a teasing kiss, while his expert hands moved enticingly across her body, touching every curve. He pushed her gown off her shoulders and nestled his lips between her breasts.

With every beat of her heart, Sabine gloried in his touch. She ached for him to master her body as he had before.

Suddenly he pulled back, his hand touching her swollen stomach. "Forgive me, for a moment I forgot about the child. I would not want to hurt you."

She pressed her hand on top of his. "Do you want to feel the baby?"

His eyes widened in wonder as he felt movement beneath his hand. There was a tightening about his heart that he could not understand. "The baby moves within a woman's body. I never knew this."

Gently, he moved his hand across her stomach, in awe of his own creation. "Now the child becomes real to me. I never thought about it as a living person."

At that moment, the child moved again. "'Tis a miracle!" he said.

As if he had no control of their movements, his hands moved to tangle in her hair, and he turned her face to him. "Is it so bad that you carry my seed within your body?"

"As you said—a miracle."

With silken words, he whispered in her ear. "I thought I would never hold you like this again."

She could not speak because her heart was so full, and she was enveloped by his warmth.

"But we have unfinished matters," he went on.

"What do you mean?" she asked, her hand gliding across his shoulder.

Garreth caught her chin and forced her to look at him. "Why did you leave me—the real reason?"

"I . . . had to."

"That is no answer."

"I was afraid of you." She raised her head, her eyes seeking his. "And I wanted to punish you."

He gently ran his finger over her lips. "Didn't you know that I could never have harmed you? And if you wanted to punish me, you succeeded."

She moved away from him, but he clasped her shoulder and drew her back. "I want you, Sabine, and you want me. It may not be love—call it what you like, but it's strong and it's real. I will have you if it will do no harm to the baby."

She melted against him, giving in to the urgency of his touch. "It will do no harm," she said, unmindful of anything but the desire that flamed in his dark eyes.

He rolled to his back, carefully bringing her on top of him to rest against his body. A thrill vibrated through her as he supported her while arching upward and sliding into her body. His movements kindled fire within her heart, and she surrendered breathlessly to his probing invasion.

Her fingers curled in his hair as she boldly pressed her mouth against his, drawing a moan of pleasure from him.

"Sabine, Sabine," he whispered, "you're in my blood, and I am in yours. We will never be free of each other."

Her lips parted to receive his kiss, and she groaned as he satisfied her aching body. She was unaware that he kept his raging desire under control, fearing he would do harm to her or the baby.

Searing passion carried her to dazzling heights. Her flesh tingled, her mind soared. This was where she wanted to be—this was what she was born for, to give and receive pleasure from her husband.

Long afterward, Garreth held her in his arms. Neither of them would speak, because there were no words that could express what had happened to them.

"It will be like this every time for us," he said at last.

"Yes," she agreed.

At last he sighed and untangled himself from her, turning his back. "Good night, Sabine."

She had the feeling that he had been waiting for her to say something—but what? "Good night."

Turning her head, she stared at moonlight spilling through the window and casting shadowy patterns across the floor, until at last her eyes drifted shut and she slept.

When she awoke, it was morning, and Garreth was no longer beside her. It was almost as if she had dreamed him.

Ysabel entered cheerfully, carrying Sabine's breakfast tray. She took in the tumbled condition of the bed, and smiled to herself. "The sun's shining and it feels springlike."

"It's warmer here than at Woodbridge, yet spring is still weeks away."

Ysabel propped the pillows up for Sabine and then placed the tray across her lap. "Have you and his grace plans for the day?"

"If his grace has plans, they do not include me. I feel time heavy on my hands. At Woodbridge, there was much for me to do. Here, the well-trained servants go about their tasks quietly and efficiently, needing no instruction from me."

"I suspect the servants have been trained by his grace's mother."

There was a knock on the door, and Ysabel opened it to Mrs. North. "His grace has instructed me to make ready the room across the hall for her grace. I've had the room cleaned and aired and a nice cheery fire is burning in the hearth. When you are ready, I'll have her grace's trunks moved."

"Very well," Ysabel said. "I will let you know."

She closed the door and turned to see the distress on Sabine's face. "Did you know about this?"

Sabine shook her head. "No." She looked down to study her hands. "It suits me well enough to have my own bedchamber. I am restless at night." She glanced up at Ysabel. "It's what I wanted, is it not?"

Ysabel knew Sabine was feeling dejected. "I daresay his grace is doing what he thinks will make you happy. You did demand your own rooms," Ysabel reminded her. "Should you fault him for honoring your request?"

Sabine pushed the tray aside and grabbed her robe. "I don't want to eat. I would like to bathe and dress now so I might see my new quarters."

Ysabel sighed, wondering if Sabine would ever allow herself to be happy.

Sabine's bedchamber was well furnished. Priceless tapestries adorned two walls. The bed hangings and curtains were of purple velvet, trimmed with golden fringe. The chairs and couches were of ivory silk, while a Turkish rug brought the conflicting colors into harmony.

Mrs. North told Sabine that after the wedding the dowager duchess had overseen the redecorating of the chambers with Sabine in mind. That was little comfort to Sabine, but she settled into her new suite with no notion why Garreth had banished her from his chamber after he had been so insistent that she share his bed. Had he meant to hurt her? If so, he had succeeded.

Never one to lament for long, Sabine busied herself in preparing for the baby. She selected the three rooms that had been Garreth's nursery, and began making them ready for her baby.

The bright moments in her life were when she heard from Richard. Lately his letters were filled with enthusiasm. He wrote of his many friends and his love of his studies. She was lonely for him, but she would see him in the summer. Winter had finally loosened its grip on the land and there was a promise of spring in the tepid breezes that swept across the fertile valley. In protected areas grass had begun to sprout and turn green, and the skies were blue and cloudless.

It was in March that Sabine received a letter from Garreth's mother stating that she would be arriving at Wolfeton Keep within the month. Sabine was happy and a little apprehensive—at last she would meet the dowager.

Garreth had been away for three weeks. He'd informed Sabine that the Archbishop of Canterbury had urgently requested his presence in London.

At night when she was alone, she agonized over the thought that Garreth might be with Lady Meredith. It was no more than she deserved, she admitted. After all, had she not driven him away with her pretended aloofness?

32

Archbishop William Laud stood with his hands clasped behind him, his face barely masking his concern as he conversed with Garreth. "This woman— this Lady Meredith must be located with all haste. Her actions are merely stirring up memories that are best left in the past. His majesty wants this entire affair over and done!"

"As do I, Your Excellency," Garreth replied, trying to be tolerant of yet another demand from the king.

"We have heard that Lady Meredith has made threats against her grace. I don't need to tell you what his majesty's enemies can make of this."

"You will forgive me if my first concern is for my wife. Assure his majesty that every precaution has been taken to protect her and to locate Lady Meredith."

"This is a pretty muddle."

Garreth was weary of trying to please the king. He had ridden hard to reach London, and had not seen a bed in two days. "If there is more we can do, Your Excellency, you will have to tell me."

"As you know, his majesty is in Scotland. He's asked that you remain in London until he returns. While you wait, we want you to make yourself visible. Accept every invitation, attend every ball. The lady will surely get word that you are in London and show herself."

"It might draw Lady Meredith out of hiding, and it could keep her away from Sabine," Garreth said. "However, I do not like to be away from my wife at this time. The birth of the baby draws near."

"I assume you have her well protected?"

"I do, Your Excellency."

"Then we shall set a trap for Lady Meredith; you, of course, being the bait."

Garreth crossed his long legs and stared at the archbishop. "I agree to your plan. But know this—I shall not tarry in London past two weeks."

William Laud picked up a quill, scribbling notes. "Where will I find you?"

"My London house, Blackthorn Hall."

"Be alert, Your Grace. This woman could be anywhere."

"I'll find her," Garreth vowed. "She has a debt to pay, and she'll pay it."

The archbishop saw the dangerous glint in Garreth's eyes. He would not want to be Lady Meredith if she fell into the duke's hands.

Sabine awoke and stretched her arms over her head, while she watched the first light of dawn reflect off the wall of her bedchamber. She struggled to a sitting position, which was no easy accomplishment. Her stomach was fully rounded, and she felt clumsy and awkward.

After she had breakfasted, she went to the nursery to make certain it was ready. As she ran her hands over the rosewood cradle that had been Garreth's, she tried to think of him as a baby. What had he been like—would her baby look like him?

Ysabel appeared in the doorway, her face flushed with excitement. "Her grace has arrived."

"Garreth's mother!" Sabine dashed down the corridor to her chamber and glanced at her reflection, patting her hair into place. "I had not expected her until next week. I look a sight."

Sabine picked up a lace cap and placed it on her head, hoping to look matronly. "I have wanted to meet her for so long, and now I am nervous. What if she doesn't like me?"

"She has gentle eyes," Ysabel said. "And I could tell that she is also nervous about meeting you. Perchance she is worried that you won't like her. She's waiting in the small salon."

"I'm ready," Sabine said, walking toward the door.

Slowly she descended the staircase, not wanting to take the chance of falling. She paused before the closed door of the salon with her hand on the handle, gathering her courage. Then she entered the room to find Garreth's mother standing near the window.

Sabine took a step, and the movement caught Adrienne Blackthorn's attention. She turned around, and Sabine looked into the kindest eyes she had ever seen.

"Sabine, my dear," the dowager said, rushing forward. "How long I have waited for this day."

Many times Sabine had pictured the dowager duchess

in her mind. She had thought of her as tall and imposing, not as the petite woman who now stood before her. Her dark hair was shot with gray, and her eyes were dark like Garreth's, but soft. She smiled sweetly, almost shyly, at Sabine.

"My dear, you are so lovely. I knew that your hair was red, although I have never seen that particular shade before—it's magnificent. Oh, would it not be marvelous if you have a daughter with your hair?"

For some reason, Sabine wanted to cry—her mother-in-law's kindness overwhelmed her.

Adrienne Blackthorn hesitated for only a moment before she enfolded Garreth's wife in her arms. She could feel Sabine relax against her and tightened her arms around her.

"Your Grace, I am so glad to meet you at last."

Adrienne held Sabine away. "Let me get a closer look at you." She touched a red curl. "You cannot guess how happy I am about the baby. I had begun to despair that I would not hold Garreth's child in my arms before I died. And, of course I wanted to know you."

"I feel we already know each other," Sabine said hesitantly. "Your letters were always such a comfort to me, Your Grace."

"No, no—we will have not titles here, Sabine. If you call me Your Grace, I shall have to call you Your Grace, and what a muddle that will be. Can we not be Sabine and Adrienne?"

Sabine drew in a relieved breath. "I would like that, Adrienne."

"Where is that son of mine?" she asked, looking toward the door.

"I'm sorry to tell you that he's in London. Had he known you were coming, I'm sure he would have been here."

"That suits me. This will give us a chance to get to know each other without interference."

Sabine could not help but laugh. "Are you weary from your journey? Would you like to rest?" Then she hesitated. "I should not have asked you that, this is your home."

Adrienne took her hand. "No, my dear. You are now the mistress of Wolfeton Keep. I am but a guest, and that is as it should be. In truth, I have been looking forward to moving into the dowager house across the park. It's quite lovely, much smaller, and easier to manage."

"But—"

Adrienne shook her head. "No argument. I have always wanted to travel, and now I have the time. Would you deny me that pleasure?"

"No, of course not. But you will not leave until the baby is born, will you?"

Adrienne's eyes were shining, and she looked relieved. "Not if you want me with you."

"Oh, yes, please—I would very much like to have you with me. I know so little of giving birth. In truth, I'm sometimes frightened of having this baby alone."

"Then, my dear," Adrienne said, removing her hat and tossing it on a chair, "I shall be happy to stay. Truth to tell, I would have been disappointed if you hadn't asked me. I believe you and I are going to be great friends."

Sabine found Adrienne Blackthorn to be every bit as charming as her letters. So it was that the two Blackthorn women settled down in Wolfeton Keep to await the birth of the baby, and the return of the man they both loved.

*   *   *

Sabine had been having sharp pains in her back all morning, but had not mentioned it, thinking it would go away. Now it was getting worse as she and Adrienne walked in the garden.

Suddenly Sabine paled and gasped for breath, clutching her stomach.

Adrienne took her hand, clearly worried. "My dear, is it the baby?"

"I believe so." She gritted her teeth. "The pain is . . . intense." Sabine licked her dry lips. "Adrienne, it's too soon. The baby is not due for yet another month."

"Nature has a way of bringing this about. Try not to distress yourself, my dear. It would seem that I perfectly timed my visit."

Adrienne helped Sabine to a bench and then hurried through the kitchen door, calling for assistance to get Sabine to her bedchamber. When she returned to Sabine, she found her doubled over in pain.

Ysabel and Mrs. North entered the garden and the three of them helped Sabine into the house, up the stairs, and into bed. The physician was sent for, but he was away, and it was doubtful he would return in time to deliver Sabine's baby.

Adrienne watched Sabine doze between pains, and she raised troubled eyes to Ysabel. "What shall we do? Should we send for the village midwife?"

"I will attend her grace," Ysabel said with assurance.

The dowager looked doubtful. "Are you capable of delivering a baby?"

"Be not concerned—I know what is to be done."

"Very well. Between the two of us, we will see Sabine though this."

Ysabel touched Sabine's stomach. "She has suffered so much in her life, Your Grace. Would that I could bear this child for her."

"She is dear to you."

"Indeed, Your Grace."

At that moment, Sabine moaned and opened her eyes. She tightly gripped Adrienne's hand until the pain subsided.

"Rest when you can, my dear," Adrienne urged her. "You will need all your strength."

In a haze of anguish, Sabine looked frantically about the room. "Ysabel—I want Ysabel!"

The old woman came to her. "I am here—all is well."

Sabine sighed and seemed to relax. On into the night she labored. When the first streaks of dawn lit the sky, she gave birth.

Ysabel gently handed the child to the dowager. "'Tis a girl."

Lovingly, Adrienne wrapped her new granddaughter in a soft blanket and then cradled her in her arms. "I have never seen a birth where the baby does not cry," she said, softly kissing a tiny fist. "You are a wonder, Ysabel."

Ysabel did not hear her. She was watching Sabine with troubled eyes. "Is there still pain?" she asked.

Sabine rolled her head and tried not to cry out. "Ysabel, help me!"

Adrienne handed her granddaughter to Mrs. North and came back to Sabine. "What's wrong?"

"She should not be having this pain. Wait!" Ysabel cried in amazement. "What's this? There's another baby. Why did I not see this?"

Several minutes later, a second child was born. Ysabel was smiling happily as she handed the baby to Adrienne. "Your Grace, you have a pair of them. This one is a grandson."

Adrienne was so happy she was crying. She moved to Sabine, a baby nestled in each arm. "Garreth will be so pleased about these beautiful babies! He is the father of a beautiful daughter and an heir. God be praised—twins!"

Sabine smiled and touched each soft, downy head. "I cannot believe twins!" She felt happiness bubble up inside her, and a strong motherly love for the tiny infants.

"You must rest now, my dear," Adrienne told Sabine. "The long ordeal is over."

Weakly, Sabine turned her face to the wall as the sleeping draught Ysabel gave her began to take effect. There was a smile on her face as she drifted off to sleep.

Garreth greeted Captain Barkley, who had just come from Wolfeton Keep. "Is all well?" he inquired.

"Yes, Your Grace," the captain said, trying not to look pleased at the news he was delivering. He was told not to say anything until the duke had read the letter.

Proudly, he handed his grace the letter. "It's from her grace."

Garreth looked puzzled when he saw the handwriting. He had supposed it would be from Sabine. "My mother?"

"Yes, Your Grace."

"Does it require an answer?"

"I believe so, Your Grace."

Garreth broke the seal and read to himself.

My Son:
This is a glorious day, because before dawn, Sabine gave you two precious gifts of life. Yes, my dear Garreth, you not only have a lovely daughter, but a son as well. Twins! They are small, but appear to be healthy. You

can imagine our dilemma. Now we need two of everything. Be joyous in your heart, for this is a great day for the Blackthorn family.

Garreth reread the letter to make certain that he had not misunderstood. "A son *and* a daughter?"

Captain Barkley was smiling widely. "Yes, Your Grace. The Keep is buzzing with activity, and there is much pride in the village for the new little lord and lady. The church bells rang for an hour, announcing their births."

Garreth was stunned by the unexpected event. Then he smiled proudly, wishing he could shout the news to the whole of London—he was a father! A Blackthorn heir and a daughter had been born! He found himself anxious to see them.

Stephen entered the room just as Garreth was giving Captain Barkley instructions to saddle his horse. When Barkley left he spoke to his friend. "I'm going home. You watch for Eugenia here. I must be with Sabine and the babies."

Stephen's eyes widened. "Did you say babies?"

It was clear that Garreth's mind was on other matters. "Yes, Sabine had twins—a boy and a girl."

Stephen slapped him on the back. "This is wonderful! Imagine you a father—and twins, no less." Stephen was grinning. "Your wife can never do anything the ordinary way, can she?"

"It would seem not."

"My compliments, my friend!"

There was a sudden urgency in Garreth's manner. "I must leave now. If Eugenia hears of this, there is no knowing what she might do."

"Yes, go home, Garreth. I'll send word if I hear anything more about Eugenia."

*   *   *

Sabine was recovering under the watchful eyes of Ysabel and Adrienne. Three wet nurses had been engaged, and Adrienne had miraculously rearranged the nursery to accommodate both her grandchildren.

It was long after dark, and Sabine had heard the clock chime the ninth hour. She entered the nursery and spoke to the nurse. "I'll take my daughter. You may leave us alone."

The nurse thought it was too soon after the birth of the twins for the duchess to be out of bed, but she dared not say so. "As you wish, Your Grace."

Sabine lifted her crying daughter in her arms and walked back and forth across the floor, attempting to quiet her. She paused to glance at her son, who had his little knees drawn up under him and was sleeping soundly.

"Sweet one, why can you not be good like your brother? See how well he sleeps, even through your crying?"

The sound of her voice seemed to calm her daughter, and the infant nestled against her.

Garreth stood in the darkened doorway with a tightening in his chest. Nothing had ever touched him as deeply as the scene he was witnessing. Sabine wore an emerald green velvet dressing gown, and her glorious red hair spilled down her back. Her beautiful face held a new maturity, and he caught his breath at the softness he saw in her eyes when she hummed softly to the baby. He suddenly wanted her to look at him with that same softness.

"Truly the little mother," he said, stepping into the room.

Sabine could feel her heart beating in her throat. "I . . . did not expect you."

His voice sounded detached. "You did not think I would hasten home to you?"

Their eyes locked, and there was a long silence.

"I think you did not return to see me, Garreth."

He moved closer, wanting desperately to catch a glimpse of the baby she held in her arms, but somehow reluctant to show his feelings. He stopped several paces from her. "I suppose you will scold me for not being here when the babies were born."

"I shall neither admonish nor advise you. In your defense, you could not have known they would be born early. I say only this to you; they are your son and daughter—flesh of your flesh—that should mean something to you."

Did she not know how proud he was of her and his babies? Could she not see that he wanted to reach out and touch her flaming hair, to touch his lips to hers, to hold her to his body until the trembling inside of him ceased?

"I have a great interest in their welfare," he said at last.

By now the baby was sleeping, and Sabine laid her in the cradle. Garreth looked from one baby to the other. He moved closer and reached out to touch a soft head.

"I have much to learn. I never knew babies could be so small." He was shaken with an unbelievable feeling of pride. He had not expected to feel this strongly about his son and daughter.

"They are smaller than most because they were born early."

"Mrs. North informed me that was usual with twins."

"So I am told."

"Which one is which?"

"The one you are touching is your daughter." She nodded to the other cradle. "That is your son."

He moved to stand over his son and took the tiny balled fist in his hand. "It is hard to imagine that he will ever grow as tall as I."

"He will though, Garreth."

"What are their names?"

"I did not name them because I was sure that you might want to use family names."

"A thoughtful gesture." He moved in a leisurely way to her side. "We shall decide their names together. Do you have any preferences, Sabine?"

"I would like to name our daughter after my mother and yours. Of course, you will want a family name for our son."

He reached out and laid his hand on her arm. "I have a vague memory of your mother, having only seen her twice, and then for such a short time. She was very beautiful. What was her name?"

"As you know, she was French. Before she married my father, she was Lady Ryanne de Chavaniac."

"A lovely name." His eyes moved to his daughter. "Lady Adrienne Ryanne Blackthorn. Yes, I like it."

"I would like to call her Ryanne."

"Lady Ryanne Blackthorn. Yes, that will be her name." Garreth moved to his son. "My father's name was very English. Have you any objections to Edward Thayne Blackthorn, the eleventh marquess of Huntley?"

She looked down at his hands that were clasped on the rung of his son's cradle. She remembered how it felt to have those hands hold and caress her.

With relief, she nodded. "It's a good name. I like it." She moved to the door. "Good night, Garreth."

"Yes," he said watching the way the candlelight glinted on her hair, and wishing he dared touch the soft tresses. "I suspect you should not yet be out of bed. I believe it takes time for a woman to heal from childbirth."

"I am strong, Garreth."

He turned away from her and muttered under his breath. "I have known that about you."

She left and made her way to her room, wishing she was as strong as she pretended. All she had wanted to do was run into his arms and have him hold her, until the fear and uncertainty went away.

33

Adrienne found it difficult to leave her grandchildren. She held each baby, kissing them tenderly, and then handed them to their nurse. She brushed a kiss on Garreth's cheek. "Take care of yourself and this lovely family."

He smiled. "I shall, Mother."

She turned to her daughter-in-law. "I'll miss you, Sabine. You have become very dear to me."

Sabine tried not to show her sadness. "I shall miss you, Adrienne. Have a lovely holiday in Florence, but return to the Keep soon."

Adrienne bent close and whispered in Sabine's ear. "I'll give you and Garreth the summer to make things right between you, and that's all I can promise. I have become attached to my grandchildren, and I fear I shall make a nuisance of myself."

Sabine kissed her mother-in-law's cheek. "You could never be that."

The dowager duchess climbed into her coach and waved good-bye.

"I shall truly miss her, Garreth. Your mother is an extraordinary woman."

He was offering his finger to his daughter and smiled at the child when she clasped it. "Yes, she is. As are all the women in my life."

"I believe we should get the children back to the nursery now that they have seen their grandmother on her way. I think I shall go riding. I haven't ridden since the babies were born."

Garreth looked at her quickly. "Take Captain Barkley with you."

Sabine waited until the nurses carried the babies inside before she answered Garreth. "I don't need an escort," she said haughtily. "Are you afraid I might run away again?"

He was still reluctant to tell her about Eugenia's threats. "It had crossed my mind."

Sabine was glaring at him. "Whereas I might leave you, I would hardly leave my son and daughter."

His jaw settled in a stubborn line as he looked at her. "Nevertheless, you will take Captain Barkley with you."

She drew in an angry breath, but said nothing more. With her head high, she moved quickly toward the stable, thinking Garreth was still trying to punish her. He never allowed her to go out alone. Was he really concerned that she might leave?

Garreth watched her for a moment, then went inside and climbed the stairs to the nursery. The wet nurse smiled at him. "Her little ladyship won't go to sleep, Your Grace."

He peered at the child, who was rosy and healthy. "So it would seem."

"They are beautiful babies, Your Grace."

She held the child out to him, and he hesitated for only a moment before he took his daughter from her. He smiled down at the tiny girl who wriggled in his arms. "I believe she knows me."

"Of course she does, Your Grace. If you don't mind my saying so, your daughter does not eat like a lady, and can even eat more than her brother."

Garreth smiled at the little cherub face. For the first time, she smiled at him and his heart was so full he could not have spoken at that moment.

His son chose that moment to howl loudly. Garreth handed his daughter to the nurse and lifted the boy in his arms. When he held his daughter there was softness in his eyes, but when he held his son, pride ripped through him.

"So you thought your sister was getting all the attention and decided to protest, my son?"

The tiny Lord Blackthorn stopped crying at the sound of the deep voice, and looked right into his father's eyes. For just a fleeting instant, Garreth had the sensation that he was looking into Sabine's eyes, though he could not have said why. "They seem to grow more alert every day."

The nurse chuckled. "They are quite alert for only eight weeks old, Your Grace."

He placed his son back in the cradle and looked at each child before leaving the room.

The nurses and the servants were aware of his frequent trips to the nursery. For some reason he always came when the duchess was absent.

*　　*　　*

The night sky seemed on fire as jagged spears of lightning shattered the darkness. Sabine tossed on her bed in the thralls of a terrifying nightmare. She was reliving the night she had fled Woodbridge. She was running, running, trying to save Richard from death. "No," she moaned aloud, "NO, THEA!"

She sat up in bed, her heart pounding, her gown wet with perspiration. She took several steadying breaths, wishing she could rid her mind of the fear.

Suddenly a shaft of lightening struck with a force that rattled the windows and shook the ground. Without thinking she jumped out of bed and ran for the one pinnacle of safety—Garreth. She burst into his bedchamber to find him sitting in a chair with papers spread on his lap.

He came to his feet, seeing her stricken face.

"Sabine?"

"I—the—storm. I—"

He held out his arms, and she ran to him. His arms closed around her like a soft band of protection against anything that might harm her.

He could feel her tremble and sensed her fright. "Did you have a bad dream?"

She could only nod.

"I won't let anything, real or imaginary, harm you."

She nestled her head against his chest as the sound of the steady beat of his heart calmed her. She raised her head and looked into soft eyes.

"I feel ashamed. It—was like the night at Woodbridge."

He lifted Sabine into his arms and carried her to his bed where he laid her down, then pulled the covers over her. Sitting on the edge of the bed, he took her hand in his. "You have no reason to feel ashamed, Sabine. You have more courage than ten men." He brushed a wayward curl from her face. "I'm glad you felt you could come to me."

She swallowed several times but could not speak, and he could see that her terror was real. "Do you want to sleep with me?" he asked.

She nodded.

He closed his curtains so she could not see the storm and blew out the candle before getting in bed beside her. Gently he pulled her into his arms. "Do you want to talk about it? We never have, you know."

"I often have the dream. It's like living that horrible night over and over."

He cradled her against him. "You spent the night in the flooded stream, with a broken leg, and yet you managed to keep your brother from drowning. I know of no one so brave, Sabine."

His praise warmed her. "I was not brave—I was frightened."

Garreth touched his lips to the pulse beat just below her ear. "You even faced me, Sabine, thinking I was the one responsible for the tragedy."

"I . . . know the truth now. But I am sometimes frightened, Garreth, knowing that I still have a faceless enemy."

He tensed. "What do you mean—what enemy?"

"The woman, whoever she is, that wanted me dead. I have tried to tell myself that she was only an imaginary danger invented by Thea's confused mind."

His arms tightened about her. "Don't think about it now." He tried not to think of the soft curves pressed against him. What Sabine needed was understanding, not his unbridled passion. "Suppose we speak of something pleasant, Sabine."

She raised her face to him, although it was dark and she could only see his outline. Dare she tell him what had been bothering her since the birth of the children? There would never be a better moment than now when he was gentle and understanding. "Garreth, I want to have my children christened by Father Santini as soon as possible."

She felt him tense. "My children will not to be brought up Catholic, Sabine. The difference in our religion has a new wrinkle, does it not? It reaches out for our children."

She had to make him understand how deeply she felt about the christening. "I implore you, Garreth, allow me to have them christened, and I will speak no more about this with you. I know no peace, fearing that my children may lose their immortal souls. If you allow this one thing, I will ask nothing more of you."

"You ask much, Sabine."

Desperate words ached to be spoken, but she must keep calm. "Can you not guess how I feel about this matter, Garreth?"

He could. He still carried an image of her kneeling in the chapel in Paris. That day he had watched her without her knowing it, witnessing her devoutness as she had prayed. Finally he relented. "I shall allow the christening only if you have the priest come to Wolfeton Keep for the rite."

Sabine could hardly believe that he had agreed so easily. "I will send for Father Santini tomorrow. Thank you, Garreth."

He stroked her upper arm. "Would that all your wishes were so easily satisfied, Sabine. But mark this well, I only agreed to a christening. I will have no Catholic priest dwell within Wolfeton Keep."

Sabine knew this decision had been a difficult one for Garreth, and she would press him no further at this time. "It will be as you wish."

In gratitude, she moved forward and brushed her lips against his cheek, then pressed her face to his.

He took in a deep breath as the sweet smell of her dulled his mind. "Sabine, I brought you to my bed to render comfort, but if you continue what you are doing, I'll be more than a comfort to you," he warned.

Daringly, she turned her body to his, pressing her thighs against him.

His breath was hot against her lips. "Do you tempt me, or strive to make me mindless?" His arms went around her, and he positioned her tightly against him so she could feel him throbbing against her aching body. "Is this what you want of me?" he asked, his hands tangling in her hair as he brought her face to his.

"Yes," she answered breathlessly, offering her lips to him.

"I want you, and you want me—beyond that I dare not question," he said.

There was only a groan from her as he rolled her over, parted her legs, and rising, slid into her, the hotness of him burning into her mind.

His mouth caressed hers, while his body mastered her trembling flesh. Murmuring her name, he rubbed his lips against her and then deepened the kiss with a bruising force. She sensed that he was trying to hold back, and she knew he feared he would hurt her.

"Garreth, I am healed from the births," she whispered.

With a painful intake of breath, he drove deeper, his hips moving against her in such a way that invited her movements. Her body was singing in perfect harmony with his, and she knew that something out of the ordinary was happening to them. This was beyond lust and body hunger—it was love—a need for possession and total surrender.

Garreth was unaware by what name he called her.

"La Flamme, now I possess you as you have possessed me. You are mine at last."

Her hands slid over the corded muscles of his back. And she was unaware that she answered him in French. "*Oui*." She looked deeply into his eyes. "*Oui*, I am yours."

With excitement raging through their bodies, they breathlessly rode the wave of passion, spiraling upward to a height obtained by so few. They moved together, breathed together, and at last, reached a quaking satisfaction together.

He held her tightly until her body ceased to tremble. "You will no longer sleep apart from me," he said in a soft voice.

"Never."

He pushed the soft curtain of her hair aside and lay his lips inches from her mouth. "You are mine."

"Yes."

There was no need for further words.

Garreth cradled her tenderly against his heart until she fell into a peaceful sleep. Long after she slept, he held her, amazed that she had surrendered so easily. There was still trouble between them, but tonight she had come willingly into his bed.

His lips touched her brow. "You will no longer have the nightmares. I shall keep them at bay."

She sighed in her sleep and curled tighter into his embrace.

Garreth did not attend the christening, but then Sabine had not expected it of him. Little Ryanne cried when Father Santini anointed her with water, but Thayne merely looked bored. Afterwards, Sabine felt a great weight lifted from her shoulders. At last, her children's

immortal souls were not in danger. In her heart she
thanked Garreth for his kindness in allowing it.

Sabine's life had settled into a familiar pattern.
Garreth was away most of the day, and she was now
confident enough to take over the duties as mistress of
Wolfeton Keep. She was glad that her mother had
trained her well. When she had doubts about anything,
she followed her mother's example.

At night, Garreth would take her in his arms and
she would welcome his touch. But after their bodies
had been satisfied there was always a wall of silence
between them. The tension was building, and uneasiness hung in the air. Something had to happen soon—
they could not continue as they were for much longer.

Sabine's mornings were spent directing the housekeep-
ing, inspecting the kitchens, and making menus for the
coming week. In the afternoon she could always be
found in the nursery with her children.

The weather was wonderfully pleasant as the mild
days of spring held the hot days of summer at bay. Sabine
was seated on the floor of the nursery, with Thayne on
her lap. He laughed and gurgled at her, while tugging at
a red curl. He squealed with delight when she held him
above her head, singing an old French song.

Garreth stood in the doorway, observing the domestic
scene. Sabine had been more than he'd expected in a
wife. Under her watchful eye, his home ran smoothly,
and she always found time to be with his children.

He came into the room and took his son from her.

"He grows stronger every day." He nodded to his
sleeping daughter. "I believe she has our son as baffled
as her mother has baffled her father."

Sabine's calm gaze met his. "You are mistaken. Our

son has a strong mind; he is merely patient like his father and allows his sister the greater part of everyone's attention."

He looked at her in surprise. "A pretty compliment?"

"Your tolerance is what I admire most about you. Of course, there is a point when you reach the end of your patience, and anyone who would test you beyond that is a fool."

He laughed. "You have ofttimes tested me to the limit, Sabine."

She decided to change the subject. "Can you tell them apart? They look very alike."

"Of course. Thayne's hair is noticeably darker than Ryanne's, and he is slightly larger. While their features look identical to most people, I can distinguish them with no trouble."

Sabine was surprised that he knew them so well.

"If you will excuse me," she said, walking to the door, "I will go below and see to your supper. I didn't expect you home until later."

"I have a surprise for you," he said, laying Thayne in his bed.

"Oh?"

He watched for her reaction as he spoke. "A courier arrived today from King Charles. He and Queen Henrietta will be arriving for a visit one week hence."

Sabine could only stare at him. "Their majesties are coming here?"

"Yes. And we are fortunate that we have time to prepare for them. The king seldom gives advance notice of his visits. Will this be a hardship for you?"

Sabine was already beginning to calculate in her mind the meals she would serve. "How many in the party, and how long will they reside with us?"

"There will be some seventy people, counting servants and lords and ladies of the Court. The message says that they will remain with us for two days. Do you feel you can play hostess to so large a gathering?"

"Yes, of course," she answered, feeling less sure than she sounded. "My mother trained me well for just such an occasion. You will have no reason to feel concern, Garreth."

"No," he said, his dark gaze softly sweeping her face. "You are quite capable in all things."

34

Sabine was busy from morning until night. The royal suite, where three previous kings of England had slept, was her first task. It was stripped to the bare furnishings, washed, polished, and shined. In a trunk, she found bed coverings that had been woven with the royal crest. These were cleaned and placed on the bed. Crushed flower petals were soaked in oil of mint sewn into small packets, and placed in hidden nooks to make the rooms smell sweet.

Everything was sparkling clean, and all the bedrooms made ready for the guests. Sabine opened the huge dining room, as well as the large salon. She talked to the head huntsman about arranging hawking for the ladies, knowing that Garreth would plan hunting parties for the gentlemen.

Extra women came from the village to help in the kitchen. Fruits and vegetables were gathered, fish and game prepared—grain was milled and baked into loaves of bread, blocks of cheese were prepared and butter was churned, ale, wine, and casks of brandy were stocked in the pantry, cattle were slaughtered and preserved in salt, pork and deer was roasting over the fire. Great pots of stew were bubbling over the fireplace, while capon and quail were stuffed to be baked to a golden brown.

Sabine had brought many of her mother's recipes with her, and she instructed the cook to bake French tarts stuffed with spices and nuts and covered with a sweet cream sauce.

Tomorrow, the king and his entourage would arrive, and Sabine had assured Garreth that everything would be in readiness, but had she forgotten anything? She went over in her mind everything her mother had taught her. She could think of nothing that had been left undone.

Wearily, she went up the stairs and into the nursery because she had not seen her son and daughter all day. Thayne was asleep, but Ryanne was kicking her feet and gurgling. Sabine lifted the child in her arms and sat in a chair by the window. The baby curled up, closed her eyes, and fell asleep. Sabine felt her own eyes drifting shut, and she soon fell into an exhausted sleep.

She awoke with a start to find Garreth standing over her. He took Ryanne from her and laid the child in her cradle. He then lifted Sabine in his arms and carried her down the corridor.

"You have worked diligently to make my home shine, little mistress. It's time you rested."

Entering his bedchamber, he deftly undressed her and slipped her nightgown over her head. Then he lifted her into the bed and lay beside her, holding her with tenderness. She nestled her head against his shoulder, falling asleep. No nightmare would haunt her tonight.

* * *

Sabine had chosen carefully what she would wear for the meeting with the king and queen. Ysabel laced her into a dark green silk gown with frilly white underskirts. Her hair was pulled away from her face and fastened with emerald clasps.

A deafening noise broke the silence as the king's cavalcade rode over the wooden bridge into Wolfeton Keep.

Mrs. North hurried up the stairs, and was puffing to catch her breath when she knocked on Sabine's door. "Your Grace," she cried, her eyes bright with excitement, "his majesty has arrived!"

Sabine rushed from the room and down the stairs to join Garreth, who already stood on the steps, ready to receive their illustrious guests.

He gave her a warm smile. "Have no fear, his majesty will be the one who's nervous when he sees you."

Sabine hardly heard Garreth because the king was already before them. He looked older than she remembered. She knew of the difficulty he was having with Parliament and the insurrection involving the Scots— also, many of his own lords were rebelling against him. He looked haggard, and she found herself pitying him.

"Your Majesty," Garreth said, descending the steps to greet Charles Stuart. "We are honored by your visit."

King Charles laughed jovially. "It's been too long since I've been to Wolfeton Keep. As we rode through the woods, I saw game aplenty."

"Yes, Sire, this mild weather has made for good hunting. I believe you will not be disappointed."

"Gads, who is this lovely creature?" the king asked, moving up the steps.

"Sire," Garreth said, "You remember my wife, Sabine."

The king's eyes held a light of amazement. "This was

the little girl I met at Heyworth Moor?" He clasped her hand much as he'd done that day. "She's a beauty." The satisfied look he gave Garreth as much as said that Garreth should thank him for such a winsome match.

Sabine dipped into a curtsy. "Welcome to Wolfeton Keep, Your Majesty."

"Quite so, quite so." His attention turned to the woman who was dismounting. "Your Grace, may I present you to the queen?"

Queen Henrietta was petite and pretty with dark hair and eyes. Her smile was sincere, and she offered her hand to Garreth before she turned to Sabine.

"We are pleased to meet you," she told Sabine graciously.

Sabine curtsied and then spoke in French. "You are most welcome in our home, Your Majesty."

"Ah, you speak my language very well, Your Grace. I would almost believe that you were from France."

"My mother was French, Your Majesty, and I believe you know my aunt quite well. Before her marriage, she was Margretta de Chavaniac."

The queen was delighted. "Of course, Margretta is my dear friend. She wrote me concerning you. I hope everything was resolved to a happy conclusion."

"It was, Your Majesty, and I thank you for your notice."

"You must encourage your aunt to come to England. I have missed her dreadfully." In a move that signified marked favor, the queen linked her arm through Sabine's. "I have long wanted to see Wolfeton Keep. Will you show it to me?"

"It would be my pleasure, Your Majesty."

The banquet table sparkled with golden vessels. When everyone was seated, a servant appeared behind each chair with scented water and a towel for washing hands. Course after course was served, and everyone ate with relish.

Sabine sat to the right of the king, while Garreth was on the queen's left.

"Your wife is charming, Garreth," the queen observed. "I am quite taken with her. Is it not amazing that she gave you twins? You are the envy of us all."

"Indeed, Your Majesty."

The desserts were served, and Queen Henrietta clasped her hands in delight after she took a bite of the sauce-covered tart. "But this is wonderful! I have not tasted tarts such as this since I was a girl in France. Garreth, your wife is exceptional."

Garreth looked down the table, where Sabine appeared to be keeping the king amused with her wit. Pride swelled in his chest, for there was no denying that Sabine was playing to her most critical audience tonight, and she had so easily enthralled them.

The banquet ended, and the king insisted the men would not be separated from the ladies. So men and women alike migrated to the large salon, where they were entertained by three minstrels and a juggling act. Confections were served from golden platters, then delicious spiced wine, another of Sabine's mother's recipes, was offered in crystal goblets. Everyone praised the evening, but none louder than the king.

When the king and queen were at last ready to retire for the night, King Charles took Sabine's hand. "You are a gracious hostess, Madame. I have seldom been so well entertained."

The queen brushed her lips against Sabine's cheek and smiled at her husband. "Magnificent. I almost felt as though I were visiting France tonight."

*   *   *

The hour was late, and silence had settled over Wolfeton Keep as everyone sought their bed. Sabine made a last tour of the kitchen, making certain everything was in readiness for the next day.

Wearily, she climbed the stairs and walked down the corridor with the intention of going into the nursery, but Garreth stepped out of the bedroom door and closed it softly behind him.

"The children are sleeping soundly, and so should you be." He slipped his arm about her waist and guided her toward their chamber. "You made me proud, Sabine. But you also have me amazed. Is there no feat you cannot accomplish?"

He opened the door and she preceded him inside. She was pleased by his compliments. "If I was successful tonight, my mother deserves the tribute. I did only what she trained me to do."

"Their majesties were most impressed with you. I believe they will be singing your praises for months to come."

Since she had sent Ysabel to bed hours ago, Sabine unpinned her hair to let it cascade down her back. "All I want is to sleep."

Garreth came up behind her and placed his hands on her shoulders. "The king is taking credit and boasts that he brought us together."

"His majesty has much to answer for."

Garreth's hands dropped away. "Yes, so he does."

Sabine yawned, and then looked apologetic. "I have arranged for the ladies to hunt with bow and arrow tomorrow since the queen expressed that she is partial to the bow."

She climbed into bed, and Garreth pulled the covers over her. Before he could undress and get in beside her, Sabine was fast asleep.

*   *   *

Sabine wore a wine-colored riding habit with a matching brimmed hat. She smiled at the queen, who looked lovely in a blue habit trimmed with silver braid.

"Had I known we would enjoy ourselves so much, Sabine, I would have insisted on spending more time at Wolfeton Keep. You are an excellent companion," the queen said.

Sabine nudged her mount forward to keep pace with the queen while the other ladies fell in behind. "You must return often, Your Majesty."

Queen Henrietta applied her whip to the horse's rump and shot out ahead, and Sabine raced beside her. "We shall certainly do just that."

After they had ridden for a while, the queen halted her mount. "I see our husbands, just there, shall we join them?"

"If that is your wish," Sabine answered.

As they approached the king and his lords, the queen halted her horse and stared in amazement. "Who is that?" she asked, pointing with her whip handle to a nearby ridge that jutted out over a stream. That woman is not one of my ladies. Is she of your household?"

"I do not see anyone, Your Majesty," Sabine said.

"There just above the incline—the woman with the poised bow."

"I see her now, but I don't recognize her from this distance, Your Majesty."

In that moment, Sabine gasped, for the woman aimed her arrow at one of the men. At first, Sabine thought it was the king himself, but when the arrow flew, Sabine cried out as Garreth slumped over and fell from his horse.

Sabine didn't remember riding across the meadow to her husband, or sliding from her mount. She ran to

Garreth and dropped down beside him. Blood stained his doublet, and she gasped, fearing the arrow had pierced his heart!

She took his head in her lap and touched his face while chaos reigned about them. Several men had ridden after the woman, and others gathered about Sabine and her fallen husband.

"My love, my love!" Sabine cried as Garreth's eyes fluttered open. "Do not die. I love you so."

"Your Grace," the king said, touching her shoulder. "We should get him to the Keep as quickly as possible."

She leaned forward and placed her lips against Garreth's mouth, while his blood soaked her gown. "Do not worry, my dearest love, I will not allow anything to happen to you," she assured him.

Garreth tried to speak, but no words issued from his lips. There was such sorrow in his eyes as he looked at Sabine. He reached up to her, but his hand fell away and he went limp.

"Please," Sabine cried in desperation, looking beseechingly at the king. "Help my husband."

Several men came forward and lifted Garreth's body, and he was handed into the stalwart arms of Captain Barkley.

"Take him along slowly," the king commanded.

The queen led Sabine's horse forward, and the king himself lifted Sabine into the saddle.

"He will be all right, Sabine," the queen said, squeezing her hand.

Sabine was too stunned to think clearly. "I must find Ysabel," she said, with a last look at Garreth. "She will know what to do." She kicked her mount forward and raced for the Keep.

When she arrived, word had preceded her, for Ysabel was waiting on the steps.

"Is his grace's injury serious?" Ysabel inquired, hurriedly.

"Yes." Sabine jumped from the horse. "Very bad." There was pleading in her eyes. "You must help him, Ysabel!"

By now, the rest of the party had arrived, and Ysabel took one look at Garreth and ordered him to be taken to the kitchen.

Sabine ran ahead of them, ordering the servants out of the kitchen. She waited fearfully as two men brought Garreth in and laid him on his side across a long table.

"I'll want the basket from my room," Ysabel said, looking at Sabine. "Since you know where it is, it would save time if you fetched it."

Without pausing, Sabine ran from the room, knowing Ysabel would do all she could to help Garreth.

Ysabel looked up at the men who gathered about the unconscious duke. "I already have my basket, I merely wanted to get her grace away from here so she would not see what I must do." Ysabel then pointed at Captain Barkley and one of the other gentlemen. "You two stay— the rest of you leave."

"Now," she explained as the room cleared, "I'll need you both to hold his grace still while I remove the arrow. It's good he isn't conscious."

She deftly broke off the shaft, and then, gripping a sharp knife, cut Garreth's jerkin away. "Keep a grip on him, this is going to hurt."

Garreth groaned when Ysabel pushed the arrowhead through his back. Blood ran freely from the wound, but at least the arrow had been removed.

"The flow of blood is cleansing," Ysabel said, crushing a handful of yellow roots and rubbing them on the wound. "He has lost much blood, but the roots will stop the flow."

With the help of the two men, Ysabel was able to bind clean white linen about Garreth. "'Twas a clean shot, and luckily caught only his shoulder. A little further, and it would have pierced his heart. His grace will recover nicely, although he'll be sore for a few weeks."

Ysabel turned to Captain Barkley. "The two of you will carry his grace upstairs to his own bed." Then she looked at the second gentleman. "You kept your head and took orders well. By what name are you known?" she inquired.

"Charles Stuart, Madame, at your service," he replied, lifting Garreth's legs while Barkley took his head and shoulders.

Ysabel was embarrassed. She had seen the king only from a distance and hadn't recognized him. "I am sorry I was so presumptuous, Your Majesty."

"Have no worry, Madame. I have seldom seen such healing hands as yours. How would you like to join my service?"

She shook her head and smiled slightly. "I am flattered, Your Majesty, but my place is with her grace."

Sabine came rushing down the stairs, momentarily startled when she saw the king helping Barkley carry Garreth. "Ysabel, how is he?"

"There is nothing to worry about. He will recover."

"You would not just say this to keep me from worry?"

"I have ever been honest with you, Your Grace."

Sabine raced ahead and flung open the door to the bedchamber. When Garreth was laid on the bed, she dropped down on her knees and clasped his hand. "I shall remain with him," she said.

"Have no thought of anything but your husband," the king told her. "I shall play host in Garreth's stead, and the queen is quite capable of entertaining the ladies."

Sabine's eyes were brimming with grateful tears. "Thank you for your kindness, Your Majesty."

She was not even aware when they withdrew, for her attention was on her husband. Garreth's lashes rested against his pale cheeks. She touched his velvet soft hair and pressed a kiss on his lips. For this moment, he belonged to her alone.

"I love you," she whispered. "I loved you the day you came to me when my mother died, and I loved you in Paris. I didn't think it was possible, but I love you more now."

Her voice reached Garreth from his fog of pain.

"I shall always regret what I did to you in Paris. When you recover, I'll make it up to you, my dearest love."

He did not open his eyes as he felt soft, warm lips touch his. He lay very still, and his heart was gladdened at Sabine's declaration of love.

35

Dressed in her black riding habit and black-brimmed hat with a red plume, Sabine allowed the groom to help her onto a horse.

"Spinner here will give you a nice run, Your Grace," the groom told her. "Would you like me to ride along with you? There'll be a storm coming."

She glanced at the dark clouds that were gathering in the east—they were still some distance away. "Thank you, no. I shall return by luncheon."

He touched the brim of his hat. "Very good, Your Grace."

Sabine rode up the hill and across a wide meadow. She ran the horse for a while and then slowed him to a canter. When she saw the large lake ahead, she rode in that direction. She had been curious about the lake since first seeing it from the bedroom window.

She could see a small pagoda and thought it strangely out of place in this setting.

As she watched a flock of blackbirds take flight and wing their way across the sky, her thoughts turned to Garreth. He had not remained in bed but three days and then he insisted he had to go to London. He ignored Sabine's warning that such a journey might open his wound. He had been gone for a week now, and she was miserable without him. It had been glorious nursing him, taking care of his needs.

Sabine glanced at the dark sky, realizing that the storm was gathering about her. She could never make it back to the castle before the rains came. The wind tore at her hat, and she had to keep a hand on it or it would be ripped from her head.

She heard the sound of a rider and glanced up the slope to see Garreth. She watched him dismount and come toward her. How handsome he was in a green leather jerkin, buff-colored breeches, and high leather boots.

"Did not you see that a storm was brewing, Sabine?"

She smiled. "I did. But I don't melt, Garreth. I have been rained on before."

He returned her smile. "You are always going to be a rebel, are you not?"

"I hope so. I would not want you to think me commonplace."

He shook with laughter. "You commonplace, my lady wife? Hardly. I never know what deviltry you will be about. I believe since the day I married you it was ordained that you would keep my life in turmoil."

"Is that what I do?"

He nodded at her with mock solemnity.

Her laughter was musical. "Then you should consider locking me in one of your towers, Your Grace, and losing the key. Or perhaps you could put me on a ship back to France."

He pretended seriousness. "All this I have already considered, but my children need a mother."

"It appears that we are at an impasse then."

"It would seem so."

The rain came suddenly, and it fell in torrents, peppering the water in the lake and swirling it into waves that lapped against the bank.

Garreth pulled Sabine from her horse, gathered her in his arms, and ran toward the pagoda. When they reached its shelter she expected him to place her on her feet, but instead he held her, his gaze moving over her face.

"You are the most fascinating woman I have ever known, Sabine."

His eyes locked with hers, and she could hardly speak.

"You must put me down. I am certain your wound still pains you."

"Not at all." There was a sparkle to his eyes that she had not seen before. "You were a good nurse, and Ysabel is an exceptional healer."

"Yes, she is. She cured my limp."

"She has what the fairy folk refer to as healing magic."

Rain fell about them, and lightning flashed across the sky, but Sabine was no longer frightened of storms. Garreth had chased all her fears away.

He set her on her feet at last. "We could be here for quite some time, Sabine. These storms can last indefinitely."

"How did you find London?"

"Dull. Except that I saw Richard. He'll be arriving in two weeks to spend several months with us. He said to tell you that the de Baillards will be visiting in July."

"I have missed my dear friends. You do not mind, do you?"

"I welcome anyone who was kind to you when you needed friends."

She glanced up at him and found his eyes on her face. "What else did you do in London?"

"I had an audience with King Charles and Queen Henrietta, and listened to them praise the beauty and virtues of my wife." He turned her to him. "Sabine, have you any notion of the identity of the woman who wounded me?"

Her brow creased in a worried frown. "I have given it much thought, and have concluded the woman was not one of the hunting party. She was aiming directly at you."

"It was Eugenia Meredith. Since she tried to have you killed before, I thought she intended to try again—all the while, it was me she wanted dead."

"That was why you would not allow me out alone?"

"Yes."

Sabine trembled, thinking how very nearly the woman had succeeded in taking Garreth's life. "Why did she do such a thing?"

"She was demented."

"You once loved her."

"No, Sabine, never. You must believe that."

"I believe you, Garreth. What will they do to Lady Meredith?"

Garreth raised her chin and his eyes locked with hers. "You need never fear again. She's dead, trampled by her own horse as she tried to get away from the king's men."

Sabine looked away from him, but he forced her to look at him. "Sabine, Lady Meredith was the woman who helped my cousin, Cortland, with the raid on Woodbridge."

"I had come to suspect as much, although I did not want to say so. It was a fitting end to her," Sabine replied, having little sympathy for the woman who had caused the death of her father and had almost killed Garreth.

She walked to the other side of the pagoda and turned back to him. "Garreth, there are many things I wanted to speak to you about, but I have not had the courage."

He looked doubtful. "I have not found you lacking in courage."

"I have never forgiven myself for what I did to you in Paris."

In two strides, he stood before her. "You mean by deliberately making me fall in love with you?"

"Yes." She lowered her head, no longer able to look into his dark probing eyes. "And wanting to hurt and humiliate you."

He tried to keep from smiling. "You did all that and more, Sabine. There is but one question that burns in my mind, and I must hear you say the words, while I look into your eyes. Do you love me at all?"

She could not speak.

Garreth laughed and gathered her close. "It is wrong of me to tease you, Sabine. I know you love me, and don't deny it."

She laid her head against his shoulder. "How could you not know?"

"Especially since you so recently admitted it to me yourself."

She raised her head and looked at him. "When?"

He placed his cheek against hers. "When I was wounded and you thought I was unconscious. I was sorely tempted to kiss you then, but it was much nicer listening to you say how much you loved me."

There was no longer reason for pretense or false pride. "I do love you—I suppose I always have."

He reached into his pocket and withdrew the ring he had given her on their wedding day. "Will you wear this, knowing that this time it is given with love and not out of duty?"

She nodded, too choked to speak, as he slid the ruby ring on her finger.

He shook his head. "Oh, my Sabine, how far we have come to find happiness, when all the time, it was right where the king had commanded it."

She lay her face against his chest and planted a kiss there. "What shall we do now?"

His smile was devastating. "It's simple—I love you and you love me—is that not a beginning?"

She closed her eyes as his arms tightened about her. "Yes, oh, yes."

"Little did I know that the night I fell in love with La Flamme, I was in love with my own wife."

She stood on her tiptoes and brushed her lips against his. "You will not tell anyone about my past?"

Humor danced in his eyes when he saw her uncertainty. "No, we can hardly admit that the duchess of Balmarough is in fact the famous La Flamme."

He pressed his cheek to hers. "There will be those who will comment that you resemble the mysterious actress."

"Yes," she said smiling, "and I shall most certainly act indignant, and you will insist that they apologize for daring to make such a comparison, and as my husband you must challenge them to a duel."

Garreth laughed softly. "Not me. You are the better swordsman."

They both laughed and then he became serious. "To me you are many women in one. You are the lovely little Sabine—the exciting La Flamme, and my duchess who conquered a king. Most of all, you are my wife and the mother of my children."

The rain hammered against the slanted roof, and

lightning illuminated the sky, but Sabine and Garreth did not notice. They were locked in each other's arms, unrestrained happiness at last fusing them together.

"I have never told you," she said, as his lips brushed her cheek, "that you once came to me as an answer to a prayer."

He looked at her quizzically. "When was this?"

Her expression was serious. "It was the day you appeared behind me in the little chapel in Paris. I had asked for a sign—for someone to help me and Richard—I looked up and you were there, my love."

He gave her a smile that warmed her heart. "I was compelled to seek you out that day. Little did I know that a higher power guided my steps."

She nestled in his arms, glorying in his strength. "This is where I want to be, Garreth."

He laughed and held Sabine to his heart, his dark eyes soft and loving. "It would seem we have no choice. We were first commanded by a king, and then by God's higher power. It must be ordained that we love each other."

Her heart was too full to speak.

"Will you pledge your love to me for all time, my lady wife?"

"Forever," she promised, her eyes glowing.

He lowered his head to capture her lips. At last, they had overcome all the obstacles that had kept them apart.

They were as one mind, one heart, one love.